THE LEGACY OF THE NINTH

The Legacy of the Ninth

Paul Anthony

The Right of Paul Anthony to be identified as the author of this work
has been asserted by him in accordance with
the Copyright, Designs and Patents Act of 1988.

~ ~ ~

First Published 2008
Copyright © Paul Anthony 2008
All Rights Reserved.

Cover Photography © Kathryndinsdale.co.uk

First published in Great Britain in 2008 by
Paul Anthony Associates
www.paulanthonyassociates.co.uk

By The Same Author

~

In Fiction…

~ ~ ~

The Fragile Peace

Bushfire

~ ~ ~

In Poetry…

Sunset

~ ~ ~

Author's Note

It was during my frequent visits to some of England's most northerly museums that I realised how much we had discovered about our ancestors, and how the complex world in which we now live was shaped by events occurring centuries ago. Of course, not everything is known about the people who walked our planet two thousand years ago; but there are those amongst us who have spent their lives rummaging through the debris of the past to give us an indication of how things once were. History proves they were often right and sometimes wrong. Dealing with fact and opinion and weaving them together to make sense of things is a time consuming never-ending business. It's not surprising, therefore, that these earth detectives sometimes inspire us to think of how things might have been.

And so, in the writing of this book, I give a very special thanks to those historians, curators, geologists, botanists, architects, archaeologists, and earth scientists who found the remnants of the Roman Empire and inspired this story. It would be wrong of me not to acknowledge those farmers and landowners of Cumbria and Northumbria who have preserved the border lands and the Roman heritage that is embedded into our very heartlands.

A handful of characters referred to in this literary invention take their names from historical figures that died about two thousand years ago, but some of the places mentioned in the forthcoming pages are real enough. This story is, however, pure fiction: the product of human imagination and a naïve dream that one day there really could be peace in the Middle East.

You see, out there in the desert, long ago, a change of wind direction and a twist of fate might have transformed things forever…

Paul Anthony

To Margaret – Thank you, for never doubting me.

To Paul, Barrie and Vikki – You only get one chance at life. Live it well, live it in peace and live it with love for one another.

To my special friends – Thank you. You are special.

…… Paul Anthony

PROLOGUE
~ ~ ~

'Still running?'

Yes, he was still running. Back out on an open road, pounding the tarmac. Rivulets of sweat cascaded from his forehead, skirted his eyebrows, and flowed down the contours of his sun-tanned face before streaming onto his throat and disappearing into the cotton of his black running vest. It was his day of rest and relaxation; there were precious few. It was his private time: a time to hone his body and relax that weary mind. Despite a fire mounting in his lungs, Billy Boyd forced a smile, which was brief enough to be polite and neighbourly enough to be tolerated, and moved gingerly to the offside of the lane. Stepping over a pothole, he lengthened his stride.

'Still running, John,' replied Boyd smoothly as he wiped a droplet of perspiration from his chin and deposited the offender on the thigh of his black running pants. 'It's supposed to be good for you but I'm not so sure.'

'Meg won't want you a physical wreck, lad! Mind how you go, Billy.'

'I will, John. Look after yourself.'

Throwing a casual wave in the air, Boyd strode passed the farmer and checked traffic at the end of the lane. With a burst of speed he was across the carriageway and into a broad country lane that was bordered by the luscious green fields of the Eden valley. The fields were fenced but where there were no fences the meadows were edged by dry stonewalls. A patchwork of undulating meadows ran down to the River Eden where mud and debris had washed onto the bank from the previous month's flooding.

Boyd was back. He'd returned from secondment in London; his days in the Special Crime Unit were over. Back in uniform, pounding the streets, he was still fighting crime. He had been promoted. He was Chief Inspector William Miller Boyd in charge of the uniform section: new ground for the specialist undercover officer. The hustle and bustle of New Scotland Yard was a long way from the rural bliss of Cumbria. Yet the peace and quiet that his team in Scotland Yard had warned him to expect was not apparent. Since returning to Cumbria, his working days seemed endless. There simply weren't enough hours in the day. It was one thing after another and all work and no play had left Boyd jaded and stressed out. Even Meg, the woman he loved so much, the nurse he'd recently made his wife, had warned him. Now he knew how she felt. His job was making him a total pain to live with. She'd kissed him goodbye that morning, pushed him through the door, and told him to relax in his jogging shoes before the job totally destroyed him. Cumbria or Scotland Yard? It didn't make any difference to Meg. She'd told Billy Boyd to get his act together before their marriage really turned sour. Boyd needed time to relax. His smart suit and fancy silk ties were a thing of the past. Even his jeans and sweaters were consigned to the rear of a wardrobe. He was 'uniform' now and his plainclothes image had disappeared. His dark blue uniform hung in a wardrobe for the day whilst his hat and truncheon, and a pair of brown leather gloves, were on a sideboard in his house. Even his trusty black boots were crying out for polish in the back hall and those shirts were in need of an iron. It was his day off. He was running. The police force was right out of his mind. He was off duty for a week, a whole week, and he intended to spend time running and getting fit. He wanted to find solace in his mind and perhaps take a glass or two down at his local. He would switch off from the police force and the rest of the world. To hell with them all, thought Billy Boyd. It was his private time.

He ran to the Moor.

Boyd felt a breeze strike his face, felt the freedom of his solitude, and a spring in his heel. He ran as freely as the wind with his mind and spirit in perfect harmony. His dark hair quivered behind him, his blue eyes checked the road beneath his feet, and his square chin pointed the way ahead. At thirty-nine years of age Boyd sensed middle age reaching his body, and he hated it. He sprinted down a lane until he reached a farm where he saw a ditch in a field. The lane was straight, bore no bend, and ran parallel to the ditch. The tarmac ran downhill, slightly, enjoying shelter from hedgerows of hawthorn, bramble and honeysuckle.

A fox scuttled across a field in the distance; its bushy tail visible on the skyline, and deer foraged unseen in a wood that came into view as Boyd descended the hill. A badger burrowed deeply into the soil and nourished her family far from the prying eyes of the lonely runner. On high, a buzzard hovered, searching for an unwary morsel below. The broad expanse of sky was bright and clear blue with only an occasional white puff of cloud visible.

Jogging down the lane, he increased his speed as he felt the ground open up before him. He recognised the vallum on the offside of the road, knew the word vallum was taken from the Latin and means 'wall'. Here, the vallum was no more than a shallow ditch lying about twenty yards from a hawthorn hedgerow, behind a dry stone wall, inside a field. He knew the vallum represented the vestige of Hadrian's Wall. Yet on the Moor where he ran Boyd couldn't see the brickwork and mortar that had disappeared from view centuries earlier. All that was left was a shallow ditch in a field that was said to shroud the remains of the vallum, but it hadn't always been so shallow. When the Romans originally built Hadrian's Wall there had been a ditch on either side of the structure, and the ditches had been made quite deep and broad. The vallum puzzled Boyd. No one seemed to know why the Romans built a ditch either side of their wall.

Stepping out briskly, Boyd thought about the deer and badger that roamed his Moor. He thought about the vallum and the Romans as the land fell gently towards the bed of the Eden valley. Striding out now, Boyd thought of those tragic road accidents and those mangled limbs he'd so sadly removed from the road that week. Then he thought about Meg and decided on flowers and a candlelit dinner for two to make it up to her.

He turned right and ran towards Carlisle, by-passed the Wallfoot hotel, reached a roundabout, deviated left, and sprinted through the hamlet of Linstock. Here, houses were a quaint mixture of old and new, and village bungalows were festooned by the glories of summer with a hundred blooms in every garden. Climbing roses and a variety of moss embraced older, more substantial, houses. Yet the glory of this hamlet lay in the gardens and village green at its centre. Boyd crossed a bridge over the motorway.

Crossing a cattle grid, he twisted left onto a rough track leading down to the River Eden. He ran along the riverbank until he reached a suspension bridge near a confluence with the River Petteril. Boyd eased off, ignored the bridge, and held his course on the riverbank. Sensing the skyline before him, he recognised the buildings of the Civic Centre, the castle and cathedral. The modern office buildings and ancient structures stood proudly above the Eden. He felt he could reach out and touch them; they seemed so close. Yet the sheep around him would have him believe he was in the middle of the countryside. Such was the glory of Carlisle: sheep in a park less than half a mile from the hustle and bustle of a new Millennium. Jogging around the cenotaph, gradually scattering a flock of sheep, he savoured deep grass beneath his feet. Then the rough path eventually met parkland once more but then its surface suddenly changed to tarmac. He thought about the park, its river and that cathedral. It was his release from violence and anger; and his liberation from the frustration of dealing with those whom he had pledged his life to suffocate. Such thoughts would deflect his mind from those drugs and burglaries, and the heartache of a city. Such thoughts would kill that stress burning his mind and racking his body.

He reduced speed as a hill appeared, shortening his stride. Sweat ran onto his body and his legs stiffened. His heart thumped and his lungs exploded as he gritted his teeth and powered up a hill to Brampton Road. His arms were like pistons as they drove his body up a steep incline. With a quick glance to left and right, he steamed across a main road and clawed his way up Well Lane. His knees pranced high yet his feet merely kissed the footpath when he felt the sharpness of the incline. The hill threatened to go on forever. Boyd winced at the thought of steep hills and running forever. When he reached the top of the hill, he was in Stanwix village, he was spent.

Turning left, inhaling deeply, Boyd filled his lungs with oxygen and broke down to a walk. Worn out, he padded towards Stanwix School with his hands on his hips, repeatedly gulping in air. He saw a sweet shop next to the school and decided to replenish himself. Entering the shop, Boyd removed a coin from his bum-bag and bought a tablet of chocolate. Boyd felt stiffness in his legs and burning in his lungs. His back felt rigid; tight and tense in its movement. Sweat rolled from his shoulders and he felt the sun caressing his bare skin. His heart thundered; his head swam; he was spent.

Boyd sat, feeling burning from the soles of his feet. Those blisters would be fractious by the time he had completed his run. Delving into his bum bag again, Boyd found his sunglasses and put them on. A self-satisfied smile gradually wrinkled across his face. He was determined to enjoy that sunshine. Then, carefully, almost reverently, he removed a black bandanna from his bag. He folded it into a triangular shape and wrapped its base to his forehead. Tying the bandanna tightly at the back of his neck, Boyd knew he would stop the sweat from rolling into his eyes and, in any case, the cloth would protect his head from the sun. Then he fingered the tablet of chocolate in his hand. Strangely, the tablet of chocolate felt unusually heavy. Perhaps it was exhaustion from his running. Resting his back against the school wall, Boyd heard children playing noisily inside a playground. Then the sound of music drifted through an open window of the Rose and Crown public house, nearby. The smell of good ale invaded his steaming nostrils and then suddenly a trumpet sounded. Turning casually, Boyd examined a sign erected outside Stanwix School. It was a Protestant school.

Religion?

Boyd wondered why schools always carried a sign showing their religious affiliation. Religion? Religion seemed so important to so many people and yet it puzzled this man who had no religion.

Boyd speculated on whether any of its pupils were Catholic, Muslim or Jewish. What a mixture of religions, thought Boyd. Surely there was a potential for conflict? Boyd wondered if the school allowed the followers of Islam to surrender to the will or law of God. Did Muslims in school read the Koran? Boyd pondered on whether the Torah, the Pentateuch, the Scriptures, was read by Jews in school. He wondered if the Bible was read by Catholics and Protestants and queried if religions were taught at all since the foundation of morality surely lay in such teachings. Yet Boyd had no firm religion to speak of. He was neither a disciple nor an agnostic. He fancied each individual could make up their own mind; yet he bore no grudge against those staunch bigots whom he found difficulty in understanding.

Reading the sign, he learnt Stanwix School had been constructed on the site of 'Petriana', an old Roman fort completed during the first century. He knew from his own school days that Emperor Claudius had invaded Britain in AD 43. Checking the sign once more, he explored an image of a Roman soldier sat astride a horse.

Turning, Boyd saw the River Eden and a bridge crossing from Stanwix to the city centre. He saw Carlisle castle and its battlements proud on the skyline, and he saw a cathedral dominating the very soul of Carlisle.

Boyd felt tired, heard his heart beat slower, and his lungs reduce in their effort. His legs stiffened further and his perspiration waned. He felt his eyelids grow heavy and surrender to fatigue and stress; those worries encroaching upon his mind: Meg, the worries of a city and its riots, the worries of it all. Spent, Boyd lay back against a wall and drifted down the abyss of his mind.

The tablet of chocolate loosed from his grip.

The tablet… The tablet of chocolate… It had all started with a tablet. It had all started with a tablet of rock, a handy-sized tablet of rock from a far-off continent. That's what started it all, thought Boyd.

And David, of course.

If it hadn't been for David; none of it would have happened. None of it would have been possible; if it hadn't been for David.

Boyd held the tablet of chocolate in his hand. It was the same size as that rock. Boyd knew what had happened since David. Boyd had been part of it, lived it, and was racked physically and mentally because of it. It was the events of Tullie House and those drugs and riots; and the castle that caused his mind to crash into turmoil.

Now, in his moments of reflection, he wondered what had happened prior to David. Where had that tablet come from? What was the story of that tablet? What story would David have told Boyd had they only had time together; time to walk, time to talk, together?

Thinking of David and the events of it all, Boyd found some words forming in his mind. He thought perhaps this story had started centuries earlier. Perhaps the story was of other people from a far-off continent: a different place, a different time. Perhaps David would have told him; had they had more time together; told him David's story.

1
~ ~ ~

David's Story:
Dateline: AD 73: The Negev Desert.

Desert sands caressed the earth, whispered in silence, conspired together, and then shifted endlessly in the cool breeze of a dying night. Gradually, dawn broke over the countless dunes that forever changed the Negev landscape while desert creatures scurried to their hidden lairs to escape the rising sun. Lazily, almost reluctantly, a deadly scorpion scuttled beneath a flat rock to await its prey. Then, it was as if there was a hesitant stillness in the air: a peaceful serenity that seemed to accept the presence of the mighty rock, and the camp of leather tents that spoiled the landscape.

Two men: one old, one young; had stood since dawn, watching, and searching the desert for any sign of movement from the tents of leather.

The two men watched the scouts arrive on horseback and dismount, and then watched them come and touch the foot of the rock far beneath them. Scouts came every morning to touch the rock and take their turn to watch the same two men standing on the battlements above. The scouts watched the two men as they waited for the sun to rise above the camp of leather tents, and above the mighty rock. It was a game of touching, of prodding, and of watching, and the sun continued to rise.

'It never rains,' declared Eleazar.

'No, it is surely the way of the desert,' replied Jacob.

'The sun bears down endlessly: burning a barren land, scorching an infertile earth; until she prays on the wind for a drop of rain, a hint of dew. Yet there is not enough dew to quench my thirst.' Eleazar's brown eyes penetrated deep dark sands beneath him and his voice carried quietly to a young man standing by his side. 'In the beginning there was only peace and solitude. There wasn't even a single footprint in the sands of time. No, there was just a desert and a million grains of sand that held no memory of before and no prediction of the future; until man was born.'

'You sound so sad, Eleazar,' said Jacob, anxiously. 'Why is this so?'

'It is because I grow old. My time draws to an end, Jacob.'

'Don't say such things, Eleazar. You are our leader. You cannot die. Eleazar ben Jair will live forever.'

Eleazar shrugged a smile. 'Hear me, young Jacob. There are things I must tell you before I die; before my time runs out. You must listen to my voice and pass on my words to the generation who follow you. It is the way of man to pass on his words so that those who follow will remember and learn from the past. It is a lesson you must learn; a legacy you must pass on.'

'Why is it so, Eleazar?'

'When God revealed himself to Moses and the Israelites on Mount Sinai the word of God was spoken from The Master to His disciple. The word of God has been preserved in the spoken Torah that we call *Mishnah*. It has been learnt and memorised and passed on in an unbroken chain from master to disciple, and now it is preserved in our very faith for all time. It is our Torah: it is our way. It is as strong as the written Torah: the written Scriptures that have been handed down through the generations of our people. Together, the written word of our scriptures and the spoken word of our *Mishnah* make our Torah strong. It is our legacy, my young friend. It is our legacy and yet I am troubled by those Roman scouts beneath us, this siege, and a vision I see in my troubled mind.'

'Pray, what is it that troubles you, Eleazar?'

'This land... Our land...'

'What of these lands' asked Jacob?

'It all began long ago... So long ago.'

'What do you mean?' asked a puzzled Jacob.

'The Canaanites were first to arrive, Jacob. They dragged their hopes and religion with them to the Promised Land. They were people of the Hebrew tribe and their faith became our religion, Judaism. They settled these lands and a nation of city-states was born. Later, the Philistines invaded. The Philistines and Arab Caliphates drove out the Hebrew and claimed these lands as their own. They denied our faith and renamed our lands Palestine.'

'I know this to be true, my leader.'

'The sands recognised the change, Jacob.' Eleazar's eyes scanned the far horizon, searching the desert wastes. 'The sands witnessed the birth of unrest in these lands. The sands whisper, shimmer, and blow with a breeze of uncertainty. Through the centuries this has become a place for war. At night the sands howl in contempt at the shattering of peace and solitude. Then the Romans arrived, invaded, and extended their vast empire. Seven years ago we, the people of Judea, rose against the might of Rome and their Gods of falsehood. For our troubles

Emperor Vespasian sent his son, Titus: a devil by any standards, to destroy the rebellion. Four years later Titus razed our Holy City of Jerusalem. The second Temple was destroyed, all except the western wall. Yes, it is true. The great works of David and Solomon lie in ruins. We were lucky! We managed to escape and find our way here but that was over two years ago and we have been besieged by these Roman Legions ever since. Every day their scouts ride around us and threaten our very existence. I am tired of the siege, Jacob; tired of drawing lots for those who may drink today and those who may eat. I am tired of watching those scouts come and go on horseback. They come during the night to touch our walls and prod the rock upon which our fortress is built. It cannot last forever: the touching; the prodding, and the watching.'

Eleazar ben Jair pursed his lips and ran his fingers through the furrows of his forehead. The tiredness and stress of leadership had taken their toll on the worthy sage. His hair sprouted grey and unwieldy from his troubled head and his eyes were a bloodshot brown that seemed to rest deep within his leathered face. When he had worked sleep from his eyes, he continued to pass on his words to Jacob.

'It is because we ignored those Gods of Rome: those unworthy false Gods, that they have pursued us here. The Romans will destroy us, Jacob. They call us fanatical because we are Zealots. They want us to surrender, to capitulate. Never! Do you understand me, Jacob? Never!'

'I understand you,' said Jacob, softly.

'I command you, Jacob. I command you in the way God delivered the Ten Commandments to the Israelites. To surrender our Torah is to surrender our very being, Jacob. The Torah lies at the heart of our religion. It is the foundation upon which our faith rests. I command you, Jacob. You must never forget these words that I speak.'

'I shall never forget, Eleazar. I promise you.'

'There will be trouble in these lands one day, my young friend. These sands whisper and howl in the night but one day they will blow a desert storm that will last for years. There will be trouble in these lands when the sands explode. They will erupt in a whirlwind of frenzy and hate. Hebrew against Roman, Hebrew against Arab. Hear my words; I command you.'

Jacob held his tongue, choosing to ignore his gibbering elder: unsure of the vision prophesied, unsure of scouts who touched and prodded at the mighty rock; yet solid in his understanding of the Torah.

In the desert the sands whispered; the sun yawned. A scorpion's tail snapped through the air, stung hard, took its first morsel of the day.

'When will they come, Eleazar?' asked the younger man, concerned; his bright blue eyes searching an old man's wrinkled face for an answer he did not wish to hear; an answer he feared in his heart.

'Soon, Jacob… Soon…' Eleazar heard the worried teenager but replied in reluctant truth. 'They know we are weary from the siege. The Romans must realise our wells are nearly dry. There is only a little water left to drink and we cannot live without water from the wells. This place, our home, we are besieged by the might of Rome and I fear the worst. At night; under the cover of darkness, their scouts touch our walls, prodding and poking, looking for weak spots in the rock. During the day they tunnel and weaken our foundation, hoping these walls will collapse. Oh! Our resolve will last forever, Jacob, but even our great walls will crumble in time.'

Jacob rested his arm on the edge of a broad expanse of wall allowing his eyes to pierce the face of the elderly sage. There was a soft manner in the old man's voice: a softness that camouflaged the deepest of his beliefs; but it was a softness Jacob warmed to as he listened to the spoken lesson.

'Each night I pray for the miracle of rain, Jacob, in the hope that their chariots of war are bogged down in the sands of uncertainty.' Eleazar paused: delving in his mind for an answer to their predicament, sorting through the puzzle of religion, rooting through the enigma of war. 'Sometimes I wonder if God has forsaken us for I know that only rain or a miracle from above will save us in this our hour of need.'

Surprise crossed Jacob's face as he saw doubt in Eleazar's eyes.

The older man pointed east and settled his wiser hand on a tender narrow shoulder. 'Look out there, Jacob. Is that a sandstorm I see gathering? Look, the storm gathers near the camp of leather tents. Do you see?'

They stood on Masada's tallest battlements looking out across the barren wastes of the Negev desert as the sun began its climb towards the ninth hour of the ninth day of the ninth month. Masada was indeed formidable. Sat perched high on a hill, the isolated structure was virtually impregnable from three sides where sheer cliffs dropped down towards the rolling sands. Every fifty yards, or so, a reinforced stone turret interrupted a line of walled battlements and offered further refuge to defenders.

The Zealots lived inside the mighty walls of Masada with their rich and splendid synagogue dominating their daily worship. Morning, noon and night, they worshipped. It was as if their very souls depended on the worship of their God. The eminence of the great synagogue contrasted sharply with a scattering of humble wooden storage huts that contained a dwindling supply of food and everyday items. Inside the caves, carved from the rock, lay hidden personal belongings and a large collection of Holy literature that was revered by the God-fearing militants. There was only one entrance to Masada and it was situated at the top of an incline protected by a narrow rocky approach: a snake-like twisting path.

The view across the landscape was breathtaking: quite spectacular.

But in the distance, Jacob made out a faint blur of dust rising from behind scattered mounds of low-lying sand dunes. The blurred smudge of dust rose from where they knew the camp of leather tents had been pitched.

Eleazar gasped as he caught sight of the rising haze. Then the haze gradually became a cloud of dust that swelled from where leather tents had been pitched: the leather tents that housed their enemy at night, and sheltered their enemy from the chill breeze of a desert night. It was those leather tents from which Roman scouts came each morning that God sent.

'I prayed last night,' murmured Jacob, following Eleazar's pointed finger as the dust cloud gathered and frothed on the distant horizon.

'Did God answer your prayer, Jacob?'

'He told me we would win. He told me Masada would last forever. We shall defeat these Romans, Eleazar. God has told me this.'

Eleazar turned and looked his young friend deep in the eye: quizzical, almost disbelieving. Eleazar rasped, 'Did God tell you that we should fight these Roman dogs of war with our bare hands, Jacob? Did he tell you that? No, I suspect not for we have no weapons save our great Torah. It is one of the great Commandments, Jacob. Thou shall not kill.'

Jacob looked away, ashamed; his pride hurt from Eleazar's rebuke; his spirit dented. There were no more softly spoken lessons from the old man of wisdom. Jacob heard only a rasping tongue of condemnation from the leader of the Zealots.

Jacob asked, 'So we must surrender to the men of Rome and pay homage to their many Gods, their false Gods?'

'No surrender!' barked Eleazar, snapping angrily at his impassioned confidant. 'We shall never surrender, Jacob. Not in a million years. This is our home. We are the rightful owners of these lands. King

Herod the Great built this place: his villa fortress. Herod cut this fortress from the very rock itself. It is our land. It is God's will.' And then softer, almost soothing, Eleazar muttered, 'We shall never surrender. No! Not to any man.'

The sun continued its rapid ascent into the heavens as dust and sand billowed in the distance, bubbling larger, fermenting with intrigue.

Eleazar said, 'You are a mischief, Jacob, but we shall not surrender.'

A cloud of dust broadened and darkened the sky above the dunes.

Jacob turned as if to take his leave but then changed his mind. He moved towards Eleazar. Jacob felt nervous, looked somewhat tense, and fidgeted slightly before he managed to speak. 'I have made an altar from this stone, Eleazar. When I die, I will take this altar with me to my resting place. The altar will comfort my soul on my journey to the Heaven of Peace.'

'An altar! Let me see your work, Jacob.'

A flurry of cloth produced a small tablet of stone from inside Jacob's robe. There was a glint in Jacob's eye. It was his way of asking for forgiveness; his way of impressing Eleazar; as he gently caressed the tablet of stone with his fingers. Jacob wiped the sculpture with the corner of his black, dusty garb and handed it to Eleazar. The mysterious tablet measured nine inches in length, six inches in width, and three inches in depth.

'Are you a beggar hiding food? What do you call this strange piece of work that you produce from your pocket, my young friend?'

'It has no name, Eleazar.' Jacob's voice was now keen and eager. 'It is a tablet from Masada. It is my legacy: all that I own, all my faith, all my religion. My God is in this tablet; this altar of stone. Look closely at how my flint has made these lines.'

Eleazar gathered Jacob's stone in his craggy, arthritic hands and examined a design that brought pleasure to his eyes. The tablet showed an image of the fortress of Masada. Part of the tablet, the bottom right hand corner, bore the carving of an irregular-shaped candlestick: a Menorah. Turning the craft towards the light, testing its rough surface with his frail fingers, the old man's eyes glinted and smiled at Jacob's handiwork.

'When you are encased in your sarcophagi your burial chamber will carry the mark of a Menorah with you. You are indeed ingenious, my young friend.' Eleazar laughed, approvingly. There was a smile from

Eleazar. 'Perhaps this tablet of yours has mystical powers, Jacob.' Eleazar contrived a sudden wink. 'Perhaps it will grant you eternal life, Jacob.'

Jacob nodded his head vigorously, happy to please his elder.

'The Menorah is used in our celebration of Hanukkah. When I die the carved lines, which show a nine-branched candelabrum, will help my soul to celebrate Hanukkah here in Masada. The Romans may defeat us but in my death I will celebrate the victory of the Maccabees over Antiochus Epiphanes. I know the victors were Hasmonaeans but I learnt their family name as Maccabees. Do you remember the legend of the Maccabees?'

'Of course, I know it well, my friend. It is no legend, Jacob,' counselled Eleazar, scholarly. 'These words I speak are true. Antiochus the Fourth, Epiphanes as he was known, was once King of Syria and ruler of all Palestine. He fought the Egyptians and captured Jerusalem many years ago. So many years ago it was even before I was born.' Eleazar twisted a smile at such a thought and continued, 'Like the Romans, Epiphanes denied our faith and made Judea worship the Gods of Greece. Our priest, Mattathias, and his sons, the Maccabees, also fled to these mountains just like we did. Later, when they were strong, Judas Maccabee led the people of Judea in a struggle for freedom against the Syrian warlords.'

'And restored Jerusalem to our faith when those Syrian armies' were hammered into defeat and the valiant Maccabees drove them from the Holy City,' interrupted Jacob, smiling in triumph.

'Correct,' beamed Eleazar. 'Your words carry truth.'

'The Maccabees then rededicated the new Temple of Jerusalem using a nine branched candelabrum, a Menorah. There is a Feast of Dedication and a Festival of Light when we celebrate Hanukkah. In death, I shall have a light to show the way, Eleazar. The beam will light my celestial path and I shall walk through the gates of Heaven with pride in my heart.'

'You have learnt your lessons well, my young friend,' replied Eleazar, clasping an arm around Jacob's neck as his eyes took in the intricate flint work. Chuckling, he added, 'Let us hope it is many years before you need your tablet with its image of Menorah.'

'It is good that after only ten years and five I am still learning,'

'Yes. It is good, my young friend. Very good!'

Jacob held out his hand to receive his tablet.

'Keep it safe, Jacob,' nodded Eleazar. 'Keep your tablet safe. For you know what we must do when they tear down our defences?'

Acknowledging his unrivalled leader, Jacob bundled his stone into the furls of his robe and looked out from the battlements to the ground below. 'Look down there, Eleazar,' pointed Jacob. 'The Roman soldiers have set fire to one of their tunnels again. Surely that will not burn our rock?'

'No, Jacob, but if their tunnel is built well then fire will consume earth, heat the rock, and eventually fracture the stone. These Roman engineers have found a way to bring down our walls and I have no antidote to heal the wound they inflict upon us.'

'Listen, Eleazar. The trumpet sounds draw nearer. It is a strange tune they play this day. What does it mean, Eleazar?'

Fingering his greying beard, the old man dusted desert grime from his robe. Worry crossed his forehead and dimmed his weary eyes; he listened to the melody and realised why the Roman cornua sounded so sprightly.

'Go to your family, Jacob. Go now, I beseech you.'

Eleazar suddenly fussed his hands like an eager handmaiden washing robes in a mountain stream. His heart beat inside his chest and his feet rocked on their soles as the sound of the cornua grew louder in his ear.

'Quickly!' roared an abrupt Eleazar, hurrying his prodigy away. 'Tell Abraham! Tell him the Romans trumpet the sound of battle! It is time!' Clasping his hands, Eleazar lifted then upwards to the heavens in final prayer; in final salutation. Closing his eyes, he whispered, 'Thou shall not kill! Oh God! It is time but we cannot fight. It is not our way.'

Suddenly frightened, discouraged by the sight of his griping leader, Jacob turned his back on Eleazar. Running as fast as he could along the stone ramparts, Jacob turned at the first stone turret and clambered down some wooden steps into the safety of the heart of Masada. Timber planks creaked in protest beneath his feet as he heard the incantation of morning prayers. Then, as a column of thin smoke slowly spiralled from a tunnel below and climbed towards Masada's walled turrets, Jacob sped towards the Temple; his toes scurrying the sand before him; his heart pounding.

'It's time,' Jacob shouted loudly, his arms waving. 'It's time. Eleazar has spoken. The Romans are coming.'

Eleazar's eyes fell, scanning from the horizon to the earth beneath him. Open-toed sandals caressed his frail feet but did little to prevent the dirt of a desert burying itself inside his fragile toenails. Below the knee, the old man checked his robe and gingerly followed the contours of the cloth towards his belt. He slowly reached to one side and withdrew a dagger: its handle bejewelled with a multitude of coloured stones. Eleazar dropped his ageing eyes on the twinkling gems and painfully grasped the hilt as if to stab the oncoming cohorts. Eleazar denied the gnawing pain in the joints of his knuckles and slowly tightened his grip on the weapon. Sounds from the desert grew noisier and balloons of sand gathered in the sky as he ordered his weary eyes on a slowly advancing army. Covering a steady incline towards their fortress, glinting in gentle morning sunlight, Eleazar ben Jair made out a centurion, and the unmistakable Standard of the Tenth Roman Legion.

'Make ready with those catapults,' commanded Domitian: a tall, angular centurion dressed in Roman splendour. 'Archers of Syria, make good your eye for the God of Fortuna will grant you sound fortune on this great day of reckoning. Fortuna will guide your arrows of revenge. Hear my words, I say unto you. I have spoken.'

Listening to Domitian's words, easing a quiver to his side, Hussein prepared his bow. Hussein had no tender fingers to ease the clay; no soft fingers to make a pot and shape the curve of an urn; no nimble fingers to turn the scriptures and leaf the pages: he was a warrior. Smaller than the centurion; his hair was black and flowing. His skin was a deep olive colour: smooth in its texture; perhaps a touch swarthy in its pigment. Hussein was just a simple Syrian peasant: a nobody simpleton from a nobody town. But he was an archer and his eyes were the dark brown eagle eyes of an assassin.

The first heavy chariot of destruction trundled sluggishly by. A dozen numeri: half-savage tribesmen from an auxiliary army, shouldered their weight against a mobile catapult under the watchful eye of Domitian: a legendary soldier who was famed in battle. Domitian stood tall for a centurion measuring five feet eight inches, perhaps nine, and his face bore no stubble from the long hot siege. His blade was sharp. His back was erect, his shoulders broad, a commander in battle. An ugly scar ran down his face from the high cheekbone near his left ear to the side of his throat.

Another heavy catapult rolled by. Two unfortunate mules pulled the ponderous machine as it gradually clambered up a rocky incline. Eight sweating tribesmen laboriously pushed, steadied and guided the wobbly apparatus as it neared the mighty gates of Masada.

Following the first catapult, and fanning out as the mouth of Masada beckoned, ranged an overwhelming array of Syrian archers.

Hussein, the simple peasant from the banks of the Euphrates, led them. The loose brown robes of his Syrian archers ran to their knees and were covered by dark cloaks knotted on their chests. Each archer carried a gladius: a two-foot long sword, sheathed at the waist. Leather quivers hung over their shoulders as they marched with their bows held low in readiness.

Behind Hussein's archers followed the rest of the Roman artillery. There were catapults, large and small. The catapult was no match for the mediocre defenders who had no fight in their belly; no weapon at their arm.

The cornuas sounded.

Increasing their tempo the archers gradually massed in front of the fortress as Hussein mustered his men and carefully withdrew an arrow from his quiver. Grains of sand gathered, rose, and clouded into the atmosphere as row upon row of marching Syrians broke into a gentle jog.

'Make haste,' ordered Domitian; his voice booming across the hordes. 'Exalt the Gods for your strength. Jupiter and Mars watch over you, my warriors of revenge. Feel not fear in your heart. Heed your leader well.'

Another signal trumpeted across the sands as the Legions vacated their campsites and marched towards Masada. Blades of retribution sparkled in the desert sun as the loose brown robes of Syria hung in terrifying waiting.

The Legionaries were the trained infantrymen of Rome: the chosen few who had conquered the known world and filled their Emperor's coffers in the process. Elegant in their dress, valiant in their fighting, they followed their Standards into battle. It was the centurions who were the backbone of their army: experienced fighting men resplendent in glorious tunics covered by protective leather thongs and finished off with shining armour across their chests. Bronze helmets, inlaid with soft leather, sat atop sturdy muscular men and an occasional coloured plume indicated the position of yet another cohort. Leather-soled half boots billowed grains of sand into the air as they neared Masada. Looming ahead of them, a thin whisper of black smoke surged upwards as the earth beneath Masada began to crumble.

Shoulder to shoulder they strode in awesome splendour. Each Legionary carried a gladius by his side and two pilums - javelins - on his back. A rectangular shield, convex in design, was carried to the front as protection from any attack. Slowly these Romans fought their battles, carefully, with the caution and patience of Job; for they were feared by all their enemies, these valiant men of war. Closer and closer, the battle lines drew nearer. Smooth leather brushed, resplendent robes danced, iron blades rattled, and then, suddenly the sound of feet pounded against the earth.

The tunnels beneath Masada wheezed; its rocky foundation groaned.

'Hooves!' whispered Eleazar. Listening, he heard a rumble; heard a prancing; heard the thunder of a horse. 'Cavalry! I see men on horseback behind those Legionaries,' warned Eleazar, shouting loudly from his vantage point, planning their response. 'But first they mean to break our walls with catapult and fire. Make ready, Abraham.'

'Tis done, my leader,' bellowed the bearded Abraham from the depths of their defences. 'May God protect us, Eleazar? The last cup is poured for those who have chosen their way. The lots have been drawn. Your order is set, by blade or by chalice. All now know my great and noble leader. It is time. It is our time, Eleazar ben Jair.'

Galloping now, cavalry horses thundered the ground as a Jewish heart beat in anger. A desert storm grew from without when Syrian feet pounded Judean soil and Roman boots heeled Herod's core.

Eleazar felt his chest swell and the soft moisture of a tear form at his eye. 'Then let it be done, Abraham, and may God have mercy on our souls.

Turning from Masada's battlements, Eleazar spoke into the heart of the desert fortress. Holding back a tear, denying a fracture breaking his heart, his voice found strength and echoed his words on the walls of the great defences. In the mystique of the hour his words boomed across the desert; across the centuries of time. 'Hear me, people of Masada. Man may burn our home, man may smash our body, but man will never destroy our faith. Hear me, people of Judea. Hear me, people of Masada.'

Eleazar, old and frail, arthritic yet brave, looked into his home, into his fortress, into Masada. Painfully fingering a dagger, he felt his skin tingle against the cold sharp iron. Eleazar ben Jair raised his dagger above his head and looked to heaven in search of his God.

The thunder of the feet and the boot and the horse replied, and invaded the ear of the Jew.

With all his strength, with all his faith, Eleazar plunged the blade deep into his heart as the first boulders whistled across the battlements into the fortress and a tongue of flame licked the edges of a crumbling tunnel.

The earth rumbled below ground as the roof of a tunnel collapsed weakening foundations, weakening resistance, surrendering to the Gods of Rome and Roman engineers. Soil split from soil, rock split from rock, and the earth opened her jaws wide.

Eleazar fell to his knees; arthritic fingers touching sparkling jewels embedded in the handle of a dagger glinting from his robe, blood weeping from his heart. As life ebbed from his soul, his whispered roar echoed through the centuries of time, 'No surrender!'

A deep red seeped from his heart and the symmetry of his pulse faltered and was no more. Eleazar ben Jair died by his own hand; jewels of death gleaming in a desert sun, protruding from a dead man's chest.

The cornuas were quiet. Yet catapults balked and bucked as rock after rock crashed into Masada's battlements. Bouncing haphazardly from the ramparts, boulders of attrition showered frantic Zealots below. Buildings crashed and splintered to the ground as more rocks hurtled through the morning air. The ground shook and a dust bowl clouded. Boulders hissed a whisper and penetrated Judea's heart. Wooden planks splintered and timber huts caved inwards as the prayers of a resolute people rent the air.

And then it rained.

Not the miracle of rain to answer Eleazar's prayers, but needles of death as Hussein gave an order, pulled back the string of his bow, and released his first arrow. His Syrian archers followed suit and unleashed a salvo of lethal arrowheads. Sheaf upon sheaf of arrows snapped through the desert air and dipped downwards into Masada's heart. Helpless men and women who had chosen to stand in defiance on the battlements and pray were first to fall, first to tumble, brought down in a torrent of angry fire.

Flames of burning arrowheads followed and found their mark igniting a handful of dry, wooden huts. Flames from above and flames from below slowly engulfed the ancient fortress.

On the ground, Eleazar's proud Zealots ran to their synagogue. They ignored the falling stonework around them as they prepared for their final mission. Dedicated to their task, stubborn and determined, they denied swirling smoke, licking flames, and cannonballs of destruction. Hurrying themselves, they neared their hour of glory, their moment of history.

The sun rose, burning, scorching, and scarring. It was the ninth hour of the ninth day of the ninth month, and the walls of the synagogue resounded to the sound of praying…

Somewhere in Masada ran a young man clutching his Menorah; his nine-branched candelabrum carved on a rock of Masada, his beam of light that would show the way...

A timber in the main gate fractured, weakened by fire, bursting open with the impact from an enormous boulder propelled from a catapult. More rocks found their target as the mighty doors of Masada finally succumbed to a ferocious onslaught.

Domitian jutted his chin and filled his chest with passion. 'Advance,' he ordered, and an army of revenge moved forward as a thousand Syrian arrows pointed the way into the heart of Masada.

Inside the synagogue, Abraham took a cup in his hands. Raising the silver chalice high, he addressed his eager, frightened audience, 'May God forgive those who violate our lands. May God have mercy on us?'

Nigh on one thousand Zealots watched as Abraham raised a silver chalice to his lips. His eyes blinked, his gullet contorted, and he drank a poison that ended his life moments later.

Outside, Hussein's Syrians had closed on the walls of Masada. Hussein ordered his archers to aim high into the sky. Their arrows flew from their bows, vertical in flight, died at the pinnacle of their flight, and then dived into the heart of Masada. When their quivers were empty, when their catapults had smashed the walls and bombarded the heart of the fortress, Hussein ordered his archers to fall back, allowing the Legionaries to complete the rout. Protected by shields from above and to their sides like a tortoise shell, Roman Legionaries smashed down the remnants of Masada's entrance. Without the loss of a man, they stormed into the Hebrew fortress with their Standards dazzling in the desert sun and Domitian at their head.

There was the silhouette of Eleazar's body lying on the battlements. Jacob screamed in horror as he ran towards the lifeless form. Young Jacob saw Eleazar's body with its rigid arm overhanging from the ramparts. He saw jewels in a dagger glinting in the sun, and then, turning, he saw Abraham's body and the horror of his death. Flinching at the sight of Eleazar's dagger, Jacob decided against poison and ran full bloodied towards Domitian. Clawing his bare hands like a jackal, Jacob screamed, 'No surrender!' Hate, anger, bravery and despair guided his zealous footsteps swiftly towards the Roman centurion. Jacob's hands clawed, his feet kicked out, and his fingernails tore at the centurion's eyes. Fifteen years of zealous dedication; a lifetime of obedience to the Torah and the Ten Commandments, forgotten in a brief second. Thou shalt not kill - Jacob wanted to kill!

Domitian drew his gladius and plunged its blade into Jacob's heart.

Young Jacob fell, dead before he hit his sacred ground.

Domitian twisted his blade and wrenched Jacob' chest apart. Smoothly, he withdrew his sword; blood smeared to its hilt. Carefully, he searched the mass of Zealots and waited for the next of their insane to attack. Carelessly, he did not see a small tablet of stone unfurl itself from Jacob's robe. He did not see the Tablet of Masada unfurl from the robe of a young Jew and drop into Masada's sand. Domitian's jaw dropped and his mouth flapped free in astonishment as without a fear for Roman centurions, without a fear for Syrian archers, without a fear for crumbling walls, one thousand Zealots committed suicide before the eyes of Rome.

There was no fear in killing one's self. There was no fear of blade or poison. Not when they had already decided, already prayed, and already asked for God's mercy. Masada's people had their faith, their religion. They had their Torah and had determined long ago upon the suicide. It was their God who was their witness. It was their God who had entered into a special relationship with the Jewish people at Mount Sinai. In return for obedience to His laws; acknowledgement of God as the only God, ultimate King and sole Legislator; the people of the lands known as Canaan and Israel and Judea would forever hold a special place in the mind of God. They believed that in return for obeying His Ten Commandments, virtue and obedience would be rewarded and sin punished by divine judgement after death. In this belief, the people of Masada knew foreign domination of their lands, and forced exile from their lands, would be remedied at the end of time when God would send his Messiah, *Mashiah*, to redeem the Jews and restore sovereignty of their lands to them. They believed all that, the people of Masada. They believed it with all their hearts and all their minds. They believed in their faith, one God, one faith. They held so zealously to that faith that they believed each individual act of suicide would hasten the arrival of *Mashiah*, hasten the return of their lands to their sole sovereignty.

They believed: the people of Masada.

A poison was drunk, burning a stomach and killing a heart. A blade was chosen, slicing a body and ending a life.

Blood gushed from open wounds, gurgling against the tortuous noises of dying men. Masada's women and children lay heaped in death across the bodies of their loved ones. Then the sands of Masada turned to a bloody red from the blade and transformed into a carpet of black robes as the soul of the Zealots ascended gloriously into Heaven. There was no rain; there was no dew; but the sands ran wet from the blood of man. No one wept. There was no battle in Masada. There was no surrender; only death in the face of defeat; by blade, by poison, by self...

Rome's Tenth Legion dominated Masada taking the fortress and standing in the ruins of a Judean dream. The auxiliaries entered with Syrians and numeri.

When blood ran dry, when hacking was no more, the General came. General Flavius Silva headed his cavalry. Trotting forward through cheering ranks on a big white stallion, he rode into a burning, broken Hebrew fortress. Flavius wondered at the power and invention of his engineers. It was his engineers who had destroyed Masada, not his infantry. With tunnels to weaken earth on which the fortress stood and catapults smashing its walls, it had only been a matter of time before the collapse occurred. General Flavius Silva smiled proudly as his soldiers waved and cheered his entrance.

The might of Rome, the Tenth Legion, had retaken Judea. The Roman Empire reigned supreme.

Hussein lowered his bow and marvelled at the power of Mars: the Roman God whom Domitian had called upon to watch over their battle: the Roman God who had sown mortal fear in the hearts of those defenders. The Syrian archer knelt in sand taking in the nectar of victory, sensing the power of the Gods, and feeling the mastery of the Roman Gods. For what kind of God would cause his followers to engage in an act of suicide, thought Hussein? A Roman God would not call for suicide, thought Hussein. A Roman God would call for revenge, for victory, for power.

There was a dull shape in the sand. Then there was a sparkle when the sun rose higher and cast its rays upon the dull shape. Hussein saw another sparkle. In the sand, beside Jacob's body, Hussein found a peculiar stone tablet. It was a strange carving in a rock, made by a flint. It was small but attractive and rested firmly in his hand. His eyes took in a carved image of the fortress of Masada and a strange heathen candlestick in its bottom right hand corner. Hussein thought: 'what is this rock? Is it an altar to a false God? Perhaps it's a keepsake in recognition of my journey from the banks of the Euphrates River? A gift from the Gods for my sister's son, Alexander?'

'Yes,' he spoke, aloud. 'When I am returned to the banks of the Euphrates, I will carry with me this rock from Masada. I will carry with me this mystical gift granted to me by the supreme Gods of Rome, gifted to me alone from these sands of Masada.'

'What is it?' commanded a voice, harsh and sour. 'What plunder do you steal for yourself, Syrian?'

Glancing upwards, Hussein saw the General on his horse and flowing coloured robes that symbolised his authority. Guards closed in, a white horse balked, and General Flavius Silva looked down on Hussein.

Domitian planted his Standard in the sand. 'Hold fast, Syrian,' commanded Domitian. A paltry smidgen of blood trickled from a freshly opened scar on his cheek.

'Pass it here,' ordered General Flavius. Hussein stooped to his knees, head down, lifted the tablet and presented it in two hands, humbled and fearful of the warlord and these master conquerors that fed him and clothed him and trained him.

General Flavius snatched the rock, studied it, turned it in his hands, and scorned the image before him. 'Take it. It is but a bauble.' General Flavius threw the rock to the ground and rode on with his guards surrounding him. There was a flick of a horse's tail and a whinny from a horse as the General and his guard moved on.

Hussein knelt in the sand, scratched in the sand, found it, fingered it, and promptly slid the Tablet of Masada into the folds of his robe. He exhaled loudly as the sound of hooves retreated from his ear. He patted his trophy in the folds of his robe and followed the warlords. He was a simple man, once a peasant now a thief. He was an assassin: an archer. Eagerly, he continued his plunder as the bloodthirsty hordes ripped open the riches of Judea and the rock of Masada fractured and collapsed into the earth.

Jacob's legacy, his guiding light, his torch-way to Heaven, was in Syrian hands, stolen from the Hebrew fortress of Masada by the armies of Rome.

*

A runner stirred beneath the sign of Petriana, beneath the picture of a Roman soldier sat astride a horse. Nearby, giggling schoolchildren laughed and pointed at the jogger sitting with his back to a wall. They poked fun at the man dressed in a sunglasses and a black bandanna. Then a teacher arrived and ushered her children into class. A shopkeeper shook his head in contempt of the man sitting with his back to a wall, smiled politely, and turned his attention to a lady and her shopping list.

The sun bore down on a tablet of chocolate. Boyd felt the tablet melting in his hand. He gathered the tablet of chocolate in his fingers as his mind searched for the story of the rock, the Tablet of Masada. Then, gradually, his tired dreamy mind wandered back through time, back to the first century and those days when the armies of Rome policed the borderlands from a fort known as Petriana.

Boyd thought about the fort of Petriana, thought about the Roman settlement of Luguvalium that became the town of Caer Luel, and thought about Caer Luel that became Carlisle. He was just daydreaming near the banks of the River Eden, on the banks of Stanwix. He was just a tired jogger, a stressed-out jaded policeman.

Boyd studied the sign in front of Stanwix School. He wondered how it had been in the Roman fort of Petriana. Boyd thought he knew and formed the words in his mind. Boyd knew David's words explained the reason for Masada, and the reason for the Tablet that had been crafted in the likeness of Masada. The words? Were they the story of Petriana? Did Petriana shape Luguvalium at all? Were Boyd's thoughts really Luguvalium's words? Luguvalium's words were the story that he would have told David, had they had time to talk, together. The words of Luguvalium's story.

*

2
~ ~ ~

Luguvalium's Story:
Dateline: AD 122: Luguvalium.

Alexander was a Syrian by birth, from Mesopotamia: the land lying between the rivers of the Tigris and Euphrates. His country had been under Roman rule since 64 BC. In the beginning Alexander's ancestors had settled on the north bank of 'al-furat' – the Euphrates, and made their home in Ar Raqqah. Alexander's predecessors learnt from their Roman masters. Indeed, a century earlier, before Jesus Christ was born, Gaius Julius Caesar built the bedrock of Roman Imperialism that was to last three hundred years. Not surprisingly, Alexander's broad family counted many who had served under Rome. When he reached maturity, when he finally determined upon his life, Alexander left his home and walked alone south through the Syrian Desert.

He walked as a boy and became a man. As Alexander grew, so did the Roman Empire. Emperor Claudius crossed the plains of Belgica and conquered the distant green island of Britannia. The Roman Empire spread across a continent: Baetica, Lusitania and Tarraconensis: south of the Pyrenees, fell. Aquitania, Narbonensis and Lugdunensis: in the plains of the Garonne, and the Loire, and the Seine, succumbed to the Roman Senate.

Alexander journeyed through barren plains in search of the riches he had dreamt of. Climbing Mount Hermon, he saw the Golan Heights and Damascus. It was in Damascus that Alexander enlisted with the Roman army under Emperor Trajan. He learnt of the Roman Gods, Fortuna, Jupiter and Mars, and abandoned his own religion in favour of the Roman icons. Alexander kept his own language but learnt the tongue of his fellow soldiers. Serving with distinction in Asia Minor and Germania, he was posted in AD 108 to Eboracum, Britannia, where the rivers of the Ouse and the Fosse meet. Alexander was respected by all around him. Tactics and strategy were his hallmarks but he was also a great fighter, valiant and bold in the family tradition. He gained promotion through the ranks to Chief Standard Bearer: 'Optio ad Spem'. He was a centurion: one of sixty centurions, each of whom commanded a 'century' of eighty men. His century was the first century of the second cohort of the Ninth Legion. He was a senior centurion and had been appointed 'primus pilus': the chief centurion of his legion. As primus pilus, Alexander commanded his legion in the absence of the Legate.

Alexander was of proven bravery; a man who was a leader of fighting men, a man respected by his century and cohort, and feared by his enemies. Each cohort contained six centuries, or four hundred and eighty men. Alexander's century consisted of ten units of eight men. Each unit of eight men formed a 'contubernium' and they lived together in the same quarters. There were ten cohorts in the legion that was overseen by six 'tribunes'. Tribunes were Roman citizens who each regulated the lives of eight hundred men. In addition, two or three hundred civilian workers supported each legion. They were generally engineers, surveyors, musicians and clerks. A 'Legate' commanded the legion and was a man of Senatorial class. The Legate spoke in the Senate at Rome and was a politician, a man who might be Emperor, and Alexander's Legate was in overall command of the Ninth Legion.

The Legion had sworn to a man to be faithful to their Emperor, had sworn never to leave the line of battle except to save a comrade's life, and had sworn allegiance to Rome, for that was the way of Rome. The Roman army that conquered the known world had structure, discipline and strength. It was formidable. It thought it was invincible.

As primus pilus, Alexander obeyed orders and led his men north to green and desolate lands where no discernible border existed. Under his Standard of the Ninth Legion, Alexander camped on the banks of the River Eden, in the town of Luguvalium. Governor Petillius Cerialis had defeated local Brigante tribes and built a fort at Luguvalium in AD 71. Governor Agricola then reinforced that fort with turf and stronger defences nine years later. As one of the most northerly forts in the Empire, Luguvalium proved one of the most important commands in the region. Ever since, occasional bands of marauding Picts had raided the settlement, damaged its fort umpteen times, and enraged Rome. About AD 80, the Romans abandoned any attempt to expand north of Luguvalium and withdrew from the frontier to consolidate their holdings. They strengthened their troublesome border by building another fort on twenty acres of land, by the River Caldew.

It was summer and Alexander's Ninth Legion had ventured north towards the lands of the Picts, the north-westerly outpost of the Roman Empire. Once the year was through, Alexander expected to receive the Emperor's Diploma of Discharge and return to Rome to live in peace.

Tired by his journey from Eboracum, Alexander rested by the Eden as twilight hovered and sand martins, ducks and kingfishers played amongst rustling reeds. He feasted on deer and hare, caught in nearby fields, and washed down the last of their raisins and dates with a superior red wine from a clay goblet. Guarding the perimeter of the camp, his sentries occupied high ground on the banks of Stanwix, north of the river, where the Legion's surveyors plotted another fort. Further north, his scouts carried out reconnaissance and gathered military intelligence.

It had been a long week and a long hard march to these unfriendly lands. Fatigue became their final friend, a friend to be shunned with the welcome advent of rest. In coming days, the Ninth Legion would be joined by elements of the Second Augusta Legion, the Twentieth Valeria Victrix and the Sixth Legion. An important meeting on strategy was to be held. This meeting was to be held in council and was of such importance that all legions based in Britannia were to be represented. Many cohorts from these legions marched with celebrated pomp and grandeur to join the Ninth at Luguvalium. Once present, Rome's military leaders would discuss orders received from the Senate: a great work was to be undertaken. Luguvalium was proud to be chosen for the great council for it was the most important centre in the north. The Legion would provide escort and security for the momentous assembly. The Ninth's Legate was charged with ensuring that the council was not attacked by an errant band of Picts. Other legions would secure the surrounding countryside while their leaders spoke. Once the grand meeting was over and food had been eaten, and wines quaffed, the Ninth would return to Eboracum and prepare for their triumphant return to Rome. Their long tour of duty was nearly over; others would finish the project.

Alexander polished his Legion's Standard, proudly arranged his armour, attended his tunic, smoothed out his leather shorts, and cleaned his coveted weapons. Beside him, on a small wooden stool, sat his uncle's gift: the Tablet of Masada. It was Hussein's astonishing present to the centurion. The tablet was small and handy-sized, measuring nine inches by six inches by three inches, and when the sun caught the handicraft, it occasionally glinted. Alexander had carried the tablet with him since the days of his youth, fascinated by its image and strangely drawn to the mystical rock. The legacy had been handed down from Hussein – the Syrian archer – to a beloved sister and mother and then promised to son and nephew, Alexander. The tablet had accompanied Alexander, man and boy, through every battle and skirmish he had fought. From his desert home in Ar Raqqah, to Damascus, to Asia Minor, to Germania, and now Britannia, the tablet had been his keepsake. Once the tablet had probably saved his life when a Briton had lunged at his stomach with a knife. Now the tablet bore a dull impression where a Briton's blade had glanced from the stone missing Alexander's belly and saving him from certain death in the process. The tablet rested next to Alexander's vine wood staff: a staff that signified his rank. Alexander weighed his stone affectionately and placed the tablet in his bundle of blankets as he settled down to sleep. He felt tiredness in his legs and stiffness in his back. He felt black invade his eyelids as his mind drifted in fatigue and he fell into a dismal abyss of unconscious sleep.

Evening stars peeped out from behind far away clouds and sparkled over leather papilos as row upon row of the legion's campsite drifted into sleep. Luguvalium closed its eyes and relaxed.

They were strange men, these men from the army of Rome. They were international, in the way of Rome. It was an army formed from conquered countries, fed and watered and trained in the ways of Rome. They spoke with a sharp tongue, the men of the Ninth: mainly Hispanic. Yet those understanding people of Luguvalium had welcomed their arrival, perhaps mindful of constant incursions from the Picts. It was rumoured in Luguvalium market place – some mile or so from the campsite – that a Roman Governor, Aulus Platorius Nepos, would soon arrive. It was whispered Governor Nepos planned to build a vast wall running from the mouth of the Eden, across Britannia. The wall would stretch to the mouth of a giant river in the east, the Tyne. At the mouth of the Tyne, the wall would end. This wall would be broad enough and strong enough to carry a marching army at four abreast and would define the boundary of the Roman Empire; thus preventing the Picts from pillaging the Border countryside.

Market traders and craftsmen spoke of a great general called Hadrian who was travelling to them from a place named Frankfurt in far-off lands near the rivers of the Rhine and Main. General Hadrian had been ordered by the Senate to supervise the construction of a wall. It was just rumour, they said, and then they had all laughed heartily. They'd gossiped no end. Townsfolk had tittle-tattled and shilly-shallied constantly. It was just speculation, wasn't it? No one could possibly build a wall in the middle of nowhere, they'd cackled. In any case, how would they make such a wall meet in the middle? They would have to build it from either east to west or west to east. If they didn't, then east and west must compromise somewhere in the middle of the moors and arrange to meet half way. They'd giggled at the prospect of a thousand Roman slaves building a wall that failed to meet in the middle. Would they build their wall close to the Stanegate Road, the road running across the Tyne – Solway isthmus? In any event, what name would they give their wall, the wall of Nepos? Some said it would be called Hadrian's Dyke, and there had been laughter. Others named it Hadrian's Folly, and there had been sniggering. Who would man the wall? Where would the guards live? How would they exist in the cruel wintry lands between east and west? And what was known of those strange people from east Britannia? Did they not speak with an accent warped beyond recognition? There had been whooping laughter again. It was just rumour, wasn't it? Either way, the townsfolk of Luguvalium looked forward to many riches that would come from being a garrison of such importance....

The invaders were marching. Men had left their homes in the far north. They had gathered in huge numbers, walked due south, and flattened the ground before them. They had arrived.

North of the Eden, north of Stanwix, they assembled in a multitude during the night. Dangerous, hungry men with long unkempt hair, rugged faces and straggly untamed beards, had trudged through lowlands in search of riches. Their dress bore no resemblance to Roman uniforms. They originated from Caledonia: a distant country north of the Borderlands. They were Picts and wore heavy coloured robes to protect them from the cold. Their robes were a dull chequered garment skirting just above the knee. The kilt, as they called it, swished smoothly with a strong movement from the hips. The Picts carried axes, clubs, an occasional bow or a lethal slingshot. Yet they wore no particular armour to speak of. They had crossed high mountains, great rivers, and deep valleys before the lowlands greeted them and a fresh, salty smell of a nearby Firth invaded their nostrils.

The men of Caledonia – all twelve thousand of them – crept cautiously towards an unmarked border that carried no wall to hinder them.

'Duncan the Bold' led the Caledonian Picts. His tall, rugged frame dominated those around him as he ordered three captured Roman scouts to be put to death by the sword. Once Alexander's scouts had been tortured and interrogated, they were disposed of. They were butchered without a prayer. Duncan had neither time nor inclination to take prisoners now that the way was clear to strike south towards the River Eden and Luguvalium. The daring Caledonian planned to delight his eyes with a view of a settlement built on the southern flank of the Eden between the tributaries of the Petteril and Caldew. It was indeed a unique site maturing within the confines of three rivers. Its attraction was obvious since between the triad of bountiful rivers lay rich and luscious green lands. Luguvalium prospered from the wealth of fertile soils, unlike the rocky, heather-clad grounds of Caledonia. Once dawn broke, Duncan's Picts would storm across the wooden bridge, which divided the fields of Stanwix and Luguvalium.

Duncan led the invasion.

Cautiously, the multitude tramped over cold barren moors until they found a deserted broken fort that had seen better days. Silently, they looked down on rows of sleeping tents below. Duncan disciplined his men, gathered his clans' leaders about him, and planned his final assault.

The first welcome chink of piercing daylight broke through a grey night as Alexander turned in his slumbers. A frenzied hand shook the centurion's broad shoulder.

'Primus pilus! Primus pilus!' A hushed but pained voice invaded Alexander's ear. 'Primus pilus, waken up! Our scouts have not returned. The God, Jupiter, has abandoned us.'

Opening his eyes suddenly, Alexander rolled instinctively and grasped the hilt of his sword. 'What manner is this that you wake me in the dead of night, Julius?'

'The guards report our scouts have not returned. Men have been sighted in yonder fields of Stanwix,' replied Julius, a trusted legionary. His stifled voice was trembling with excitement.

'Then they are fickle and still tired from our long march, Julius. Their stupid eyes play ungodly tricks in this cold and desolate land. You worry to much, my friend.'

'No, Alexander! Men gather in the dark woods, north of the river.' Urgency rose in Julius's voice. 'We are in great danger, Primus pilus. Our perimeter guards heard noises and report many legions of fighting men nearby. They carry arms and march without precision to an old wooden fort.'

'Many legions! How many legions, Julius?'

'We are outnumbered two to one or more.'

Rising abruptly, reaching for his apparel, Alexander began to dress. Sheathing his sword, he said, 'Then the God, Fortuna, has warned us, my good friend. Raise our tribune quickly, Julius, then wake our centuries. We must defend this camp for we have no orders of retreat. This ground must be held for the Emperor.'

Julius ran swiftly from Alexander's papilo and hurriedly roused the second cohort, passing Alexander's order by word of mouth as night clouds moved casually to one side in deference to the onset of bullying daylight.

When he was dressed and armed with his vine wood staff, Alexander rushed to his Commander's side and, without pretension, woke his sleeping leader.

'My legate, rise quickly! A band of Picts threatens us.'

A balding man wallowed in uncertainty, clutched night attire to his prominent gut and rose to greet Alexander. Then he burped. The legate's baldhead shook in annoyance at Alexander's intrusion. He burped again. He was such an arrogant man.

'The guards?' he asked anxiously, wiping his mind clear of wicked dreams. 'Where are our guards, Alexander? Have them deal with this band of unruly rabble. Put them to the sword if need be.'

'The guards have roused me, my legate. Our scouts have not yet returned but our sentries report an army of men in the fields of Stanwix, near the old fort that lies in decay. We are outnumbered, two to one, by all accounts. I fear for our scouts, my noble leader. I have made arrangements for your tribune to be at your side since I fear the worse, my legate.'

'An army, you say?'

'It is surely an army of Picts, my legate, an army from the far reaches of Caledonia. Only the lands of Caledonia are yet to be brought to heel, to feel our sword, to see our Standards planted in their mother earth.'

'There is no time for a council of war,' mused the worried legate. 'No time for a sacrifice at the altar before battle.' Dressed hurriedly, he barked, 'Sound the alarm, Alexander. What manoeuvre do we need?'

'Defend the bridge, my legate,' advised Alexander boldly. 'It is the entrance to this town from Stanwix and the chosen route by which General Hadrian will forge north and defend Britannia's moors whilst our great wall is being built. The waters run deep there, too deep to charge across, my legate. So our enemy must use that bridge. He cannot wade those waters without loss. Unless…'

Pausing, Alexander drew his sword and scrawled the course of the river in soil at their feet… He mapped their camp… He etched the banks of Stanwix… He imprinted Luguvalium in the soil…

'Unless our enemy moves men downstream and seeks out shallow waters, if so, we may find ourselves under attack from all four sides. I know not my enemy nor his tactic but I know how I would use such an army. I would half my force and cross in the shallows. They will surround us for they have great numbers whilst we are only a legion strong. We must remain tight and mass together. We should not disperse our men. Hold tight, I say. We must hold this bridge even if Luguvalium is lost.'

'Damn them! They could be at our rear already!'

'It is true, my legate. I advise you to mass our legion in a square formation and block that bridge over the river. It is the key to everything.'

'A square formation you say, a strange manoeuvre, Alexander?'

'If we are attacked from the rear then our square will hold until relieved or until we stand no more. I say light our bonfire now. There is half a legion camped in a fort near the River Caldew. Our smoke will signal reinforcements to our side. We should also send a messenger to the Sixth by the shores of the great lake; the lake the Britons call Ullswater.'

The legate's face twisted. He looked down at the soil and etchings made by Alexander's blade and then turned and walked towards a small table resting in one corner of the papilo. Snatching a square of beeswax from the table, he began writing a message in the soft media. Once his letter was finished, the legate read it over in his mind. The beeswax was contained within a wooden frame. The frame folded over to hide the message and could be carried easily in a pocket or the palm of a hand. Satisfied, the legate balled his fist and punched the beeswax with the imprint of his ring. Then he folded the beeswax letter over and handed it to Alexander.

'You are correct, Alexander. See to it.'

The bald man poured water from a jug into a basin, patted his cheeks with water, and dried his hands with soft towelling. He drained the last mouthful of wine from a cup and felt its distaste on his tongue.

'We are five thousand strong, our enemy is ten or more, you say, Alexander. This is not just a band of marauding Picts out for quick plunder, my friend. This is an invasion of our lands… And soon, our great council… That's just what I needed. It is a nightmare, Alexander.'

Throwing down his towel, the legate then banished his wine cup to the floor as the first of his tribunes rushed into the tent.

'Where've you been, tribune? Sleep well, did you?'

'Sorry, I…'

'No matter,' scowled the legate, turning away from the tribune and facing Alexander. 'Primus pilus! This is a stab to the heart. Invasion! Such men have no honour, my friend. Do you not agree?'

'My noble legate sees our problem well,' replied Alexander. 'Our strength lies in our discipline and training. We can hold out against the enemy but we have no reserves with which to counter-attack and push these invaders into the wastelands of the north.'

'Primus pilus, Standard bearer of the Ninth Legion, prove again how well you defend the Ninth's Standard,' said the legate.

Alexander snapped to attention.

'Raise all my centurions, Primus pilus, I order you. Use all your noble training and pitch our Standard on that bridge. Defend the Standard and defend Rome. There must be no retreat, Primus pilus.' Thoughts of retreating from the chosen place of their great council caused a cold fear to ripple through the legate's body, thoughts of his tongue failing to find words of explanation in the Senate in Rome bit into his brain. A droplet of fear, perhaps dread, leaked from his balding head. Thoughts of political ruin caused panic to swell in his gut and manifest itself in a voice of hysteria. 'Alexander! There must be no surrender! There are no orders to surrender!

'Consider it done,' swore Alexander, strapping his legate into armour of gold. 'I will take my leave, oh noble legate.'

'Wait!' cried the elderly commander. The phobia of failure in the eyes of Rome raged in the legate's mind. 'Give my beeswax imprint to our messenger. The message in the writing tells the Legate of the Sixth to ride north with all haste to help repel the Caledonian invasion. You must send our best rider south to valley of the lakes. The Sixth Legion is resting by the lakeside on the way to the great council. They must relieve us if we are to hold Luguvalium but they must also send riders south to those who march to the council. The word of invasion must be passed. You must impress upon our messenger that we stand until the Sixth arrives. Each late minute means a Roman death.'

Nodding in agreement, Alexander pocketed the beeswax, clenched his fist across his heart in salute, and retired to his duties.

The cornua sounded. First one, and then a symphony of music followed as Roman trumpets sounded action stations and Alexander's cohorts mustered to the call.

Duncan heard the sound of a faint bugle and swore. The crucial element of surprise lost at the final bridge! 'We are discovered, my clansmen,' shouted the rugged Pict. 'I shall lead you over the bridge whilst many of our number practice subterfuge. Take strength from your sword; wield well your axes of desire. Forward! Let us take this battle forward. Attack, I say. Attack!'

A multitude of Picts rose up as one and scurried towards the Eden Bridge with Duncan's tall figure leading the way.

Rome responded with Alexander's second cohort soon in armour.

A horse was found; Julius was chosen; Alexander spoke.

'Ride to the land of the great lakes, south of the settlement known as Voreda.' Alexander handed over the beeswax impression. 'Deliver this. Ride towards the great mountains of Britannia that rise towards the grey clouds. Here you will find the lake the Britons call Ullswater.'

Julius pocketed the beeswax. He carried only a spear for protection as he leapt upon his horse: it was a beautiful white charger. With neither stirrup nor saddle, he tugged masterfully on his stallion's mane as he listened to Alexander's final instructions.

'No man rides faster than you, Julius. No man this day carries any greater obligation than you. You must ride as freely as the wind and use each ascent as an eagle soars in the sky. Feed not your steed nor fill your hungered belly. When climbing hills command your charger well and think not of tomorrow's gallop, for there may be no tomorrow for us. Do this, I command you, Julius.'

Sticking out his chest, shaking his spear with arrogant pride, Julius hollered, 'Better to die for Rome than surrender to a Pict! I ride for the Ninth, Alexander. I shall ride to Rome if needs be. I give you my word; I give you my honour, Alexander.'

Alexander saluted in final tribute as a single arrow dived from the sky and drilled into soil a mere yard from where they spoke. Thin shadows flattened across the earth as more arrows filled the skies and plummeted downwards in search of the unwary.

'This day I plant our Standard high, Julius,' revealed Alexander, ignoring the attack from above. 'This day we do not move. This day is our day. Fly like a bird south to the valley of the great lakes, some twenty leagues and five or more. Deliver the beeswax message but tell the men of the Sixth that our Standard is in danger. Bring back the Sixth and you will bring us back our lives. Go, Julius... Without you... We are doomed.'

The horse pranced and bucked in anticipation as Julius flaunted his spear defiantly in the air. Turning, Julius galloped south through the streets of Luguvalium as the sound of armour and leather, and swords and shields, rattled in his ear.

Alexander watched his main chance disappear up the incline towards Luguvalium's market place before switching his mind to the coming battle. Running to a bonfire in the middle of their camp, he quickly lit a taper and inserted the flame into the heart of the wooden edifice. He stood back and watched the smoke drift into the sky, growing in strength, billowing in confusion, signalling to men at a fort by the Caldew that they were under attack. It was a plea for help. Then the fire took hold, crackling and sizzling in its birth, in its infancy.

'Hurry!' instructed Alexander. 'Mars is with us. Gather your shields. Standard Bearers to the front.'

Anxious legionaries clambered from their tents, gladius and pilum: iron and ebony, clattering noisily in confusion as the might of the Ninth Legion listened to orders trumpeting across their bustling campsite.

In nearby fields, a deer ran and a fox scuttled to its lair. An oystercatcher dipped into the reeds and buried itself in a nest. The old grey river lapped at its banks as its course meandered slowly to the Solway Firth.

As Duncan's first foot made the wooden bridge across the river, Alexander's foremost cohort barred their way. Shields in font of their chests and pilum pointed forward, their manoeuvre resembled a porcupine under attack, for under attack they were. Clerks and surveyors ran to warn the townsfolk of Luguvalium amid an avalanche of arrows falling from the heavens. Kneeling on high ground on the north bank of the Eden, archers fired high into the air searching out their quarry in the enemy's campsite. A clerk fell, skewered from behind. A musician felt the flint drill through his neck, as his throat was rendered useless by an arrow from the sky. The Ninth Legion rushed into position bolstering their porcupine tactic by lining up behind their defences with majestic strength. Yet men continued to fall, pierced by the arrows of Caledonia.

Alexander ignored the first brief encounter on the bridge. The centurion, leader of men, bravest of the brave, strode amongst his legionaries. Oblivious to the enemy, turning his back against the Picts, his contempt for the aggressor was apparent to his cohorts before him. He mounted a pile of shields lying near the Eden Bridge and stood head and shoulders above his noble legion.

'Men of the Ninth,' and courage and leadership were stamped in his voice and the manner of his standing, 'Plant your Standards well for there are no orders for retreat. Hear me! No surrender, men of the Ninth.'

Turning to face his enemy on yonder banks of Stanwix, Alexander shook his vine wood staff and boomed scorn and terror across the broad divide. 'Their numbers will never exceed the power of Mars. This day we stand with honour for the glory of Rome.'

Alexander, Optio Ad Spem, seized the Legion's Standard in his mighty fist and sank it heavily into the centre of the Eden Bridge. He shouted aloud, 'Here we stand! Here we fight! For the glory of the Ninth!'

Lungs filled with air, chests bulged, and weapons of destruction rattled and shivered in the morning sun. Battle cries went up: a throaty cheer from inspired defenders, and a lusty roar from hungry invaders.

A rabble of Pict charged across the broad bridge throwing axes and spears high into a wall of Roman shields. Screams of agony penetrated the air as a handful of legionaries fell under an array of cutting blades. More centuries took their place as yard by yard the Ninth Legion strengthened their defences and inched their way to the centre of the Eden Bridge. Some held shields high above their heads to prevent injury from falling arrows while others carried shields to their front to deny thrusting blades. Their Standard dominated the structure as the legion gathered round their charge. Alexander knew that the Standard was the rallying point. No legion had ever lost its Standard outright. If taken, a legion would fight for years to regain its Standard. To the Standard they rallied, a symbol of attrition, a noble emblem of universal power.

In the hours that followed, blades cut, blood ran red, and the Ninth's Standard stood bloodstained but proud.

Hand to hand fighting endured with the sheer weight of numbers forcing a deluge of warring men into the centre of the mighty bridge. The biggest bridge in the north, crossing the widest river in Luguvalium, creaked and shook with the weight of fighting men. Screaming, brawling warriors battled for control of the wooden structure as three thousand Picts found shallow water two miles upstream near the confluence of the Petteril. They waded through waist high water, crossed the mainstream, and turned to strike at Alexander's campsite from the rear.

Julius was galloping towards Voreda, tugging his stallion's mare, riding for all he was worth. He wouldn't let them down. He would return, triumphant, to save his friends from slaughter. Julius would be there for his colleagues, once he'd gathered reinforcements.

At the crest of a hill to the south of Voreda, Ullswater finally came into view, bathing in an unexpected spell of sunshine. The towering fells of the land of the lakes sprouted above the grey-blue tranquil waters of Ullswater. With renewed vigour in his heart, Julius mastered his stallion towards the Sixth's camp.

Suddenly, there was a narrow stream and then the branch of a tree appeared without warning, but Julius's eyes were focused on the lake below. At the last second, he ducked, yet the weeping bough caught Julius on the side of the head and he reared on the stallion. Back on its hind legs, the stallion unfastened Julius and he fell to the ground. As Julius plunged to the earth, the beeswax message slipped from his robe…

Duncan the Bold hacked ferociously, sword in one hand and battleaxe in the other. Fearless in leadership, he discarded the thrusting, stabbing javelins before him and battered his way into a wall of Roman shields. He forced the defenders backwards on their heels with a swish of his tartan and a slice of his blade. Skewers of doom clouded the light as arrow and slingshot rained down on the Ninth Legion. Screams and cries of desperation ripped apart the morning as a mob of Picts pushed forward from the north while the Ninth defended with a colossal wall of imposing shields. As the second cohort took primary position in the defensive strategy, more cohorts rushed to the fray. The centurions rapidly deployed their men amid the trumpet calls and flashing blades of battle.

Alexander fingered the handle of his weapon, its killing edge encased within a leather sheath, withdrew his gladius and sought out a giant of a man to whom the Picts were rallying. The centurion cut down one attacker, trampled over the tartan of another, and slashed viciously at an approaching tribesman.

'Forward! Forward!' screamed Duncan, taking a spear in his hand. 'Luguvalium will be ours. Forward!' His spear thrust; its iron point to kill.

'Hold fast,' ordered Alexander, in control. 'More cohorts to the Standard! Shields on high! Fortuna has granted our respite. Hold fast.'

Eden Bridge was littered with wounded, dead, fighting, and dying men. From the banks of Stanwix thousands queued to battle on the bridge, and in Alexander's eyes, there could be no retreat to the safety of the narrow streets and meandering lanes of Luguvalium. The bridge had to be held. Indeed, there could be no retreat since there were no reserves to call upon; there could be no retreat since there were no orders to retreat.

The two men locked their eyes in mortal combat as Duncan slashed his way into a wall of Roman shields. Alexander attacked the giant Pict, flaying his pilum in one hand while his gladius searched for the enemy's chest. As Duncan's multitude pressed forward, Alexander felt his pilum slip away. He felt Duncan's blade cut deep into his arm. Blood spilled from the centurion's body. Alexander fell backwards into a row of leather shields, dropping his gladius, and gesticulating in majestic defence with his vine wood staff: his symbol of authority. The staff swished through the air cutting the invader deep in his face as Alexander tried to roll beneath his second cohort's shields.

A craggy face, seethed in blood, scarred, looked down into Alexander's deep brown eyes. Duncan yelled in victory as he buried his sword in Alexander's stomach. Duncan twisted his blade, rupturing the belly before continuing onward to hack at the second cohort's defences.

Duncan trampled boldly across Alexander's body. Seconds later, a quartet of revenging javelins were thrust out from a wall of shields and embedded deep in Duncan's chest. Heaving and pushing, their pilums stabbing and thrusting, Alexander's comrades took revenge on the Caledonian leader as Roman spears propelled the heathen's body backwards into a multitude of screaming Picts. A barbed curl at the end of a pilum drove deep into the heathen's chest. The pilum broke at its wooden neck and a barbed iron point remained embedded in the chest as its shaft broke and trailed the ground. Duncan's blood dripped from the barbed curl and life oozed from his chest. Duncan died on that bridge; his body cut to ribbons.

Alexander rolled from the woodwork, threw out his good arm in an attempt to grasp a stanchion, but fell with a final groan towards the river. In the final micro-seconds of his valiant life, Alexander mustered all his remaining strength and thundered, 'No surrender.' It was his final order.

With a splash, droplets of water raced into the air and the centurion sank towards unknown depths. With a gentle, unsoundly thud, he hit the bottom of the riverbed. His body cavorted, twisted, turned, and wrestled with the gently flowing reeds of the Eden as waters turned red with his fluid and the Tablet of Masada, the rock of Judea, sought escape from his bloodstained robe. Alexander's mind raced back to the banks of the Euphrates and a place in a desert where there was only peace and quiet and solitude. His mind raced back to Mount Hermon and the Golan Heights and Damascus. His mind raced back in time, curving and spinning in a whirlpool of anguish. There was blackness in the water, a chasm in his mind, and an abyss of unknown depth. Then there was nothing.

Minutes later, defiant to the last, Alexander's body floated to the surface in the finality of his death.

His mystical rock: the Tablet of Masada: his legacy, drowned without trace in the murky waters of the Eden. The rock buried itself in the muddy sands of the River Eden. The legacy of the Ninth rested in the sands of time, as all around fought Luguvalium for the glory of the Ninth.

Charging, warring Picts made Duncan's battle-plan succeed as all hell broke out in Luguvalium. Having crossed the Eden, the Caledonian Picts reaped havoc on the five thousand men of the Ninth Legion. From all four asides, the Ninth found themselves under attack, falling back to the Standard and defending their honour as best they could.

Slingshots of slaughter, burning arrows of ruination, and the cold clash of steel, mingled with screams of injured, dying warriors as Luguvalium gave way to hordes of incorrigible Picts. Flames grew with a lick and then a lash and then took hold, burning and destroying everything in its path.

Hours later, in burning, sobbing, Luguvalium, the Standard of the Ninth was lost forever to the men of Caledonia. The Standard was seized from the bridge, never to be seen again. Yet by midday, Caledonia's marauding Picts were halved in number, held back from final victory by the disciplined, well-trained remnants of Alexander's bloodied second cohort, and a handful of men from the Caldew fort who had responded to a distress signal in the sky.

A cornua sounded in the distance...

The sound of cornua grew in the ear...

The sound of cornua grew in the ear and was accompanied by the thunder of horses' hooves...

Julius led the way, arrogantly shaking his spear, bleeding from the head, roaring revenge, galloping through the streets with the splendour of the Sixth Legion behind him. Yet his horse was broken, spent in its endeavour, and exhausted by the long gallop from Ullswater. The horse made the Market Square and promptly collapsed, stone dead.

Julius pulled himself from underneath his valiant steed as the Sixth Legion jogged into position. Limping from his fall, Julius took a shield from a dead centurion and joined the men who had journeyed from Ullswater.

A cornua sounded again. The Sixth Legion formed its battle lines.

The auxiliary infantry dominated the ground at the front of the legion. Each man stood a yard apart from his colleagues, but behind the auxiliaries, the Sixth Legion formed a wall of shields and gradually closed tightly together. Closer and closer they jostled until there was no daylight between their shields and no break in the line of shields. Eventually, they formed a shell of leather shields that was totally protected from an attack from either front or rear. They were a tortoise shell standing in waiting.

The cornua sounded and the legion stood in silence. Five thousand men heaved and panted in exertion from their journey, stood and inhaled the acrid air of Luguvalium, and stood in ordered readiness as they allowed the thumping of their hearts to subside.

The cornua sounded and the legion set off at a slow march from the Market Square. As the legion marched towards the Eden Bridge, the heat of the flames licked their shields, threatened their tunics, and warmed their faces. They saw the narrow lanes of Luguvalium on fire as they marched into a cauldron of burning hate.

The men of the Sixth Legion saw blood red fluid running down muddy gutters, yet still they held their pace at a slow march. They saw the injured, yet still they held their line and made no fissure in their shields. They could smell burning timbers and see burning flesh, yet still they made no move to help their fallen comrades. They heard the screams of fighting men and the cold clash of steel in a valley below, yet still they marched in slowness down the bank.

The cornua sounded and their march became a jog. Their metal gleamed, their Standard shone, their leather rubbed, and dancing robes swished with the speed of moving men. The cornua sounded and their march became a run. The cornua sounded and their run became a charge. Their run was held at line abreast and still there was no fracture in their wall of leather shields. The rumble of the half boot pounding on the ground drove fear into the heart of Caledonia. The mud splattered and the thunder of five thousand charging men echoed in the luscious green valley of the Eden. The cornua sounded again and the tightness of their shields fractured slightly and allowed a wall of pilum to spearhead the attack. Suddenly, they were terrifying and formidable, and magnificent in their control. Awesome, they were a mass of charging men with shields and steel thrusting into battle. The tortoise shell exploded, erupted, turned into a raging porcupine as the Sixth Legion stormed towards the bridge.

The cornua sounded and the men of the Ninth reacted to the signal in the music. The Ninth split, abandoned the ground and ran to east and west. The Ninth ducked, dived for cover, opened up a gap, and threw the sucker punch. The porcupine of the Sixth Legion stormed into the space in a masterpiece of Roman tactics. One minute the Caledonian warriors were fighting a weakened, tired Ninth; the next they were looking into a wall of colossal shields and row upon row of thrusting pilum.

The dying Ninth closed behind the advancing Sixth.

With leather shields and sharpened sword, the Sixth pushed their aggressor back to the riverbank. A throat was cut and a chest was staved and a limb was sliced to the ground. There was a roar of battle, a smell of fear, and a sobbing cry of a dying man embracing the green valley of the Eden. To the west, in the lands of the Petteril and to the east, in the lands of the Caldew, the Caledonian threat was dispatched with military precision.

Leaderless, dumbfounded by the brave, illogical courage of such defenders, Caledonia fled in retreat to the safety of her heather-clad moors.

By evening time, a myriad of glowing flames lit up the heavens, scarlet tongues of fire acted as a beacon in the Borderlands; a flag to mark the fiercest battle in Britannia's Roman history.

The fires, by the rivers, in Luguvalium, were doused. The Sixth Legion held fast the northwest frontier of the Roman Empire.

When the Picts had gone and the dying had been gathered, Julius and the few remnants of an inspired Ninth Legion stood on that bridge. They had fought for their Standard on that bridge. They had died on that bridge that day.

The Eden ran red with the blood of man.

Within a year, Hadrian arrived in the Borderlands and sent an army across the Eden to occupy high ground at Stanwix. A fort named 'Petriana' was built on nine acres of land. From that day on Stanwix grew in prosperity and splendour. In the same year, work commenced on the great wall that the Romans had planned. A thousand strong cavalry regiment moved into the fort of Petriana and policed Hadrian's Wall and the rugged, unforgiving lands of the border.

But not that day in burning, violent, sorrowful Luguvalium! Not that day when the Standard was lost. No! Not that day. Thousands died that day. But no more the Ninth… Lost in the rivers of time…

*

Stretching, Boyd checked his watch. Twenty minutes had gone and the tablet of chocolate was melting. He felt the tacky paper and stickiness on his fingers. Setting off, he jogged south into Carlisle. Boyd strode out, refreshed, smiling, with the tail of his bandanna billowing behind him in the breeze. Laughing aloud, he sprinted down Stanwix Bank to the amusement of a shopkeeper, a teacher, and a shopper clutching her list. The Chinese Gardens were on his left and the Edenside Cricket Club was on his right. The tarmac levelled and he ran like the wind across the Eden Bridge. The bridge was broad and carried four lanes of traffic on the approach to Hardwicke Circus roundabout and the box-shaped Civic Centre.

At the end of the bridge Boyd turned left and ran down a walkway to a footpath by the side of the Eden. Stepping from the pathway, he felt grass beneath his feet. The grass gave way to loose gravel, which gave way to sand situated next to the old grey river. The grass was green, the banks were serene, and flowers grew and blossomed in the sun. Sand martins, ducks, and kingfishers were at play. Boyd knelt in sand and placed his chocolate on the ground. He removed his sunglasses, immersed his hands in cold water, and felt the tingle of the current as he cleansed himself. Gone were the stress and fatigue of a troubled mind. He removed his bandanna, soaked it the cool water, and draped it across his shoulders so that his back could enjoy the soothing qualities of the Eden.

'You jogging?'

Boyd looked along the bank and saw a fisherman.

'You fishing?' replied Boyd.

'Saw you running over the bridge.' The fisherman played his rod and line as his eyes followed a float downstream. 'You're not very fast.'

Boyd thought the angler was cheeky but replied, 'If I run too fast my eyes will miss the scenery and I won't smell the flowers on the path.'

The fisherman replied, 'Poet, are we?'

'No, but then you don't seem to have caught any fish either.'

'How far have you run?'

'About seven miles! How long have you been fishing?'

'Since 1950.'

Boyd sensed banter in the words and saw a flask on the ground by the fisherman. 'Caught anything yet?' asked Boyd.

'Nope.'

'Wrong bait?' asked Boyd.

'Nope, but if I catch a fish whenever I come down to the river there will soon be no more fish to catch. One day I'll catch one and I'll throw it back so that the stocks are not depleted.'

Chuckling, Boyd sensed irony in the fisherman's words. 'It's a long time to wait to catch a fish. Have you been home since 1950?'

'Only for fresh bait,' replied the fisherman.

A yellow fibreglass canoe paddled by, carrying a helmeted youth.

Did you fill your flask when you went home?' Boyd's eyes fell again on the flask and then queried the fisherman.

The fisherman glanced at the flask by his side. Fingering his line, he pulled back his rod as he threatened a fish deep in the river. 'Help yourself, jogger. Pour two. The name is Steve, just Steve.'

'Thanks, fisherman. Don't mind if I do.' Boyd stooped down and unscrewed the flask. 'Mine's Boyd, just Boyd.' Hot, steaming tea flowed into two plastic cups. Boyd offered one to the fisherman.

'I used to work this river in the fifties.' A mitten clutched a cup and a fisherman drank in silence. His eyes chased his float bobbing on the surface of the river. Catching the current, his float disappeared underneath the centre arch of the bridge chasing a fibreglass canoe.

'How did you work this river?'

'Flood prevention, jogger! Me and my mate, we stopped the flooding you know, most of it at any rate. It was good money in them days. Now I sit and daydream and wonder if I'll ever catch a fish.'

'Long time ago, the fifties.'

'It was a long time ago, jogger. Hey! Your chocolate has melted.'

'So it has.' Boyd stepped back and threw his tablet of chocolate into the Eden. There was a plop and a strain of water momentarily raced into the air. Draining his plastic cup, Boyd stepped up the bank towards the tarmac path. 'Thanks for the tea. I prefer coffee myself. Good luck with your fishing. I hope you catch something soon.'

'Thanks! Good luck with your jogging.'

'Flood prevention, you say?'

'That's right.'

Boyd turned to run; the fisherman shouted, 'You shouldn't have thrown that tablet into the river, Boyd.'

'Why not?'

'Someone will find it one day.'

'A fisherman, like you, surely not?'

'You're wrong, Boyd. I found a tablet once.'

'You found a tablet?'

'Yes, in that river.'

'Wow!'

'You don't want to know about it though.'

'Chocolate tablet, was it?'

'I know you, jogger. I know who you are. You're the policeman in those riots, aren't you? I saw you on the telly last week.'

Boyd nodded with a half smile but offered no reply.

'You look taller in real life. You were small on my telly.'

'Does it bother you that I'm the policeman from those riots?' asked Boyd, warily.

'Nope! Not even if you're bigger in real life.'

'Good!' replied Boyd.

'Aye! I found the tablet that caused all that trouble, you know; yon Jewish tablet that caused the Tullie House affair. It was me who discovered that tablet in the fifties. Did you know that?'

'I knew someone had found it. I didn't know it was you, fisherman.'

'Steve, remember?'

'Sorry, Steve.'

'It's a long time ago, the time I found it, Boyd. I couldn't talk proper then. I was younger; things were different. I didn't know much in them days.'

Turning from his path, Boyd stepped back towards the fisherman. The old grey river slid silently by lapping at the edge of the bank, a float from a rod bobbing the surface of the water, a canoe gone. The Eden flowed in its gentle greyness towards the Solway Firth and the Irish Sea. 'Mind telling me about it, Steve?'

'Nope! Sit down, Boyd, and I'll tell you.'

The fisherman told his story and Boyd listened. It was a story of the River Eden and a fisherman called Steve.

*

3

~ ~ ~

Steve's Story:
Dateline: Autumn, 1951: The banks of the River Eden.

Summer birds were migrating to warmer climes far away. Gathering in their flocks, they set off south as the first cold nip arrived and autumn's leaves fell to the ground. The deer were no more; driven out by man centuries ago; driven out with the passage of time. All but gone from the land were the willow trees, cut down to a scant collection of fine stalwarts in the park. Yet willow was still heard when a cricket bat and a ball of leather resounded from nearby Edenside wicket. The wooden bridge once spanning the banks of the river had disappeared and four generations shopping in the market place held no knowledge of its being. The town of Luguvalium had become a thriving city while its principal river still flowed westward through Rickerby Park to the Solway Firth. Of course, the path of the river had changed over the centuries but it still separated the banks of Stanwix from the rest of Carlisle. Nothing had really changed; only the faces, costumes and buildings, and the religion of those who walked in the market place.

A torrent of muddy brown water flowed freely from rusting metallic teeth. A foot moved slightly and, with a couple of blips from an accelerator pedal, Steve jostled a dredger into position. Large rugged hands engineered two levers and spun a tiny steering wheel that caused a huge bucket to swing towards the riverbank. There was a loud clanking noise, stone intimidating metal, followed by a swirl of water and a rush of mud. A row of teeth jolted open and a collection of rocks fought for supremacy as they rolled out onto a sodden grass verge bordering the old grey river. Then the exhaust backfired and Steve's cab shook in contempt of its heavy load. Peering through his windscreen, Steve realised he'd scooped up more than just a bucketful of silt from the bed of the Eden. He'd taken rocks from the riverbed.

Pursing his lips, Steve shook his head, mystified by the rocks. According to their foreman, they should only find sand and silt.. He ought not to find any rocks. Stonework would only slow his work down and there was precious little time remaining to dredge the riverbed and remove the required amount of earth before winter set in and the horrible rains came.

Scattered leaves and an early morning chill brought a wintry promise. Winter meant snow, ice, rain and floods; a recipe for another disastrous bout of lowland flooding. And with the first fall of snow Cumbria would isolate itself from the rest of the world.

Steve drummed his fingers on his steering wheel and considered the plight of those unfortunate residents who lived in houses set back from the river. People were sick and tired of filling sandbags every year in a pathetic attempt to defeat the deplorable deluge, but he knew lowering the river bed would prevent some flooding in future years; provided he could get on with his job. Damn rocks, he thought.

Switching off his engine, Steve climbed from the warmth of his cab and stepped into ankle deep water. He was grateful to his thick woollen socks and black Wellington boots. A bitter wind whipped across Bitts Park and snapped at the Cumbrian's exposed ears. Turning up the collar of his donkey jacket, he dug his hands into his side pockets and stepped gingerly onto the embankment. There was a patch of mud and he felt himself slipping back into the river. Making a grab for the bank, he pulled himself onto dry land.

His mate, Pete, approached. 'What's the crack 'ere then, Steve?'

'I've nowt but started morning's dredging when I gets me sel' a bucket load o' stone. What's reckon t' that, Pete?'

'What's the problem then? Just dump 'em on the riverbank wid yon load o' silt. We'll git it away to the tip this afternoon.'

'Aye, I 'ear what you're say, Pete, but deeks at yon stones. There's some gay old looking rocks in amongst that lot, pal. Take a deeks at this lot.'

Pete eyed the bucket teeth distorted by the size and weight of rocks dragged from the river. He walked to the collection of stones and gazed down, mesmerised by the broken dredger's teeth and mystified by a strange assortment of masonry. The two men stood brazenly against the wind, hands in pockets, and deep in thought.

'Steve!' said Pete. 'Some of these rocks have got drawings on 'em. Words like! Could be from them fancy houses up in Stanwix. Y'know, where them rich folks live, up on't hill.'

'Let me see then, bonny lad.' Steve pushed one or two rocks onto their side with his foot and ran his thick fingers across their carvings. 'Roman! Bet ya a penny to a pun them's Roman, Pete. See! Them's not recent brickwork. Yon marks are gay ancient. I'll tell ya that for nowt.'

'Nah! My pun says Greek!' replied Pete. 'Aye, could be Greek, I reckon. Maybes' Viking. Not Roman… What do you say, bonny lad?'

'No way! Them is Roman,' insisted Steve. 'I've seen stuff like that at yon museum.'

'Museum? What museum would that be, Steve?'

'Tullie 'ouse. I went with the school once. They've got all them bricks from the Roman Wall in there. Well, all what's been found like. Reckon yon could be that Roman Wall; yon wall that 'Adrian built to keep them Celtic fans out.'

Pete laughed. 'A wall in yon river? Don't seem reet to me, lad.'

Two brains ticked over before Cumbrian logic sneaked into 1951.

'We need an architect. One of them brainy folks from up Stanwix,' suggested Steve.

Being the senior of the duo, Pete decided to take command. Thrusting out an index finger, Pete stabbed Steve in his chest and summed their predicament up. 'Roman! That's what I reckon, bonny lad. Roman.'

'You bet on Greek, pal. Make your mind up,' insisted Steve.

'Okay then. If them's Greek, you owe me a quid, Steve.'

'A quid! More like 'alf a crown and yer on,' gambled Steve.

'Two shillings and six pence! Now that's a lot of dosh these days, Steve. Sure?'

'Aye! 'Alf a crown, not a penny more,' said Steve.

Done! You'll be owing me 'alf a crown when yon architect fella says them's Greek,' said Pete.'

Together they inspected the rocks, turning them over cautiously, minding their fingers, and smoothing their cold hands over the writing. As rocks rolled from left to right, a double-decker bus crossed nearby Eden Bridge and a siren invaded Bitts Park. A screaming ambulance overtook the bus at high speed on its journey to the Cumberland Infirmary. The constant wailing of its klaxon sang even when the ambulance turned west towards Willowholme and threaded its way through Irishgate. The ambulance passed Carlisle Castle, the Cathedral, the State-managed brewery and Trinity church as the town hall clock was reluctantly striking nine o'clock in the morning.

'We'd best tell our foreman. We need an architect to take a deeks, definitely,' confirmed Pete. 'In any case, we needs ta tell yon foreman that yer bucket's buggered. Well and truly knackered, bonny lad and that's a fact!'

'Reet then. I'll do nae more 'til I knows what's up,' sighed Steve, resigned to a long wait by a cold river in a damp and windy park.

55

Zipping tight his anorak hood, Pete turned into the chill wind and made for a nearby telephone kiosk.

Cluttered documents, newspapers opened at a racing page, mucky half-filled tea mugs, and a leaking red biro festooned the foreman's desk. A splatter of dirt and a stack of late invoices added to commercial confusion. Things did not improve when a hidden telephone rang and caused his newspaper to fall from his desk as frantic fingers raced to find the offending tone under a pile of paperwork.

Eventually, angrily, he snatched the offending telephone and said, 'Works department, foreman speaking. Mike, to them wot knows me.'

Mike quickly pulled a pen towards him, cursed under his breath at its leaky mess, fumbled for a chubby pencil balanced behind his ear, and moved a yellowing writing pad nearer to his elbow.

'Roman, you say! Greek! I doubt it. Whereabouts, Pete?' Nodding in recognition, hastily scribbling notes on a yellowed pad. 'Near the cricket club, Bitts Park! In the Eden but about a mile from the Caldew... Got that... Nowt to do with Works. I'll get onto Surveyors department. It's their pigeon. Tell Steve to get back to work. We've got to get those flood defences finished before winter.'

Lifting a dog-eared internal telephone directory, Mike thumbed the pages while speaking into the mouthpiece with a 'phone balanced on his shoulder and his head crooked to its earpiece.

'No, you did right to 'phone me... What...? No, I'll sort it out, Pete. Good lad.' The 'phone moved towards its cradle but then rushed back to the foreman's ear. 'Put it back? Don't you dare, lad. It's our heritage, that is. It needs looking at... An architect? I'll get you an architect, lad.'

Mike crashed his 'phone to the cradle and immediately dialled another number. He swore once more at an unexpected interruption to his routine. A collection of papers dropped needlessly to the floor as he tried to order his telephone, his pencil, and his mess. A voice on the telephone mumbled a response but before the usual morning pleasantries were exchanged the Works foreman launched into a frantic attack.

'Surveyors? It's Mike from Works. We've rocks in the Eden where you said there should be just sand... Rocks! Do you hear me? What do you mean, so what...? Contract'll be late, that's what... Bugger all I can do about it now... You lot said sand, nowt about stone... Surveyors, call yerself surveyors... What's that? No, I think we've got some Roman remains pulled from the riverbed... I'll try Parks but I just wanted to let you lot know that you've buggered us up. Thank you for nothing.'

Crashing his 'phone down once more, Mike flicked some pages and dialled again.

'Parks department? Good… Do you do Roman remains? No! Well, who bloody well does…?' A question hung in the air before an answer was suggested. 'Right. What's his extension number…? Got that. Thanks.'

The process repeated itself. Another number was answered.

'This is the museum curator speaking. How may I help you?' A soft and cultured voice signified appreciation for the warmth of a curator's office in Castle Street. 'An architect?' He stifled a chuckle. 'No, I'll warrant you mean an archaeologist.' Jeremy, the curator, softened. 'However, if there isn't an archaeologist free, then I'll certainly bear an architect in mind.' Listening, Jeremy adjusted his spectacles and balanced them on the end of his nose. The museum curator's young heart beat faster as he considered the news from the Eden. 'Thank you. May I just take some details?' He reached for a fountain pen. 'What's your name, sir…? Please call me Jeremy. This is first class news, Mike. It may be Roman; it may not. I'll take a look myself. Now, can you kindly give me the exact location once more, Mike?' A smidgen of excitement spouted from Castle Street. 'Is it near the Edenside cricket club?'

A few moments of note taking followed before Jeremy replaced his telephone and turned to a bookshelf. He selected a book on Roman history but sighed in dismay. It occurred to Jeremy that the stonework might be ornate bricks used in the construction of some of the more elaborate dwellings built on Stanwix Bank: the hillside overlooking the Eden. Jeremy consulted his tome, checked its index, flicked its pages, and guided his eyes across a selection of black and white photographs. Replacing the book, Jeremy pocketed his ignition keys, and walked into Paternoster Row. A black cat padded across his path and fled into the museum gardens. He unlocked a green Morris Minor, fired its engine, and set off for Bitts Park.

Steve was first to sight a duffel coat, a fresh college scarf fluttering in a wind, and a pair of pristine green Wellington boots walking along an embankment. Waving to Pete, he shouted, 'Here's yon architect fella, just a young 'un, by the looks of it. He'll know nowt, mark my words, bonny lad.'

The two diggers strolled casually towards the young museum curator. There were nods of recognition as the three men stood by the river and noisy traffic rolled across the Eden Bridge.

'You the museum man?' A question loaded with begrudged respect.

'Correct, gentlemen. Jeremy is my name. I'm from Tullie House. It's so kind of you to have rang.'

There was a flurry of limp handshakes.

'I'm Steve. This is Pete. It's not kind. We've nae interest in Roman remains, pal. There's money at stake, lad. Private money, that is. We've a bet on, bonny lad. So be reet in what you say, young 'un.'

'Oh! Well, I don't know about that. Thanks for the call, though. Isn't it exciting? Are these the stones?' His eyes zeroed in on a pile of masonry and his feet set off in their direction. His green Wellington boots stopped at the stones and squelched in the mud.

'That they are, lad,' presided Pete. 'Steve 'ere says them stones is Roman; I say they're Greek. What do you say to that, bonny lad?'

'Well! We'll take a look, shall we?' A scarf fluttered and a pair of Wellington boots slithered in mud and wet grass.

Bending down, Jeremy examined their find. He adjusted his spectacles perched precariously on the tip of his narrow nose and sought to focus proceedings on the carvings. The museum curator was silent for a few moments. He offered a slight cough, one or two grunts, and a puzzled groan then he gathered his duffel coat firmly over his corduroy trousers and turned the rocks over carefully and humbly. It was as a mother tends a child. A wind whispered through Bitts Park and bit deep into the skin. Jeremy wrapped his scarf tighter, ignoring knowing smiles from hardier men who flashed their eyes at the eager bureaucrat, and then each other. The curator inspected the depths of the rocks, noting some frail vegetation that clung to the sides of the stonework. A small reference book was produced from an inside pocket. Pages were turned and comparison took place.

'These rocks have been here for many years. Look at the different colours of the soil deposits…' The onlookers examined the stone, mystified at the importance of soil deposits. Jeremy said, 'This tells you how long these rocks have been embedded in that river bed.'

Steve and Pete eyed each other in turn.

'Good fortune!' announced Jeremy, excitedly.

'Nowt good about it, lad. Them rocks have buggered the bucket teeth. We were told we were taking out silt and sand, not bloody rocks.

Machine's buggered. Well and truly knackered, it is. There'll be 'ell to pay with our foreman, mark my words, young un. Council's got nae money to repair buggered bucket teeth.'

'Sorry, I was talking to myself. This large stone looks like an altar to Fortuna, the Roman God of good fortune,' pronounced Jeremy.

'Telt ya, Pete. Thou owes me 'alf a crown,' smiled Steve, happier now, his leathery face beaming with satisfaction at his initial assessment of their archaeological remains.

Feasting his eyes over another large rock, Jeremy then took a stride towards an even larger stone.

'And this one resembles an altar to Jupiter, Father of all Roman Gods. Whereas this one…' He turned over yet another rock. 'This one looks like Myrias, the Persian God of Light. Yes, very popular with our Roman soldiers was Myrias, or Mithras, as some would say. God of Sun, you know. It's fascinating, just fascinating.'

'Persian! That's Greece, isn't it?' asked Pete, thinking of the princely sum of one half crown at stake.

'Oh no, some of the Romans worshipped Myrias,' advised Jeremy, quietly, almost to himself; his mind wandering back through countless centuries; his mind tied up with Rome and the history of its Empire. His mind neglected attention to similarities between Jewish and Roman artefact of the first century. Then a timeless wind howled in pain and cut through the air as nearby waters rippled in anticipation and Jeremy studied their find.

Jeremy continued to tickle the stones, his soft fingers caressing the smoothness of history and the etchings of a lost century. He turned a small tablet and weighed it in his palm. 'Out of place, this one,' he counselled. 'Nine inches by six by three, or thereabouts.' Jeremy angled the stone towards the sunlight. The flint work in the stone sparkled briefly and dulled as the sun rushed behind a cloud. 'It's broken in its bottom right hand corner and has a pronounced scratch across its markings.'

'Persian, bonny lad?' asked Pete.

The wind snarled with contempt and froze his bone in its coldness.

'Oh no, I doubt it, gentlemen. The break is clean and none of these other stones are particularly damaged. See! The flint work on this one looks like a Roman fort, probably a mile castle with all those turrets on it. It could be that same fort that everyone knows is there but no one has yet found. Yet these markings, below the carving of the fort, they look like some kind of candlestick in the bottom right hand corner. What a strange affair. It's a pity but the rock has fractured across the stonework and destroyed my ability to make a full analysis of the object at this time.'

'Not Viking then?' asked Pete, thinking of his half crown.

'No, definitely not!' replied Jeremy, emphatically, a crispness in his voice. 'Roman, I believe, but I'll need to validate this rock properly and arrange everything to be recovered to a laboratory. The rocks need dating correctly. There's a lot of work to do here although I'm pretty sure this is first century Roman artefact.'

'Artefact?' queried Pete.

'Artefact? It's a fancy word meaning remains,' replied Jeremy. 'I'll know better when experts from the university have studied this find. For now, we must get these remains back to Castle Street as soon as possible. I need to preserve these rocks before they're damaged further.'

Pete felt his half crown slipping away.

'Now then,' asked Jeremy. 'Where exactly did you find this lot?'

An empty palm shot out with its fingers splayed wide. A half crown changed hands, and Steve eagerly recounted the circumstances of his find. He pointed to the grey river and a buckled set of metallic teeth sheepishly peeping from the front end of a wet dredger.

'You men did well,' voiced Jeremy. A howling gale whipped at his undisciplined scarf and lashed at his corduroy trousers. 'Local historians believe that in the time of Hadrian a Roman Bridge spanned the Eden some fifty yards or so from the site of the current Eden Bridge. They think it was a wooden bridge, bound to have been made of wood really when you think about it.' Jeremy laughed. 'You men may have just discovered that site. Remarkable! Quite remarkable after all this time.'

'I found it,' replied a well-pleased Steve, the Queen's head rubbing the base of his thumb, a half crown finding its way into an old trouser pocket. 'T'was me, reet? I found yon wall in the river!'

Jeremy eased his spectacles back to the bridge of his nose and gathered his scarf saying, 'let's not get carried away, gentlemen. I think you've just contributed to our heritage and that's wonderful. A little more history has been uncovered, I suspect. Excellent!'

Steve sniffed and ignored Jeremy's ridiculous remark. Clownish student type; what did he know, thought Steve? The half crown was pocketed. The ale from the nearby Malt Shovel public house virtually tasted Steve's lips. He'd be drunk for a week on half a crown.

The wind dropped when a tide turned on the nearby Solway Firth. By afternoon, the latest Roman remains had been prudently labelled, photographed in situ, and carefully crated in wooden boxes. A wagon arrived, trundling through muddy grass. Some workmen lifted the crates into their wagon and the banks of the river were once again bare. The artefact was transhipped to a basement in Tullie House Museum. The dredgers dredged and the search for more stones continued. It was all to no avail. Nothing else was found, either that day or in the years ahead.

Deep in the sands of the River Eden lay the bottom right hand corner of the Tablet of Masada. It was abandoned, forgotten, unfound. In the heart of winter, rain and snow fell but there was no more flooding and two dredgers earned the thanks of a river-bound city. The secrets of Eleazar, of Judea, of Jacob, of Hussein, of Alexander, of the Ninth Legion, lay wrapped in an abyss of denial and error.

Under lock and key, snug and warm, the Tablet of Masada slept in the hallowed grounds of Carlisle's premier museum. Quietly and without reverence, the mystical Hebrew stone nestled next to its long-forgotten enemies, the altars of the Gods of Rome.

*

There was a ripple of white water and a grey flash of dorsal fin followed by a tingle of excitement from a fisherman and a jogger on the riverbank. With an exuberant heave on his rod, Steve played his line and felt the fish yield. Reaching down, smiling broadly at his unexpected success, Steve collected a landing net and moved towards his fish.

Boyd nodded, then laughed and asked, 'So all these years have gone by and you're still pulling things out of the Eden, Steve?'

'Trying hard! This is the first bit of luck I've had for years.' There was a gentle plop as a captured fish entered Steve's net.

'Ever studied history, Steve?'

'No call for history, just fishing,' replied Steve. 'Why do you ask?'

'Well that piece of rock you found in the Fifties was eventually named the Tablet of Masada.'

'Masada!' Steve knelt down on the grass and took hold of his fish. The tail fin splashed noisily as he caressed the belly of his fish. 'Are you telling me that after all these years that rock really was Greek, not Jewish? Am I half a crown out? What's half a crown in new money?'

'Oh no! Masada is an old Jewish fortress. First century actually!' said Boyd. 'An Israeli archaeologist discovered its remains in the Sixties.'

'Big deal!' scorned Steve, his eyes feasting in delight on his magnificent prisoner. 'What's so important about this Masadamba place?'

Boyd closed with Steve and peered into his landing net. 'Masada! It's a Hebrew fortress lying in the Negev desert, been hidden there for years.'

Steve's hands followed his fishing line towards the body of his fish. Gently, he examined a hook protruding from the jaw of the fish. Quiet now, it was as if the fish was a dull statute.

'Yes,' continued Boyd. 'Masada! It's a place synonymous with suicide; a word that stirred a nation, a legend that enshrined a revolution.'

'That's what the fish just did,' laughed Steve.

'Pardon!' puzzled Boyd.

'Committed suicide! I can't remember the last time I caught one.'

Boyd chuckled and said, 'you see, Steve, there was a mass suicide in Masada. It's been compared with the Holocaust of the Second World War.'

'And that was barbaric,' said Steve. With a twist and a tug Steve removed a curled hook from the mouth of his fish. 'Horrific even!'

'So now you know why Masada is such an important part of Jewish culture, Steve. It's a shrine of peace.'

Steve crawled carefully through the grass and reeds and gently liberated his fish into the grey waters of the River Eden. Then, standing, he watched his fish glide into the Eden's depths, free.

Boyd said, 'I had you down for a fry up with chips tonight, Steve.'

'Like I said, Boyd. Don't deplete those stocks. He's a young 'un. I put him back so that he can enjoy a bit more of life.'

'Then I got you wrong, Mister Fisherman.'

'And that archaeology man, he got it wrong too, Mister Jogger.'

'Yes, but it didn't cost him his job. In fact Jeremy became chief curator at Tullie House. I met him you know.'

'Nice bloke, bit young as I remember,' remarked Steve.

'That's how I know the story of the Tablet of Masada, Steve. Jeremy told me his side of the story.'

'Jeremy's story! What did he have to say?'

Jogger and fisherman looked into the serene waters as if searching for a fish that had somehow miraculously escaped into freedom.

Turning to Steve, Boyd said, 'Jeremy told me about David and his visit to Tullie House...

*

4

~ ~ ~

Jeremy's Story:
Dateline: Spring, 1991: Tullie House Museum, Carlisle:

With springtime in the season and a whistle on his lips, David hurried across the road and eyed the magnificent grandeur of Carlisle cathedral. A host of daffodils, a cluster of crocuses, and some welcome sunshine heralded his arrival in Castle Street and escorted his stroll towards the cathedral entrance. Occupying a dominant site in Carlisle city centre, next to Paternoster Row and Tullie House Museum, the Cathedral represented the power and glory of the Protestant Church; yet David wasn't a Protestant, despite his zealous belief in God. David was Jewish: he was a Jew.

Despite his apparent blissful whistling, David felt homesick and longed for his family in Tel Aviv. Although yearning for his Israeli homeland, he worked hard studying for an honours degree at Manchester University. It was the last year of his degree course.

David's family were thankful their son was studying in England. Although far from the family hearth, he was safe from the fear of war, and safe from Saddam Hussein's scud missiles. David's family remembered how in August 1990, some 540,000 of Saddam's Iraqi troops invaded Kuwait and devastated the country. David returned to his home in Tel Aviv that Christmas when Israel was at peace; the State of Israel refused to be drawn into a conflict that threatened to destabilise the Middle East. As time went by the Iraqis rejected calls to relinquish Kuwait and the United Nations were obliged to intervene, appointing an American General, H. Norman Schwarzkopf, to lead the allied response. Operation Desert Shield was born.

In January 1991, America, Saudi Arabia, Britain, Egypt, Syria and France, responded to Saddam Hussein's ugly offensive with a 500,000 strong Coalition army. Attacking the Iraqis, the Coalition drove their enemy back to the border. As the Iraqis retreated they burnt Kuwait's oil wells, desolating the land. The desert was on fire, burning and scorching all before it in an inferno of mindless antipathy. To make matters worse, Saddam's elite Republican Guard dug in on the border and held the advance. Determined to strike at the heart of Iraq, General Schwarzkopf skirted Saddam's crack troops and headed north as British and American Air Forces pounded enemy defences. Meanwhile, in an attempt to divert the attacking forces from the Iraqi - Kuwait border, Saddam Hussein chillingly launched his scud missiles at Israel and Saudi Arabia. Saddam launched his scud missiles against Tel Aviv from mobile carriers lying near the Israeli border with Jordan. In a further onslaught, he launched more missiles from mobile carriers lying in the southernmost reaches of the Negev desert. Arab fought Jew as the desert sands erupted in a cauldron of burning hatred. The desert was on fire and its storm knew no boundaries. Scud missiles rained down on the civilians of Tel Aviv while at the same time a further bombardment was launched into Saudi Arabia from inside the Iraq - Kuwait border. Still, Israel steadfastly refused to enter the war but gratefully accepted American air support. The world worried that Israel might unleash an atomic bomb against Iraq, and worried that the Arab countries of the Middle East might turn their attention to the lands of Israel. Saddam Hussein's attack on the Jewish nation was seen as an attempt to change the very course of the war. Perhaps the Iraqi leader hoped that Arabs belonging to the Coalition would turn against the Jewish State; perhaps he hoped that the Arabs of Syria, Egypt and Saudi Arabia would join forces with him and destroy Israel. It was to no avail, the Coalition forces tamed Iraq and Saddam Hussein was defeated in February 1991. The desert storm boiled, simmered, and then died in the sands - but at what price?

David remembered that night in February; the night before he was due to fly back to England and his university studies: the horrifying night when his family wandered into the street to watch American Patriot antimissile missiles race into the darkness and blow Saddam's scuds out of the skies. His family were lucky to be outside watching Patriot missiles destroying the incoming terror. It was while watching those warring fireworks that a stray scud honed in on Tel Aviv. The scud was launched in the Negev desert. It climbed into the darkened skies, roared to its apex, evaded Patriot missiles, and whispered silently in its earthbound flight. Then the scud dropped onto the roof of David's house and smashed his home into smithereens. His house exploded into a thousand pieces. The thump of Saddam's scud blew David through the air and onto his back. He rolled in the street until his back collided with a wall and he felt a sharp pain rip along his spine and detonate inside his head. His mother, father, brother, and his grandparents were blown off their feet with the blast from the scud. They were lucky; they only sustained cuts and bruises and aching muscles while their home was taken away from them: destroyed by an Arab scud. When their house became a crater, when they had wept all night, David returned to England and his studies and left his family searching for a new home.

The threat of war was never far from Israel and the terrorist threat proved a constant plague. Arab suicide bombers demolished schools and town centres in the name of Jihad: the Holy War. There were times when Palestinian terrorists wreaked havoc with their hit and run tactics, and there were periods when youths scowled hate at those who were Jewish. In England, David was safe from Saddam's scuds and his parents were happier.

There was a youthful spring in David's step but his mind was in turmoil. The nerves in his spine were tingling and his head would occasionally pound. His outwardly mobile appearance only hid an aching heart: a heart that was stinging from the jibes of those who ridiculed his attempt to grow a beard in imitation of his elders. His inner torment swelled from the ignorant, deranged insults directed at his faith. His heart throbbed with contempt for those who scorned the black trimmed hat that adorned his head. Contempt and affront burnt away at his religious beliefs.

David didn't tell his parents of the jibes, the insults and the ridicule, and he didn't tell them how difficult it had been for him to keep up with his university studies. He never mentioned his inability to compete with other students, of struggling to sustain the energy desired, and of those tingling nerves in his spine and the occasional pounding in his head. He sent no words to his parents, no letters home, and no telephone calls. David didn't want them to worry about Saddam's scuds returning and him not keeping up with his studies and falling behind the others. He didn't want them to worry about there not being much chance of a first class honours degree unless a miracle occurred. His parents knew if the Iraqis ever attacked Tel Aviv again, then at least David was safe across the seas. Hadn't they suffered enough, his family? Grandparents who spoke of a Holocaust in fearful hushed tones and a brother who feared the Arabs and the hit and run terrorists? Hadn't they suffered enough? He didn't tell his parents of the problems and turmoil in his mind. He had an assignment to do: an important one. It was an assignment that would make or break his degree course. His assignment had to be correct in its research; in its structure, in its writing. To fail would confirm the failure of his course. There would be no first class honours degree and he would return home in shame and failure. He could not return home in failure. Not David!

Steadying his hat in a sudden breeze, David felt his long black tailcoat swish round his knees. He walked through the cathedral grounds, strolling casually through the fresh lawns and early spring flowers, before visiting a café in the fratry. Ordering black coffee, he drowned it with sugar and rattled his cup with a frenzied stir. The drive from Manchester had proved enjoyable for the archaeology scholar. He had found solace in his journey north, marvelling at the tumbling fells of rural Cumbria as the motorway carved a path through Tebay Gap, marvelling at the sheep and patchwork fields that were bordered by picturesque dry stone walls; the sheer beauty of it all. Refreshed, he gathered his thoughts and his papers and stepped out into the sunlight to begin his research project.

Ancient Norman battlements soon came into view. The walls had dominated Carlisle's skyline since the twelfth century when Henry the First visited Carlisle in 1122 and ordered the site to be fortified with a castle and towers. The resultant fortress proved a solid obstacle to invading Scots in the following years. Indeed, some historians reckon Carlisle itself changed hands eleven times during its long, often violent, history. Frequently Scottish, Carlisle was now unquestionably English. But one of the castle's finest boasts was the imprisonment of Mary Queen of Scots. During the reign of Elizabeth the First, Mary Queen of Scots was incarcerated in Queen Mary's Tower in 1568. Although she was only imprisoned in the castle for two months, before being transferred to Bolton Castle, she occasionally walked from the southeast postern gate, which was situated immediately below her quarters, to the main gatehouse on the southerly approach to the castle. The route she took became known as 'The Lady's Walk'. Here, she watched her retinue playing football on the castle green while promenading with her lady friends. Settled as the early British community of Caer Luel, Carlisle stood on the River Eden and occupied ground adjacent to the tributaries of the Petteril and Caldew. Throughout the years, the meandering, sweeping Eden had flowed quietly behind the castle, hiding its secrets and minding its own business. Now the red and white flag of English Heritage fluttered proudly from the castle keep and waved to Eden's deep and murky waters as they surged westward to the Solway Firth and the quiet freedom of the Irish sea.

Turning up a slight incline, David sensed an automatic door open as he approached the museum. Tullie House museum was a splendid Jacobean building with an excellent reputation for visual display: a superb collection of ancient relics, enjoyable modern amenities, and, above all, good taste. The museum had been extended since its days as a Jacobean town house: its contemporary design coincided with the time of the Gulf War and a recently completed extension catered for a huge tourist influx.

Selecting a handful of coins from his pocket, David paid a small fee, received a ticket and brochure in return, and nodded politely to the cheery female face. The receptionist directed him upstairs towards a local history section. Ignoring a burly security guard, David casually explored the freshly plastered corridors of time. Studying the contents of the display cabinets, he learnt how the ancient Romans once lived in the thriving city of Carlisle: the settlement the Romans had called Luguvalium.

Creaking floorboards identified his slow walk through the exhibition room. Listening to a tape playing softly in the background, the scholar visualised himself dressed as a Roman centurion. His lessons informed him that the grounds on which both Carlisle Cathedral and Tullie House Museum stood were once the site of a Roman fort. David recognised a variety of weapons on display, including specimens of pilum, gladius, shields, axes, daggers, and bow and arrow. There was even a model of an old Roman catapult, and a uniformed guide, here and there, to help and inform. David noticed the altars to the false Gods: the Gods of Rome, as he scouted the halls. He scowled playfully at the altars to the false Gods, and then he snarled at the showcase and really meant it. He snarled at the altars to the false Gods because the Gods that were worshipped by the Romans were false. David knew there was only one God, David's God. Scrutinising the altars, David saw that the carved stones were all different shapes and sizes. Some of the stones were portable and some were unwieldy. They were all Roman stones.

The sizeable collections of interesting remains were recovered locally. Some of the rocks were found near Netherby, north of the city, while others were found during excavations of Hadrian's Wall, between the Solway Firth and Northumbria. Strangely, there were few remains recovered in Carlisle itself; save those dragged from the Eden in 1951 and a handful of titbits from Stanwix. Urban development over the years had merely shrouded history - for the time being.

As David walked the corridors of time he saw that the plastered walls bore colourful posters showing places of local interest, together with a variety of absorbing facts that directed his attention to Birdoswald Roman fort near Gilsland. The Romans had obviously occupied this region to some degree, thought David. Perhaps one day the true story of the Roman occupation of Carlisle might be known - but it was unlikely.

Turning a sudden corner, David ascended a short flight of wooden steps and found himself walking on a section of Hadrian's Wall replicated for posterity. Polished floorboards yielded under his weight and a spotlight shone brightly from the ceiling and focused his eye. For a second, he was blinded by the light! For a brief mystical second, the light shone obliquely, as if it were a flash of light from a flint. Then the light shone as if it were a laser beam boring deep into his mind. David flinched, raised his hand, shielded his eye, and then dismissed the silly moment of mysticism and concentrated on the curious catapults and basic artillery weapons of early Roman armies.

Fascinated, the nostalgic archaeology student withdrew a pocket notepad, flipped a pen top, and began to write furiously. He copied plans of how Hadrian's Wall, its mile castles, turrets, vallum and hinterland, had once looked. His assignment on Roman artefact and the history of archaeology would improve considerably with such research, he thought. Writing quickly, his pen scratched the paper in time with his brain. He turned a page, then turned another page and wrote. When he had written for a while, he tried to visualise the past in his mind.

Time moved swiftly forward bringing a hungry stomach and a parched throat. A change of wind direction pointed the castle's flag north towards Stanwix village, an exclusive housing estate north of the River Eden.

Afternoon arrived, a strong breeze enveloped the city and a wind began to blow outside the museum, chasing litter in the street.

Tired from his reading, writing, and studying, David folded his notepad. Yawning aloud, to the amusement of a few onlookers, he retraced his steps towards the museum entrance. David had spent most of his morning in Tullie House and still hadn't visited more than half of the exhibition. It was time to take a breath of fresh air and a bite to eat. For a brief moment he had forgotten the jibes and ridicule that was the product of wearing your faith for all to see. He had wandered through Luguvalium without a homesick thought for his family, not a homesick thought and not a jibe or an insult from his fellow man.

David checked his brochure, seeking the door to a natural history section and a garden of herbs near a sunken Roman shrine. He searched for a signpost to the welcome sunshine. There were no signs, only glass cabinets containing the altars to the false Gods: the Gods of Rome. There was a card placed in front of a cabinet. Reading the card, he saw that the contents had been recovered from the Eden during a dredging operation in 1951.

When he read the card, he lifted his eyes to see the mark of a Menorah. Mortified, David stopped in his tracks.

A Menorah! There in a cabinet, carved on a stone that was broken at the bottom of the right hand corner! The Menorah was pushed to the rear because it was smaller than the others. It was bullied by the false Gods; out of place amongst the Roman altars and a Jacobean house with its creaky floor, surrounded by bright spotlights and colourful posters and the noises of Luguvalium echoing from plastered walls, and the corridors of time.

A Menorah! Not seven branches, not eight branches, but uniquely nine branches, and it was fractured across the base. Fractured and broken yet to a knowing eye clearly a nine branched candelabrum used in the Feast of Dedication and the Festival of Light. It was a nine branched Menorah used in the celebration of Hanukkah.

It was unmistakable and mystical and devout. It was spiritual and memorable and cried out for attention and understanding in a Roman city that housed no Jewish population to speak of. What's more, the Menorah formed part of a larger picture, a carving of a fortress: a fortress David knew well. The bright spotlights that illuminated the find drilled through his eyes and deep into his sanity. His brain spiralled into turmoil as crazy, silly, stupid thoughts ripped his turbulent mind into shreds. His brain faltered with the stress of the moment and a laser beam from a ceiling spotlight that bit deep into his intellect. There was an explosion in his mind, far away, and a scud in his mind blew his logic into smithereens. There was a crater in his brain and his mind was in Tel Aviv rolling along the dust and striking a wall and feeling a tingle of nerves in his spine. His sanity exploded with the slur of a false religion. The thoughts in his mind persuaded him that somehow, someone somewhere was conspiring against him in a land far away from home.

There was David anchored to a museum floor; yet his brain was far away in Tel Aviv thinking of a scud missile that turned his home into a crater of frightening memories. There was David rooted to a museum floor; yet his head was reeling and his eyes were rolling. His heart was aching and he was suddenly so tired, so tired of schooling and his fellow man. He was suddenly so tired as his brain plummeted in decline. He was tired of the jibes and insults and ridicule. He was exhausted when his sanity spiralled towards Tel Aviv and that crater of frightening memories, mystical memories from the past: memories which filled his mind and filled his brain. There was Israel born in the desert of Judea; but the Jews had been plundered by the Romans and were at war with the Philistines! And there was David's brain, locked in the past in a day called today.

There was Israel still frail from a butcher called Nazi, and David was too young to remember such wars. Israel was a thief, a taker of lands! Palestine was homeless, kicked out by the Jews! David was homesick, his mind taunted by strife! Israel was searching for peace with the Arabs and David was so old that he knew the Maccabees and Hanukkah and Masada because that was his faith: his arrogant, old, ill-tempered, glorious creed. He knew about Masada and the suicide and why a Menorah could not live with these Gods. He knew about his home and his prayers and the sound of those scuds. He knew about his family and the horror when those scuds hit the roof of his home. He remembered the altars of falsehood and fear. He knew about Jupiter and Fortuna and Mars. With those scuds from above and those lies of the past, he was dreading the future as he remembered the past.

With a tear in his eye and suffering in his head, he clenched his fist and drove it into the glass cabinet with all the power and strength that his proud old cantankerous religion could muster.

An explosion of glass pierced the air as splinters of wood and a dozen shards caused a hundred fragments and an alarm bell screamed from a control panel on a plastered wall. David howled in defiance and hatred as blood spurted from his balled fist and spilled onto a wooden floor.

A burly uniform sprinted up the stairs.

With a clatter the museum doors flew open and the wooden floorboards surrendered to the presence of a burly security guard, running, with his arm outstretched and a glint in his eye. The wind outside blew harshly and shook a pane of glass in a window frame. The guard heard the museum windows resisting the gathering winds, and saw David's head rolling from side to side like a man possessed. The guard saw broken glass on a floor and heard alarm bells screaming in agony. Then he saw David's hand inside a cabinet and his fingers tracing a carving that was a broken Menorah.

There was a touch from trembling fingers as David caressed the stone tablet. It was his Masada. It belonged to the Jews. Not the Romans.

Loud and clear from the lips of Rome... 'Thief! Stop thief!'

Loud and clear from the lips of Arabia... 'Thief! Stop thief!'

Loud and clear from the lips of a guard... 'Thief! Stop thief!'

Mystically, strangely, divinely, Israel was sobbing from the wars of the past while David was crying with a bleeding hand. Israel was in torment while David was in pain, and his mind was still exploding in a thousand different directions: still plagued by torment and fear, and that inexplicable noise inside his head. The alarm bells were ringing with scorn and contempt and then there was a flurry of fists and arms and feet. David's escape was denied when suddenly the guard was laughing and smiling and calling him a Jew-Jew boy. Then David threw a punch to the guard's face. There was a squeal from the guard and David watched a sarcastic laugh become a bloody nose, dripping, swollen, ugly and bruised. There was glass on the floor and blood on the wall. There was a security guard snarling then laughing at an easy catch. Then there was the sound of a siren arriving and a blue beacon flashed from a big white van that carried the word 'police' on its side. Suddenly, Jeremy, the curator, appeared in the room. He pointed towards David and two policemen ran towards the would-be thief. Gruff hands secured David's body and a pair of handcuffs hurt and bit into his skin.

Broken glass was trodden underfoot as David was bundled downstairs through the doors and into a police van. A hinge on the back door of the police van squealed in delight as David's body was propelled into the back of the van. Then there was a jolt from the van and a siren sounded as it lurched off with David rolling from side to side and his back colliding with the walls of the van, and still, that tingling in his spine and pounding in his head. His skull was hitting the sides of the van but his brain was somewhere else, smashing into a wall in Tel Aviv as it rained scud missiles.

Minutes later, they were at the police station. It was brick built with bars in the windows and a massive iron door that opened into a corridor and seemed to lead into a tunnel of despair.

A sergeant appeared with a brass key to a cell. He was an unkindly sergeant who didn't understand: an unkindly sergeant without either the time or inclination to listen, and then there was a bang and a clatter as a cell door closed and Jeremy nodded his approval and thanks to the police.

There was a silence that followed with David alone on a bunk; a peace that followed with David and his solitary mind. In the silence and peace of a lonely cell David's mind continued to tumble and turn. It took time for David to realise there was no-one listening in the corridors of time. There was just a wind circling in solitude and whimpering in a tunnel of despair. David was alone on the bunk of his cell when he nestled his aching head with shaking hands.

Eventually, he looked up. There was anguish in his bloodshot eyes when he cried out aloud, 'M A S A D A'...!

*

'Thanks for that, jogger. Bad tempered type, wasn't he?'

'Who? Jeremy or the fish you've just released, Steve?'

'No, David! He seems to have got all worked up about this religious business. No need really, is there?'

'Well, some people get excited about all manner of things, Steve. Some people even get a little euphoric at times.'

'Euphoric?'

'Yes, you know. Excited! Exhilarated!

'Funny, Boyd, but when I'm alone…'

'When you're alone, what?' asked Boyd.

'When I'm alone that can happen to me, but only when I'm fishing. Sometimes I can sit here by the river all day and get so carried away with my fishing that I forget what time it is. Wife goes mad when I'm late! She carries on a treat at me. Says I'm a daydreamer. You see, Boyd, fishing relaxes me so much that, for me, it's as if I was in my own private world.'

'I get the same feeling when I'm running, Steve.'

'Running! Impossible! You can't get euphoric running, jogger.'

'You think not, Steve?'

'Then tell me how it happens, Boyd. You being a champion jogger and all. You're the slowest man I've ever seen on Eden Bridge.'

'Do you know what I say to sarcastic fisherman, Steve?'

'Me, jogger! Sarcastic!'

'Loose thumbs!'

'Pardon me!'

'Loose thumbs, Steve. Running starts in the thumb. If your thumbs are loose then your wrists will relax and your shoulders will follow suit. If your shoulders are relaxed then your frame will be supple and your legs will be flexible and easy to run with, provided you stretch before and after a run.'

'You a medical man too then?'

'No, but my wife is. She's a nurse. But I've been running for years.'

'What's this pain barrier people talk about then, Boyd? Never had any call for a pain barrier myself, not when I've been fishing, but I've heard people talking about it on the telly.'

Boyd looked into a blue sky, far away into distant wispy clouds as he told Steve what it was like to face the pain barrier.

'The pain barrier attacks and strikes into your body and penetrates your mind with its depravity. The wind tears into you when you run into its very core. You can sense it slicing your skin, tearing your body. Its deep bite cuts into your face and its teeth chew at your very essence. It's like a cancer burning through your body and mind, ravaging your very soul.'

'Bloody hell, Boyd. I didn't think jogging was that dangerous,' laughed Steve.

'When the wind drops, when you've beaten the elements, your legs release their inner strength. Stretch out and you feel so supple and flexible.'

'Never get much of that fishing.'

'Sometimes it's the wind that zaps you down like a weakling. But it can be heat, rain or snow. Whatever, when you finally overcome the point of exhaustion, Steve, your mind and body settle into total relaxation. That's why Meg sent me running.'

'Who's Meg?'

'My wife: the nurse. I told you I was married, didn't I?'

'Must be if you've got a wife.'

'She's brilliant. I'm lucky to have her, Steve. You married?'

'Just! Wife says if we divorce she'll cite the fish as the other woman.'

'Mine thinks the police force is more appropriate.'

'Women! They're always twining about something.'

Boyd shook his head and laughed. 'Now I know why Meg insisted I went for a run this morning. She knows about the pain barrier.'

'She's very lucky then. Are you going to finish telling me or not?'

Smiling now, Boyd said, 'When your mind and body lock together in perfect harmony, you can fling yourself along in a state of total euphoria. It just happened to me when I was crossing that bridge.'

'Thought you looked slow.'

'Speed has nothing to do with it. It's in the mind. Thanks, Steve. Thanks, Meg. You've both been a real big help.'

Steve turned, looked around, and said, 'I don't see any Meg, Boyd.'

'I do. You see, when your mind and body are in perfect harmony your mind drifts away and looks down on your body. That's euphoria!'

'Wow! If you're right, then I'll have some of that. If you're wrong, you're one hell of a crazy man. Give up jogging, Boyd, before it gets to you.'

Boyd laughed and said, 'Your mind leaves your body when you break the pain barrier, Steve. It soars into the sky like an eagle over the river: an eagle supreme. The exertion changes to a feeling of complete relaxation. You can sense the stress in your mind change to a state of total tranquillity. There's a harmony about your body and soul, and you're wrong, I'm not crazy. It's the truth. Ask any marathon runner.'

'What were you thinking when you came over the bridge, Boyd?'

'I was thinking that Stanwix had proved more than far enough for me. I was totally gone, Steve, finished, spent! I'd reached the point of exhaustion and then gone beyond it. But now I can see it all so clearly.'

'See what?'

'The last nine days of my life! Now I understand why the past framed the last nine days of pain and stress, and heartache. I understand it now. I've lived through it; been part of it.'

'Sounds bad! Could be jogger's disease, medical man. You'd best ask your wife when you get home.'

'No! She might tell me to take up fishing, then where would I be.'

'You going to tell me about the last nine days of your life or are you going to stand there being euphoric all day?'

'Now I can explain it, Steve. It's all so clear now. It's the Legacy of the Ninth and it's my final story....'

*

5
~ ~ ~

Boyd's Story.
Dateline: September 1ˢᵗ, Present Year: Istanbul, Turkey.

Captain Nicholas Crosby's blue silk handkerchief poked cheekily from the breast pocket of his white lightweight suit. The wisp of luxury identified with his blue silk tie and plain cotton shirt. Walking briskly towards a shopping complex, he allowed one hand to rest casually in his trouser pocket while his other hand fidgeted unnecessarily with the knot in his tie. The double vent in the hand-tailored cloth of his suit jacket flapped gently in a morning breeze as he made his way down a slight incline.

Heading towards the Grand Bazaar, he paused at a junction and waited for traffic to clear before crossing the carriageway and making his way towards a pottery shop. Crosby did not look back over his shoulder until he was on the bridge: the bridge that crossed the River Bosphorus. It was only when he was on the centre of the bridge that he glanced over his shoulder, crossed the road, and continued his journey to the pottery shop. Taking care on the bridge, he warily looked at faces and cars as they approached, and then instantly stored the images in the back of his mind for future use. Walking without precision, he slowed his pace, almost to a saunter at times, and seemed quite relaxed in his mannerisms. Neither did he march with a military bearing in his step. He had learned to shelve such pretensions when his career was transformed from combat officer to military intelligence agent. Gone were the uniform and cap badge of his regiment; gone were the pomp and circumstance of marching bands on a parade ground. He heard no more the harsh rasp of a sergeant major barking out orders to new recruits; no more the slither and slide of an unseen reptile in the jungle of Belize. Gone was the street patrol from the alleys of Londonderry; gone was the camouflage of an urban soldier and jungle warrior. Now his masquerade was a white lightweight suit and a blue silk tie in a land of sunshine. Captain Crosby had rid himself of the uniform of his regiment in favour of the undercover suit of the Intelligence Corps.

Glorious sunshine straddled the Galata Bridge and intensified a blue sky overlooking the Golden Horn: a narrow inlet, which formed a natural harbour and led to the commercial centre of the city once known as Constantinople.

Born in Brampton, Cumbria, in the Sixties, Nicholas Crosby had enlisted in his local regiment and seen service in Belize and Northern Ireland before applying for an attachment to Military Intelligence. Indeed, he didn't really apply for the intelligence posting at all. Rather, the regimental top brass responsible for 'special duties' selected him. His sharp mind and analytical prowess had been noted, it seemed. His understanding of the intelligence world and an ability to combine snippets of information with proven fact bore testament to those gut feelings that underpinned the mad methodology of his work. He knew why they had chosen him: those grey suits of Whitehall and those shadowy people from Thames House and Vauxhall. He knew why the talent spotters of the Ministry of Defence, the Security Service and the Secret Intelligence Service, had selected him. It was the Arabic tongue he had learnt from his father: a man with olive-coloured skin who had taken an English wife, and English name, and settled in the county of the Lakes. And it was a lightly browned skin, which his father had bequeathed him, that interested the Intelligence Services, made him stand out above the others. It was his Arabic; his ability to blend into a chosen background, and his previous experience in running a network of informants and agents into the heart of the Provisional IRA, which were the reasons why he had been selected for an undercover assignment in Istanbul.

In London, and back home in his regiment, he was Captain Nicholas Crosby. But in Istanbul, he was an undercover agent posing as a managing director of an import-export firm.

Istanbul is a beautiful place to be a managing director of a false company, thought Crosby. The city was an attractive location to set up a company that traded legitimately and was funded by the British Government entirely as a cover for more clandestine operations. It was those special operations, of which he was in command that provided the reason why he was stationed in Istanbul. He was there to run counter terrorist operations into the Middle East and as far as British Intelligence was concerned, Crosby was in charge of Station Bosphorus.

Istanbul is a unique city lying on both sides of the Bosphorus: the strait separating Europe from Asia. To the north of Istanbul the Black Sea shimmers and to the east lays Kocaeli Province, and the road to Iran, Iraq, Syria, Lebanon, and Israel - the Middle East cauldron. To the south the Sea of Marmara washes the shore and to the west rests the province of Tekirdag, and the road to Greece and Bulgaria. This extraordinary region is a centre of unique intrigue. The Straits of the Bosphorus witness

50,000 vessels passing through its waters every year. The majority of vessels are super-tankers each carrying some 80,000 tons of oil from the Caspian Sea to the world's commercial centres. The Straits also host every movement of the Soviet Black Sea Fleet, a matter of significant interest to Crosby's colleagues in their intelligence world. Istanbul is the city of the Blue Mosque; the Topaki Palace; the Ottoman Sultans and the Mosque of Sulieman the Magnificent. It is the city of the St Sophia Cathedral; and a horde of fish restaurants, nightclubs and spice markets. Istanbul is a magnificent city: the place where Asia meets Europe, where east meets west.

Walking this great divide between two major continents, Crosby made for the pottery shop. Increasing his pace, stepping from the bridge, he crossed between the flow of traffic

At a tailor's shop, he stopped, looked in a display window, and saw a tailor's dummy adorned with soft fabric. He realised the soft fabric was of linen and its exquisite cut formed a snappy beige-coloured suit. Noticing the garment carried a hefty price tag, his eyes moved casually to a pair of shiny leather shoes and a collection of silk ties resting on a glass cabinet. With a slight turn of his head Crosby scanned the road behind him and somewhere in his brain a library of images, collected on Galata Bridge, was compared with those faces now surrounding him. Warily, Crosby ambled on and stopped at a shop where its window display was of soft woollen fabrics. Pausing, he appreciated the contours of loose cardigans and casual sweaters. Then he whistled at their unattainable price and strolled on. Crosby walked on and was seen only by those around him as a man window-shopping in the gentle Istanbul sun.

At the Arab quarter - near the Grand Bazaar - Crosby faltered. His hand moved from his trouser pocket and tamed an apparently unruly lock at his forehead. Then he stopped, and watched. He saw the pottery shop but he would not enter the building.

In London, and back home in his regiment, people were cosmopolitan, but in the Arab quarter, they were Moorish and of Middle Eastern appearance. Here in Istanbul dark skins and outlandish features manned market stalls and a wave of different languages flooded the Arab quarter. Dark eyes flashed and a tourist paused as a market trader sensed a bulging wallet. Brown cloth rolled and silver trinkets glinted in the sun. Two tongues jabbered and their hands flourished in the barter of the moment.

Motionless, self-disciplined, Crosby waited.

He saw in the skins of the Middle East the terrorist organisations of Abu Nidhal: the Palestinian Liberation Organisation, and Hamas, and Hezbollah, and he sensed the great war between Muslim and Jew. As part of the struggle between Muslim fundamentalists and western liberal democracies, he recognised those dark-coloured skins as the enemy of his faith, his politics, and his religion. It wasn't that Crosby considered himself to be a racist, far from it. Rather, his instincts warned him to be wary of those potential agents of the intelligence services of Syria and Egypt, and Iran and Iraq. For in this melting pot of the Middle East, Crosby saw a potential for the Mossad of Israel and the Central Intelligence Agency of America. And they both could be an enemy as well as a friend.

In the Arab quarter, Crosby was cautious because he knew this was where the Middle Eastern Intelligence war in Istanbul was played.

Pausing at a collection of silver trinkets, he allowed his fingers to play across a leather belt that hung loosely from one side of a market stall. An Egyptian trader approached him, spoke first, and then offered a price and tried to hold his eye.

Fingering the leather belt, Crosby felt its texture, appreciated its design, and haggled its price as he watched the pottery shop. Smoothing soft leather with the back of his hand, he checked its buckle and continued to watch the pottery shop. He examined the exterior of the pottery shop and a pavement café nearby. He watched a street artist sketching adjacent market stalls, followed his eyes, and saw they were concentrated on a sketching pad. Then he watched a lead pencil flow across a sketching pad and reproduce an image of the market place. He observed a woman sitting on a bench watching some market stalls and tending to her shopping bag. Watching her eyes, he saw they did not move from her bag. He tried the belt around his waist and haggled its price with an Egyptian trader as his eyes scanned a café and stalls. When he had checked the street he replaced the belt and dismissed the Egyptian with a wave of his hand: a dismissal to match inferior goods.

It was an irrelevant gesture as far as the Egyptian was concerned; another suit walked into view. Another wallet ripe for plunder presented itself. A tongue jabbered and the Egyptian's hands flourished and a selection of silver trinkets sparkled in their offer. A prospective customer offered a price. There was wild gesticulation, and then a rushed barter before the price change turned into an unsavoury argument.

Crosby was looking in those windows again. The captain of intelligence was watching reflections from the windows. He looked into the shop windows as he moved slowly through the bazaar. Studying these reflections, he watched the body movements of those around him. His field of vision did not leave these reflections, or those shadows falling at the corner of his eye. His eyes did not seek contact with another, not for one moment. He watched only the images of these reflections until he saw that he was not followed. Not until then did he enter the shop.

The display in the window was bright and lit by the rays of the sun that fell onto the shop front; but deep inside the belly of the shop there was a veiled shadow and a quiet that extended no welcome. Yet in the gloom Crosby could easily make out the shapes of pots, vases, urns, and candlestick holders. Moving to the rear of the shop, Crosby recognised earthenware and terracotta; then he took in the smell of Turkish cigarettes lingering in a distinctly still air. In the quiet he heard a shuffle of feet and a cough from an elderly man who was alone, smoking. The elderly man was an Arab who carried no smile to his face; no curl to his lips, no hint of recognition. The Arab who owned the shop only nodded to the man in the white lightweight suit and blue silk tie. Then the Arab looked casually over Crosby's shoulder towards the front door. It was just a casual look of no particular consequence, but it was enough to satisfy the shopkeeper that no one had followed Crosby into the shop.

The Arab stubbed out his cigarette and approached Crosby.

Two hands, gnarled and wrinkled with age, veins standing out, frail, offered a pot to the captain of intelligence.

Crosby didn't barter. He didn't need to take such a precaution in the empty shop. There was no excited haggle over its price as they stood alone in their silent dealing. Removing his wallet, thumbing some notes from a leather compartment, Crosby knew their arrangement. He offered some notes. There was a nod of thanks, no words spoken, and then two frail hands passed over a pot and took his money. The money disappeared into the folds of a robe. Another Turkish cigarette was removed from a crush-proof packet and a lighter sparked its flint. A flame cast a shadow in the gloom and then cigarette smoke curled lazily towards a ceiling as the unsmiling Arab inhaled.

Crosby was gone from the shop carrying his pot.

Ambling through the Arab quarter, he carried his urn back towards his office: the import-export office set up by the British Government.

With wrinkled hands, an elderly Arab counted his notes and replaced them in the fold of his robes. Sitting quietly in the darkness of his shop, smoking, he thought of his son in the desert wastes of the

Lebanon. His son's message from those desert wastes had been delivered to the captain of intelligence. The old man dusted his collection of earthenware hanging from the walls of his shop and allowed his mind to stray to his son.

Crosby did not hold his pot urn tight at his side. Rather, he carried it loose with one arm cradling his vase, casual, as if it were no more than a trinket from a market place. It was as if it were a gift bought from the bazaar for a friend, a lady friend perhaps. To hold it tight and close to his body, and to walk quickly with his urn, would signify urgency in his walking and importance in his buying. So he ambled with his urn loose at his side, unimportant, no hint of urgent destination. Carrying it loose by his side, walking to his office, he played his intelligence game.

When Crosby was inside his office, convinced he had not been followed from the pottery shop, and knew he was alone, he set down his pot urn on a table. On the table sat a desk lamp, a blotting pad, a telephone and his newly acquired urn. The urn had a small base that grew progressively to wide shoulders. There were two handles at either side and they gradually narrowed to a slender opening. It was an amphora in its shape: in the style of the ancient Greeks and Romans.

Crosby ran his hands around the amphora's shoulders and felt the work of a fine blade. Allowing his fingers to drop towards the base he felt more knife work and knew there was a hidden message carved in the clay amphora. It was the message he had been waiting for. Crosby read the message carved by the son of an elderly Arab who owned a pottery shop in the Grand Bazaar.

There were no words for Crosby to read, not in the proper sense. The writer had chosen to communicate in a manner similar to that of the Sumerians, and in the style of the ancient cuneiform. The Sumerians had once occupied the lands of Mesopotamia between 3000 and 2000 B.C. Their culture spread to Egypt, Syria, Persia and Asia Minor. Quite simply, the Sumerians communicated in the written form by cutting lines into clay tablets. Characters were simplified into single images and strung together in a line of pictures that they called cuneiform. Crosby preferred to call their system 'picture writing' or 'pictography' but the maker of the amphora knew of Sumerian culture and had devised a method of urgent communication. Their arrangement was not without problems since pictures were sometimes ambiguous and could only be read easily by someone with an understanding of the cultural background of the creator. Crosby was such a man.

Turning his amphora around, Crosby examined all the carvings he found. Then he turned the object over and studied the base. Occasionally he would turn his amphora towards a desk lamp so that he might get a better feeling for the work of the blade. Eventually he understood the carvings, and their meanings. Scattered throughout the amphora, but in the manner proscribed by Station Bosphorus, Crosby saw carvings of a pomegranate, a man with a javelin, a bird, a small bear, and a star.

Opening a drawer, removing a wooden-handled hammer, Crosby laid it on the table. Then he took a newspaper from a drawer and laid it next to his hammer, spread out the newspaper, and laid his urn upon its sheets. Using the hammer, he smashed the urn at its shoulder. The pot disintegrated and fell onto the newspaper with an earthy clatter. The message was safe in his possession. Crosby destroyed the carvings having memorised the Sumerian cuneiform: the picture writing, in his head. It was necessary to destroy the amphora, thought Crosby. He would never jeopardise his source in the desert. Crosby could not keep the amphora on his desk and advertise the pictures. There might be only a few who knew of Sumerian culture but images spoke for themselves, and with time and patience an enemy could decipher the cuneiform. Crosby could not take such a chance. Bundling the newspaper tight, he made sure the remains of his amphora were destroyed with the repeated thud of his hammer.

Crosby knew the cuneiform had been crafted in the desert wastes of the Lebanon. He knew the cuneiform travelled by hand during one day and one night to Istanbul. The son of an elderly Arab had loaded the urn onto a rust-infested wagon on the outskirts of the security zone separating Lebanon from Israel. The son passed his load of pot urns and terracotta onto a cousin who drove their load back through Turkey to a sister. The sister took their load north back to Istanbul and their shop in the Grand Bazaar while the cousin returned to the Lebanon with an empty wagon to await their next consignment. The amphora was recognised and placed in the rear of their shop on the south side of the Bosphorus by an elderly Arab who smoked Turkish cigarettes and awaited the arrival of the captain of intelligence.

Crosby knew the code name of the sender. It was Danu, his agent in the desert wastes of the Lebanon.

Crosby marvelled at the pottery shop family, marvelled at their courage. They had been spying for the Secret Intelligence Service of Her Majesty's Britannic Government for fifteen years. He knew how Danu's family would be treated if they were ever caught working for British Intelligence, if they were ever caught spying for the British Imperialists, and the Zionist State.

They would be tortured slowly. No fingernails to fret over. They would be pulled out and skewered in the process. No toe nails to cut fine. They would be pulled out. No testicles to swell in the moment of lovemaking. They'd be flattened out, squeezed, and skewered in the process. No nipples! They'd be burnt with a cigarette lighter and stretched by twine that hung from a tree. Then they'd be kicked to death like a dog, left to lie in the desert sun, a feast for the birds of prey, and the teeth of a desert jackal.

It was the custom of the Arab terrorist and the method he chose to torture a traitor. It was the way of those at war with each other.

In the secret war that British Intelligence fought there was no technology in the desert, no portable dish to set up satellite communications with GCHQ at Cheltenham: the British electronic listening post. No short-wave electronic button pad to bounce an encrypted signal to the British listening post in Cyprus. No one-time pad to leave beneath a chosen desert rock in the hope that Crosby's men would retrieve their coded message before the Arab terrorists did. It was far too dangerous for such things. Everyone was watched on the desert roads that were patrolled by the Syrian army every hour. In the desert such intelligence was transmitted by word of mouth, the spoken words, handed down from one to another. Yet reading images carved in the Lebanon, gasping with apprehension, Crosby's intuition told him what he must do. Scrutinising the pictures, analysing them, Crosby assessed their significance in his gut.

There was a flutter in the pit of his stomach as he deciphered a name carved by Danu. Crosby made for the communications centre in a cellar beneath his offices.

Looking into an oval mirror, which was fixed to a sparse dressing table, the woman smiled wistfully back at her reflected image. Thoughtfully, she combed her long black hair and inspected her rounded face, her long smooth nose, her dark jewelled eyes, and her soft olive complexion.

There was a Jordanian passport on the table in front of her. Opening it, she leafed through its pages to the photograph of a female who was *Yasmin al-Amin:* Yasmin, the trusted one. The photograph had been taken six years earlier, just before she arrived in England. She decided her passport photograph did not do her justice at all. For indeed, she thought she was much prettier than the tiny coloured rectangle trying to force a smile from a dull page. Analysing her photograph carefully, she realised the lines in her face were a little younger, and, for a brief moment, she wondered how long it would be before old age started its harsh process of chiselling deep grooves of time into her skin. Suddenly, she snapped the passport shut. Yasmin al-Amin, if that were her name, for she had never set foot in Jordan, set aside the passport of deceit and looked again at the oval mirror.

Nodding slowly towards her mirrored reflection, Yasmin knew immediately she had succeeded. She had indeed become vain and thought it was right for her to think that way. Becoming vain had not been easy for Yasmin, but the colonel had taught her so well. Six years after her arrival in England, Yasmin was well and truly vain, often a little selfish in her ways. She combed her hair well and used expensive cosmetics and luxurious perfumes of the western world to good effect. She wore very well a buttoned silk blouse and belted skirt that rode just above her knee whenever she sat down. It was what the colonel had told her she might wear.

Abandoning both her hairbrush and passport, she switched on her transistor radio and listened to the thriving music. It was loud, raucous, western, and occasionally sexy; and at times she did not understand the meaning of all the lyrics; but she knew some of the words were likely to corrupt her. Yasmin had learnt to take pleasure from soft lipstick and subtle eye shadow, and scented perfume; but the sensuous music had been a tremendous challenge for her. The music could have corrupted her and might yet bring about her downfall. The colonel told her to pretend to enjoy such music; to dance to the incessant beat; to sway in time with its rhythm, and to laugh at the sexy words. She had succeeded, so far, but she wouldn't allow such music to corrupt her heart and mind.

It was not Yasmin's way.

Yasmin was a Muslim and believed in Islam, adhered to it, and lived by it. Yet the colonel had told her to forsake Islam and deny the Koran. Moreover, the colonel had insisted she denied the calling of her ancestors and it had wrangled with her from the very beginning. Yasmin was a follower of the Koran, which she regarded as the speech of God to Muhammad, mediated by Gabriel, the angel of revelation, and therefore infallible since God is its author. Yasmin worshipped one God, unitary and omnipotent, who created nature through an act of mercy. There were no malfunctions in nature since God had meant to create nature subservient to humanity. The ultimate purpose of humanity is to be in the service of God, she thought. Yasmin believed she was in the service of God who would construct a society free from corruption. God had created, consequently He would sustain and guide until the Day of Judgement when all would be gathered and judged solely according to their deeds. Yasmin knew that if she were successful, she would go to the Garden that was Heaven. But she must not be corrupted by wealth, power or pride. The Koran taught her that ideal human endeavour was to reform the earth and deny humanity where it was too proud, petty, narrow-minded or selfish. Accordingly, and against the colonel's explicit orders, she endeared herself to the five duties known as the 'pillars of Islam.'

Six years ago the colonel gave her a Jordanian passport and the name Yasmin al-Amin. Because he trusted her, the colonel taught her to abandon Islam and embrace the ways of the capitalist west. It was for the good of Islam, he told her, and it would ensure her a better life in the land of paradise that surely awaited her. She complied with the colonel's orders in the knowledge her life of service would sustain and deepen Islam.

Now she lived in a flat in Cullercoats sandwiched between Whitley Bay and Tynemouth on the northeast coast of England. Once a tiny fishing village, Cullercoats boasted a small harbour, a lifeboat station, and steep cliffs that swaggered outwards then stumbled to a crescent-shaped sandy beach below. Whenever Yasmin was lonely or in need of her one true God, she walked down past Saint George's church onto the seafront. Finding a pier near the lifeboat station, she strolled along the jetty that strutted arrogantly into the greyness of the bleak North Sea and looked towards the horizon. It was impossible to see her home in the Middle East, of course, but she often wondered if the gulls soaring high above ever visited her desert valley. There, quietly, without the knowledge of the colonel, she carried out her duty of daily prayer. Privately, by tongue and with full consent from her heart, she spoke into the wind, 'There is no God but Allah and Muhammad is his prophet.' She was alone at the end of the jetty as the North Sea pounded the sea defences below her and exploded in a shower of surf above her.

Then she would think of what the colonel had said, and she would rededicate herself to his orders.

It was the colonel who recruited her, taken her to a new home in the desert valley, trained her, taught her, and placed his faith in her ability. The colonel had provided money for travel, arranged flights, acquired tickets, and briefed her: she was to do nothing to attract attention while she lived in England. She would call herself Yasmin and find accommodation with the money provided. Yasmin should look for a job where she might meet people and learn of their ways. Listening, agreeing, Yasmin complied. On arrival in England, she was to read, on the first day of every month, a certain daily newspaper. She was to read the personal columns, ordered the colonel. If a message appeared for *Yasmin* from *Ray*, she must obey every printed word.

For twelve long months Yasmin bought the newspaper and looked for a message. It was not until the second year of the occupation of her flat in Cullercoats, in the thirteenth month of her stay in England, that she saw a message. Yasmin followed the instructions in the personal column and two weeks later she met Ray outside the main entrance to York Minister.

It was perhaps an unusual place for two Muslims to meet one another: a Protestant edifice of such renown. Yet given that Ray was merely a cover name for an Intelligence officer working out of an Arab Embassy in London, and Yasmin was a deep cover agent for a Palestinian terrorist faction, then there seemed to be a certain understandable misdemeanour in their actions. Both were intent on leading false lives.

The meeting in York proved the first of many. Each time they met, Yasmin told Ray of the people she had met during her employment at the estate agent's office in Whitley Bay. He asked whether she had met any politicians, any military people, any police, or any Jews of importance. Yasmin answered Ray's questions and when asked she supplied photographs of the houses in which they lived. It was all Ray asked of her, and all the colonel had taught her to do: to search out the enemies of the Palestinian people so that revenge might be exacted when the time was right. Until then, she was to report upon Jews she met, police she knew, politicians she encountered, and military people whom she became aware of in the area.

Yasmin stood up and stepped away from the oval mirror. Smoothing down her skirt, she reminded herself that in Cullercoats she was known as Yasmin Baker. The name was much more convenient.

Reaching behind the sofa, Yasmin Baker removed a black plastic bag. Inside her bag were photographs of houses, newspaper clippings, a video of a local television news program, and a slender box, which was about a foot in length. Gripping tight her black plastic bag, she set off to meet Ray. He had asked for the articles she carried. Yasmin would deliver them. It was what the colonel had instructed in the valley of *al-Biqa:* the Bekaa.

By the shallow waters of the Litani river, in the Lebanese valley of the Bekaa, walked a solitary man. He walked with purpose through the valley, which was bounded to the north and east by Syria and to the southeast and south by Israel. But to the west, the Mediterranean Sea bordered the Lebanon, which was dominated by two mountain ranges separated by the valley and the river he walked beside.

The colonel had briefed him, explained the plan that had been made during the previous six months, told him what must be done, what to do and how to do it. And then revealed what he was about to do would further their cause and ultimately restore their lands to the one true faith. The colonel pointed out the way to journey and the method of travel, and then he withdrew quietly and left the man to walk and pray alone.

The lone man walked through groves of pomegranate, stands of fine pine and cedar trees, and climbed the sides of their beloved valley to a high place where a deep reddish brown rock jutted out from the cliff top above the Bekaa. He had walked since before dawn to arrive at his high rock and now he looked down on his native land and spoke aloud to the wind, 'There is no God but Allah and Muhammad is his Prophet.'

It was the man's ritual to pray. He was a Muslim of particularly extreme beliefs, and a follower of Jihad: the holy war.

Each day the man made his necessary ablutions before climbing to the high rock to speak with his God. He prayed before sunrise, in the early afternoon, in the late afternoon, after sunset, and before midnight. Each time he prayed, he imagined the position of the Kaaba, in the great mosque of Mecca: the city where Muhammad was born. He had once visited the Kaaba, a windowless cube-shaped building in the courtyard of al-Haram, in Mecca, Saudi Arabia, near the Red Sea. He marvelled at the southeast corner of the Kaaba, built by Abraham, and looked upon the Black Stone, which was given to Abraham by the angel Gabriel.

Now, the man faced due south, in the direction of the Kaaba and prayed alone.

He prayed to Allah for many things but always recited the Koran, for it was infallible and undeniable in its strength, truth and purity. But each time he prayed to God, he thought of Jihad, and the Islamic goal of reforming the earth, by armed force if necessary, in order to assume political power and implement the principles of Islam throughout the globe.

The Muslim, extreme in his outlook, zealous by nature, unlike others belonging to his religion, believed in Jihad. He adhered to it, and lived by it.

Passionate, fervent and intense, the man prayed before sunrise for a good right eye. In the early afternoon he prayed for a firm left forearm. During the late afternoon he prayed for a strong right shoulder. Before sunset he prayed for commitment. Prior to midnight he gave himself again to Allah and ordered his mind and body to take no sound precautions for his personal safety. Each time he prayed, he thought of his courage and asked that it might be strengthened still further.

Then he stood and recited details of the plan given to him by the colonel. Committed, he looked out across the valley and memorised every specific detail of his mission. He held no fear of what lay ahead. He had undertaken such operations before and knew there was a likelihood that he might die during his assignment. Were he to die in the holy war in which he was engaged, he would not die in vain. He held no fear of death since his passing would merely ensure a better place for him in his next life. He was prepared for martyrdom and hoped it would be that way. It was the highest accolade for a man like him to be given: martyr. To the intended victim, he held no personal grudge or hatred. The victim was truly irrelevant in the greater scheme of things. The victim was from a country corrupted by wealth, power and pride. The intended victim was merely an instrument of that nation. The man knew the nation would not reform itself and would not give back the taken lands. For himself, in the final moments of his ultimate glory, he had decided in his prayers to take no specific precautions for the safety of his own soul. He would die for his beliefs, if necessary.

He prayed again, one last time.

Again, he entrusted the minutiae of the operation to his memory; and then turned north. As he walked away he looked over his shoulder at his beloved Bekaa.

His name was Namir and he was a killer of men.

In the communications centre, in the depths of Crosby's office, there was a secret encrypted keyboard. Switching on the apparatus, Crosby removed its protective dustsheet. Once the passwords had been entered and contact was proved, Crosby began to transmit the contents of Danu's message to the men in grey suits: those men in London. The carvings on the amphora had been deciphered. The picture of a pomegranate revealed that Danu was in the camp in the Bekaa valley. The image of a man with a javelin warned of an assassin. The carving of a bird revealed the assassin was in flight. The figure of a small bear was a reference to the star constellation known as Ursa Minor: the Little Bear. The star depicted above Ursa Minor was the Pole star. Ursa Minor was angled towards the Pole star and showed a northerly direction. The letter on the base of the amphora was N for Namir.

Danu's pictures were a warning.

Namir had left the camp in the Lebanon where the terrorists were training... Namir was headed north... Namir was on the move...

Pushing his pen across some papers, Boyd slurped on stale coffee from a plastic cup. He spluttered and swore at the liquid. Then a horn blared in the Carlisle traffic and he closed his window. It was dark outside and he should have been at home with his feet up in front of the fire watching a video. At this time of night, he ought to be sipping a glass of Murphy's beer while Meg ravaged her Port wine. But he was too busy with his damn paperwork. He'd be with her soon though, when he'd emptied that infernal plastic tray.

A telephone rang and he grasped the instrument with his free hand. It was the Chief. Boyd acknowledged, listened, asked no questions, and nodded his head in agreement. He spoke in the affirmative, replaced the telephone, set aside his paperwork and emptied the contents of his cup into a rubber plant. With an uncomfortable sigh, he retrieved his briefcase from the desk. It was late and he'd been ordered to travel to London. An appointment had been made for him. It was a briefing and it was urgent.

Boyd was on the move.

*

6

~ ~ ~

Dateline: September 2nd, Present Year: The City of Carlisle, Cumbria.

The wind blew gently, soothing a tarmac surface that methodically channelled a late afternoon downpour into Carlisle's gutter drains. A gentle wind and a heavy shower killed a disagreeable smell of exhaust fumes that usually hung in the atmosphere at the junction. Now there was an agreeable freshness seeping through the early evening air.

Cross depressed brake and clutch together and gently brought his vehicle to a standstill. He slid the gear stick into neutral and listened to his car engine ticking over. Ahead of him, a red traffic light graciously held the queue. The sun was down and evening played but there were only two cars on the street: his and the other.

The other was a 'Beamer'.

It was a two litre black BMW, sleek and shiny, with four males on board, and it was standing at the traffic lights basking in Cross's headlights and a pool of light from a nearby street lamp. Two men sat in the front and two in the rear. The pair in front kept their faces straight ahead but Cross noticed how those in the rear were itching to look round. A head moved. It was just a very slight twitch from a neck, but enough to make Cross narrow his eyes and zero in. Cross scanned the neck that twitched nervously. Hair on this head seemed to be close cropped, coloured black, and perhaps a little greasy in its texture. The neck was thick, maybe even chubby, and it seemed to roll onto the owner's collar and overflow in two layers of skinny blubber. The flesh of this blubber was a dark, dirty colour, not the pink-white flesh of a pure Englishman. A gold stud was barely discernible in a left earlobe.

His was a police car.

Sergeant Cross considered it to be his own personal property and woe betide anyone who messed with it. Cross's patrol car was big, shiny and white. It was indeed awesome. Chequered on its sides, it carried radio aerials and a sleeping blue beacon on its roof. Inside, a radio hummed quietly from a dashboard; but it certainly wasn't a tune. Suddenly a harsh female voice crackled over the airwaves and said, 'Suspect'.

Nodding, merely confirming in his innermost beliefs, Sergeant Cross looked ahead and pierced the back of a skull with his knowing steel eyes.

In the Beamer, a measure of blubber on a neck rolled slightly and resettled, and a gold stud quivered in anticipation.

A lazy dog stirred as a clipboard flew into the rear passenger compartment and Constable Bannerman tightened his seat belt. Rocky was a pet, rejected by its previous owners once it proved incapable of sniffing out the odour of drugs, and made redundant by budget-conscious managers. Their drug squad dog was a reject but to those men in that police car, Rocky was Cross's pet, and God help anyone who thought otherwise. Disrespectfully, their canine friend sniffed at Bannerman's clipboard, yawned, and then went back to sleep. Rocky was apparently bored with life.

Grasping the transmitter, Bannerman acknowledged their radio message with a curt 'Roger' and then turned to Cross, the driver, 'On the straight. Take the Beamer on the straight, Cross. It's suspect! Worth a check.'

Nodding once more, Cross slipped quietly into first gear as a red traffic light disappeared and a green one shone an advance.

Both cars moved off as a neck stopped twitching and blubber settled on a collar.

The Beamer pulled away first and turned right into Warwick Road, slowly, normal. It was trying to look natural, not interesting at all. Cross followed the growling black monster; his eyes locked on target; his lips pursed tight in concentration.

'Now, Cross.' An arm extended from a dark blue tunic and Bannerman's middle finger pressed a switch. 'Let's give them a little message, shall we?' Another finger hit a button and a siren blurted out their presence, just one short blast. 'Now they know we're here, Cross.'

Rocky pricked his ears up, yawned again, and allowed his tail to flap noisily against shabby cloth upholstery.

Pulling out casually Cross caught up with the Beamer. Once alongside Bannerman swivelled his head and eyed its driver, gesturing with a palm for the Beamer to stop. Then, overtaking, Bannerman reached for a switch. A 'Stop' sign flashed from their roof as they pulled the car in. Cross held the steering wheel, his grey eyes on his interior mirror, watching, waiting, searching their faces, and wondering.

They cruised to a standstill, slowly, routine, with their tyres kissing the side of the kerbstones and obscuring some precisely painted double yellow lines.

Bannerman released a catch on his door and stepped into a pool of rainwater shimmering in the early evening light. 'Wait one, Cross. I'll call you if I need you.' A neon reflection saw the big man move from their police car and a splash from a puddle fell onto a double yellow line.

Cross nodded at the only constable in the force who didn't call him Sergeant. Colleagues might describe such a transgression as an insult to Cross's rank; but it wasn't a problem for Sergeant Cross. It couldn't be. Bannerman was like a brother to him.

Two engines purred like tigers as Bannerman walked back and snapped, 'Vehicle stopped,' into a radio dangling from his lapel.

Restless, Cross caressed neutral and moved his left hand to the parking brake, then back to the gear stick. The fingers of his right hand found his ignition keys and threatened a plastic fob, but his engine kept on turning. Cross was fussing like a Bengal Leopard at feeding time. His steel grey eyes intimidated a mirror as he watched the Beamer, wondering. Only the trim of his eyebrows, below his jet-black hairline, bounced back from the bottom corner of an interior mirror. Something wasn't right. He could feel it in his nose, sense it in his mind. He lived it every day. It was the reason he was the kind of policeman he was.

Rocky yawned again, flicked a tail haphazardly, from left to right, and set big gooey Labrador eyes at his master, Cross.

The first splash of evening rainwater fell on their windscreen.

Inside the black growling Beamer there was an air of unease and a building brick on the floor. Then there was a rustle in a bag, a hand down a leather seat, and a squirm. Nervously, a look behind confirmed the first flush of panic. Streams of sweat slowly trickled down the young driver's forehead as he sought instruction from an older youth in a rear seat: the one in his mid twenties with a swarthy outlandish complexion: an Arab in illegal possession of drugs. It was an Arab with a fatty neck, which rolled down onto his collar in two layers of blubber, who carried the drugs: an Arab with a revolver under his sweaty armpit.

'Jo-Jo, why did you stop?' asked the Arab.

'I've not much option, Yasif,' replied Jo-Jo, nervously. He was looking at Yasif's reflection in an interior mirror. 'It's Bannerman. He's the hardest cop in town and I think he knows my face.'

'Listen to me, Jo-Jo, and listen up good. I don't want them to see my face. Mow him down when he gets near enough, Jo-Jo. Understand?'

'Mow him down We'll have every copper in the country after us.'

'I don't want them to see my face, Jo-Jo. Go! We can't take a chance. Go!'

Bannerman approached Jo-Jo's door in quick time. Bannerman was in the roadway, bending down and looking through the driver's window. In a split second, his eyes found Jo-Jo and scanned the passengers with his built-in copper's radar. The Beamer's engine was still running; its engine throbbed in his ear. The driver's hand reached for a gear stick. A knee dropped; it could only be to the clutch. The driver's window still held tight. Bannerman tapped on the window. There was no response. There was just a blank expression on the driver's face.

Bannerman shouted, 'Cross!'

With a screech of tyres the Beamer roared backwards. Jo-Jo heaved on the brake, slammed in the clutch and came to a standstill. Fast hands rattled through his gears, crunching into first, and then Jo-Jo lurched forward at speed with the rear of his Beamer snaking and twitching in a frantic, near panic-stricken escape.

Cross heard a shout and Bannerman's splashing feet. He leaned over, flicked the passenger door open and then set off in pursuit as Bannerman threw himself into the moving police car, reached for his radio handset, and shouted, 'Chase on, Cross!'

Cross nodded. There were no words offered, just two steel grey eyes narrowing down a street zeroing in on a disappearing black, shadowy Beamer.

A Labrador yelped. He was up on all fours and his tongue was out panting. At last, Rocky was somewhat disturbed.

'Down, Rocky!' Shouted with vigour.

Rocky knew Bannerman's voice but he searched for a response from his indisputable master, Cross. There were no words spoken from Cross, just silence and a fierce engine roar.

Rocky sat on his hind legs, voiceless, obedient, waiting, watching, and sensing that something was wrong.

The growling Beamer had stolen a crucial yard, was well down the road, and had powered on through those city streets. Traffic lights flashed, red, green and amber, and silver shop lights lined an escape route as the street lights cast a thousand neon pools on a tarmac surface.

A blue beacon flashed and joined a chaos of lights. The roof aerial leaned backwards with the quickening from take-off and a siren sounded as Cross gripped the wheel. Bannerman hung on as a bend disappeared and the back end of Cross's police car twitched in vengeful anger. The radio croaked but an engine thriving, a siren bleating, and Rocky now barking, killed its futile transmission.

The traffic lights were shining red but Jo-Jo didn't seem to care as one dangerous Beamer stayed loose on the road. It was approaching the red, oblivious to other colours on display.

Rain fell, trickling in a drizzle, splashing on a windscreen, and on a long straight in Lowther Street Jo-Jo ripped through those red traffic lights and sped away from Cross and Bannerman, and a Labrador called Rocky.

Cross hit his accelerator. A metal pedal pressed the carpet above the floor and his patrol car engine screamed in devastating pursuit.

Casually, a group of drunken youths wandered from a bar and saw a fiery Beamer, heard, then saw a chasing police car, and raised two fingers at the men in blue.

Bannerman saw their faces. He knew their names and he saw their gestures, and he traded insults with one finger held erect. 'I'll be back. Enjoy your last pint?' mouthed in displeasure. It was such an irrelevant remark but then Bannerman took everything personal.

Ignoring Bannerman's interruption, switching off from the outside world, Sergeant Cross just placed his mind on his job and carved through twilight traffic with a gentle twitch at every overtake.

Jo-Jo moved to the offside lane of three and hurtled past a bus, car, and pedal cyclist, before diving dangerously towards a right-angled nearside corner. Turning, Jo-Jo narrowly missed the front end of a taxi; he was so perilously close. Blaring horns accompanied a cacophony of angry insults.

Cross saw Jo-Jo's Beamer turn. He slammed the brakes, swung his steering wheel savagely and drove down the inside lane, headlights flashing with such stunning wrath.

Bannerman spoke quickly into his police radio. He was advising his control room and telling his tale as their squealing siren penetrated the receiver's ears.

Heads in the rear of Jo-Jo's Beamer came into view once more as Cross gained ground down a slope towards a roundabout. Red brake lights shone from the rear of the Beamer as its nose dipped and then swung into the offside lane heading north. A puff of blue-grey exhaust gases escaped a tube as the panicking Jo-Jo gauged some traffic lights and slow moving traffic as he approached the roundabout.

Then the traffic lights changed to green.

A police van driven by Constable Martin appeared from the west, its driver's eyes searching for and then finding two racing cars hurtling towards the roundabout that dominated the city. Another blue beacon circled the night as the police van waddled slowly into the centre lane. Martin was trying to reduce traffic flow, trying to hinder Jo-Jo's black Beamer, trying to slow the chase down.

Bannerman radioed an intercept, 'Now!' He saw it happen and saw it fail. Encroaching onto the roundabout, the Beamer mounted a paved area with a fierce bump and clung to the kerb, passing Martin's police van on its offside. The van's offside mirror jutted towards the Beamer, and then it buckled into pieces when the Beamer's nearside wing mangled the glass and the mirror fell to the ground. A shattering crash sprinkled the tarmac with fragments of glass and snippets of debris. Another puff of exhaust fumes escaped as a lower gear was taken and Jo-Jo sped away through the gearbox, laughing, exhaling in temporary triumph.

Grimacing, Cross took second gear and sliced through traffic up on the kerb directly behind Jo-Jo's black Beamer. Rubber regained tarmac and Cross's car springs jolted as the pavement groaned farewell. Excited, Rocky bobbed on the back seat and growled at the car in front. Then Bannerman whinged as the tyres found purchase and Constable Martin's mouth dropped, rigid, all aghast in a brief moment of passing.

The road fanned out into three lanes north over Eden Bridge.

By the centre span, chased and chasers were touching sixty-five miles an hour as traffic opened up for the Grand Prix event. Pedestrians stopped to stand and stare. More traffic lights emerged, ignored in the frenzy, rejected in the hurry, abandoned in pure desperation as the drug couriers sped away tracked by police.

Eventually there was an open road; two chariots tested their skills.

Jo-Jo held the crown of the road with Cross weaving to left and right, climbing all over his tail. A left hand turn up a hill followed, sudden, a late manoeuvre from young Jo-Jo but not late enough as Cross replied and stuck to the back bumper as only he knew how. Then Jo-Jo lost control and over steered. His back end twitched and his tyres lost their grip, spinning and spitting loose gravel in defiance. A wall appeared. The rear end of the Beamer slid, unchecked, towards the brickwork. Then metal crunched as Jo-Jo's black chariot clattered an offside wing and wounded its rear bumper on the sandstone boundary.

Jo-Jo faltered, loosing speed with a metal bar dragging on the ground and an occasional spark from the tarmac, and two heads turning anxiously from their rear seat.

Rocky barked as Bannerman screamed into his radio and planned their next move. Cross remained silent. He was solitary in his driving. He was the one in the cockpit, alone at his wheel.

Another police car careered down the hill towards the battling motors; its flashing blue beacon drew towards the damaged Beamer.

'Yes!' screamed Bannerman in triumph. 'Gotcha!'

With an abrupt thud, Cross slammed on the brakes when he saw people appear.

Frustrated, the Beamer moved dangerously onto a footpath scattering an old man with a walking stick, a woman with a pram, and a child with a pink teddy bear.

A hand appeared turning the Beamer's sunroof to an open position by rotating an inside handle. Then a mask appeared at the rear window and a figure wearing the mask emerged, vertical, looking out through the Beamer's open sunroof.

Caressing the brake pedal, Cross pulled back and allowed the Beamer ground.

Bannerman cursed and the police car coming towards them jammed on its brakes and slewed to one side with the Beamer held in the middle. Jo-Jo was the meat in a sandwich. The Beamer was trapped.

The masked face turned and sought Cross's car. Cross was too far away from the mask to be an easy target. Yet half on a footpath and half on a road, the Beamer angled towards the police car blocking the road ahead.

The police car inched forward, blocking the road further, narrowing the escape gap, and threatening the Beamer and its occupants.

Suddenly the masked face had a building brick and an arm drew back and threw the missile towards the stationary police car. Turning sickeningly, soaring through the air, the stone found its mark and the police car's windscreen exploded in a shower of glass.

The arm disappeared; the mask dropped down and an open sunroof closed as the Beamer drew level with a police car slewed across the road.

The police driver saw the brick, then shattering glass, and was out of the chase as the Beamer rolled by on a footpath with its bumper dragging and clanging near a terrified child with a pink teddy bear.

At the top of the hill the road took a bend to its left with Cross again chasing and ignoring broken glass littering the road. A 'thumbs up' came from an unfortunate policeman as Cross inched past his wreckage and a woman screamed with a child in her hand. A pink teddy bear lay in a gutter, forlorn, abandoned, and then a child screamed uncontrollably.

Rain was now falling and lancing the tarmac but the Beamer was nowhere to be seen. Jo-Jo and company had vanished into thin air!

Driving silently into Stanwix village, dogged by bad luck, Cross and Bannerman searched for the Beamer. They saw the Crown and Thistle public house; Stanwix School and the sign of Petriana; and a newsagent. Turning on a car park, they retraced their steps.

'Just sit quietly, Cross' advised Bannerman. 'They'll show up in a moment or two.'

Cross pulled into the kerb and switched the engine off.

'Perhaps we need him, Bannerman,' said Cross, pointing towards the sign of Petriana and a Roman soldier sat astride a horse.

'One horsepower! I think not,' replied Bannerman with a wry smile.

'I was thinking of the cavalry actually.'

'Wait one,' scolded Bannerman.

There was silence save for Rocky panting and whimpering in the back seat and a clock ticking quietly from a dashboard.

Two minutes later Cross fired the engine and they drove towards the Art College discussing how the Beamer had escaped. Constantly circling, they were convinced that Beamer was there to be found. They drove on, just searching.

There was a flash of a car's headlights in the distance.

'Go left! Left, left, left,' screamed Bannerman.

Cross complied as his car shook in fury and a radio crackled with others responding to chaos in the night.

'Right! Right, right, right. There it is, down that hill.'

Cross heard Bannerman, swung his steering wheel, and saw a shower of sparks as the Beamer's bumper bounced on tarmac. Down a hill Cross's patrol car sped with its lights flashing and its siren blaring in the dark. A line of parked cars surfaced but the Beamer held the crown of the road and zipped down the middle to a junction in sight. The clanging noise of torn metal accompanied the sound of thriving engines and sparks flying haphazardly from a broken bumper.

'Move it, Cross. They're pulling away,' protested Bannerman. Cross killed the complaint with an icy glance as Rocky panted and his tongue drooled with delight.

With a clamour of brakes and a rattle of metal the Beamer made the junction, ignored a temporary red traffic light, and swung left shattering a family of traffic cones warning of resurfacing work. Red and white cones flew into the air and bounced from a garden wall into Cross's path.

With a sickening crunch some plastic crumpled and died beneath Cross's patrol car sump.

The Beamer smarted and took another left to reach a main road.

Rejecting the brake pedal, Cross cradled the handbrake and Bannerman closed his eyes. There was a flick to right and then left as Cross snapped on the handbrake and felt the rear of his patrol car career round at full speed with his foot hard on the accelerator pedal and the engine screaming in triumph.

There were only yards between these two chariots now as the chase gathered pace and rain pierced down. Within minutes they were back on the bridge with the Eden beneath them and rain falling from above.

'Back towards the roundabout,' screeched Bannerman into his radio.

Up ahead, Cross saw fireworks as the Beamer's bumper finally surrendered and flashed on tarmac before rising into the air. It was loose, adrift, a missile in flight.

'Christ!' mouthed Bannerman, his hands in front of his face waiting for a smash, expecting the bumper to hurtle through their windscreen.

Cross wrenched the steering wheel and hit the brakes. The bonnet dipped. Cross swerved. The bumper sailed over the police car dislodging its blue beacon, aerial, and a stop sign from the roof.

'Christ!' shouted Bannerman again.

Rocky wagged his tail and barked in anger as some debris obliterated on the tarmac behind them in a shower of silvery sparks and plastic entrails.

The roundabout came into view again as the Beamer held the middle lane and tore through city traffic on its frightening getaway. Cars filtered off as the crazy chase carved through a line of vehicles and headed west towards the estate. Cross remained silent, his brain on the game, steel grey eyes on his quarry as he ordered his broken car in breathtaking pursuit.

Heads turned; tongues wagged. The Beamer made its escape dominating the dual carriageway as Jo-Jo struck out for the new estate. He was making for home, clogging it as fast as he could. Flat out for freedom!

'He's still there!' screamed Jo-Jo. 'Throw those bags out, Yasif. Dump it!'

'Why? Are you crazy, Jo-Jo?'

'Give them the drugs, Yasif. Throw it out. They'll stop for the gear.'

'No way. Drive!'

'We'll never make it, Yasif,' protested Jo-Jo. 'Throw the gear out.'

'Ten grand! It's worth ten grand, you fool. Keep going, Jo-Jo. Do as you're told or you'll regret it. We'll drop the car on the estate and run for it.'

'You don't understand, Yasif. That was Bannerman. He's infamous.'

Yasif's skin embraced a trigger guard, curling a finger round the killing tool. The coldness in his voice filled their car and stung its occupants. 'When I'm ready. Listen to me, Jo-Jo, you chicken shit English. The next time I tell you to mow a man down, you do it. Now drive!'

Jo-Jo felt a metal barrel kiss his neck, heard the tone in Yasif's voice, sensed the threat, and hurried on through city traffic.

A green light beckoned as Yasif pressed the digits and spoke to a girl on his mobile 'phone. He was cool and calm betraying no harshness as he ordered the girl to do as she was bid.

'This is Yasif, my pretty little girl. We're coming up onto the estate, Trish, but we've got company.'

'I can hear sirens in the background, Yasif. Have you got the gear?'

'Yes. Don't worry about the police… Just worry that what I tell you to do, Trish, you get right.'

Sensing menace in Yasif's voice, Trish squirmed, 'I'm listening.'

'This is what I want you to do…'

The menace in his voice shivered an eager response. Trish ran from their house to contact the dealers, nearby.

'The new estate! They're making for the new estate,' advised Bannerman.

A voice on the radio acknowledged and organised a response.

Bannerman cut in, 'West on the dual carriageway, speed… Eighty-five plus. Four up and still going strong. We can't catch it.'

'Roger, message timed one nine three zero hours… All units! All units make for the new estate and prevent entry. Suspect vehicle is a black BMW, two litres with rear spoiler, headed west at high speed. Current location Castle Way towards the new estate. Four males on board, fail to stop for police… Be advised… Origin of report indicates vehicle seen acting suspiciously… Occupants have already immobilised one panda… Exercise caution… Standing operating procedures required, Bannerman!'

'Caution!' retaliated Bannerman. 'They're bloody lunatics for Christ's sake. They must have robbed a bank.'

Rocky barked in agreement.

'Down!' and was banished by Bannerman to the depths of the car.

'It must be a bank job, Cross. They'll do a runner. Get closer.'

There was a silent response from Cross as his car took top gear and briefly left the ground at the summit of a slight hill. They were afloat in the air with no traction, no driving, but it was only a split second then the tyres bounced on tarmac and their suspension earned its keep. Like bees chasing honey they came from all over. There was a dozen flashing blue lights joining the carriageway and blocking all the exits.

The BMW held fast, shot up a hill, and swung round a roundabout.

With Cross in hot pursuit the Beamer tore down a long straight road. Swinging from left to right, Jo-Jo overtook everything in sight with Cross glued to his tail at every twitch. An elderly pedestrian took one step onto the road and then jumped backwards quickly as the two cars thundered down the road at breakneck speed. With a screech of brakes the Beamer turned into an estate that only a few years earlier had been a lazy patchwork of green meadows where sheep had once grazed.

Bannerman tightened his seat belt and whispered, 'Standing operating procedures dictate we should not enter this estate without prior approval, Cross.'

'I don't recognise no-go areas, Bannerman.' Cross snatched a lower gear, snarled, and hurtled the vehicle forward as they spun round a corner at sickening speed.

'Me neither,' laughed Bannerman.

A maze of terraced streets, obscure passageways and concrete walkways, met the entourage as the Beamer took a left into the new estate. The car wound its way through narrow streets bouncing over some bumps placed by the council to reduce speed. It passed some neatly trimmed gardens and freshly painted wall surrounds, ignored the floral curtains and smoke spiralling from chimney pots.

Cross gave chase with headlights flashing, a siren warning, and rain beating down on a windscreen. Over the speed ramps they jolted and lurched as all available units entered the estate. Tilting to left and right, the chase continued. The cars drove without a care; narrowly missing parked vehicles, colliding with kerbstones, ignoring speed ramps, cutting corners.

The sound of tyres screeching and hearts beating filled the ears of the chariot men.

On the bends, brakes squealed and tyres bit tarmac. On the straight, a flickering needle rushed towards the extremity of a speedometer. The chariot men were like shadows in the night, racing, skirting the ground lightly, and almost flying like hovercraft. Curtains twitched from frightened windows as shrieking sirens and growling engines penetrated every home on the crime-ridden, poverty-stricken, estate. Deeper and deeper the chase penetrated the very heart of the desperate community.

Neatly trimmed gardens gave way to desolate tiny squares of barren wastes. Once, flowers had breathed here. Residents had watered them and taken pride in their estate. Pebble-dashed homes, with white lace curtains gracing their windows, gave way to rows of wooden hoarding that had been erected by the council to prevent them from being smashed by stones and petrol bombs. Smoke, spiralling lazily from chimney pots, gave way to empty and derelict shells where only drug addicts, prostitutes, and handlers of stolen property survived. The road gave way to red brick dead houses in the centre of the estate. It was a place where no one wanted to live.

Darkness fell when the streetlights suddenly snuffed out. The only light in the place where no one wanted to live shone from the car headlights that Cross commanded.

A dark swarthy face in the Beamer turned and glanced at the chasing police car. There was a hint of blubber twisting from a sweating neck. Two shaking hands gripped a steering wheel. The gun barrel quivered in anticipation, and then a voice spoke into a mobile 'phone, 'Now!'

Cross reached wooden hoardings, knew the derelict houses, sensed a change and suddenly saw shadows as the Beamer turned off the road. It was all in a flash of speed. The Beamer hopped over the footpath and drove through a gate into a park. Suddenly, there were no pools of amber to reflect their way on darkened tarmac. There were neither cats' eyes nor white painted flashes to reflect the centre of the road. No people, no cars, no lights! It was a trap in the rain in a park surrounded by derelict houses where no one wanted to live.

Rain fell and the grass muddied.

They never knew how many missiles hit their patrol car. Cross and Bannerman just heard the noises of glass breaking and metal twisting when a deluge of objects hit their motor and Rocky yelped with fear.

Closing in, the mob bombarded the struggling patrol car. It was trapped in a downpour of wooden staves, sticks, stones, and rusting metal pipes. Its windscreen erupted within seconds. The roof bulged inwards as an empty beer keg, thrown from the roof of a derelict building, tumbled awkwardly through the sky and made its mark. A long jagged pole thrust through a side window and pierced the air between Cross and Bannerman.

Turning his steering wheel, Cross frantically slammed the accelerator down, but the tyres carried no grip on the rain-soaked muddy grass. Thrusting the gear stick into reverse, Cross hammered the accelerator as hard as he could. Wheels spun; rain fell. Mud splattered into thin air as Cross's car faltered in a park where no one played.

Flames gathered on the car bonnet when the first bottle shattered and burning liquid spilled into the vehicle. Fire raped shabby upholstery and licked savagely at the occupants. All that could be seen from inside the police car was a hundred flashing evil dancing shadows and a torrent of fiery projectiles lancing down with the rain.

Bannerman screamed into his radio. Cross wrestled with the controls. Rocky yapped and bared his teeth. Sticks and stones pelted down on trapped men.

The Beamer had gone. It was out of sight. They'd escaped. They were free.

A headlight exploded as a bottle atomised a glass lens and the light was no more. The other headlight died as a half brick buried itself in a glass unit and extinguished the light. A jeer filled the park. The mob bayed with pleasure, howled for blood.

The Beamer hopped out of the park and swung into a parking area behind a row of new shops. Yasif stepped from the Beamer as Jo-Jo ran from the estate in a cold sweat. Two other passengers stepped from the car and looked at each other, a question in their eyes as Jo-Jo's panic became obvious.

Yasif sensed tension, realised the problem and knew what to do. He spoke quietly, 'Not now, boys. I made a mistake. Chicken shit English! It won't happen again. Disappear for now, Aden. You and Rollo, be there at twelve noon tomorrow. Make sure you bring Jo-Jo with you.'

The two men nodded in agreement. Turning his collar up, Aden walked off in the opposite direction to that of Rollo. The young driver was nowhere to be seen.

Alone, Yasif unscrewed the Beamer's filler cap and threaded a torn piece of cotton into its petrol tank. A flame grew from his cigarette lighter and touched the cloth. He stood back and watched a flame race up the cloth and dart down the filler tube. A dull explosion followed and a cloud of black smoke preceded the flames that quickly burnt the black BMW. Within minutes the BMW had turned into a toasted metal chassis as violent flames engulfed its upholstery and devoured a leather dashboard. Fire ripped through the Beamer destroying any fingerprints or forensic evidence that might have lingered.

Trish approached carrying her mobile 'phone. She curtseyed as Yasif walked towards her and then she began to laugh aloud as his face broke into a toothy arrogant grin. Her long black raven hair swung across her shoulders. She pocketed her 'phone in a sheath at the belt of her jeans. Her hands went out to greet him.

'How did I do, Yasif? Was that what you wanted?'

Yasif reached his hand beneath his armpit and allowed his fingers to touch a trigger guard and a gun barrel. Then his fingers felt a bag of drugs hidden inside his clothes. A smile crept across his lips. Yasif took Trish in his arms and kissed her. Trish devoured him for only a moment before she thrust her hand inside his clothing and touched their drugs. She laughed and kissed him again, full blooded on his mouth with her hands combing his hair and her body thrusting into his. Yasif ran his fingers down her back, spread them, and caressed her buttocks. He looked back at the flames climbing from the park. Trish laughed. Yasif smiled and walked away from the park.

In the park, Rocky barked in fury, Bannerman screamed in horror, and sirens wailed in the distance. Another window smashed and voices pleaded for salvation as petrol seeped into the car burning upholstery and scorching blue tunics. A salvo of bricks and stones hammered down on the ambushed vehicle. Pale and anguished, their faces were ravaged with fear. Hearts thundered the beat of frightened men as blood rushed and adrenaline rose to fever pitch. Terrified, they could not escape the downpour of debris seeking to desecrate them.

'Officers down! Two missing!' Police radios warned of misery.

'Officers down! Car on fire!' Police radios confirmed their ordeal.

A police van slithered to a halt, siren in anger, blue light in rage, and with a metal grille laid over its windscreen. Officers ran from the vehicle wearing crash helmets and carrying short shields.

Cross, bleeding and burning, seized the moment. He kicked the driver's door. Determined, he pushed, heaved, and bounded from the car amidst a barrage of missiles. Dragging a screaming burning Bannerman from the car, he felt a building brick strike his back. Falling to the ground, exhausted with the effort, Cross was wrecked by tension and pain. With a supreme effort, Cross rolled Bannerman in the mud and smothered the flames scorching his uniform. Spitting petrol from his mouth, Cross sensed burning hair and plunged his head into the muddy waters of the earth, killing the fire. He lay on the ground and coughed at smoke attacking his lungs. Above him rain pelted down and soaked his clothes to the skin. A tail swished and he heard Rocky barking at his feet. Then Cross heard the splashing boots of reinforcements and saw lights. Blue lights! The stress of the moment detonated inside him. He didn't see flames or missiles or petrol bombs smashing at his feet. He didn't hear abuse, breaking glass, or tyres exploding with heat. He just saw blue lights and a metal grille on a windscreen and helmets and shields. Turning, Cross knelt on the ground and saw those evil shadows running in the flames. He guided Rocky, ordering the dog with a voice of wrath. 'Go! Go, Rocky! Go!'

Rocky needed no second telling, no order, and no advice. The magnificent animal, rejected by drug squad because he had no sense of smell, bounded into the mayhem.

The Golden Labrador, ignored flames, missiles, screams and bottles.

The pet Cross should not have had inside his patrol car leapt into action. The reject bounded into the park, his master's bid to do, in the rain, in the flame, in the mud of a park where children didn't play.

Rocky barked, sirens wailed, and shadows slid into the night as quickly as they had arrived. Rain fell; mud splattered, Rocky leapt. The dog's teeth gnawed, a youth screamed, and flesh punctured as Rocky bit an arm holding a Molotov cocktail. Biting deeper, the arm became pulp as Rocky tore away in frenzy and the crowd panicked.

Flashing lights heralded more reinforcements.

They charged into the fray. Police retaliated and the crowd retreated. Police charged and shadows fled into the night. The crowd vanished…

Yasif was gone from the park where no one played. Jo-Jo's Beamer was gone from streets where no one wanted to live. There were no drugs to find nor gun to know of. Suddenly, it was over. Sirens and screams ceased and a silence filled the park. The silence of the night was spoilt only by a dog barking, a youth howling, and a burnt out police car smoking in a park on a rainy autumn night.

Boyd didn't really enjoy his visit to London. The afternoon briefing had droned on for hours and had been saturated with political correctness and polite tones of needless conformity.

As arranged, after the talking, he walked into the west end and met Anthea and Dee-Dee: two old chums from his undercover days on the Special Crime Unit in New Scotland yard. The three friends ate well in a French restaurant and drank far too much. Boyd opted for Murphys, to the disgust of a middle-aged waiter, but Dee-Dee surprised everyone with a bottle of champagne to celebrate his promotion to sergeant. Anthea spoke of a rapturous love affair with a Portuguese policeman called Raphael, and then promptly updated her colleagues with their latest wedding plans. Dee-Dee and Anthea both asked Boyd about Meg, sent their love, and said they would visit the north soon. Anthea even promised to write that week with wedding invitations, but the trio's get together eventually came to an end. Their meal proved the high spot in Boyd's long day.

Finally, Boyd bought Meg a souvenir from a street trader's stall before returning to his hotel. A tee shirt again, thought Boyd. Now that will really impress Meg. Big Ben again. Still, she could always put it with the others he'd bought over the years.

It was in the lonely confines of his hotel room where Boyd 'phoned Meg and spoke of undying love, promised her faithfully he'd be home next day, and then told her he had thoroughly enjoyed dining with Anthea and Dee-Dee. When the call ended Boyd took to his bed and lay with his head on a pillow.

Restless, he thought of what those men in grey suits had said to him. They'd gathered around a highly polished walnut table dominating an office overlooking the River Thames and told him what to expect as they disclosed details of the event. Boyd listened keenly when the itinerary moved north but up until then he'd been relatively nonessential. A London policeman, a portly gent with a ginger moustache and a bellyful of self-importance, had sat next to him at the walnut table. They'd listened to what was said, and then the London policeman told

Boyd his trip from Cumbria to the capital had hardly been worthwhile. It was small peanuts, said the moustachioed London policeman. It was hardly worth travelling all the way from Carlisle to the capital, offered London's finest, just to hear a nonessential part in the visit of the Minister from a foreign country. Boyd's part in their security operation was fairly minor: a brief visit by a VIP, a foreign diplomat. It would all be over in a couple of hours. The Minister would shake a few hands, smile a few smiles, and say the right thing in front of camera. All Boyd was required to do was to keep the lid on things up north for a couple of hours and then it would be back to Chequers for sherry and biscuits; perhaps a stroll in the garden before supper.

Boyd had smiled politely, nodded mistaken agreement, and regretted his naïve acquiescence.

Had they laughed to themselves? Had he heard a snigger behind his back? Had that moustachioed London policeman shared a joke, at his expense, with others at the conference? Or was Boyd's mind playing tricks? Just look after things up north for a few hours. Any action, any real problems of diplomacy, will be in London. Don't worry. Minor part to play. It was if they were trying to make a fool of him.

Boyd blistered when he switched off the bedroom light ands buried himself beneath the covers. He tossed and turned wishing he'd taken the sleeper from Euston up the west coast to his home on the edge of the Lake District. Lying awake, he listened to those voices in his head. Hardly worth you coming down for this briefing, Boyd. You needn't have come down from Carlisle, Boyd. Silly of you to have rushed down really, Boyd. Just a couple of hours for the VIP visit; keep the lid on things up north, won't you. There's a good chap, Boyd.

Boyd didn't feel like a good chap.

The tide turned and she walked from the pier to her flat. It had been a long day for Yasmin and she needed the luxury of sleep. The meeting with Ray in Gateshead's Metro Centre had tested her.

They'd met in an Italian restaurant in the Mediterranean Village. Crowded with shoppers and tourists, Ray kissed her on the cheek when they met and made out as if they were lovers. Yasmin chose pasta because it seemed appropriate in the cosy Italian setting. He selected a salad. Ray needlessly paid for their meal before it arrived and asked if she was all right for money. She'd smiled, rejected his offer, and listened to him lecturing - Ray says this - Ray says that. He went on and on, and the more she listened to him, the more she thought him bossy and arrogant.

She heard his orders though, had to. It was what the colonel had instructed.

As their meal came to an end, he asked for the package. She pushed a black plastic bag beneath the table and allowed Ray to take it. Ray didn't check the contents, didn't need to. He trusted her. He apologised for his rudeness and explained he needed to meet an acquaintance. Then, abruptly, as if he was late for an appointment, he left her alone to finish off her pasta. .

Ray walked off carrying the black plastic bag.

Yasmin was annoyed. Ray was a professional intelligence officer and she was his agent. Yet they both knew better than to curtail a meeting in such a manner. The choice of a restaurant in a crowded place was fine if they were to be seen as lovers engaged in idle conversation. But lovers don't meet with a kiss and then part with a rude explanation. She'd been left alone in a crowded restaurant to finish her meal. It was as if they had endured a lover's tiff. Ray had drawn attention to her and she could not forgive his ineptitude. The restaurant staff might have wondered why their meal had been paid for so soon. Surrounding customers might have noticed Ray's sudden departure. She would not meet him again in such circumstances. She thought Ray unwise and wondered how long he had been in England. He had become complacent with his stupid orders and strange choice of rendezvous, and his professional status was now in tatters. At least that's what Yasmin thought, and the colonel had trained her. The colonel would have lambasted Ray, had he known of his amateurism. No, she thought Ray totally unprofessional. The colonel had told her she would be in safe hands. Yasmin wasn't so sure. She didn't like his manner, his arrogance, and his swift departure.

Yasmin followed him from the Mediterranean Village and watched him take the train from the Metro station into Newcastle.

She tracked him and a short time later watched Ray waiting outside Newcastle railway station. A black BMW motorcar arrived containing four men. The car stopped outside the railway station opposite a litterbin. Ray walked towards the BMW and deliberately dropped her plastic bag next to the litterbin, near the vehicle. Then Ray walked on without so much as a word to the occupants of the black car. Moments later a young boy jumped out of the driver's seat, collected the plastic bag, and threw it in the back of the car. Yasmin watched from the safety of a telephone box outside the taxi rank. As the BMW drove off, she saw Ray drive out of the railway station car park in a Mercedes Benz motorcar. She didn't expect to know everything that was going on, such was the nature of being a spy. But she thought it strange that Ray behaved in such a manner. She followed him so easily and he had not noticed her surveillance.

Then, worried at such incompetence, Yasmin returned to Cullercoats. She didn't trust Ray. She didn't fully appreciate why, at that precise moment, but she thought Ray might be dangerous.

Late at night, in the Special Branch office of Newcastle's central police station, a film was developed in a dark room of the photographic suite. The film was of a man and woman sat in a restaurant in the Metro Centre. Another shot showed the same two people parting abruptly. A third shot revealed a man driving out of a railway station car park in a Mercedes Benz motorcar. The car carried diplomatic number plates.

7

~ ~ ~

Dateline: September 3rd, Present Year: The City of Carlisle, Cumbria.

'Come in and sit down.' Chief Inspector McMurray's condescending hand beckoned entry as his pen nib hurriedly scribbled across a batch of documents. 'I've read your reports and I'm not impressed.' Rejecting his work, McMurray gathered a sheaf of papers and dumped them in a plastic tray as he scrutinised the approaching officers.

Bannerman took his seat first with Cross reluctantly following suit. They sat in high back chairs, which were no more than wooden straitjackets, as they watched Chief Inspector McMurray loll backwards into his executive swivel throne.

McMurray eased his chubby posterior into a more comfortable position in the plush leather upholstery that signified his status. He set his pen to one side and prepared his pipe. It was one of the remaining privileges of ageing seniority that he held dear. Digging deep into the bowl he loosened some spent tobacco with a pipe cleaner. When he had eyed their discomfort and sniffed disparagingly, he decided to teach the two men a lesson in patience. Black ashes tumbled from his overturned pipe and spilled into a glass ashtray as he glanced at the two men. Sniffing again, he removed a cloth pouch from a side pocket in his tunic and scooped fresh tobacco into the bowl of his pipe.

They waited for his words as awkward seconds ticked into minutes.

'Fat, arrogant bastard,' thought Cross to himself.

Fingering fresh tobacco, McMurray tamped it down into the bowl and thought it was time to remind them he was boss.

Bannerman shuffled his feet nervously. The feet wore size ten shoes and he stood six feet five inches inside them. Broad across the shoulders, he was quite muscular despite a slight paunch around his midriff. A chiselled square chin gave him the appearance of a man older than his twenty-eight years while a crop of microscopic ginger hair sprouted from a rounded skull and crept dangerously towards his ears. His mouth engaged in most of the action for at times he gabbled on endlessly about the most unimportant of things. From a distance, he looked almost bald. Up close, no one told him so. His friends called him 'the big man' but enemies called him 'the screaming skull'. In contrast, Cross remained a statue with his eyes fixed on the pipe bowl watching

McMurray's every move. Cross was smaller than Bannerman: a mere five feet eleven inches tall in his size nine boots. Bushy jet-black hair flowed untidily from the sergeant's head. He'd had lived twenty-seven unwise years and a deceptively proportionate build tried hard to conceal his sinewy body. The quieter one of the two, Cross seldom spoke at length or expended unnecessary energy. Indeed, he was laid back to the point of total relaxation and yet at times he carried a short fuse to a fierce temper. His steel grey eyes sat deep in a face that rarely portrayed any emotion, but behind his eyes ticked a brain as sharp as a razor, and just as dangerous. He was not a man who suffered fools gladly, and often it showed. Most people called him 'Cross'.

With a subdued tick, the second hand of a wall clock swept onwards. A desk and a grey carpet separated McMurray from the two men and tried to compliment the dreary pastel emulsion frowning from a wall into the heart of his office. Bookcases groaned from the weight of law books encircling the gathering while a sombre pink shade embraced a light bulb, which drooped from the ceiling, in a pathetic attempt to bring colour to McMurray's working environment. It failed.

Rattling a matchbox, McMurray began his sermon with a strike of a match on sandpaper. The head ignited and hovered over his tobacco. With a puff and the continued threat of a match, McMurray disappeared in a cloud of smoke. He re-emerged seconds later when his palm waved away lingering remnants of tobacco smoke and he jutted the end of his pipe towards Bannerman and Cross.

'You were both lucky not to be seriously injured,' said McMurray, his pipe triumphant at last. 'You should probably be in hospital.'

'We were lucky. It didn't warrant the worry of a long stay in a hospital bed. I discharged myself after treatment,' said Bannerman.

'Mmm! Yet you both know my rules. Standing operating procedure dictates no one enters the heart of that estate unless it is during an approved operation. I am in charge of policy and administration in this police station. You failed to obey the policy laid down. Your operation was not approved by me. You two cowboys disobeyed standing orders and took on the whole damned estate, didn't you? Well, I've no sympathy for either of you. You're a sergeant, Cross, for God's sake. You, of all people, should have known better. When Chief Inspector Operations gets back he'll chew you both into little pieces…'

'Boyd?' asked Cross.

'He's Chief Inspector Boyd to you, sergeant!'

'Indigestion...' muttered Cross.

'What did you say, Cross?'

'He'll get indigestion.... Chewing.'

'Don't interrupt!' snapped McMurray. 'Listen to me, you cheeky young upstart! You know the rules, don't you? The estate is out of bounds unless prior approval is sought. When you disobey my rules you can expect to be punished. As a result of your inadequacies' one of my police cars is totally burnt out. It's a complete write off. Another has had its windscreen put out and one of our vans needs a new offside mirror. Four of my officers sustained minor injuries from thrown missiles and you two are lucky to be alive.'

'We didn't start the riot,' said Bannerman. 'They were waiting for us. It was planned. Can't you see that? They were waiting with petrol bombs and a beer keg, the works. It was a trap. Do you understand what I'm saying?'

Their questions went unanswered. McMurray slid an ashtray nearer and continued his sermon. 'Furthermore, the estate is still simmering this morning. The situation is not totally under control. I'm told there were sporadic incidents of disorder during the night. A couple of shop windows were put in and a half a dozen cars were broken into. Car radios stolen, personal belongings rifled, the usual.'

'Any prisoners?' asked Bannerman.

'After your fracas in the park the mob dispersed but regrouped elsewhere. An hour of blatant disregard for authority followed. Three cars were found burnt out on the estate. One of the vehicles is a BMW; probably the one you were chasing. A check on its engine number shows the vehicle is legitimate but the last known owner of the car died about a year ago. It looks as if the car has been used by a series of joy riders ever since.'

'A pool car left on the streets for anyone to use?' suggested Bannerman.

'Probably! An informant using the code-name 'Mad Mary' reported the BMW parked on the estate at various times and in various places. The woman wouldn't give her address or answer any questions about herself. She saw the Beamer parked on the edge of the park on two or three occasions. A few days ago the car was parked up at the back of some shops. She thought it was strange, possibly abandoned. As the car didn't appear to have an owner she 'phoned its details in and suggested it could be used in crime. The Intelligence unit has her code-name on file but access to her full details is denied by order of Chief Inspector

Operations. Young God Almighty is flexing his muscles it seems. The Intelligence unit put the Beamer on their list for a stop check, that's where you came in.'

'She was right about the Beamer,' interrupted Bannerman. 'So when we checked the car on our radio, it came back suspect?'

'Yes, but whether she was right or not is immaterial. The BMW was torched and any chance of getting fingerprints has been destroyed. The point is if you hadn't chased that bloody car onto the estate there wouldn't have been a mini riot last night.'

'Mad Mary smelled a rat! We reacted to her tip-off, that's all. Any prisoners?' asked Bannerman again, persistent. 'It's important - Getting prisoners! It shows you mean business.'

'Your riot has caused me more than enough headaches this morning. The press have been on and so have Headquarters. Explain this! Account for that! I'm bloody sick of justifying everything. Even our local member of parliament has taken an interest. You should have ended the incident once the speed of the chase became too dangerous to undertake in safety. What you don't catch today, you catch tomorrow. You know that. No! Not you two. Heroes! Bloody heroes! People like you just don't realise how much mayhem is caused by over-reacting. The chase ended up with an orgy of crime and I'd much prefer a quieter life.' Tobacco smoke clouded towards the ceiling signalling anger in the air. 'Do you understand me? Do you realise the trouble you've caused?' snapped McMurray.

'Mad Mary was still right though. Any prisoners?' asked Bannerman: persistent. McMurray seemed reluctant to answer.

Ignoring Bannerman's repeated query, McMurray thrust an accusing finger towards Cross. 'The dog, Cross! That bloody dog of yours! No pets in police cars! It's a simple rule and it's my rule. No pets allowed anywhere near the police station. Do you hear me, Sergeant?'

Turning his head away, Cross gazed out of a window and caught sight of the early morning traffic threading its way down Rickergate towards the Civic Centre. A sigh oozed from his lips as he tried to picture Rocky attacking McMurray and taking a toothy bite from a large behind. A rare smile rippled across his sullen cheeks.

'What's so funny?' asked McMurray, working his pipe furiously.

'The dog took a prisoner,' murmured Cross with a hint of sarcasm. 'Rocky made an arrest. It was a good one too. A petrol bomber!'

'Petrol bomber, was he? That prisoner will probably sue us. You set a dangerous dog at that youth. The kid is in hospital right now, savaged, cut to ribbons. Your so-called pet is not a police dog; it's a bloody reject from the drug squad. It's a pet, for God's sake. Try explaining that to the court. The defence will call it unauthorised arrest! They'll probably put the dog down. If they don't, I will.'

'Rubbish!' offered Bannerman.

'Rubbish or not, there'll be a court case. I'll be writing reports forever. We haven't a leg to stand on. What were you thinking of, Cross?'

'Self-preservation! I thought I'd take a prisoner before they burnt us alive.'

'Tell that to the court.'

'I will. Don't you worry.'

'It won't make any difference, Cross. Whether he's convicted or not, we'll be sued to kingdom come in the civil court. If we're lucky we might get the chance to settle amicably out of court, but I wouldn't bank on it.'

'Provided we're proved wrong,' muttered Cross.

'If there's a court case, Cross, you're finished. You'll lose your stripes and you'll never get them back.'

'We'll have to wait and see what happens then,' replied Cross.

'Either way, it's trouble; paperwork I can do without.'

'It'll be a long time before that kid throws another petrol bomb at the police,' quipped Bannerman. 'A very long time.'

'It's not that he shouldn't have been arrested,' conceded McMurray, with a begrudged sigh. 'It's the unauthorised use of your dog that is in question, Cross.'

'What about the unauthorised use of petrol bombs?' retaliated Cross.

'The youth has made a formal complaint against you both. This matter is now in the hands of our discipline department. Reasonable force is one thing, deliberately setting a dog on someone is quite another.'

'It was self defence,' emphasised Cross.

McMurray ignored such a possibility and leaned back into his chair as a tobacco cloud continued to swirl above him. 'Once Chief Inspector Operations is back from London, you can look out. It's his responsibility since this is an operational matter. At the moment, I'm in charge. I'm putting you both on foot patrol until a decision is made as to whether or not you should be suspended from duty.'

'You're joking?' queried Bannerman, his eyes wide in disbelief.

'I never joke,' replied McMurray, brusquely. 'Now get out and get rid of that bloody dog.' A hand dismissed the pair and immediately sought a sheaf of papers resting in a plastic tray.

'I want a personal interview with Chief Inspector Operations when he returns from London,' said Cross.

'If that's what you want, Sergeant, I'll arrange it. I'm expecting him back later today, probably this afternoon. The discipline department have reminded me that I am in charge of policy and administration. Not that I need reminding, of course. Since this incident stems from an operational matter I am obliged to wait for Young God Almighty to scrutinise events upon his return.'

'Can I ask what Chief Inspector Boyd is doing in London?' said Bannerman. 'Young God Almighty, I think you called him.'

McMurray sniggered a reply, 'It was of course a slip of the tongue, my way of revealing his unquestioned authority to you. Well, I suppose you may as well know since there's to be yet another press conference on the matter. Chief Inspector Boyd is in London receiving a final briefing regarding a State visit. Apparently some high-powered Israeli minister of something or other is visiting the United Kingdom to discuss the Middle East peace process with our Prime Minister.' His backside shuffled uneasily in his chair. 'During the visit an Israeli minister is taking time out to come to Carlisle and receive the Masada Tablet from the city council. We've known about his visit for some time, of course, but it's only just been decided which Israeli minister is to receive the Masada Tablet on behalf of the Jewish State. Now the minister is known we shall be made aware of relevant security implications in respect of that person. The individual may need a bodyguard while he's in this country. It's quite usual for visiting V.I.P's to receive some form of protection, although I doubt whether such a person will be at risk in this country. It all seems quite irrelevant to me. Rather a waste of time going all the way to London for a briefing, I suspect. But then who am I to argue with London. It's going to be rather a high profile affair now, I understand.'

'Oh yes, the Masada Tablet!' acknowledged Bannerman. 'I read about it in the Cumberland News. When was that, 1990, 91, 92? Doesn't matter. It was in all the papers and on Border Television as well, if I remember correctly. Anyway, a few years ago some student, an Israeli, was in Tullie House Museum when he discovered an altar belonging to the Jews. It was a rock from early Israel, something like that. The rock was Jewish and someone had put it in the Roman section of the museum by mistake. Bit of a balls up, wasn't it? Do you remember that incident, sir?'

McMurray mellowed slightly and then sniggered, 'Yes, quite vividly. In fact, I was the sergeant who arrested the young Jew you're referring to. I was stationed in the west of the county then but I was sent here to cover sickness. There was an incident in the museum. I was driving the prisoner van that day. God, that seems years ago now but I remember the incident well. You never forget those you arrest, do you? I was promoted to inspector shortly after that.' A match struck and hovered once more, intimidating his tobacco. 'He was charged with criminal damage. The Jew boy, I mean. Apparently Jewish altars of that period were very similar to Roman altars, or so the papers said. There was quite a fuss about it all. The kid smashed Tullie House up and thumped a security guard. I don't remember the finer details. It's all to do with Roman remains and ancient history, I believe. The kid wrote to his Embassy when he got out, that's what got the ball rolling. All pretty boring, if you ask me.'

'I see,' said Bannerman. 'So boring we now have a State visit to contend with?'

'Yes, well,' replied McMurray, 'Water under the bridge. The tablet did belong to Israel and Carlisle City Council will hand it back during a formal ceremony at Tullie House. Hands across the sea and all that. The Roman city returns a Jewish artefact, etc. etc. It's good publicity for Carlisle and for the Israeli minister, I suppose. The place will be full of tourists that day, mark my words. I expect national television will want to interview a senior officer. That's my job, of course. Perhaps I'll remind everyone who arrested the Jew. If it hadn't been for me, the tablet wouldn't have come to light. It's good for our local economy, don't you think so, Cross?'

Cross displayed no interest in either the State visit or the Masada Tablet. Contemplating, he privately considered the medical implications of inserting a pipe into an arrogant rectum.

'No, of course you would have no interest in matters of culture, would you, Cross? My problem is the estate is simmering and we have a bloody State visit at the end of this week. That's a problem we can do without. Thank you very much!'

McMurray paused to service his pipe again.

Bannerman said, 'If Chief Inspector Boyd has any sense he'll be clubbing it in the west end of London tonight.'

Cross interjected, 'Could you answer me one question, chief inspector?'

'If I must,' replied McMurray, looking daggers at the younger man who had an uncanny knack of getting right up his nose.

'Where were you when those petrol bombs were being thrown at us on the estate?'

McMurray flustered in a cloud of tobacco smoke that erupted from his pipe as a strangled cough escaped an unprepared throat.

'Never mind,' rescued Cross. 'I think I can guess.'

Cross stood up and walked towards the door.

'Foot patrol, both of you,' ordered McMurray, recovering his composure; yet willing to let such a confrontational remark slip by unanswered.

Bannerman watched Cross's receding shoulders, looked at McMurray, rose from his seat, and followed Cross into the corridor.

A door marked 'Chief Inspector Policy and Administration' slammed shut as Cross and Bannerman walked down the passageway.

'You can't resist antagonising people, Cross. Why couldn't you just leave it?' There was no need for that last remark. Try to be politically correct otherwise McMurray will cause trouble for you. He'll eat you one day, Cross. Eat you for breakfast.'

'Politically correct? I'd rather say it as it is.'

'Well don't, and don't go upsetting Young God Almighty when you see him,' cautioned Bannerman.

'Since when did you get a licence to call Boyd Young God Almighty?'

Bannerman chuckled a reply, 'I didn't, but I know there is no love lost between our two chief inspectors. One comes from the west of the county and the other is from the east. They're obviously rivals. It's easy to play McMurray off against anyone, believe me. I do it all the time, Cross. Sometimes it's even fun. They never compromise.'

'McMurray is a pratt,' spat Cross.

'We both know the man is a pratt but you don't have to dig at him.'

'Correct,' replied Cross. 'He's a pratt. I know it, you know it, and we all know it.'

'They say even Young God Almighty knows it.'

'Boyd, Chief Inspector Operations? He's younger than McMurray, that's why McMurray is jealous. Boyd got promoted to Operations. McMurray thought the job should have been his. McMurray won Policy and Administration, thank God. Talking about God, Young God Almighty hasn't been here long enough to know what's what,' advised Cross.

'Perhaps,' warned Bannerman. 'McMurray has a lot on his mind. If the bosses are planning a State visit then the last thing they want is an estate boiling over into a riot. No wonder he's worried. All we need now is a murder and then the cat will be well and truly in amongst the pigeons. We're hard stretched enough as it is.'

'Come on,' said Cross, stepping briskly through some double doors. 'We've got work to do.'

Bannerman followed and placed a hand on his partner's shoulder. Stopping in his tracks, Cross turned to face the big man with a close-cropped ginger skull.

'Don't let anyone tell you ability and rank go hand in glove, Cross. McMurray looks after paper clips, toilet rolls, and policy and administration. The London man is our man, Cross. Young God Almighty will sort this lot out for you. The complaint, I mean.'

'I doubt it, McMurray has been around a while,' replied Cross. 'Boyd is newly promoted and hasn't worn a uniform for years. He's a scruff gear man. Specialist undercover work, they say. All this lot will be new to him. Riots, disorder on the estate. He won't have a clue, will he? Worst thing is, he won't want to upset headquarters by supporting us, won't want to jeopardise those shiny new pips of his. The man's still learning what uniform is about. He'll be just like all the rest of them. Me! Me! Me! That's all he'll be interested in.'

Bannerman tried to keep pace with his smaller comrade as they strode out.

'Reckon he's a Freemason, Cross?' asked Bannerman. 'Boyd, I mean.'

'Don't you prattle on, Bannerman?' Cross exhaled a loud sigh and then said, 'Pound to a penny he is.'

'How do we find out?'

'Watch the lodge on Thursday night, Bannerman. Touch of surveillance should do it. Start at seven finish at eight, clock he whole lodge.

'Sounds boring. I thought it was a secret society.'

'Nothing's secret anymore, Bannerman. Just stand in the shadows.'

The two walked on in silence. Walking the full length of a corridor, Cross strode past a rest room and clicked his fingers. There was a soft bark and Rocky leapt from a carpet and joined Cross at his heel. At the end of the corridor, the three entered a parade room.

'Where are we going?' asked Bannerman.

'Foot patrol, the man said.' Cross's key rattled as he opened his locker door.

'What about Rocky,' asked Bannerman?

Cross's flat cap, with its black and white checked band, sailed into the rear of his locker coming to rest near a vacuum flask and a police helmet. 'What about Rocky,' quizzed Cross, mischievously? 'The dog saved us once, he can do it again.' Cross bent down and ran his hands affectionately through Rocky's golden hair. Rocky's neck went back and Cross lovingly caressed the dog's throat with his knuckles. Rocky's tongue drooled out and began to lick Cross on his face. Cross smoothed back Rocky's ears and stroked his back saying, 'Easy boy, easy. No-one's going to touch you.'

'That reminds me, Cross. Thanks.'

'Thanks! What for?'

'Saving my life last night,' smiled Bannerman.

'You would do the same for me, Bannerman,' said Cross.

Bannerman turned and rummaged in his locker. Not a word was spoken as both men readied their equipment. Bullet proof clipboards and a pile of leaflets about traffic law were buried in a locker. Batons and gas canisters were selected and buried inside their uniform. Changeover complete.

'Wouldn't you, Bannerman?' quizzed Cross, suddenly worried by Bannerman's inability to reply.

'Would I?' replied the big man. A brief moment of silence followed before both men burst into laughter.

'Let's take a walk up the street,' laughed Cross. 'Time to take the sun.'

Bannerman shook his head, 'I'll buy you a pint tonight, Cross. We can celebrate our transfer to foot patrol. I enjoyed traffic but what the hell.'

'You'll buy me more than a pint, Bannerman. When we finish duty we're straight in the pub. The first one won't touch the sides. The second one will swill the smoke from my throat and the third one… Well, I might even taste the third one.'

'Time for a session, Cross. I'm your man,' smiled Bannerman. 'Stuff McMurray and his police force. It's time for a stress break in the pub.'

Cross donned his helmet; Rocky fell in line. The sound of footsteps replaced a chuckle of laughter when the rear door of a police station closed tight and two men and a dog set off for a walk in a Roman city.

The estate was new in comparison with the rest of Carlisle. Built in the Eighties it extended the city boundaries, clawed back the lush farmland of Eden's valley, and proved a disaster. Constructed around a once-proud park, in a typical grid formation, its new houses were at first occupied by those who had waited patiently on the local housing accommodation list. Later, homeless from North East England and Central Scotland occupied some of the houses, but as the estate expanded; its occupants grew in disparity. Strangers, people from the Midlands and North West Lancashire, moved in, sought work, settled in their various guises, and tipped the unique balance of fellowship that had once been the trademark of the estate. When a recession bit deep, the local economy suffered its fair share of misery. As a result, the estate's social fabric lay in tatters, ripped by unemployment, poverty, crime, and drug abuse. It had all seemed to happen so quickly, without rhyme or reason.

There were no flowers in the park anymore. The blooms had been trampled underfoot when a rampaging mob had run from the police. Patches of grass were scorched here and there, completely burnt black where a police car had been attacked, and still damp from a Fire Service jet that had killed the flames. The ground was littered with household debris and the flotsam and jetsam of life sustained in a stark existence. Broken vodka bottles, cider bottles, and discarded beer cans lay besides spent hypodermic needles, stub end joints of cannabis, and crumbling building bricks. Black iron railings bordering the park were rusted brown, sometimes loose and bent where idle hands had tried to rip them from their moorings to use as spears against blue uniforms. There were no children playing in the park. The swings and seesaw, which needed a realistic coat of paint, stood idle and slowly began to rot; and the park-keeper seldom visited his park. He was too afraid of being attacked and robbed by unruly elements drifting in and out of the estate where no one wanted to live. When it rained pools of water lay in hollows and ditches, failing to drain away as landscape designers had planned. The concrete pathways were cracked and bordered by straggly weeds that needed a hoe. Plastic litterbins were full and overflowing, sometimes melted where a vandal had set a mindless fire. Where litter lay, a wind occasionally blew and regularly wafted debris into the air. The wind whistled through the scorched park and brought a lingering chill to its pathways.

It was such a desolate place.

A widow woman walked alone in the scorched park as a shrill breeze nipped at her ankles. Mary Forsyth knew the park well and walked its ragged paths every day to exercise her Alsatian. She felt safe. Her bitch was big and sprightly and bared its teeth at those who dared approach. Tugging her leash, she patted her dog.

Of local origin, Mary lived in a house where smoke escaped from a chimney pot and her garden bore grass that had once been trimmed to perfection by her dearly departed husband. There was even a pink rose bush in a tub near her front door. Slightly better off than some of her neighbours, there were lace curtains in Mary's front window. In the centre of a window ledge sat a potted plant, an Irish Shamrock that had travelled well. The Shamrock always sat in the middle of her window ledge, unless she moved her plant to water its roots. But Mary Forsyth was known to be a bit of an oddball when it came to looking after plants. She only watered her Shamrock at particular times and told her neighbours that tending to a Shamrock involved many a strange Irish custom. They laughed at her and thought she was harmless. The young and unsure visited Mary Forsyth for advice and were welcomed by a lonely woman who needed people to talk to. The old and infirm visited her for comfort and were welcomed by a widow woman who recounted the smile of her late husband and told of how he had returned one Christmas with a Shamrock. Mary made coffee and tea and baked tiny fairy cakes for the young and unsure, and the old and infirm. Mary Forsyth knew everyone on her estate; they all popped in for a chat, a coffee or tea, or a tiny fairy cake. People on the estate were good folk, she thought. Mary knew some of them received only a pittance from the Social Security to live on. There was no work. Many folk turned to crime and drugs to get by. There was no steady employment to speak of; the social fabric was dying with the straggly weeds. Mary thought there were more good folk than bad folk on the estate where she lived, despite what everyone said. Mary Forsyth knew everyone, made it her business to know everyone. She listened to both young and old when they drank her drinks and ate her tiny fairy cakes. She heard young ones gossiping and criticising older ones, listened to older ones scolding younger ones, and heard it all when she served drinks and tiny fairy cakes. Then she walked her Alsatian in the park and wondered if the girl would contact her about that black BMW and those strange looking men who had started all the trouble on her streets. Of course, she couldn't prove they started the trouble. She looked at her watch and reckoned it was time to return home.

The Alsatian sniffed its nose to the ground and pulled on its leash.

No one knew that Mary Forsyth had agreed to be Boyd's eyes and ears on the crime-ridden, poverty-stricken estate. Her life wouldn't have been worth living if those on the estate knew she was a police informer. She was mad to help them, quite mad.

The widow woman walked through a scorched park where children never played and decided it was time to water her Shamrock plant. The girl would come soon.

Mad Mary headed home.

Delving into an inside pocket, Boyd removed a notebook, flipped through its pages, and carefully removed a sheet of paper. Fumbling in the breast pocket of his suit, he pulled out a pencil. Annoyed, he began to write but the train's motion did not help the good ordering of his pencil across the paper. As the train rocked gently from side to side Boyd glanced out of a window and recognised the countryside. They were approaching Crewe.

His mind returned to that London briefing and the problems before him. He drew, on his sheet of paper, a map of the road from Carlisle airport to the city centre. In his mind he counted the number of junctions between leaving the airport and arriving at the venue. Closing his eyes for a moment, he visualised driving the road as he counted the number of junctions and bends where a car would need to slow down in order to negotiate a corner. He drew a cross on his paper, here and there, where high ground was situated, where bad bends existed, where bad junctions criss-crossed his route; and where a car would have to slow down. When he had drawn a map from the airport to his venue he turned his piece of paper over. On the rear he drew a map of the road from the city boundary to the venue. Again he ordered his pencil to show junctions, bends and high ground.

When he had finished his drawing, Boyd walked from the first class section of his train to a buffet car. Steadying his walk in a rolling carriage, he rocked from handrail to handrail before locating a steward. A few pound coins were exchanged for two cans of beer and a forced smile. Returning to his seat, he looked out of his window and remembered that Intelligence briefing in the office overlooking the Thames.

Boyd looked again at his piece of paper and both maps he'd drawn. It's a start, he thought. Stretching back into the comfort of his seat, he considered his briefing and that information, wondered how reliable the source had proved in the past. Rubbing his chin thoughtfully, he speculated on whether Namir was bound for Carlisle, London or Chequers? Or was Namir just missing in the desert? He tried to guess how often the agent runner met his source of information, and how good the source really was? For that matter, thought Boyd, how good is the agent runner? Then he dismissed his opinions with a whimsical bite of his lip. But he knew if the agent runner were a rank amateur, then British Intelligence was probably wasting everyone's time with useless information. He'd asked who or what the source of information had been, and he'd been virtually disowned by a man chairing their briefing. Boyd had suggested it might be helpful if the police knew where the information regarding Namir had originated. Blanked again, he'd been told parting with such information might endanger lives. With a security clearance well above *Positively Vetted Top secret,* Boyd had thought British Intelligence might have been more helpful. It wasn't to be. What's more, Boyd didn't blame them one little bit. In their shoes, he would have preserved his source at all costs.

The source of the information was undercover, decided Boyd. Undercover: the word flowed through Boyd's blood and fed his very being.

Reaching forward, flicking a top from a can, Boyd swung its contents into his mouth. The beer tasted good and swilled the inside of his mouth before rushing down his gullet. He drank again, this time more slowly as he savoured its taste and doodled on his paper. Scrawling subconsciously, his doodle suddenly took on a character and shape of its own. Boyd had scribbled the childish outline of a gun on his notepaper!

As he studied his immature artwork, Boyd wondered how he would plan an attack, were he a killer of men? Where would a murderer choose to attack, and which weapon might an assassin prefer? Gun or bomb? A sniper's rifle or a bomb with a timing device in its mechanism? Close range or long range? Hit and run or suicide attack? Proxy bomb, car bomb, nail bomb, oh, how many kinds of bombs were there? How many ways could you kill a man? It was Boyd's dilemma to assess which weapon, which method of attack, Namir could choose.

Boyd set aside his drawing and looked out of his window. He thought back to an American President who had been shot by a man in the crowd, an Israeli leader who was also shot by a man lurching from a group of well-wishers, the motorcade in Dallas when Kennedy was tragically killed by a sniper, and a British Prime Minister whose sleep was destroyed when a bomb exploded in a hotel room in Brighton.

It seemed a simple matter to kill those in high places.

I feel it in my mind, thought Boyd. It looks too easy; this man will come.

The train stopped with a sudden lurch and a virgin can of beer shifted towards the edge of the table. Boyd grabbed his can, looked out of the window, and saw the platform of Crewe railway station. The hands of a clock were approaching noon.

Would he come by train, thought Boyd?

Boyd remembered Crewe railway station from years ago. He knew Crewe and the Cheshire countryside surrounding its railway community, remembered it from his undercover days. It was one of many places he'd come to do a job and then moved on, silent in the night, like a scorpion stinging his victim and moving on to do another job. He recalled those days in the Special Crime Unit in New Scotland Yard, his undercover squad. He'd been an undercover officer in London, too. If he were undercover now he would know what to do, he thought. He'd spent most of his working life undercover. Now they'd put him in uniform and he hated the rigidity of life in a blue straitjacket. He preferred his jeans and tee shirt and the undercover life, scruff gear man chasing terrorists and international drug smugglers.

Boyd considered the route as he toyed with his rescued beer can. The Israeli Minister seemed in most danger when he walked from the aeroplane to his car, driving a predictable journey from the airport to the city, or when he was in the company of those he trusted: a confidante or even his own bodyguard. A killer might use a knife, a bullet or a bomb. He could choose to kill at close quarters with either a knife or a handgun, but an assassin could opt for a long-range attack if he decided to take a sniper's stance. In the main, that's how terrorists killed important people, thought Boyd. That's why it looked so easy. Wrestling with his mind, Boyd thought carefully about explosives and bombs. He would need police motorcyclists to guide the very important person's vehicle through traffic. His charge could not stop, should not present a sitting target for a bomb, and ought not to present a target in the cross hairs of a sniper's rifle. Boyd needed dogs to sniff out explosives that might blow the intended victim to smithereens, and a team of officers to search roads and streets; litter bins and sewers, and to explore car parks and telephone kiosks dominating the area of the visit. It was a thankless task but he required these people to prevent a sniper killing the intended victim. Ordering these requirements in his head, Boyd decided on what he must do to protect his charge, to prevent an attack. It was trivial, wasn't it? Just keep things under control for an hour or two, there's a good chap. Nonessential really, fairly routine visit, they'd told him. Then they'd laughed behind their backs at him. Treated him like a fool, hadn't they?

Then why a briefing if it was trivial, thought Boyd? Why a briefing about a man who had left the desert wastes of the Lebanon to travel to the United Kingdom to assassinate a high-powered Israeli minister. Who was important here, the potential victim or the assassin? Or was it just an overriding belief that an assassination attempt could only take place at Chequers, London, or Heathrow airport? Is it complacency on behalf of the Intelligence people, those grey suits that are never questioned because their track record is said to be supreme, beyond accountability?

'Tickets, please.'

A voice brought Boyd back to the present; he rummaged in his suit pocket for a voucher. There was clip of his ticket and the guard walked on.

Boyd thought back to when he was undercover with the Customs people and bought drugs from a dealer who'd been arrested shortly afterwards. Shaking his head, he thought about his undercover days with the American Treasury people when he'd bought counterfeit money from a dealer who'd been incarcerated immediately afterwards. Then he remembered the time he was undercover with Interpol and bought guns from a Russian who'd also been arrested. They'd all been arrested thanks to his undercover role. He'd saved lives and all that irrelevant claptrap and he knew it was because he found it easy to step out of the role of a stereotyped big-footed copper. He knew he was good at undercover work because of the manner in which he lived his role. Boyd hated the conventions of conservatism and embraced a free spirit within him. The free spirit within him was trapped in a problem he'd inherited at a briefing in London. Who the hell is the source of the information? Who is this man, Namir?

To beat this man him, thought Boyd, I must think like him...

The Arab's hair shimmered black when his neck rolled its swarthy blubber onto his jacket collar. His collar sprouted from a black fleece blouson that covered a dark silk shirt. A pair of charcoal-coloured trousers finished his clothes, matched the pigment of his skin; and complimented a dark depravity occupying his mind. Taking a rear entrance, Yasif nudged a door open, crept through the back kitchen, and stepped warily into the body of the house. Pausing cautiously, he stood still and listened. A gold stud in his ear quivered in the half-light as he allowed his eyes to become accustomed to the dim light. Edging forward, he felt adrenaline rush through his blood when his footstep crunched on broken glass. Startled, Yasif froze in the centre of the room and listened to the silent, empty house. He heard only his lungs heaving and falling as he scanned the abandoned building.

A patch of rising damp dominated one of the walls in the lounge and stopped abruptly where plaster had cracked. The wall gave way to a filthy pink skirting board, which bordered the room, and tried to limit an unusual animosity oozing from the house. Old newspapers covered wooden floorboards in a futile attempt to absorb the dampness. Perhaps these scattered newspapers had been the only carpet the previous occupants could afford, Yasif didn't know. Yasif neither knew nor cared; he remained indifferent to such trivia. The room felt cold and unfriendly despite a large fireplace that focused his eye. Upon its mantelpiece lay an overturned candlestick from which wax had dribbled from a burnt out candle and soiled a pamphlet advertising double-glazed windows. Grimacing, Yasif doubted whether anyone on this estate could afford such an extravagance. A solitary light bulb dangled from a thin line of flex that grew out of the ceiling and a crack in the plaster ran the full width of the ceiling and down towards the remnants of a curtain rail that bore no drapes. The windows were boarded yet they allowed a chink of daylight to penetrate the room and cast a lone ray of sunlight onto a soiled floor. In one corner of the room lay a crumpled empty beer can and a stale crust of bread. Allowing his eyes to wander into a hall, Yasif saw a heap of junk mail lying unopened on the cracked linoleum.

The situation suited Yasif perfectly: an empty house on an estate where no one wanted to live.

Yasif took in the dank smell of his derelict shell as he slowly removed his foot from some slivers of broken glass. Filling his nostrils, Yasif detected a faint odour of shaving lotion.

'Rollo?' quizzed Yasif.

'I'm here, Yasif,' replied Rollo.

A stout man emerged from the hall and stepped into the lounge. Rollo was born in England and in his early twenties. His father was Syrian and his mother English. Between them, they had bestowed upon their only son the gift of appearing as a half-caste. Rollo stood five feet nine inches tall and carried light brown hair, swept back and unruly. His grimy locks flowed all the way to broad shoulders. He was clean-shaven yet swarthy in his facial demeanour and his body alluded towards an ungainly plumpness where a growing paunch tried to climb over his leather trouser belt. Despite his age, it was a virtual roly-poly figure that filled the doorframe in which he stood. Rollo wore soiled denim jeans and a brown leather jacket zipped to his chin, and he smelled of cologne that wafted from a freshly shaven face and invaded Yasif's nostrils.

'I could smell you,' said Yasif. 'Aden and Jo-Jo, where are they?'

Jerking his thumb backwards over his shoulder, Rollo replied, 'They're here, Yasif, just as you ordered.'

Jo-Jo strolled arrogantly into the room. His thumbs dug deeply into the waistband of his jeans as he looked down at some yellowing newspapers strewn across the floor. Jo-Jo was the youngest in the house and the only pure Englishman present; if there was ever such a mortal. At nineteen years of age Jo-Jo had not yet matured in either the physical or mental sense. Long lanky legs supported a frame towering six feet tall. His thin build complemented his narrow shoulders and a shallow stomach. Strutting to one corner of the room, he attempted humour as he prodded a stale bread crust with his foot.

'Nice place you have here, Yasif. Is this all there is for the party?'

Scowling, Yasif slowly backed away towards the kitchen door. His eyes followed the young Englishman's every move. Then he flashed his eyes at the hallway as Aden entered.

Pressed denim jeans and a blue polo neck sweater followed Jo-Jo into the room. Aden grew an inch less than Jo-Jo yet his proportionate build sprouted muscles where Jo-Jo only enjoyed puppy fat. Aden was six years older than the Englishman and of Middle Eastern extraction. His straggly fair hair covered the tops of his ears. A twitch of his head found Yasif. Aden nodded.

'It's the last supper,' said Aden.

Yasif noticed deep blue eyes embedded in Aden's eye sockets. When Aden's eyes flashed, an earthquake rumbled inside his head and the power of a demon awoke.

Devilish eyes filled Aden's face and pierced the rear of Jo-Jo's skull. A curt moustache drooped at the side of his lips when he spoke. 'It's the last supper, Jo-Jo, and it's your last supper,' repeated Aden.

Jo-Jo had placed himself in one corner of the room. Yasif, Rollo and Aden closed in and formed an arc behind him.

'Last supper?' queried Jo-Jo with a quirk, a sarcastic grin. 'There's not enough there for an alley cat. Come on; let's do the cut. Give me my share of the take, tell me when our next collection is and I'll be on my way.'

The youngster turned, held out his hand, and offered it palm upwards to Yasif.

Ignoring the gesture Yasif nodded at Aden as Rollo moved casually forward and broke the ray of sunshine adorning the cluttered floor. The cast of light was broken.

Jo-Jo sensed an atmosphere and realised he was cornered, perhaps by design, perhaps by accident. He did not know. The grin on his face suddenly broke when he felt contempt in the air.

'You were employed by me to drive a car from Carlisle to Newcastle to collect a package,' said Yasif. 'You were told to return to Carlisle and take us to certain areas where deliveries would be made. You were recommended to me as a good driver, a man who could drive fast and would do as he was told. I was told you could be trusted. I was told wrong.'

'Yeah, I was a little edgy when the cops came after us. Bannerman was one of them. He takes things personal. Big hard man! Believe me, when Bannerman and that other guy are on to you, you've got no chance. Word is, they've got a drug dog. But I got you home safe with your drugs on board.' Smiling arrogantly, Jo-Jo shrugged his shoulders and said, 'There was no need for your gun but I'll give that a by. I'll say no more on that gun. Now all I want is paid for my time.'

'You panicked when all you had to do was keep cool and play it safe,' continued Yasif. 'You lost it totally when they got behind us. You were a fool when you dumped our car and ran away. You forgot to torch our car with petrol in the boot. You were on the verge of hysteria all the way through the job. I told you to mow the man down but you couldn't, could you?'

Sensing torment in Yasif's voice, Jo-Jo stepped forward as if to move into the centre of the room. A belly rolled and a belt buckle strained as Rollo reached out and grabbed Jo-Jo's arm. Spinning round, Jo-Jo glanced at Rollo, looked into Aden's eyes, and saw a devil dancing in his black pupils.

'Hey, man! Like I didn't want to get stopped. I should have turned off and avoided the city centre. I realise that now but I didn't know you would take it so seriously. Give me a break, man. Don't take it personal. We got away clean, didn't we?'

Yasif fingered a tube in his trouser pocket and felt the metal thread with the tip of his finger. There was a nod from Yasif and then Aden pushed Jo-Jo into a corner as Rollo closed with the Englishman. Rollo's knee shuddered into Jo-Jo's groin. With a sickly thud Jo-Jo coughed, doubled up, and fell to the ground on his knees.

'When I said mow the man down, you couldn't. When I said torch the car, you couldn't. You ran like the coward that you are. You ran like the chicken shit Englishman that you are.' Yasif withdrew a tube from his pocket and asked quietly, 'Who did you tell about our visit to Newcastle railway station?'

'No-one, Yasif,' gurgled Jo-Jo.

'Who did you tell about the driving I gave you to do?' Yasif fingered a metal tube: a silencer, in his hand. The silencer turned and screwed tight to the barrel of his gun. 'Speak up, chicken shit English.'

'No one, man. No one knows, man. I've kept clean. I told no-one.'

'I don't believe you.' The end of a silencer led the barrel of Yasif's gun to Jo-Jo's head. 'Tell me again chicken shit Englishman.'

'Listen to me, man,' said Jo-Jo, cold fear rising from a shallow belly, drying his throat, twisting his tongue in discomfort. 'Without me you were nothing. It was me who gave you the drugs network on the estate. It was me who pulled those dealers together and got the money together and made it all happen for you.'

The nose of Yasif's silencer pressed cold into Jo-Jo's temple.

'It was me who introduced you to Trish, man. It was me who…' Yasif's silencer retracted an inch, no more. A smile cracked on Jo-Jo's face. 'It was me who made it all happen for you, man and I'm the one who…'

Yasif pulled the trigger.

The retort was no more than a dull thud. A bullet entered Jo-Jo's temple near his right ear and penetrated his brain a microsecond later. A small calibre missile ripped through Jo-Jo's skull and exploded in a climax of freedom from the upper part of his skull, above his left eye. A hole appeared in his head and his body slumped to the floor. There was another dull retort as a second bullet drilled into his forehead. A third bullet broke Jo-Jo's sternum and filled his chest cavity with death. Jo-Jo died within seconds.

Blood spurted onto the lounge wall and joined a patch of dampness rising from a dank skirting board. Blood splattered and ran onto an empty fireplace, and then ran along a collection of soiled newspapers that carpeted the floor.

Yasif took a step back and said, 'Chicken shit English. Remind me to kill you better next time.' He wiped a smudge of blood from his hand: the hand that held a gun.

'Don't stand so close next time, Yasif,' advised Aden, shaking his head.

'You could do better?' retaliated Yasif, snapping his words.

'Yes,' replied Aden, defiantly. A devil danced in his eyes and his pupils seemed to dilate and burn in their madness. Aden wrenched the gun from Yasif and stood over Jo-Jo's body. 'About this range, that's all.' There was a brief flash, a hint of flame, followed instantly by a dull retort. A fourth bullet entered Jo-Jo's dead body. 'Then there's no blood spurting about onto your clothes. Understand?' said Aden.

Removing a handkerchief from his pocket, Aden unscrewed the silencer, rubbed a cloth over the gun, and then placed the weapon on the floor near Jo-Jo's body.

Yasif smiled and his toothy grin gaped at Aden. Then Rollo allowed his belly to billow over his belt buckle as Aden stepped over Jo-Jo and the three men broke into laughter. It was trivia, unimportant, irrelevant. What could be important about the killing of a man? In the eyes of the killers, it was trivia: how a man was killed and from what range, trivia!

When their laughter had died, they arranged Jo-Jo's body in a pose. Panting with his exertions, Rollo dipped his finger in Jo-Jo's blood and scrawled some words on a wall near a fireplace where dampness rose from a pink skirting board. An ugly crack in the plaster looked no better when it was adorned with the words that Rollo had scrawled. They laughed again.

'He didn't have to die,' chuckled Rollo.

'He'll never know why he didn't have to die,' smirked Aden.

'Jo-Jo isn't important,' replied Yasif, biting harshly. 'He was killed only to cause confusion, to divert attention. He's irrelevant, my friends, and so were those drugs.'

'Then why bother about them?' asked Rollo.

'The drugs will put money in our pockets, that's all. These English pound notes will smooth our stay in England. Just a sideline, Rollo. Let's not forget why we are here.'

A silence followed in an empty house on an estate where no one wanted to live. Rays of sunlight tried to break through a window but evil inside denied daylight its glory.

'Come on, boys,' said Yasif. 'It's time to make ready for the brother of our cause. The brother comes soon and the reason he comes is important.'

They nodded in agreement and turned away from Jo-Jo.

'Aden, make that call tomorrow,' said Yasif. 'As arranged.'

The three men walked from an empty house where a fourth man lay dead. Jo-Jo's blood trickled slowly across a yellowed newspaper and stained its print. His blood ran into a shallow pool and broke the shadow of evil that filled the house.

*

8

Dateline: 4th September, Present Year: Daybreak, The City of Carlisle.

Chief Inspector Operations was back at his desk ploughing through his documents, and he was tired. Unscrewing the cap of a vacuum flask, Boyd poured himself a coffee, heavily sugared, no milk, and checked his watch. It was approaching seven thirty in the morning and a dawn raid on his paperwork had succeeded in emptying his in-tray and filling his out-tray.

Boyd yawned, drank, and guided a fountain pen over his papers. A scrawl of a signature and an occasional question mark filled his time before he killed an errant blob of ink with a slip of blotting paper. Reading about burglaries, vandalism, petty thieving and dozens of nuisance calls, his mind buzzed as he caught up with events that had occurred during his brief absence. He saw the names of those who were either wanted or suspected of criminal offences, whose photographs were posted on the briefing board so that they might be recognised and arrested. Finally he examined a report submitted by Louise: the girl who was undercover in the city. Locking her report in a wall safe, he returned to his seat and slurped his coffee. The strong blend dripped and a stain smudged one of his documents. The air filled with expletives as he shuffled his papers. Then Boyd recognised the signature of Chief Inspector Policy and Administration. McMurray's signature ran neatly and precisely across the memorandum stapled to Cross and Bannerman's reports. Setting down the cap of his vacuum flask, Boyd put his pen down and leaned back in his chair. His feet rose from a carpeted floor and relaxed on the edge of his desk as he lay back into his deep leather seat and read the words of Cross, Bannerman and McMurray. There was a clear description from Bannerman, an uncompromising argument from McMurray, and a reasoned explanation from Cross. Boyd worried on such problems: the quandary of a rising crime rate and a riot; various issues associated with McMurray, Bannerman and Cross; and the relationship between the three men. Boyd knew in his heart he would eventually have to stamp out the bitterness growing between the three men, realised a sour relationship was not good for business. He needed a team that would pull together, not pull apart. Damn them for their stupidity, he thought. Damn them for not working together.

The minute hand of a wall clock moved on with a surprisingly loud thud that broke the silence in his office. Sighing at another wasted minute, Boyd felt jaded. He had a feeling it was going to be a long day.

An Alsatian bitch was on a leash, straining at her neck, tongue drooling, and shoulders hunched tight as she pulled Mary along. Mary wore wispy greying hair and was small and slender, not at all muscular; yet she was strong enough to order the dog to heel despite the fact her body was approaching its fiftieth anniversary. The Alsatian was younger, of course, no longer a puppy but still full of energy. Walking through the park in the early morning, Mary went to collect a newspaper and exercise her dog.

The sun was rising and a wind was blowing gently.

Suddenly, the Alsatian became stubborn. She would not move an inch and strained on the leash with her shoulders hunched tight and her paws clinging to the ground, steadfast. Pulling on the leash, Mary shouted, 'Heel,' but her Alsatian would not obey, obstinate bitch of a dog.

The Alsatian's nose twitched, sensed a faint smell, flared its nostrils, and broke free from Mary. Bounding along a weed-strewn footpath, she ran for all she was worth. With her great paws clawing at the ground, she scampered to a broken fence where some houses bordered the park. It was the houses that were abandoned, derelict shells where no one wanted to live.

'Heel!' Ignored.

Quickening her pace, Mary followed her Alsatian.

'Heel!' She shouted. Ignored again. Cantankerous animal.

Cursing at the obstinacy of the canine form, Mary chased her dog.

Mary's Alsatian had scared a rabbit and she was chasing it like there was no tomorrow. The Alsatian's eyes were glazed and her great paws were relentlessly eating up the ground between herself and her quarry. The rabbit dodged and swerved, zigzagged, and then made for long grass as fast as it could. A white patch on its behind, on its rear, bobbed frantically and gestured its escape route as Mary's growling Alsatian closed in for the kill. There was a parting in long grass and Mary's dog howled. Then the dog balked, met the long grass, sniffed, and barked in despair.

She'd lost it. Damn rabbit!

The dog growled at the essence of the rabbit, and barked again at the rabbit gone.

'Heel!' Acknowledged this time.

The Alsatian turned, gave a final yap at the long grass, and then ran to Mary with its leash trailing on the ground wrapped up around its front paw, whimpering in defeat, tongue drooling. The widow woman scolded her Alsatian, mildly, took up the leash and continued their walk.

Moments later, Mary and her Alsatian walked passed a house where Jo-Jo lay as they made for nearby shops and a minute's idle chatter with a local newsagent.

Breakfast time soon approached with a newspaper bought, a dog exercised, and a rabbit free to live another day. Returning home, tramping across the neatly trimmed grass of her garden, Mary removed a key from a purse and opened a door to her house. She watched her Alsatian scamper into the hallway and lap at a bowl of water before she closed the door of the house behind her. Walking into her lounge, Mary removed a Shamrock plant from a window ledge.

Bannerman's head thundered. It was the ninth pint of beer, which had washed down double vodka that had done it. Cross fared no better as he looked blankly at the table. The table was in the station canteen and carried two cooked breakfasts. It was nine o'clock in the morning and there was a rumble of thunder in their heads and a stomach-churning smell of fried tomatoes attacking their delicate nostrils. The toast was soft and allowed butter to drip and form a tiny pool of yellow grease on the edge of Bannerman's plate.

Without any warning, not even a mumbled excuse, an arm stretched across the table and snaffled a jar of marmalade as Bannerman looked on. The arm belonged to one of the new traffic patrol team: the cheeky one with spots on his chin and short-cropped hair. They were just youngsters, thought Bannerman. That new team in the big white patrol car were just kids, still wet behind the ears. Six years service between them, if they were lucky, thought Bannerman. Maybe seven. What did they know about traffic? They were the choice of McMurray, of course, but then come to think of it, what did he know about traffic? Two out, two in, that's the way it was when you upset McMurray. Arrogant bully of a man, thought Bannerman.

There was a snigger from a cheeky lad with spots on his chin and short-cropped hair as the top of a marmalade jar was flipped open and a knife attacked its contents.

Sombre, Bannerman studied the new traffic patrol team who had snaffled his jar of marmalade and were sniggering at the two men with hangovers: the two men who were transferred to walking the streets in the wind and rain while the new kids on the block enjoyed the relative warmth of a cosy patrol car.

Hostile, slowly twisting his face towards his young rivals, Bannerman allowed his eyes to drop to the marmalade jar. Then he looked at the snaffler of his marmalade, deep in the eye, penetrating, cold, questioning. Bannerman coughed slightly and allowed his eyes to drop once more to the jar of marmalade.

The sniggering stopped abruptly.

Bannerman scowled at the snaffling of his jar of marmalade, but then let it go with a dismissive wave of his hand. Perhaps he was getting too old, even at his age. Perhaps these youngsters were no longer afraid of his screaming skull and a sergeant who was always cross. Maybe the elders were loosing their touch?

Sergeant Cross shook his head, seemingly detached from proceedings. Lukewarm coffee tasted foul in his mouth but his bacon was crisp, just as he had ordered. Pulling his plate closer to the edge of his table, Cross slid some crispy bacon into a napkin at the side of his plate and palmed it. Rocky would have a treat that morning and to hell with their marmalade and the new traffic patrol team. What did they know about driving? They were just kids. They'd never been in a high-speed chase before, never driven on the edge of insanity. They were just kids, boy racers in blue uniforms. Cross decided they weren't real drivers, not like him.

Filling a glass from a jug of water, Sergeant Cross took two tablets to soothe away a thunderstorm in his brain.

The city was awake. The sun had cast its rays on the Eden. Morning had arrived.

Louise was driving an unmarked van: an old grey one with a clapped-out engine and a noisy exhaust. A puff of dirty black smoke grunted from its exhaust pipe as her van moved along the dual carriageway with the city centre disappearing in a rear view mirror. The body of the van hung low on its springs, creaking with the weight of its underbelly. The exhaust was done for but the brakes were okay. Not the handbrake though, it was faulty, needed adjustment, and didn't hold tight on very steep hills. The front bumper was twisted and a small dent spoiled the front wing of the van. Inside her van it was a rubbish tip. Old coke cans, crisp packets and finished-with newspapers littered its passenger foot well. The rear part of her van, the part where she spent most of the time on her back, or on her belly, was a little more comfortable. It was carpeted, thick pile, coloured grey, like the exterior of the van; but a little grimy. The van's tax disc was out of date, had to be to blend into the estate, and it was pushed down below the rim of the windscreen where it couldn't be easily read. There weren't many vehicles taxed in some parts of the estate. There was no money for tax discs. Cash for drugs and buying stolen property on the cheap, but no money with which to tax a car, pay a television licence, or try some pretence at legality.

Louise was just a slip of a girl really. She was nearer to thirty than twenty and closer to five feet four inches tall than she would prefer to be. Although, brown eyes and one or two freckles on her cheeks characterised one hell of a sense of mischief. That's why Boyd had picked her for an undercover job, of course, her sense of mischief and looks that killed the usual image of a conventional policewoman. A fashionable bob shaped her light brown hair and a parting creased her hairline in the middle, just above the line of her nose. The bob was short, neat, and seemed to fit well the face of an undercover lady. Convenient, her hair could be tied up on the top of her head, brushed to one side and then restored, or swept back off her face. It could even be enhanced with a false ponytail wandering down her spine. Her bob was adaptable since she had already learnt how important it was to change her appearance. She wasn't known at the local police station though. Boyd had organised that when he'd set up his Intelligence unit. Recruiting Louise direct from a training centre, Boyd had selected her months before he'd left Scotland Yard, before he'd even moved north himself, and he'd argued with the Chief over the girl and won. Only the Chief knew about Louise, and Boyd. The Chief had agreed to let Louise move to the city and get bedded down in a flat to develop her undercover role prior to Boyd moving back north. Sent to London, she'd been trained in the necessary arts, now she was Boyd's undercover officer in the city: his secret weapon against burglars and drug dealers. All she did was lie on her back, or on her belly, and keep watch and talk to Boyd's informants. That's all she did. It was a trivial job, really, living on your own, working alone; but she was living life on the edge.

Driving onto the estate, Louise threaded her way through the streets and bumped her way over some speed ramps. The van's engine protested, the exhaust backfired, and the springs of her van groaned. Louise drove around the estate until she saw the house and its bare window ledge. Cruising slowly past, she realised there was no plant in the window. When there was no Shamrock plant on the window ledge, Louise knew Mad Mary had information to pass on to the Intelligence Unit. Louise would meet Mad Mary at the appointed time and place. A signal had been made. Checking her watch, Louise drove past Mad Mary's house without a second glance. Her old grey van hung low on its springs with the weight of its underbelly dragging it towards the tarmac. Louise would make the noon meeting.

Aden walked from a rented house on the edge of the estate and strolled towards the town centre.

There was an elderly lady struggling with a big plastic bag. She wore a grey raincoat and lugged her bundle towards a launderette. Aden scrutinised the lady carrying her bag into the launderette and watched her dirty washing overflow from her bag onto a counter. Pausing by the launderette, Aden studied the woman in the grey raincoat. He watched as she emptied out her black plastic bag. The soiled dress, skirt, knickers, tights and sweaters sprawled onto a work surface inside the launderette. Then there was a dirty look from the lady. Mind your own business, she thought, as Aden seemed to inspect his image reflecting from a launderette window.

The launderette manager thought the olive-coloured man was very conceited. Loved himself, didn't he? The man regularly paused at a launderette window, always preened himself, invariably smoothed his hair, and continually turned his face to left and right checking his profile. Such a vain man, thought the manager of the launderette.

Aden smoothed his hair and walked on. Using a zebra crossing, he dodged between the traffic flow before looking in a post office window. There was a wooden sale board immediately behind the post office window yet the red paint of the wood did not deny those reflections that Aden was searching for. He searched those reflections bouncing from the glass, those images of people around him, and then he knew he was alone. No one had followed him from his or her rented house near the launderette; no one had followed him across that zebra crossing; he was free. He was sure their house was not under surveillance. Why should it be? Feeling secure, he walked on.

Walking along a line of terraced houses, Aden strolled along a footpath. At the end of the terraced houses he took a sharp right-handed turn towards a garage. He stopped abruptly a yard from where he had turned, near the junction, leaned his back against a wall, and waited for a man running or a woman walking. He expected a follower to walk round the corner of terraced houses and bump right into him. He waited for a surveillance officer to stroll casually by. Perhaps someone tailing him would walk on the other side of the road, perhaps not. He didn't know, but he didn't take any chances.

Aden thought if he were followed from their house on the edge of the estate then those tailing him would show out very soon. He would know them by their height. If it were police who tracked him then he would look for lofty people. Tall men and women in the police carried confidence in their eyes, assurance that came from wearing a uniform and using the authority vested in their office. They might be young and stocky, perhaps fit and muscular, he had been told. He would see them looking for him and he would look into their eyes to see a hint of recognition reflect back, and he would know. He would know if he were being tailed. If it were government people following him, the Intelligence people, then that might be different. They might be smaller and older and there would probably be more of them. If it were the Intelligence Services tracking him then he would still catch them out because they did not know the streets like he knew the streets. They were usually London people, they only knew the capital, he had been told. He had walked these streets for a time and a half since they had arrived to do the job and now he was learning the alleys, roads and parking areas. He knew the streets and parks encircling their estate had made it his business to appreciate the streets, as if his very life might depend on it. He'd learnt these streets and checked out those reflections. Now he paused at a corner and knew he wasn't followed.

Walking on, Aden stopped at the corners and studied the reflections. Then he took a bus, but only to see who boarded the bus with him. It was the way Namir had trained him: the way Namir had said it should be.

When Aden was tired of the bus, he waited for the traffic to slow down, to crawl in low gear, and then he jumped safely from the bus to a pavement. Then he walked on, paused at some windows, and resumed his counter-surveillance. When he was totally sure of his solitude he made for a telephone kiosk.

Midday approached.

Finding a telephone kiosk, Aden made a call. When his call was answered he removed, from his pocket, a piece of paper that Yasif had given to him. Aden spoke the words written on the paper to a reporter who took his call: a journalist. He told the journalist where the body of a man called Jo-Jo could be found. Then he told the journalist why Jo-Jo had been killed and by whom. When he had spoken Yasif's words and heard excitement rising in the journalist's voice, he smiled to himself in quiet satisfaction. But when the journalist started to ask more questions, he folded Yasif's words, put them in his pocket, and replaced the handset. Then he hurried back towards a house on the edge of the estate.

A hinge screeched in need of a squirt of oil when the door banged shut and Aden walked from the telephone kiosk. The call had been made. He walked away.

An old grey van with a noisy exhaust drove by. Aden looked at a girl driving it. He examined her face as she drove past but he did not see the brown of her eyes search out his features. The girl driving the van ignored him. She seemed to be just a slip of a girl, he thought. There was a backfire from the van's exhaust and a puff of oily black smoke clouded from its exhaust pipe.

Aden crossed the road, laughed to himself, and made for their rented house.

A bus shelter stood opposite some gardens on the edge of the estate. The shelter was built with red brick but its canopy was of corrugated iron rusting at its corners. Louise stood in the bus shelter and watched Mary walking towards her carrying a tattered old shopping bag. An Alsatian dog trotted at Mary's heel with its leash hanging loosely from the woman's wrist. The woman looked tired. Her face was drawn and lined with fatigue.

Mary strolled into the gardens and sat on a wooden seat beneath a gazebo, opposite some flower beds where the essence of late blooms caressed midday air and floated softly to her nostrils. The Alsatian settled by her feet, obedient for once. She did not acknowledge Louise standing in the bus shelter. The girl would come soon, when it was twelve o'clock, noon.

Louise stood, casually, watching from the bus shelter as traffic chugged by. Looking down the street and into the gardens, she noted the lay of the land from her bus shelter. Louise studied the slender woman with greying hair sitting on a wooden seat relaxing by the flowers, and watched her stoop down to take in their fragrance. A dog kneeling at Mary's feet ignored the blooms. A couple of children walked by kicking a tin can between them and eating ice creams, but no one else ventured near. When Louise was sure Mary was completely alone she walked across the road and made for a wooden seat beneath a gazebo.

Louise sat down next to Mary. They talked. Neither heard the town hall clock strike twelve.

Mary did the speaking and Louise did the listening. Mary told Louise about a boy called Jo-Jo who had been dabbling in drugs for over six months. She spoke of cannabis resin and ecstasy tablets he sold on the estate, how word had slowly filtered round the estate that Jo-Jo was selling drugs, and how he had built up a network of drug users. The users relied on Jo-Jo: he was the one with contacts in the drugs world.

Louise listened to the story of Jo-Jo and how he had grown from a small-time supplier to the main dealer on the estate. When the estate's supply of cannabis suddenly dried up, heroin became readily available in large quantities. Overnight, Jo-Jo turned into a real fast buck hustler. Louise made no notes, could not be seen to be writing on paper as she talked to a woman from the estate. She continued to listen and memorise the story Mary told her. Louise learnt of a girl called Trish who became hooked on Jo-Jo's heroin.

Mary spoke in hushed tones and whispered of the amounts of money involved in buying and selling drugs. She told of boys and girls, men and women, who came to her house where she dispensed coffees, teas, and tiny fairy cakes. She spoke of people who gossiped about Jo-Jo and Trish, and three strange looking newcomers with olive coloured skins. It was Trish who became hooked on Jo-Jo's heroin and went on to sell more drugs in order to feed her own habit. A man called Yasif had befriended Jo-Jo and then met Trish. Jo-Jo had since disappeared from the streets. He was apparently doing a bit of driving for someone called Yasif. Just a bit of driving, probably to do with drugs, they said. Mary had dispensed more teas and coffees, made more fairy cakes, passed them round, and learnt of the gossip on the estate. When she had told Louise of what she had heard, she told her of what she had seen. She told her she'd seen some men with olive coloured skins going in and out of abandoned houses. She wondered why? Hiding stolen property probably. She told Louise she'd made a call to the police station and used the code-name given: the code-name Mad Mary. Then Mary laughed, telling Louise she did not like the code-name Mad Mary although she agreed it suited her. She told Louise she'd reported the black BMW: the Beamer. She'd telephoned in about it once she was satisfied that Jo-Jo and the three men with olive coloured skins were using the vehicle. She'd lived on the estate long enough to smell a rat. Listened and heard enough to know that these men were up to no good. There was something wrong with these people. They were into drugs; they were into buying and selling stolen property. Couldn't prove it, of course, just knew it to be correct from the teas and coffees and the dispensation of tiny fairy cakes.

It was tittle-tattle that she spoke of, thought Louise. Just tittle-tattle from an estate where idle hands helped themselves to tiny fairy cakes and loose tongues exchanged gossip that was probably half right and undoubtedly half wrong.

'Sort it out, Louise, if you can. There's a good girl,' she said. 'Those three foreign men live in a rented house opposite that launderette. Well, so I'm led to believe. That's what the good folk on the estate say. They haven't been there long, just moved in, they say.'

Louise nodded and withdrew her hand from the neck of the Alsatian, shied away from the teeth now bared before her, frightened.

'Try and make the estate a better place to live, Louise, if you can. There's a good girl. It might be trivial to you but it's not trivial to me. I live there, you know.'

Louise heard Mary's voice but saw only an Alsatian's teeth. Louise gritted her teeth, opened her lips, and flared her nostrils at Mary's dog. The freckles beamed on the high point of her cheeks as she snarled at Mary's Alsatian.

'Tell Boyd, Louise. I've known him since he was a young copper wet behind the ears. Tell Boyd, won't you?'

The Alsatian barked, retreated from Louise, frightened. Louise closed her teeth.

'Tell Boyd, Louise. He'll know what to do. There's a good girl.'

Louise nodded again but held her eyes on the Alsatian, now retreating.

'One day she'll stop playing games with you, Louise. She'll bite your hand off and I will say I told you so. The poor thing can't work you out.'

'I'm just a pussy cat, Mary.'

'Miaow,' replied Mary.

'Time to scratch,' said Louise.

'Mind how you go,' said Mary, gathering her shopping bag, her Alsatian, and her thoughts. 'See you next time, same signal.'

Mary was mad to talk to police when she lived in an estate that was ridden with crime, thought Louise. She was mad to talk to police. If anyone found out on the estate, discovered the reason why a Shamrock plant kept on moving from a window ledge, discovered the relationship between Louise, Mary and Boyd, then Mary would be in really big trouble. She probably wouldn't survive twenty-four hours. Mary was mad to talk to police, wasn't she? Just mad, Mad Mary.

'Take care, Mary. See what you can find out about those foreign looking men. Are they English or what? Try to find out about those drugs? Where did Jo-Jo go? Can you find out about that girl Trish? How big is her habit? See what you can pick up, Mary. Soon as you can. Don't leave it too long. I'll tell Boyd. Don't you worry. I'll tell him, Mary. Take care. Look after the dog.'

'Miaow,' replied Mary.

Mad Mary was gone from the gardens as the big hand of the town hall clock was rushing towards the Roman numeral of one.

There was a click of a radio and the sound of a female voice.

'Go ahead,' replied Bannerman. 'We're near that location now. A derelict house, you say. What number?'

There was a whistle of static from Bannerman's radio followed by a broken female voice that snapped out an address. Bannerman looked at Cross and shrugged, 'Why is it always near to finishing time when you get a job to do?'

'Divine intervention?' suggested Cross, his eyebrows rising in mild irritation.

'We'll take that call,' said Bannerman into his radio. 'We'll be there in a few minutes.' Bannerman turned and headed towards the address.

'Message timed at thirteen hundred hours,' replied a female voice.

A wind was gathering as the first drizzle of day fell to the streets and shallow pools of rainwater began to form in the gutters.

'A dead body?' asked Sergeant Cross.

'So they say. Apparently a journalist has rung in to report he's received an anonymous call. There's a dead body in a house. It's probably a false call, a stupid prank. It usually is. You know what some folk are like!'

'Overdose!' suggested Bannerman.

'It'll be some poor kid who's died from an overdose,' replied Cross. 'Why do they always die when it's nearly finishing time? Have they no respect for the living? Have they no respect for my hangover?'

'Divine intervention, Cross,' laughed Bannerman. 'Come on; let's get a move on. If it's not a false call then we'll be busy. There'll be a doctor to pronounce death, an undertaker to arrange, a body to identify, relatives to inform, and a coroner's report to fill in. It's going to be a long afternoon. Smile nicely at the doctor who certifies death and you may get a couple of free tablets for your headache!'

They stepped between the flowing traffic with Rocky trailing Cross's ankle, tongue drooling, head to the ground, sniffing. Rainwater grew and a wind blew and rippled the surface of a dozen shallow pools.

'Could be a trap?' mused Cross. 'Things aren't settled down on the estate. It could be like the last time when we chased that Beamer. They could make mugs of us again. I can still see that iron railing crashing through our car window and I still feel the heat of burning petrol. We should have signed ourselves sick for a week and left McMurray to sort his own problems out. Fat bastard of a man! We came back to work too early, Bannerman. No one thanks you for busting your balls nowadays. Do you think they've set us up again? A false call, two coppers in a derelict house, trapped. What do you think? You're the one with brains. Are the scumbags on the estate after us?'

'We'll soon find out.'

The two men threaded their way through alleys and walkways, turned into a street, and neared the address. The windows of the houses were boarded up and all the gardens were bare of flowers. Grass in the gardens grew long and un-cared for and it was as if every garden was a repository for litter and the unwanted flotsam and jetsam of life. They found the house and checked its number scrawled in chalk on a front gatepost. When they had circled the house and checked its rear garden, when they were sure there was no one waiting to attack them, they walked down the front path towards the house. The path was strewn with weeds reaching towards the desolate garden, reaching towards soil that was tuning into mud as a drizzle swelled to a downpour.

'Let's send Rocky in first?' suggested Bannerman.

Cross nodded, approached a front window, and knelt down. There was a slight fissure in the wooden boards that covered a pane of glass. Cross peered through the break and allowed his eyes to focus on a thin space in view. Moving his head slightly, from left to right, he made out some old newspapers covering the floor in a haphazard fashion. Then, walking to the front door, Cross poked his hand through the letterbox and felt the wisp of a spider's web. He knelt down, rattled a letterbox, and looked through its slender opening. He saw a bare staircase leading to the upper floor. The house was abandoned, derelict, and silent. It was a little eerie.

'Come on, Rocky.'

The Labrador pranced and followed Cross to the rear of the house. Cross knelt at the rear door and smoothed Rocky's neck as he listened to the silence emanating from the shell of the derelict. The rear door was ajar and led into a bare kitchen.

Pushing the door further open, Cross saw broken glass. He nuzzled his dog and whispered, 'Go, Rocky. Seek it out, Rocky. Seek it out. There's a good boy.'

Rocky snorted, circled Cross, and then padded into the room with his tongue drooling and his head dropped, sniffing.

'I think we're safe,' said Bannerman.

'Perhaps we're being stupid,' replied Cross. 'Sending in Rocky because we're frightened of being attacked. Let's not tell anyone about this, Bannerman!'

'Why take chances? It'll take two minutes, Cross.'

There was a sound of Rocky barking from within. The bark dropped to a whimper and then Rocky appeared at the rear door and circled again with his tongue drooling and his tail flopping against a wall. Rocky barked again and scampered into the front room, barked again, turned and came back to Cross and Bannerman.

'He wants us to go inside,' said Cross. 'He's found something.'

Bannerman withdrew his truncheon from a belt on his side and moved swiftly into the room behind Rocky. Cross followed, fumbling for his radio, or a torch or a truncheon, and hoping to God he wasn't going to be attacked again.

'Jesus!' said Bannerman, stopped in his tracks.

'Bloody hell!' from Cross.

Rocky barked and pranced, head bobbing, neck up and down, eyes wide, nostrils flared, barking again.

'Good dog,' said Cross. 'There's a good dog.' He caressed his dog for finding a body on the floor before them.

Rocky ceased yapping, sniffed at Cross's feet, and padded across to the body.

The body was of a young man who had been shot four times. He was stone dead and his blood had stained the wooden floor in a grotesque demonstration of death. Propped up against the cracked plaster of a wall, his body was situated near a broad fireplace, which boasted a single wooden candlestick and a greasy mantelpiece. The body was hugging the wall, gruesome in its finality, abandoned like the derelict house. There was a gap between the body and a trail of blood running across the soiled floor towards a hall, a staircase, and the front door. It was odd that this young man should bleed against the cracked plaster of the wall; odd he should not bleed in the space between where he hugged the wall and a pool of blood lying in the centre of the room. It was odd, very odd indeed, they thought. It wasn't the body and blood, and a space on the floor where there was no blood, which had shocked Bannerman and Cross.

It was those words scrawled in blood on the cracked plaster of a wall that had stunned them.

'*Shot by Bannerman.*'

The bloody red letters formed into three words, faint, and they stretched long with the supposed final movements of a slender finger. The tip of the young man's finger was red, bloodied, as if he had painfully scrawled those faint words on the wall. It was as if he had hugged a wall and scrawled his final words with the blood of his body. It was as if he had named his murderer in the final seconds of his death. He was dead, shot four times. He must have been dead within seconds of four bullets entering his body and ending his life. But there was only stunned silence as they looked down at the body and Rocky lay down at their feet, disinterested now. Even then, Bannerman and Cross sensed it wasn't right. Dead people didn't write the names of their killers on the cracked plaster of a wall, couldn't write such a thing with four bullets in their body. It was obvious he had been killed in the centre of the room where he had bled, and then he'd been dragged to the wall. Even then, Bannerman and Cross knew his body had been posed; his shoulder propped against a wall deliberately. And a space on the floor where there was no blood confirmed it.

Neither man spoke for what seemed an eternity.

Cross and Bannerman could only look at a body posed and those words scrawled on the cracked plaster of a wall. '*Shot by Bannerman.*'

Rocky stood, whimpered, and licked Cross's hand, proud of his find, proud of a body he had found at the order of his master.

'Bollocks!' said Bannerman. 'Bollocks! Bollocks! Bollocks!'

'Shot by Bannerman,' said Cross, softly. 'Shot by Bannerman! What the hell's going on, Bannerman?'

Bannerman shook his head and knelt down by the boy's body. At first, he did not touch the body, did not feel its face, and did not smooth its clothes. He did not finger blood in the cracked plaster of a wall, and he did not search the body. He studied the manner of a body leaning against a wall and followed the legs that ran down to the shoes on the feet. Where the shoes met the floor, a newspaper was torn and the dust of a floorboard was gathered. It was as if the body had been dragged, a short distance, towards the wall. Next to the boy's ankle lay a handgun. The weapon was within reach of the body.

Bannerman raised the dead boy's chin with his finger and slowly turned the face towards him. Then he looked into the boy's face.'

'It's the boy who was driving that Beamer the other night, Cross. It's the kid who was driving, for God's sake.' Bannerman thought for a second or two and then said, 'I know him! Where've I seen that face before?'

Cross said, 'The gun! It's not suicide. Did the murderer deliberately leave the weapon behind? What's going on, Bannerman?'

There was a sudden crunch of glass and the lightning turn of Bannerman's head. A camera flashed and a photograph of Bannerman's face was captured kneeling beside the body of a boy called Jo-Jo with the words *'Shot by Bannerman'* scrawled in blood on the wall.

'Thanks, boys,' shouted the reporter. 'The call was right then. A body! Dead, is it?' His camera flashed again and the reporter darted into the room. 'Named him yet, have we? Know who it is, do we?' The camera hung from his shoulder as a pencil poised above his notebook. 'Got a cause of death yet, boys? Looks nasty. Got a time of death? Suspicious is it?'

Rocky growled and barked with the camera flash, then yapped at the reporter's feet. The reporter jumped backwards, startled by Rocky's presence, swearing aloud.

Cross palmed the camera down, and pushed the reporter out of the room. 'Out, you bastard. What do you think this is a bloody playground? Out, you clown! Call yourself Press! You're a disgrace!'

'Murder scene, is it?' croaked the reporter, grappling with his notebook, pencil and camera, as he nervously eyed Rocky.

Bannerman clicked a radio hanging from his lapel. His voice was dull and lacked the usual fire and strength of its tone. 'Control! Reference your last. We have a dead body and a journalist at the scene. We have ourselves a problem. Get Mister Boyd up here right away. This is a murder scene.'

Yasif rolled casually from Trish and breathed out hard from their lovemaking. He wiped sweat from his forehead as he watched her bosom gently rising and falling. Her breasts were like sharp mountains with the firmness of her nipples still visible.

Rolling onto his back, he fingered the stud in his ear. Then he glanced at an alarm clock sitting on a table. It had gone five and was pushing for six. Beside the clock lay a hypodermic needle. The syringe was empty but it would soon be filled again, once she was awake and craving for a fix. He looked at Trish: a pretty English girl with long black raven hair that cascaded from her shoulders and flowed down her back. She would have been really beautiful once when heroin hadn't held her body in a vice-like grip. Now her face was lined, drawn, and greying, beauty gone. He looked at her sad nakedness as she dozed. Then he nudged her and she turned to face him.

Smiling, her hands automatically trickled down his chest and ran over his stomach towards his groin. A tongue darted from her lips as her hand slid slowly down.

Yasif gripped her hand tight and shook her, ignoring the track marks in her arm: veins where heroin had been injected with a needle, places where the fluid of death surely ripped away at her insides.

Her eyes flickered, her brain sparked, and she returned to the land of the living with a cheeky smile.

Trish wasn't important, thought Yasif. She was nothing to him, just a temporary plaything. She was just a heroin addict who still managed a firm set of buttocks, a pretty English girl, but not much more. Heroin in exchange for sex! It was a perfect arrangement and helped pass the time while they waited. But she was unimportant. She was irrelevant, trivial, and temporary. He kissed her on the lips. She would be dead within a week, he thought. Dead from the overdose of heroin that he planned for her.

There was a rap on a door and Aden stormed into their bedroom. His eyes roamed over the woman's naked body. The sound of a television playing loudly followed him into the room.

'Yasif! We're on the news. Come on!'

Yasif rolled from the bed, grabbed a thin towel around him, found his sandals, and walked quickly into the lounge.

It was a pretty girl who was reading the news on television. As her face disappeared from the screen, a camera shot of the estate appeared.

'Police today sealed off part of an estate on the edge of Carlisle following the discovery of a body in a derelict house. It is understood that a journalist is helping police with their enquires but he is expected to be released shortly. Police refused to confirm that the body of a young local man, a resident from the estate, was found inside a derelict house. For a report on today's events and the recent disorder that has broken out on the estate, we go live to our North West correspondent.'

The figure of a dark suited man holding a microphone flickered onto the coloured screen that Yasif, Aden and Rollo watched.

'Thank you, Angela. I can tell you that tonight tension is rising here on the estate in Carlisle. It started two days ago when it is alleged that heavy-handed policing resulted in sporadic outbreaks of disorder evidenced by burning cars, smashed windows, and looted shops. The discovery of a body in a derelict house will do little to restore peace to the area, and little to persuade public confidence in the police. Allegations abound tonight that the body discovered in a derelict house is that of a local man, who, according to one source, managed to scrawl the name of his killer in his own blood on the wall of the house in which he was found. Police refuse to confirm or deny that the name scrawled on the wall is that of a local policeman...'

Yasif smiled and patted Aden's shoulder. Rollo nodded in approval. There was a satisfaction in the house, a smug satisfaction that comes with causing deliberate confusion.

Trish staggered into the room, rubbing her eyes.

'It's Jo-Jo,' said Yasif.

'What about Jo-Jo,' said Trish, semi-drugged, dazed, and confused.

'He's dead,' said Rollo.

'Dead? How?' asked Trish, zipping her denim jeans tight.

'Killed by the police. They say it was Bannerman,' said Yasif.

'What? Killed by the police!' said Trish, buttoning her blouse, running her fingers through her hair.

'Listen,' said Yasif. 'It's on the news, Trish. Listen.'

When she had heard their words and seen their pictures, she sobbed for Jo-Jo. She sobbed for him and shook for him until Rollo removed one hundred pounds from his wallet and thrust it into her hands. The tears were rolling down her cheeks for the death of her friend and she didn't know why. Perhaps it was the heroin in her blood that confused her, dazed her, and threw her mind into discontent. Perhaps she didn't know why she was crying, sobbing for the death of her dealer friend. She saw one hundred pounds and took the money and didn't know why it should make her happy. Why did she need money when she had Yasif and a needle that was never empty?

'For you,' said Rollo. 'To help you forget Jo-Jo.'

Trish looked up at Yasif. He nodded to her, sanctioned the approval of her acceptance of Rollo's money, and smiled.

'For you, Trish,' said Yasif. 'The murder of Jo-Jo by the big tall policeman must be avenged. Jo-Jo's death must be avenged.'

She felt confusion rippling her mind. Why was Jo-Jo so important?

'Take the money, Trish. Jo-Jo must be avenged otherwise there can be no China White. Do you hear me, Trish? There can be no more powder until Jo-Jo's death is avenged. No heroin on the estate.'

'No fix? You can't do this, Yasif. The kids need their fix. They live for it. You can't deny them their fix, Yasif. Hey! What's going on?'

'Spread the word, Trish. Tell the kids who killed Jo-Jo. Tell them Bannerman killed Jo-Jo. Tell them there'll be no white powder on the estate until Jo-Jo's death is avenged. Tell them Bannerman was responsible!'

Yasif turned his eyes from her face, shunned her, and then walked past her into the bedroom. Not so much as a glance. The bedroom door closed tight behind him.

Trish watched him go. She was speechless in a stupid kind of way, moronic being that she was. She'd spent her whole life taking from people, manipulating them, and bleeding them dry. Now she felt abandoned, tossed to one side. Snatching her coat from a peg on the door, she was gone from the house near the launderette. Walking, confused, clutching one hundred pounds in a shaking hand, Trish spread the word. She didn't know why! It was her addiction, of course, and a life of taking, never giving. Selfish woman in selfish times! She spoke to the addicts who relied on Jo-Jo's heroin. There was no China White on the estate. There would be no more heroin until the police had gone from their streets. It was too risky to do any dealing.

By midnight the word had been spread.

'Jo-Jo escaped Bannerman during a car chase the other night.'

'Jo-Jo was carrying our heroin.'

'The heroin has disappeared and Jo-Jo has been killed.'

'The police have killed Jo-Jo.' The word spread.

'Bannerman killed Jo-Jo.' It was said. 'The big hard man!'

'Bannerman must have stolen our drugs from Jo-Jo.'

The word spread. Idle gossip fuelled an epidemic of dangerous words. The words were like a fire out of control.

When Trish had seen the kids of sixteen and nineteen and twenty three years of age gather at street corners, when she had seen the first petrol bomb fly through the air into the windscreen of a parked car, she returned to the terraced house.

The house was quiet, deserted, abandoned. The Arabs had gone from her house. Closing the door behind her, she walked towards the bedroom. It was so quiet without them. Panic set in and she rushed towards the bedroom, kicking open the door. The wardrobe was open and bare. Yasif was gone. She checked the time on her alarm clock. Then she saw a hypodermic needle on the bedside table. Yasif had not forsaken her, good man that he was. He'd left her syringe filled with the clear fluid liquid of heroin.

She sat on her bed; content, happy to be taking again, not giving. She seized the needle, rolled up the sleeve of her blouse, and plunged the heroin into her arm. It was as if the heroin was her reason for being. Groaning, with the last drop of fluid gushing through her blood, she lay back onto the bed and looked at the ceiling. The fluid twisted, turned, and burned inside her. The heroin found its mark, penetrated her very soul, and took her to another planet where the only sound was her lungs heaving as they fought the evil within her. In the morning she would be dead, overdosed from the pure strength of Yasif's heroin. Murdered by heroin and the deliberate overdose Yasif had fixed.

Outside, in the wind of the night, cars were burning and a mob was looting and stones were being thrown at the police.

'Bannerman!' they screamed. 'We want Bannerman!'

A car braked gently and came to a standstill outside the shop. It was dark, cloudy, not even a star in the sky. The driver got out of his vehicle and went to the boot. He removed an empty beer keg and set it down on the footpath. He rolled the keg along the pavement and then hoisted the metal cylinder through the shop's plate glass window. Immediately, there was an almighty shriek from an alarm box on the wall. Not at all perturbed, two hands reached through the window display and pulled some clothes from a tailor's dummy. Turning, the burglar placed the stolen clothes in his car boot and lit the taper of a petrol bomb. He threw the bomb into the body of the shop and watched as flames gripped the fabrics and grew in ferocity.

The floorboards caught fire, and then the walls, and finally the flames licked the ceiling. A bell continued to scream from an alarm box as the raider drove away from the burning fancy dress shop.

The Bosphorus sparkled neon blue in a late evening moonlight that cast shadows of awe from the Galata Bridge. Istanbul was preparing to close down for the day, ready to close down the day and open its nightclubs and restaurants where the people of Turkey would feast their last meal and dance their last dance. Such a starry, moonlit night, above the Galata Bridge.

Crosby walked from the pottery shop carrying an amphora, carrying a hidden message from his agent, Danu. He carried the pot urn loosely by his side and made for his office where the cuneiform would be studied and the amphora shattered by a hammer. The captain of intelligence strode through the music and romance of Istanbul, and ignored the carved pictures adorning his amphora.

When he had reached his office and deciphered Danu's pictures, Crosby was disappointed with the message. Puzzled, Danu's message meant nothing to him. When Danu had reported Namir was missing then that had been looked upon as high-grade intelligence by the men in grey suits. It was good quality information because everyone in the Intelligence world knew Namir was an assassin. Namir was suspected of shooting dead a Jewish diplomat in Belgium, and of planting a car bomb killing an Israeli Military Commander who had chosen to holiday in Cyprus. Namir was suspected of delivering an overdose of high-grade heroin to an American envoy in Cairo, and he was suspected of a dozen or more assassination attempts. When Namir abandoned his valley in the Lebanon, withdrew from the desert wastes that befriended him, left the safe haven that the Syrian army protected, then the Intelligence Services of the west knew something was on. When Namir moved, they all moved. When Namir left his safe haven Crosby knew the Arab was on the loose, was chasing another target, and was going to kill again. It was just tittle-tattle Danu had picked up from the valley, the desert, just tittle-tattle. It was trivial tittle-tattle that had saved lives for years, thought Crosby. A loose word heard, and reported, could mean a change in security arrangements; a change to a route or a change to a visit or a holiday. Tittle-tattle from the desert kept people alive, even when the message was carved on a trivial pot urn.

Crosby shook his head in despair and read again the pictures from Danu. He walked to his communications unit and encoded a message into an electronic dispatch machine. Once he had checked its content he pressed the transmit button and sent Danu's message to the men in grey suits in London.

Who is Yasif, wondered Crosby? Who the hell is Yasif?

*

9

~ ~ ~

Dateline: September 5th, Present Year: The Kocaeli Province, Turkey.

When his machine chattered back at him, Crosby acknowledged London, tore the message from a teleprinter, and cursed. He pondered on the flimsy in his hand for a while then unfolded a road map and took a long hard look at the layout. Finally he grasped a telephone and rang the old man at the Grand Bazaar. Shaking his head in disbelief, Crosby closed down the communications unit and secured his office. He had no time to lose. Walking quickly, his face twisted a smile as he reminded himself of the irony of the situation. It was the usual case of hurry up and wait.

Crosby didn't seek the luxury of sleep at all; sleep was out of the question; just a snatched hour while he waited patiently for Danu's father to leave the wagon on a truck stop on the outskirts of Istanbul. Although he was tired, he followed his orders. It was the way of his regiment, and the way of the Secret Intelligence Service he was now part of: to follow orders given.

Reaching beneath the driver's seat, he felt the bundle, sighed with relief, relaxed, and drove through the starlit night. The wagon's driving mirror was fractured diagonally from corner to corner and its reflected image was that of a desert storm. At least it seemed that way to Crosby as he glanced in his cracked mirror, studying the dark haze of sand that rose from the rear wheels of his wagon. He was driving the wagon used to transport pot urns from the Lebanon to Istanbul's Grand Bazaar. It wasn't so much sand in the image of his mirror as a cloud of frothing dust. But he wasn't in the desert. He was on a road out of Istanbul, east of the Bosphorus Straits, driving through the Kocaeli Province. He checked again his fractured mirror. There was no one tailing him. No one followed him from his company office near the Grand Bazaar, and there were no unwelcome headlights in his rear view mirror. He was alone in the darkness, alone at the steering wheel.

Crosby drove through the naval base of Izmit: the capital of the Kocaeli Province lying to the north of the productive tobacco growing areas of Turkey. Then he turned south and drove through the farmlands of Sakarya. When it was still dark, when he knew for sure that he was not followed, he stopped by the side of the road and applied the handbrake tight.

Crosby stripped naked.

He carefully bundled his designer suit, Italian shoes, and his silk shirt into a black plastic bag. With less concern, he bundled his underwear, socks, and his leather belt into the same bag. Then he dismounted the cab and buried his black plastic bag in a ditch by the side of the road. Naked, he buried the bag with his hands, felt the earth in his fingernails, and then rubbed the dirt on his hands and face. He ran the soft soil of Turkey through his hair, dirtied his finely combed tresses, and covered his body in the soil of the land. Still naked and shivering slightly, he returned from the ditch and climbed back into his wagon. Stretching beneath the driver's seat, he pulled away a package left by Danu's father. He unfolded it, threw away its paper wrapping, and examined the contents. It was a brown coloured djellaba, cut long, loose, and hooded. Dressing quickly, he immediately felt comfortable in the robe and thought his father might have been proud to see his son dressed in the garb of a Syrian Arab.

Padding himself down, he made sure he carried no English cigarettes, no English money, and no telltale tiny article that might give him away to an enemy. He wasn't wearing the usual silver medallion around his neck and he'd left his Armani wristwatch behind. There wasn't even a wedding ring on his finger. When he had stripped himself of the western world he spoke aloud in Arabic, twisted the words from his mouth, and found again the tongue of his father. It was the reason he had been recruited all those years ago. Gone were the Englishman and his fineries, gone was the pretensions of his regiment, and gone was the stuffiness of the Service. He was back to his origins and he was ready.

Firing the engine, Crosby set off south.

The empty wagon rattled at top speed but Crosby had received his orders in encrypted mode in the communications unit of his false company. He'd run them through the decode procedure before reading a flimsy hard print in English. When he'd understood his orders, he'd popped the flimsy into a shredder and heard its metal teeth chew them into an eternity of destruction. The orders received on his secret machine from London were simple: face to face with Danu, face to face with his agent, face to face in the desert. Find out what the hell is going on in the Lebanon. Discover what on earth is going on with Namir. And what is Danu really trying to convey through his silly carvings? Go face to face with Danu in the desert. Don't break your cover; don't jeopardise the company, and don't let the enemy take you, but find out what Danu knows.

It was going to be a cool night, a hot day, and a long drive.

Putting his foot to the floor, Crosby pressed the accelerator hard and felt the rattle of his empty wagon. He praised the Lord for the pottery shop shopkeeper who had loaned the wagon, praised his own father for the gift of an Arabic tongue, and headed south for a face to face with Danu.

Boyd removed a crumpled notepaper from his leather wallet. Unfolding his pencilled notes, he smoothed out their folds with his narrow fingers pressing firmly against the hard wood of a table beneath. He looked up when a door pushed open and a chill draft invaded the room as Bannerman and Cross sauntered in and took their seats amongst other officers. There were men and women, uniforms and detectives, about fifty or more sitting ready for Boyd's briefing. The door swung lazily on its hinge before it eventually closed tight behind them with a gentle click. A black plastic chair angrily scraped the floor when one of the sergeants present grew impatient and moved closer to mumble in the ear of a colleague. A partially filled coffee cup was set down on the floor, spilled, and left a slender ring of contempt on the tiled floor. The mumble grew and a whispered chatter gradually embraced the room.

'What have you got there, Boyd?' asked McMurray, whimsical, leaning over from his seat behind the top table.

'My briefing notes,' replied Boyd with a grin. 'I wrote them on the train coming back from London. The map is out of scale, of course, but we'll get there. Perhaps you could... You any good at sketching, Mac?'

McMurray disapproved, shook his head, smirked at the crumpled paper and rough pencilled notes and said, 'Certainly not, you'll have to do that yourself.' A tobacco pouch slapped against the table. McMurray's hand rummaged inside his tunic and a pipe was produced. 'You look a bit amateurish, if you don't mind me saying. Are you seriously going to present a briefing from a scruffy piece of paper, Boyd?'

'Yes, I certainly am,' smiled Boyd. 'I've briefed people in worse circumstances than this. But that's another story.'

'Take a tip from me, Boyd. I'm an old hand at this game. It's your first briefing here. Most of these officers know you but some have never met you. Some of them have never even seen you before. They know about you, know more than you think, and probably know what colour socks you wear. You're still new to them though. You're the new man returned from Scotland Yard. Five weeks ago you were wearing filthy jeans and a beer-stained tee shirt in some scruffy part of London that half these officers have never even heard of. But they'll eat you if you use that piece of scruffy paper. They'll eat you for breakfast and spit you out, Boyd. Watch out!'

'No smoking,' replied Boyd, nodding at McMurray's pipe. 'If the men can't smoke in the briefing room then neither can you.'

'It's a pipe for God's sake, Boyd. Loosen up, Goddamn you.'

'This is my briefing and it's your no smoking policy that's plastered on every wall of the nick. Thou shall not smoke. Now listen up because the answer to your question is yes, I am going to use this crumpled piece of paper to do my briefing. You may have forgotten but I spent all yesterday afternoon, and most of the evening, at the murder scene. When I eventually got home, it was late. I walked through my front door and immediately answered the 'phone.'

'Called out again?'

'Believe it! I turned right round, went back to the estate and tried to organise our response to the disorder. Bloody riot, the press are calling it. Not yet a bloody riot, but it's not far off, let me tell you. Although you wouldn't know, never having been there. Anyway, I'm tired, short of sleep, and long on bad temper. Be warned, Mac.'

'You should have 'phoned me, Boyd,' said McMurray, unusual sincerity in his voice. 'I would have turned out.'

There was no answer from Boyd, only a blank disbelieving stare towards Chief Inspector, Administration and Policy.

'How many persons did we lose through injury?' asked McMurray.

'Three!' replied Boyd. 'One with cuts and bruises; two with concussion. Both concussion cases were detained overnight in the infirmary. It could have been worse, much worse. It seemed to simmer for a while, little groups forming here and there, and then as night fell and the pubs closed violence broke out. Windows smashed, one car overturned, and then there was a sudden fire. We moved in, had to really, couldn't not move in. Control called me out. By the time we had sufficient numbers and a proper game plan sorted out missiles were flying, one or two petrol bombs, but mainly sticks and stones. Ten minutes of running disorder, ten minutes of hand-to-hand fighting and then it was all over. Hardly a riot but then you can do a lot of damage in ten minutes.'

'Any prisoners?'

'Three in the traps, Mac, and they're all under seventeen.'

'Kids! They'll be back on the streets in no time.'

'Perhaps! I've got the duty sergeant talking to the prosecuting solicitor. If we can keep them in custody, then we will. Three isn't good enough though. Not good enough. We were like Gurkhas. Not a prisoner in sight. But come to think of it, half a dozen Gurkhas would have won us the day. No, Mac, the boys should have taken a bag full and given a clear signal to anyone out there.'

'Orchestrated? The riot, I mean?' asked McMurray.

'I would say so, Mac!' mused Boyd. 'If things don't settle down soon, I'll need to rethink our strategy. I don't want to overreact, but then I don't want to go too easy either. It's a difficult decision to make when all those cameras are on you and the press are watching your every move.'

'Stressful?' There was a forced smile forming at the corner of McMurray's lips.

'I'll let you know when the headaches start, Mac. At the moment I can do without a murder enquiry as well.'

McMurray looked pensive for a moment and then said, 'If I were you, Boyd, I'd pull right out of the estate. Don't get involved in any fighting. Treat it like a no-go area. Just don't send anyone into the estate and there won't be a problem. You can't overreact if you don't react at all. There's an old police saying, isn't there? No arrests mean no problems. Multiple arrests mean multiple problems. Back off, Boyd.'

'Give them the streets, Mac. You must be joking?'

'No, I'm serious. Belittle the problem and it'll go away. Face up to it and it'll get bigger. Think about it. Why make a rod for your own back?'

'I don't agree with you but unfortunately I need your help.'

'You need my help, Boyd?' twisted McMurray, sarcastically. Then with a taunt, he said, 'My advice is to go back to your jeans and tee shirts.

'Can you keep your eye on things here while I'm thumping the pavement and sorting out this murder?'

'Of course, I can. The Chief made his choice; operations are yours, so operate. The policy and administration are mine, so I'll run the business while you play toy soldiers. Just don't get in my way, Boyd, and don't try any London tricks in my nick.'

'We're going to get on fine, Mac, just fine. Who knows, we might even end up liking each other.'

'Don't hold your breath, Boyd.'

'I won't, but if I need to empty your nick to kill this disorder I will.'

'What with?' McMurray lifted his pipe and sucked on its empty bowl. He chuckled as he cradled his pipe and then set it on the table next to his tobacco pouch. 'You'll need every available officer on the murder enquiry, Boyd.'

'We'll see, shall we? It's your job to enforce that no smoking policy and mine to catch a murderer and kill the riots.'

Murray threw a hostile look.

Boyd rapped his knuckles on the table. 'Attention everyone.'

There was a discontented grunt from McMurray; hurt by Boyd's piercing tongue. Grasping his pipe, McMurray sucked on an empty bowl.

'Thank you, ladies and gentlemen.'

The room settled down when Boyd stood to his feet and pinned his crumpled piece of notepaper on a wall next to a dry wipe board. A latecomer entered the room, rushing, and perhaps a little anxious. The latecomer was young, wore no tunic, carried no helmet, and was decidedly scruffy, thought Boyd. The sleeves on the latecomer's shirt were rolled to his elbow and a button on the collar of his shirt was undone. In his left hand he carried a black clip-on tie: the anti-strangle type.

'You got a problem, constable?' asked Boyd.

'No. Sorry, mate. I'm a bit late.'

'You don't understand me, young man. I'm not yet your mate; I may never be your mate. Your problem is that you are a member of this police force yet you wear no tunic, carry no helmet, and wear no tie. Indeed you look as if you slept in those trousers last night. Your problem is that you need a tunic, a helmet, a tie, and some pride in who you are and what you do. Out! Come back when you are dressed properly and you know where you belong. Smarten up, young man! Double quick!'

The youngster gulped and retreated sharply. The door closed tight.

A murmur of disapproval seemed to linger in the room. Bit snappy with the youngster, wasn't he, the new boss? Bit keen with the latecomer, wasn't he, the new man? Bad tempered? Trying to impress, was he, the new man from London? Hypocritical! The London man who dressed like a down and out, five weeks ago? Short on memory. Long on bad temper. Thinks he's in the Scots Guards that one.

Boyd selected a black marker and then reproduced from a crumpled paper some sketches he had made. There was a silky scrawl of a marker pen across a white surface. 'I'm no artist but this will have to do,' he said.

There was a giggle from the rear seats and was that a sly comment uttered from the fourth or fifth row? Boyd let it pass.

Boyd's eyes visited his crumpled paper then turned to the board and guided his marker across its surface. Lines and crosses and curves appeared on the board. The word airport appeared in a square and the roads to a venue were drawn. A venue appeared in a square and junctions were drawn and crossed the lines. They were roads and bends and vantage points in Boyd's mind, and in the mind of the killer. The sketch was the killing ground in Boyd's mind, and in the mind of the killer.

When he had finished his lines and crosses and curves, and had revisited the piece of crumpled paper, Boyd turned to face his audience.

'Good work on the estate last night, thank you.' Boyd lied and tried hard to hide his disappointment at only a handful of minor arrests. 'This morning I want to fill you in on what is in store for us over the next few days. Firstly, to recap, Jo-Jo's body was found yesterday. He was shot dead from close range. Four bullets! His body was deliberately posed against the wall of a derelict house and his allies would have us believe that PC Bannerman is responsible for his death. I spoke to the forensic scientist last night. Put simply, Jo-Jo was killed at short range, probably died within minutes, if not seconds, of the bullets entering his body. Where he fell, he bled. He was then dragged to a wall and posed for our convenience. The murderer no doubt wrote PC Bannerman's name on the wall. There are some fingerprints in blood on the wall. The fingerprints are not Jo-Jo's and they're not Bannerman's. They probably belong to the murderer. No doubt it was the murderer who telephoned our journalist friend and told him where to find Jo-Jo's body and who was responsible for killing him. The question of irresponsible press behaviour is not my concern. The Chief will be taking that up with the editor and television people and anyone else he can make listen. Whoever wanted to wind us up, stretch us to the limit, certainly knows where to hurt us. Once the media had the story that police were responsible for a murder, then… Well… You know the rest. Mayhem on the streets; a violent protest, some would say. Others would say a convenient excuse for criminal devilment.'

'I hope you told the Chief it wasn't Bannerman.' The question was from an older detective with panache for interruption, and a gravelled voice that sought confrontation with Boyd.

Boyd flinched at the interruption. He was used to listening and taking orders and following his orders to the last letter, even undercover. Even though he was an independent, he still followed orders set down.

'There'll be time for questions later,' replied Boyd, patiently. 'But as an aside, I can tell you PC Bannerman was out drinking when the forensic scientist states Jo-Jo was killed. PC Bannerman has an unbreakable alibi...'

'Checked it have you?' interrupted the gravel-voiced detective again.

Boyd ignored the remark. 'And fingerprints that don't match. PC Bannerman couldn't be killing Jo-Jo and drinking with Cross and a pub full of people at the same time. That's why PC Bannerman is still with us today.'

'And a God Almighty headache to go with it,' cracked Bannerman.

Boyd smiled, and noted Bannerman's face, and the size of the man with close-cropped ginger hair.

'Did you really think someone here would kill Jo-Jo?' From a uniform: a sergeant this time.

'I was investigating that possibility, yes,' revealed Boyd.

'Do you really think one of us is involved in his murder?' It was from the same uniform sergeant.

Boyd flinched and wondered if this was a cross-examination.

Then it was the detective voicing his opinion again. 'Don't lose sleep over a scumbag from the estate.' There was a chorus of approval and a mumbled hushed cheer from the rank and file.

Boyd winced again. It was his first briefing and they were taking over. They were taking over his first briefing, his orders, and his reason for being. Who were these people? Who did they think they were? Did they think they were a law unto themselves? Were these the kind of people who lived under their own rules? Were these people who had forgotten that their calling was their religion? Had they no faith in leadership? Where was the faith he expected from such men and women?

Boyd snapped at last. 'You don't solve murders by speculating. When you join the police, your fingerprints are taken. You all know that.' He began to walk into their midst. 'The fingerprints are locked away and put in your personal record.' Boyd probed their faces with his penetrating eyes, turning, confronting them. 'I told the forensic boys to work through the night and compare the fingerprints found in blood with the fingerprints of every officer in this station.' Then Boyd returned to his desk, turned, and challenged them, 'Yes! Every officer! Anyone got a problem with that?'

There was hush in the room: a resentful hush. Slowly, gradually, a cold air of distrust filtered through the rank and file of the briefing room. There was a cough and a backward movement of a body and a swivel of a head. Exchanged glances signified a horror not experienced before. They were above suspicion, weren't they? Who gives a damn about some dead druggie scumbag on the estate? What was so important about some dead druggie scumbag on the estate? Let it go, Boyd.

'Bloody upstart,' whispered a sergeant. 'Bastard in the first degree,' whispered a constable at the back of the briefing room. Bloody trouble this man, thought McMurray. 'Hypocrite,' whispered a gravel-voiced detective. It was as if Boyd had breached the boundaries of an established relationship, broken a friendship before it had started, and overstepped an unseen mark.

Boyd thought he could hear whispers and mutterings, thought he could see startled worry on stressed-out leaderless faces, and thought he could see an occasional look of contempt. What were they whispering out there in the rank and file? What right has this newcomer to delve into their past, to check their fingerprints? Who did he think he was, London man from a squad no one gave tuppence for? London's man! Who did he think he was? What right had this upstart from London to suspect them?

'Negative result,' finished Boyd. 'It's what you'd expect, what I'd hoped for, and what needed to be proved. You're all in the clear.

'So far!' Thank God for that,' murmured Cross.

Boyd smiled the acknowledgement and noted Cross's face. 'No! Someone out there is making trouble for us. At the moment I don't know who, but I'm going to find out. Before I give you the duty roster and my plans to counter tonight's likely disorder, I need to brief you all on events taking place on the ninth of September.

'Clever bastard with those fingerprints.' The whisper, too loud, caught Boyd's ear.

There was a groan from his audience and a sniggered laugh at a loud whisper heard. Then there was insolent chatter from those who knew best.

'London's man is over the top. London's man is going to impress his friends from the capital, at our expense,' it was whispered.

'London's man will put a red carpet out for the Scotland Yard boys. He'll go right over the top, to impress,' it was whispered.

'London's man is becoming a pain in the arse. London's man should sod off back to Scotland Yard,' it was whispered.'

Boyd ignored the wayward whispers, ignored the mutterings, not quite heard, and knuckled the table again, loud. The rap brought a slow silence to the room. He allowed the silence to wallow and seep through the briefing room, until only the sound of breathing could be heard and a slight grumble of a chesty cough. The riot wasn't the only thing getting out of hand, thought Boyd. They weren't used to being led, these people, he thought. Perhaps he should explain things better. Perhaps he was a poor communicator. Perhaps he should go out and come back in. They seemed not to like his style of leadership and it was his first briefing. There was a wall being built between them. He must break down the wall, he thought.

'The Israeli Foreign Minister flies into London on September 7th. He will be conveyed to Chequers for a meeting with our Prime Minister and the President of the United States of America. Their agenda is simple: an update on the Middle East Peace talks accompanied, no doubt, by a declaration of continued resolve to bring about peace in that region. On the 9th of September, their talk's close, photo opportunities will have been seized upon, and the Foreign Minister will fly into Carlisle airport. On arrival at the airport, out near the village of Crosby On Eden, the Minister will be brought swiftly to Tullie House museum, here in the city. At Tullie House museum he will be received by the Mayor and invited to tour the museum. He will, of course, accept that invitation; the protocol has already been established for the visit. The Minister will tour the museum and there will be a short ceremony in the foyer to hand over the Tablet of Masada. I'm not going to elaborate on the history of the Tablet or the reason for the visit. I think you are all well aware of press reports concerning the visit and the Tablet. While the Minister is in this City, his safety will be of paramount importance to us. The Israeli Foreign Minister will be our number one priority that day. Second best will not do. All understood?'

There were one or two resentful nods of acknowledgement accompanied by a plethora of blank bored faces. They were correct, thought a sergeant in uniform, Boyd really was going to look after this man like no one ever had before. Boyd was going to impress his mates from the Yard, wasn't he? Boyd was going to go right over the top and make them look like fools, wasn't he?

'The atmosphere in this room is a little claustrophobic. Or to be precise, I detect that you lot couldn't give a damn about the visit of the man from Israel. Well I do and from now on, so do you.'

'A Jew, is he, the Israeli?' It was from the gravel-voiced detective.

'The Jew boy will be the one wearing a skull cap to keep his head warm,' quipped a uniform sergeant.

'Wasn't Hitler a Jew boy?' From the fourth row, shouted. Septic humour, sour laughter returned.

'Zip it!' From Sergeant Cross, loud and sudden. Then Cross turned his head; he was angry and seething with annoyance. 'You lot are ignorant.'

'Will London police be looking after the man or his own people?' asked McMurray, turning his head from Boyd and leaning back in his chair. Get even time, thought McMurray. 'We've enough to do without running around providing security for bloody foreign visitors, Chief Inspector Boyd.'

'Guests! They're guests in our country,' reminded Boyd. The Israeli Foreign Minister is a guest and it's our job to protect him and make sure things go well.'

'I'm sure your Scotland Yard friends will find your sentiments exactly what they require,' spurned McMurray. A derisive smile twisted at the corner of his lips as he shuffled his large posterior on the seat. McMurray's smile was seen and shared by the audience.

'Special Branch will provide protection. We will support the Branch,' explained Boyd.

'Unnecessary, I say,' countered McMurray. 'It's not worth it for a trivial little visit that will all be over in about two hours. Most unnecessary.'

Boyd dropped his marker with a resounding clank on the table; then his fist thumped the dry wipe board. Pausing, he thought back to why the visit of the Israeli Minister had been arranged; cast his mind back to David: the Jew who had watched scud missiles destroy his Tel Aviv home: the Jew who had smashed a glass cabinet and touched a rock and found the Tablet of Masada. Perhaps it was easy to understand how ridicule and ignorance blurred the mind. Boyd cast his mind back to a conference and a portly, moustachioed London policeman, and a woman who had chaired a meeting with those grey suits who had sniggered behind his back. Was he alone; was this a bad dream, he thought?

'Trivial, is it?' asked Boyd. 'Non-essential? Irrelevant?'

'Well…'

Boyd cut McMurray off. 'Perhaps you will allow me to finish? The bad news is good intelligence has been received to the effect that whilst the Foreign Minister is in the United Kingdom there will be an assassination attempt on his life.'

Suddenly, there was a murmur of growing interest from around the room. There was the lift of a head, a flash of an eye, and a spark of interest.

'I believe this assassination attempt will take place here in Carlisle,' announced Boyd.'

'How do you know that?' McMurray again.

'Because I feel it in my bones and it's the place I would choose to kill a man if I were the killer,' said Boyd.

'Oh, you feel it in your bones, do you?' said McMurray. 'You, a killer? I doubt it; but your bones, yes. Maybe it's arthritis?' A chortle from the rank and file, fifth, maybe sixth row.

Boyd rounded on McMurray. 'In London and Chequers you have the Prime Minister and the President of the United States of America, and that means a hundred bodyguards and every piece of electronic gadgetry you can imagine to protect them from terrorist attack. High fences, alarms, cameras, aerial surveillance, uniform patrols outside, plain clothes patrols inside, bodyguards in every corridor, need I go on? Up here in the north, you've got open roads, open fells and more space than you can imagine. Here, this is where I would kill, here.'

'I don't agree,' McMurray again, frowning, shaking his head.

Bannerman's elbow nudged sharp into Cross's side.

'I don't give a damn about what you agree with, Chief Inspector McMurray, and what you don't agree with, for that matter. I came to brief you not to argue with you. All I can smell in this room is complacency and arrogant, self-centred, self-opinionated, bad attitude, small time, narrow minded bullshit.'

There was a silence in the room as Boyd's voice raised a decibel.

'In fact, from what I've seen so far some of you in this room couldn't police your way out of a paper bag. Carlisle's finest? Don't make me laugh. You can't even dress properly. All talk and no action. That's what you're all good at. Good old fashioned Cumbrian bullshit. But why did I end up with a complacent herd?'

McMurray's mouth flopped open and his pipe hit the table. A chair scuffed with the slight movement from a body of a fat policeman. Bannerman winced. Cross smiled and dropped his head. Then there was a slight grumble of a chesty cough from one in the audience.

'Yes, complacency with a capital C. Now, listen to me and listen good, this is how we will protect this man…'

When he had pointed at his lines, crosses and curves, and explained their meanings, he turned once more to his audience.

'Tonight! Expect more problems on that estate. I want one team on the estate and three teams on standby.' Boyd scrawled the names of four sergeants on the board and then said, 'Team leaders! Keep up with the plot or you're no good to me.'

There was a sharp intake of breath as one of the sergeants saw his name on the board.

Boyd shouted, 'PC Bannerman and Sergeant Cross?'

Two hands rose into the air.

'Good! I've heard your names mentioned, seen your names on reports, now I know your faces. No more street work for you two.'

'Well, that's your first step in the right direction,' shrilled McMurray, victory etched in a smile beaming across his face, from ear to ear. 'I've already grounded them both, Chief Inspector Boyd. Didn't you read that part of my report?'

'Bannerman and Cross, I have a special assignment for you both. I'll see you in my office after this briefing,' said Boyd, ignoring McMurray, ignoring a snigger from the fifth, maybe sixth row.

'I should sort that dog out too, if I were you,' advised McMurray. 'Put the damn thing down. Scrawny mongrel!'

The door swung open and a young constable wearing a tunic and carrying a helmet appeared with a sheepish look on his face. He wore a tie.

'Much better,' said Boyd. 'Always wear your uniform with pride, young man. It is the symbol of your authority. It is your honour and your dignity. Wear your uniform as if it were part of you. If you look good people will have faith in who you are and what you do. Understood?'

There was the nod of a head and half a smile that was glad to claw back the lost yard. 'There's a 'phone call for you, sir.'

'Thank you. I'll take it in my office. Sergeants, step forward. Get your teams organised and memorise those sketches inside out. I want everyone to know that route like the back of his or her hand. I want everyone to know I mean business. By the time you've swallowed all that, the duties for tonight will be on the clipboard in the Intelligence unit. By nine tomorrow morning an operational order for this security visit will be with every officer in this building. Stand with me and stand beside me, but God help you if you stand in front of me. Chief Inspector McMurray, the launderette is where dirty washing is cleaned, not in public. Next time you want an argument, my office.'

Boyd was gone from the briefing room. He walked into a corridor and into his office and a waiting telephone. The hinge on a door creaked.

There was the strong scent of a silent sweating fifty lingering in the room. A pipe was gathered and a tobacco pouch opened. A bowl scooped fresh tobacco and McMurray's fingers pressed the flake down into his bowl. A match was struck and a thin curl of smoke hovered in the air of the room. 'Testing times,' smiled McMurray, to no one in particular. 'Testing times.'

Cross stood. Bannerman followed.

Cross, seething with anger, walked across the floor of the briefing room and stood in front of McMurray seated at the table. McMurray glanced up at the man with bushy jet-black hair. Then McMurray stared long and hard into Cross's face, virtually challenging Cross to react.

Waving his arm slowly in the air, in an arc, Cross wafted smoke from McMurray's pipe, breaking the circles of smoke with his hand.

'You could choke on a pipe, chief inspector. Just as you could choke on the claws of a dog trained to kill!'

Cross turned and was gone. Bannerman followed suit. McMurray's eyes drilled into Cross's back and then he shook his head as the door closed noisily behind the two men.

'Good, Louise,' said Boyd, cupping the 'phone to his ear, alone in his office. 'Heard about the murder, have you?' His eyes narrowed and scanned a broad desk before him. 'Good! No, that's good. Hearing about the murder on television is good. You have the same knowledge of the murder, as Joe Public does, no more, no less. That's good. Don't worry that you don't know everything.' Boyd smiled, scanned his desk and saw a pad. 'I know, it's not easy, is it? How was Mary when you finally got to see her?' He nodded into the telephone and pulled the writing pad from the corner of his desk. He took up a pencil from a jar near the telephone. 'Known her for years. Good cook! She's a cracker of a woman but don't touch her dog. It's an Alsatian if I remember well. Big teeth! She was my first informant when I joined the job. Some kid pinched a plastic gnome from her garden. I caught the kid, recovered the gnome, and became a hero in her eyes. Well, not really a hero, just a gnome catcher. She never forgot me, even when she moved to the estate years later. She was one of the first contacts I went to when I returned. I thought she might want to help. What did she have to tell you?'

Boyd listened and wrote, scribbling with a pencil floating on his pad.

There was a sudden knock on the door of Boyd's office.

'Come in,' shouted Boyd. Covering the telephone mouthpiece, he beckoned Bannerman and Cross into the office. 'Take a seat, boys. I'll be with you in a minute.' Boyd pointed at a kettle and coffee jar on a tray in the far corner of his office. 'Switch it on and make three. Black for me, no sugar. Not my usual but it's want I need right now'

Boyd's ear returned to his telephone as three mugs rattled in the far corner of his office. Swivelling in his chair, Boyd hoisted his feet to the edge of his desk and scribbled again the words from Louise.

'Jo-Jo, Trish, three foreigners, all olive skins... One of them called Yasif... Anything else?' Boyd's quiet question, cupped in the palm of a telephone, private, wasn't for hearing by makers of black coffee, no sugar. Not for public consumption, the words of an undercover officer.

'That's all,' said Louise. 'There's nothing else to tell. She made the signal, I saw her, and she told me. I thought you'd want to know why Mad Mary 'phoned in about the Beamer. I thought you should know about a girl called Trish, those drugs, and these three foreigners knowing Jo-Jo. I don't really know what Mary means by olive-coloured skin. I think she just means they're coloured, not white. She's not racist and she's got no axe to grind against these foreigners but she told me Jo-Jo had been driving for someone called Yasif. Looks like Yasif was running a drugs racket and Jo-Jo was just driving for them. Makes sense, doesn't it? Or would these foreigners know their way round? Beats me! Hey, I rang last night but there was no answer from your telephone. Is Yasif Arabic or what?'

'Slow down. Take your time. Sorry, I was out, probably at the murder scene or on the estate. You did right to ring me though. Thank you.'

'I hear noises in the background. Do you have someone with you?'

'Yes, but don't let it put you off. They can't hear.'

'This seems stupid but I've been thinking and... It doesn't matter.'

'Spit it out. What's on your mind?'

'I was reading a newspaper, and then watched some television. I know there's an Israeli Foreign Minister coming to visit Tullie House. I was watching television and heard a presenter telling a story about the Tablet of Masada. Those three foreigners: the three olive-coloured skins, what if they're Arabs? Those three foreigners and the visit of the man from Israel and oh, forget it. I'm letting my imagination run away with me. I know we've got Arabs living in the city, not many, that's true. A few Egyptians, Turks, Syrians, Iranians, even a few Iraqis. There's no mosque but Arabs pass through Carlisle every day on their way to Glasgow and Newcastle. Bit of a crossroads is Carlisle, on the quiet. We've got Turkish Kebab shops and foreign restaurants. Which do you want? We've got restaurants that are Portuguese, Mexican, Indian, Chinese, Italian and Greek. I've been in them all. We've got ethnicity and skin colour and race growing out of our pavements. We've got foreign doctors and every colour and creed you can think of. We're up to our neck in ethnicity. I know if I stand outside Carlisle railway station long enough the whole world will walk by me. Forget it! What's the problem with Mad Mary's foreigners? There's no problem with Mad Mary's three foreigners. It's me… Just forget it…'

Boyd smiled and eventually interrupted. 'Forget it! Listen to me. Slow down. Slow down, for Christ's sake. What's on your mind?'

'These foreigners, Mad Mary says they live near a launderette. Says they're up to no good. You say Mary is to be trusted. A good informant, reliable, accurate, known her for years, you said. She says these foreigners have rented a place near the launderette, but I don't want to knock on doors on some made-up stupid pretence. I might frighten them away. I could risk blowing my cover.'

'No, don't do that, not just yet,' advised Boyd.

'So I ask myself, where do they live? Why are they here? Why are they here now? What are they up to? Are they in work? It's just a gut feeling I have from speaking with Mary. It's what you told me to do: to watch every day for the absence of a Shamrock plant and then go to those gardens at twelve noon and talk to her. Just like you used to do. I've met her before. She tells me tittle-tattle. I watch the tittle-tattle people and I tell you. From tittle-tattle your Intelligence unit raid houses and recover videos and chequebooks that were stolen from wherever. It's tittle-tattle and it isn't going to change the world but we're getting stolen property back, just like you said. It's tittle-tattle that keeps us going, keeps us on top. I've asked Mary to find out as much as she can about these three men. I think they could be involved in Jo-Jo's murder and somewhere there's some drugs, heroin, and there's something else bothering me and I can't explain it and I'm all mixed up but…'

'But there's something not quite right?'

'Exactly! It's the three foreigners.'

'Spot on! That's what it's all about, tittle-tattle. Sniff it out and chase it around until you're satisfied. Get on it.'

'What, just like that?'

'You make your own luck.'

'I'll work on them. I'll find them. Finding the target may not be easy.'

'How's your wheels bearing up? Is it totally knackered yet?'

'No! It's fine, rusting well. Dropping to bits. I taxed it. It's getting a new exhaust fitted today and I might even clean the windows. No one bothers my van on the estate. It looks the part.'

'What about the inside, the business end?'

'It's cramped, too tight. The box is fine though.'

'Okay, that's good. The buzz box is the main thing.'

A kettle steamed and a spoon rattled in some mugs. Bannerman delivered the coffee to the edge of Boyd's desk, no words spoken, just a puzzled look from Bannerman. Boyd nodded his thanks and grasped the mug. He seemed to take solace from the steaming liquid that tingled his lips; but he seemed to disagree with the presence of the big man.

Bannerman read Boyd's body language and retreated to sit next to Cross.

Some coffee was drunk.

'I think your gut feeling is worth following up,' continued Boyd, speaking quietly into his mouthpiece. 'I think these foreigners may be mixed up with Jo-Jo's death. In any event, we need to pull them in and check them out. We need to bottom out this Yasif guy, too. They're associates of Jo-Jo. We need to pull them in for questioning and elimination, if nothing else; but not just yet, and not by you. I'll get others to pull them in. I'll preserve your cover and your old rust bucket. No, I just want you to watch and report. Yet you're right about those gut feelings. What troubles me more is this visit to that damn museum. You did right to call me, right to report in.'

'A gut feeling is nothing much to go on?'

'No, but this is your first assignment. Make something of it. If all you do is take a drug dealer out, then fine. I want you to follow orders. The three foreigners are your targets, particularly this Yasif guy. You must look for the targets where you know you might find them. Try that launderette. I want you to target that launderette and locate those three foreigners. I want you to find out where they live? What is their exact address? What do they do? Where do they go? Who do they meet? What do they eat for breakfast? Do you understand?'

'Twenty four hours?'

'Twenty-four hours on target. Live on it. It's a murder and a gut feeling. It's your gut feeling and my gut feeling. It's about a museum visit and drugs and who knows what else, and we want a result. That's the job.'

'I'll be in touch.'

'Good.'

'Twenty four hours, you say?'

'Twenty four hours.'

Boyd's 'phone hit the cradle. Slurping his coffee, Boyd plunged his mind into deep thought and read again the notes he had scribbled from his conversation with Louise. He was oblivious to Bannerman and Cross, oblivious to the nervous anticipation they both shared. He'd switched off for a moment. Boyd slurped his coffee again.

'Boss, I'd like to explain about the other night in the park,' said Bannerman. 'Our reports, about that chase across the Eden and that incident in the park, boss.'

Boyd was drinking, ignoring Bannerman's voice, studying the words from Louise, and thinking.

'And Rocky, well, that's our dog, boss. The dog is called Rocky. It used to be a police dog, a drug dog. Well, Cross will tell you, won't you, Cross? It's a good dog; probably saved our lives, boss. Cross's dog doesn't need put down, boss. Well, you see McMurray, I mean Chief Inspector McMurray, and well he thinks that Cross and I were…'

Boyd wasn't listening. He was far away in his mind. There was not a flicker from Boyd. His eyes were closed.

'Boss!'

Still silence, eyes closed, far away.

'Boss!'

'Sorry,' sparked Boyd. 'What was that? The other night in the park? Forget it, PC Bannerman. I've read your reports, all the reports. It was always going to happen that way, sooner or later. What do you expect when you treat the estate like a no-go area? What do you expect when you give up the ground to the, what do you call them, scumbags?'

He's trivialised those events in the park, thought Bannerman. He's not interested in that chase over the Eden; he's not interested in the Beamer, thought Bannerman. He's going to support us, thought Bannerman.

'Sergeant Cross, no pets in patrol cars. McMurray is right, but you should have used the dog earlier. You seem to have sat in your car like a couple of statues waiting for that mob to pelt you. Next time you get that dog out double quick. Smarten up! Now then, I have a special assignment for you both. Have either of you two been undercover before?'

There was no reply from either Cross or Bannerman, just a confused exchange, a fluttered glance between the two.

'Probably not! But something's bothering me...' Boyd racked his brain, puzzled, eyes on both men but memory far away, thinking.

He's stressed-out, jaded, thought Cross. He's burnt out, fused, battery flat.

'I'm too tall for undercover work and he's got the dog,' said Bannerman. 'We're not undercover men, boss. We're Traffic men. You know, patrol cars, motorbikes, accident vans. Mobile, boss. We can walk if you want. I got the legs for it. We can both drive. We're the best, no one to touch us. But undercover, boss...'

'I understand. You're both good drivers really, is that what you're saying? You can still help, I presume?'

'Yes, we can help, I suppose. Can't we, Cross?'

There was a slow nod of approval from the man sat next to Bannerman.

'Yes, that's it,' remarked Boyd, almost oblivious to the conversation of which he was a part. 'That's what it was. It's been bothering me.'

'Bothering you, boss?' asked Bannerman. 'What's bothering you?'

'It was your report, wasn't it?' asked Boyd. 'It was your report that mentioned the Beamer and a gold stud in someone's earlobe?'

Boyd flurried the papers on his desk.

'I read something this week about that chase with a Beamer and a gold stud in an earlobe...'

Boyd shuffled the papers on his desk, searching, scanning the words.

'There was something about a fat neck. Blubber, you said in your report, and a gold stud in an earlobe. It was your report, wasn't it?'

Boyd thumped his fist, mildly, on his desk.

'Left or right earlobe?'

'Left or right earlobe, boss?'

'Yes, left or right? Simple question.'

'Is it that important, boss?'

'Left or right? Of course, it's important. Trivial to you, important to me. Left or right earlobe?'

'Left,' said Cross. 'Left, boss. No doubt.'

'Good man!' said Boyd. 'Where did I put those papers? The gold stud, I should have told her, I should have told her.'

'Who?' queried Bannerman.

'One of my people,' replied Boyd, scattering the papers on his desk, flinching at his mistake.

'An informant?'

'Something like that.'

Bannerman watched Chief Inspector Operations rooting for a file of papers on his desk: a file of papers that would do no more than confirm whether it was a right earlobe or a left earlobe. It was trivial, what Chief Inspector Operations, was looking for, pondered Bannerman. Pursing his lips thoughtfully, Bannerman wondered if the job was too much for Boyd. Was the stress beginning to tell? Were the murder, riot and security visit all getting to the stressed-out jaded man, wondered Bannerman?

'How can we help, boss?' asked Bannerman.

'Help? Yes, you can help. I have work for you both. I want you to make damn sure that route is searched by our teams.'

'Those search teams are good. They'll find a needle in a haystack, boss. They don't need us to show them how to search.'

'Perhaps not but I want you to drive the route the Minister will take. I want you to drive from the airport to the museum and check every bend in the road and every mound in the countryside. I want you to analyse every weak spot on the route into the city. If you analyse the weak spots, I can negate those problems with air support and strategically placed officers.'

'You've got specialists for that. You don't need us,' argued Cross.

'The specialists aren't local. I want you to do it. Use my drawing on the briefing board as a starter. Then I want you to turn that museum inside out. I want you to push those search teams until they drop. When they've searched once, I want them to search twice.'

'They won't like that, boss, not doing it twice.'

'You two have something special. I saw it in those reports I read. You two don't like to be second. You both like to win. You don't accept 'no go' areas and you both want to win. Sometimes you like to buck the system, vary the rules slightly, and even the score up a little. Am I right?'

'Perhaps.' Slow reluctance from Bannerman, thoughtful.

'Can you help me or not?'

Bannerman threw a sideways look at Cross.

Cross nodded and replied, 'The dog?'

'The dog? Good cover, the dog. Take the dog with you.'

'They said you'd be different,' said Cross. 'What do we do?'

'I want you to goad those search teams until the city is squeaky-clean. Tell them there's a bomb out there. I know it. I can feel it in my bones and I'm not the only one. I might be the worst boss you're ever likely to have. Maybe I really am an evil bastard of a man, I don't know. Hey! I might be in cloud cuckoo land. I might get the sack after all this but I feel it in my bones. There's a killer out there. There's a gun out there. Find it and find the man who wears a gold stud in his left earlobe.'

'His left earlobe?'

'You're the only two men in the city who have seen the man with a gold stud in his left earlobe. He's the key to Jo-Jo's murder, the riot, and the visit of the Israeli Minister. Find him for me.'

Camels! There were camels everywhere.

Crosby drove through the Province of Konya: the Turkish breeding centre where horses and camels seemed to outnumber human beings. Then, glancing at the great mosques of Konya, he continued east. The road was wide and straight and he made good progress. Eventually, he drove through the Province of Adana: where Pompey the Great had founded the city in 63 BC and forged a Roman military road. He drove through the Province of Hatay, and in the city of Antakya he refuelled and learnt from a tourist sign that the city was once the eastern capital of the Roman Empire, and once the centre of Christendom outside the lands of Palestine. Leaving Turkey behind him in the cracked mirror of his rattling empty wagon, Crosby crossed the border and drove down the coastal strip of Syria.

Syria's coastal plain was about a hundred miles long with the Mediterranean Sea quivering in hostile tranquillity. Pushing south towards the Lebanon, he turned inland following the course of the road. He saw a mountain range, Jabal ash-Sharqi, rising in the southeast to provide a natural geographical border between Syria and the Lebanon. He drove on towards a border crossing that led to the Lebanon as the land around him changed to a reddish-brown colour. There were few trees and the land gradually became barren and rocky with clumps of sparse vegetation. He drove on.

Crosby could see them now, in the daylight. He could see them on high ground and behind an occasional rock or a lean bush. Sometimes they stood out on all fours, quite blatant, supreme in the hot sun of a barren land. He knew they were there waiting for him if he lost his way;

knew they would tear him to pieces, limb from limb, if he didn't keep to his path; hold to his plan. He feared them, those waiting for him to make a mistake. It would be a grisly end for him if he made an error in judgement. There would surely be no tomorrow. There would be no tomorrow if he failed today. He could almost sense their presence. It was as if they were watching him from the Lebanese mountains, waiting for him, waiting to tear him to pieces if he put one foot wrong and made a mistake. He knew they would howl in delight over his broken body. They were waiting for him, the Jackals of the desert, and the Syrian Army.

Louise lay down on her bed. She settled her head against a pillow and closed her eyes for a moment, closed out four grey walls threatening to suffocate her silent existence. Sighing a lonely sigh, she drifted into a doze.

Her flat was situated about a mile and a half from the edge of the estate. The front door of her flat was painted green, flaky, and in need of urgent repair before the only coat of paint dropped off and the wood began to rot. Inside, the flat was small. There was one room to cook in, the same room to wash in, the same room to sleep in, and the same room to live in. Bed-sit land! The only window in her living room looked out onto a road leading to the estate. One of the flat's windowpanes was loose and clung desperately to a wooden frame in the advanced stages of decay. Morning condensation soaked the window ledge, seeped into its wood, rotted the frame, and ran down a wall to a damp carpet. In one corner of the room sat an electric meter. The meter gobbled up all the coins that she fed and powered both an electric fire and an electric cooker. Her tiny flat aired no welcome to a visitor, not that she had ever received visitors in her flat. It was just a place to doss down, to rest her head and 'phone home, to relax with a portable black and white television that sat on a pink plastic chair in one corner of the room, near the electric meter. The wallpaper was typical: dismal, grey embossed flowers in a grey empty room. A threadbare carpet ran to a skirting board and stopped, four inches short, curled and frayed at its edges, damp beneath a window ledge.

Restless, Louise rose from her bed and thought about what Boyd had said. She remembered when they had first met, down in London. He explained he had watched her at the training school, asked about her, enquired about her, and selected her because of her commonplace looks and her apparent independent resolve. She didn't stand out in a crowd, he explained. She was neither fat nor thin, neither tall nor small. She was neither blonde nor brunette; she was somewhere in between, he quipped. She was average in her looks, in her demeanour, just average. He liked her independent streak, he explained. He liked her Lower Second Class Honours degree in Sociology, he explained. He liked her degree obtained with the Open University, said it showed some guts to work all day and study all night. A degree in Sociology showed she was interested in people, he argued. She said lower second class was pretty damn crap, but he argued it was pretty damn good. She didn't really know why Boyd had picked her. He was a strange man, she thought, very independent, himself, in a unique kind of way. All he seemed to want was for her to be there, living in a flat, seeing his informants, watching and waiting. It wasn't even proper undercover work, she thought. She remembered when he'd travelled to London and where they'd walked in woodland on the edge of the capital and where he'd explained what was required of her. He said he would start her off handling the most trusted of his informants, handling the most basic of surveillance, handling herself, undercover. He said that one day she would have to live in the belly of her van, live in the belly of her van because it was important. He'd explained that if he ever said to her to go the full twenty-four hours then she must do it. She must find her target, must stay on her target, and must live on her target, until her job was done. She was special, he'd said. In fact, she was very special, he'd said. She had laughed in his face at the thought of being special. She was of average build, of average looks, commonplace, and lower second class. She carried a crap, below average degree, with which to do his special work, and she had laughed in his face. When she had seen the flat for the first time, she hadn't laughed. She'd cried at the thought of living alone in her flat. There was nothing special about the dismal, dank, bed-sit of a place. Her flat was lower second class.

Stripping off her clothes until she was naked, she threw the clothes, which clung to the dirt of the estate, into an empty corner of her bed-sit. She washed and then dried herself in front of a two-bar electric fire that a lecherous landlord of bed-sit land had provided. Dressing for her walk in the night, she chose black trainers and denim jeans with a dark blue roll neck sweater. Leather skin-tight gloves were selected along with a black fleece jacket that zipped up to the point of her nose and tickled her chin. Checking the pockets of her black fleece jacket, she fingered a tube of pepper spray. Special was she, Mister Boyd? She thought not.

Louise dressed for her walk in the night, dressed to follow the orders given. She would find her target; follow her target until the job was done. She would follow Boyd's orders without question because she knew how he'd lived his life, how he'd followed orders when he'd been undercover, why she'd been trained.

Closing the green flaky door of her flat tight, she checked it was locked and stepped onto a wet pavement. There was a trickle of rain and the slightest of puddles forming in a gutter. It was police weather. It was the kind of weather police in the night craved for because people didn't come out in rain. The rain was the best crime prevention device ever invented, she thought. Let the heavens open, she prayed.

In rainfall, she would walk in the night's wet shadows and find that launderette. She would circle that launderette and study the streets surrounding it. She would find the best place to watch a launderette from, without being seen herself. Then she would return to her dismal flat and sleep until early morning. When the rain stopped, when the pubs were closed, when the clubs were shut, when the milkman was delivering his first pints, she would be on her target.

She would live in the belly of a van with her buzz box.

She would be on target.

Crosby was tired, exhausted.

He'd driven most of the day, from before the time when the sun had risen to the time that was now. He'd driven since his coded machine had chattered back at him only minutes after he'd sent his last report. The thin grey clouds of night moved in when he approached the border with the Lebanon. Mount Hermon's high peak, where the Jordan River gushed to the earth's surface, lay shrouded in thin grey clouds of night and there were only a few camels on the dusty strip of road that led to the Lebanon. Uneven, unwelcome rocks bordered the road, and a thin layer of sand had blown in from the coast. There were camels and wagons and an army jeep making their slow lethargic way towards the Lebanese border. Crosby would not cross the border and drive into the heart of the Lebanon. He would wait at the border crossing for Danu to appear with a wagon laden with earthenware. He would speak with Danu and ask those questions London had sent on their secret machine. They would exchange papers and invoices and documents accompanying the load Danu brought. Then they would finally exchange wagons. Crosby would drive Danu's wagon, laden with pot urns and earthenware and bric-a-brac, back through the short strip of Syrian land into Turkey, back through the camel region, back through the tobacco growing region, back into Istanbul and the Grand Bazaar and a pottery shop.

    Danu would drive the captain's empty wagon into the Lebanon and into the security zone patrolled by the Syrian Army. The Syrian Army had taken part in all the Arab-Israeli wars since 1948 and was aligned firmly against Israel. Syria was the Arab Republic that intervened in the Lebanese Civil War in 1976 and had remained in the Lebanon ever since to provide a peacekeeping force. There, in the fertile Lebanese valley of the Bekaa, Danu would craft his pot urn and fashion the shape of his urn. There, he would etch the figures and patterns on the contour of his urn. He crafted his pot until the softness of the earth was hard like a rock and the thrill of pleasure filled his zealous eye. He was an artist. Danu would work until it was time once more to load a wagon with his pot urns and his bric-a-brac and his fancy trinkets made from the soil and water of the valley stream. He would take his freshly finished earthenware and drive again to the border where his wagon would be exchanged and his finished pot urn would be sold in the Grand Bazaar of Istanbul, in the pottery shop of his father. Danu worked in the Bekaa valley of the Lebanon where he watched people move. He watched camels and wagons and jeeps, and private cars, moving through the Bekaa valley, moving through his desert, moving between a security zone and the border with Syria. He was the eyes and ears of the Intelligence community, and he lived by his wits. He was the eye that watched the comings and goings of a Syrian army in the north, and a South Lebanese Army in the south. He was the eyes watching Israeli Defence Forces patrolling a security zone in the deepest south of the Lebanon where their border was a tall wire fence with bolted gates preventing traffic from crossing from one country to another. It was a peculiar country, the Lebanon, an occupied country. It was a war zone in its truest sense. Israeli Defence Forces did not fully trust the South Lebanese Army and the South Lebanese Army did not trust the Syrian Army. The Israelis did not trust the Syrians. No one seemed to trust the other in the various zones of power that seemed to organically filter various areas of population. It was a land of mistrust and armoured Mercedes motorcars. It was a land of constant change, constant conflict, constant religious tension, and seldom compromise. Danu was a man who saw it all, heard it all, and reported it all, and he lived by his wits, denying mistrust and denying religion. It was how it had all started, thought Crosby. It had started due to the religion of a man called Danu.

    Danu was a Jew: an Arab-Jew.

Danu wandered in the valley of the Bekaa where he listened to gunshots from a firing range, listened to the sound of grenades exploding, and listened to the detonation of a bomb, far away. Danu worked in the valley of the Bekaa where the men and women of terrorism slept. It was how it had all started, thought Crosby.

Danu drove towards the border.

His wagon was full; his wagon was creaking, laden with pot urns, large and small, and his amphora, large and small. He liked to craft an amphora, liked the shape, gentle and smooth to the touch of his fingers as he shaped its curves. The amphora was a good sell. It brought a high price in the Grand Bazaar, and it was sought after by both tourists and Turkish workers who poured oil and wine into the belly of a virgin amphora. Danu thought back to how it had all started.

Danu thought back to a time when he had returned home to his father in their pottery shop: his father who chain-smoked, old and frail, arthritis in his gnarled and wrinkled hands. That man was there, in the shop in Istanbul. The man wore a white suit, sharply cut, snappy. Very smart! He was of average build and average height. He was nondescript with coloured skin, which was neither black nor white. The man spoke with the tongue of an Arab and said his name was Nico. The man, Nico, knew Danu was a Jew, knew he had travelled from the Lebanon, knew he was from the Bekaa valley. Nico asked Danu to watch jeeps and camels and wagons and private cars, and report what he saw. It was how it had all started. Danu reckoned Nico was from Mossad: the intelligence people from the State of Israel. Danu had watched, had done what Nico - Mossad man - had asked for, and had passed trivial information down the line in a pot urn that was an amphora and their chosen way to communicate. It was the safest way to communicate for it was far too dangerous for Nico to visit him in the desert and it was far too dangerous for Danu to be equipped with electronic communications. Nico would never venture to the Bekaa, reckoned Danu. The Bekaa was Danu's backyard. Danu knew the valley and the desert that surrounded the valley, like it was the back of his hand. Indeed, the Bekaa was his home. Nico would not come to the Bekaa. Nico, Mossad's man, would not come to the valley while Danu was working for him, watching out for him. Mossad, reckoned Danu. He was working for Nico of the Mossad and now they knew all about jeeps and camels and wagons and private cars that criss-crossed the Lebanon. Now Mossad knew all about the vehicles and people who travelled from a security zone, near the Israeli border, into the heart of the Lebanon. It was the heart of the Lebanon that fostered terrorists, nurtured terrorists, and shielded them from the rest of the world. The man in a white suit, Nico, was a regular visitor to their pottery shop, always bought an amphora, and always left money with Danu's father. The money was Mossad money, reckoned Danu's father. The man in that white suit had not said otherwise until one day he had brought his father English cigarettes. Danu's father had spoken of Tel Aviv and the man in the white suit did not seem to know Tel Aviv. Danu's father was surprised and then wondered if he might be British, but British with a coloured skin and the tongue of an Arab? The man in the white suit had given money with English cigarettes: 'to help the pottery shop business, you understand,' it was explained. Danu's father had nodded, smiled, and taken both his money and his English cigarettes. 'Please, you must call me Nico,' explained the man in the white suit, and he had smiled when his money had been grasped with both hands. Later, Nico gave more money so that another wagon might be bought: 'to help the pottery shop business, you understand,' it was explained. Father listened, took Nico's money and bought another wagon. Nico suggested growing hashish, cannabis. The seeds of the cannabis plant were abundant in the Lebanon but Nico had personally supplied cannabis plant seeds. Nico explained his seeds would grow to a tall bush and when harvested would loosen the tongue of those in the valley. Hashish could be used to befriend, used to obtain access to a camp, and could be used to loosen up tongues, Nico had explained. It was how it had all started.

Danu was paid to travel from the security zone into the valley where terrorists trained and slept. Of course, Danu knew they were terrorists because Nico had told him so. Danu did not ask how Nico knew. Perhaps it was something to do with jeeps and wagons and camels and private cars that came and went between the valley in the desert and the border. Perhaps it was something to do with satellite photographs that were taken once a day: those satellite photographs that terrorists seemed to know about and fear so much, Danu didn't know. Nico of the Mossad knew, thought Danu, and he was pleased that Nico of the Mossad knew. Or was Nico an American spy? Or was it the British who Nico worked for? Did it matter who Nico worked for, thought Danu? Danu knew Nico brought English cigarettes, money, and cannabis seeds; and he was on their side. Nico was on the side of the Jew, on the side of Israel. Danu planted Nico's seeds, grew his cannabis plants, and then offered hashish and pot urns for sale. Some of his urns were bought while some of his urns were smashed to the ground in arrogant petulance. Danu continued to offer hashish grown in the valley of the

Lebanon. He offered more hashish and pot urns. Eventually, he sold his hashish but they often rejected his pot urns. He went again to their tents and bombed out buildings and sold again hashish to the bored men and women of terrorism.

They had nowhere to go, the men and women of terrorism.

They seldom left the safe harbour of the Lebanon and seldom left their camp. But every noon when it was said an American satellite was overhead, they moved into a building so that the Yankee spy in the sky could not capture their image. They lived in fear Mossad would track them down and terminate them. They were brave and frightened men and women, the men and women of terrorism. They were brave to die for a cause for which they had pledged their lives. So brave, so fearless, so violent.

An aircraft flew overhead, Israeli markings, too high to hazard a guess at its type. It was probably a fighter-bomber flying overhead, thought Danu. The men and women of terrorism would be frightened by an aircraft, they always were. They feared a Jewish bomb, a Jewish missile, and Jewish ammunition raking the Bekaa valley and the tents and bombed out hovels where they lived. They feared Israeli aeroplanes and an American spy satellite passing overhead, unseen, unannounced. And they also feared strangers who might appear in their valley. Some strangers had entered the valley once and had never been seen again. Nico would not come to the Bekaa, Danu thought. It was far too dangerous.

Who were they, thought Danu, these men and women of terrorism? Perhaps they were Hamas: an Islamic Resistance Movement who detonated the bomb that blew up New York's World Trade Centre. Or Hezbollah: the Party of God who had carried out a suicide attack on an American Marine base in Beirut in 1983. The same people who hijacked TWA flight 847 two years later. The same group who kidnapped Terry Waite and John McCarthy. Or Jihad: the Vanguards of Conquest, Egyptian Islamic extremists who were responsible for murdering President Sadat, architect of the Middle East peace process. Jihad: the Holy War. Or were they the Palestinian Liberation Organisation; people without a country; kicked out by the Jews. Homeless and Stateless. Danu thought Hezbollah had infiltrated the South Lebanese Army. Had said so, had told Nico in a messages left in his amphora. Just tittle-tattle. Danu thought the Syrian Army had an eye on the Lebanon, would take it for itself one day, when the time was right. Danu had told Nico. Just tittle-tattle. Danu understood why these men and women resorted to violence.

It was the way of terrorists to strike fear into the heart of society: to create a constant nightmare of such ferocity and terror a Government would be forced to change its policy and favour the terrorists - to bring about change by violent means.

Danu did not care to know their faction. He knew their reasons, the cause of Islamic extremism, the cause of recovering lost lands, and the cause of the Holy War.

They had nowhere to go. They lived in the valley of the Bekaa and trained with guns and bombs every day. They learnt the language of others, learnt the culture of others, learnt how to dress in the western style, and learnt the culture of the west so that they might infiltrate the great liberal democracies of the west and detonate their bombs and pull their triggers that would end a life. They practised their evil art and scorned the rest of the world.

Danu had lived in the Bekaa before the men of terrorism. Danu had made his earthenware and his amphora in the valley long before terrorists had chosen to make camp in the Bekaa.

At first they were wary of him and shunned him. When Danu pointed out strangers passing through, pointed out the regular flight of an Israeli aeroplane, pointed out bowels in the land where a cave could be used to hide from creatures of the night, or hide guns and explosives, they slowly accepted him. When he pointed to those blessed Syrian soldiers who protected his home from infidel Americans, they slowly accepted him. When he offered cheap hashish, they slowly accepted him. It had all been done slowly, over the months, so slowly. They had laughed at him all those months, just as Nico said they would. They had laughed at Danu all the months that he had infiltrated them, buried himself under their skins, got to know them, and tell Nico all about them in his messages in an amphora. They had laughed at him, pathetic-looking creature that he was. Danu was the pathetic creature who brought them hashish to kill the boredom of camp existence. They all knew Danu: a pathetic limping man, forty something, swarthy, lengthy dark brown hair that rolled and curled halfway down his back. Danu was pitiful, they thought. He was pitiful in their eyes because they were fit and strong and athletic while he was only half a man. They were killers. Danu was nothing. Danu made stupid pot urns and dragged his right leg behind him because an accident of birth had left him with a useless foot and a dead eye. He was pathetic with his limping leg and wild unkempt hair that fanned behind him when the wind blew strongly. Deplorable with his black eye patch stretching across his face and covering a dead left eye.

Pathetic, they thought, only half a man. Had it not been for his hashish they might have kicked him to death for fun, to break the boredom between the attacks they planned. Had it not been for the ridicule that they poked at Danu they might have made him swallow a live grenade, just to see what the effect on a human head was. A bloody mess, they thought.

Danu, limping half man. Half man, half blind, half creature, they thought.

Danu drove towards the border.

Crosby yawned.

The border crossing came into view. There was no broad white demarcation line across the road, no booth where a toll was taken, and no flat-roofed office where an excise duty might be paid. And there was no Coat of Arms bearing the words 'Welcome to the Lebanon'. There were two army jeeps slewed across a thin strip of road bordered by the sand of the desert, and a bombed out, broken down hovel of a building providing the only shade in the vicinity. Crosby braked suddenly when Syrian soldiers stepped into the middle of the road and signalled him to stop.

Is this the border crossing, thought Crosby? There are no signs, no way of knowing whether this is the place where Syria becomes the Lebanon. It must be the crossing, thought Crosby. Good God, they've stopped me.

There was a private car, two army jeeps and a camel at the border crossing. But no sign of Danu.

There was the ratchet crunch of a handbrake when Crosby finally brought his vehicle to a standstill. The barrel of a rifle in the hands of one of the Syrian soldiers twitched as Crosby wound his window down and told his tongue to remember Arabic.

A Syrian soldier stepped forward. 'Papers!' It was an order, not a request, from an infantryman with a rifle. His hair was black. He was of medium build and medium height, but his uniform was coloured green and he held out his hand expecting immediate compliance. There was a bored look on his face. It was as if he had carried out this routine so many times there was no more excitement in the ordering of immediate papers. A rifle dropped to his side supported by a leather sling hanging loosely over his shoulder.

The papers were produced.

'Name?' Spat out, obnoxious.

'Nico.'

'Where do you travel from?' The papers were taken. An answer was compulsory.

'Istanbul. It's in Turkey.'

'I know where it is.' Spat out.

'Sorry.'

'Nationality?' Spat out again, rude. Bureaucratic bully.

'I am a wanderer. I am but a poor man with no home to speak of.'

'Where are you going?' Nico's papers were inspected.

'I meet a man, Danu, to return his pottery for selling in the Grand Bazaar at Istanbul.'

'Danu?' His papers were turned over and inspected again. The Syrian's eye moved from the papers to the driver's face, quizzical. 'Danu, you say?'

'Yes, Danu. He makes pot urns and brings them every week so that they may be sold in Istanbul to the infidels of the west. The infidels are tourists with shit money and shit brains, but what do I care as long as the Zionist shit buy our pot urns and line my belly with good bread and cheap wine.'

A figure moved in the image of Nico's cracked mirror. Then a green uniform climbed onto the rear platform of the empty wagon. A rifle barrel twitched and the wooden platform of the empty wagon creaked beneath the weight of a Syrian soldier.

Crosby felt beads of sweat forming on his brow. He saw a soldier with a rifle on the back of his wagon, unfriendly. He wondered if he was at the Lebanese border. Had he missed something in the rear view of his fractured mirror? Had he been followed? Then he wondered if the 'phone call to Danu's father had been tapped by the opposition. Had his cover been blown?

'We will search.' The papers were held tight.

'My wagon is empty. I am not travelling into the Lebanon. I am meeting my friend, Danu. I will take…'

'I heard you the first time.' His papers were held tight and folded into the infantryman's breast pocket. Gone was the boredom on the soldier's face. 'We will search you and your wagon. Out!'

Crosby opened his driver's door and stepped down from his cab. His feet touched the ground and he felt the rough hands of a brusque Syrian upon him.

'Down! Down on the ground.' Spat out, and a rifle dropping from a soldier's shoulder, hostile.

The end of a rifle poked the small of his back. A hand grasped the nape of his neck. A black boot prodded weak skin tissue at the rear of his knee and he felt himself being propelled to the ground. His face smacked against the ground. His skull jolted from temple to temple with the sudden impact of solid earth. His eyes closed. His head swam. He felt the bitter taste of sand on his lips. Then there was a smell gouging and ripping at his nostrils. He opened his eyes and saw camel shit inches from his face. The camel dung fed on his nostrils and clawed at his throat. He turned his head and saw two Syrian soldiers prising up the empty platform of his wagon with a bayonet attached to a rifle. He heard the squash of leather and knew a soldier had climbed into his cab, was probably sat at the driver's seat searching his cab and his belongings. There were at least four Syrian infantrymen, he thought.

'You are new on this road. This vehicle comes every week, but not you.' The soldier again, standing above him, now with his knee pressed into his back, now with his hands padding down the captain of intelligence: the man from British Intelligence. And the deep smell of fresh camel shit was inside him and he was gagging.

'I am new. I am Nico. I am to meet Danu…'

'Silence.' Spat out, a knee compressing his spine, hands roaming from his legs to his hips to his chest, searching his clothes and his body, padding him down.

'I do nothing wrong. I come to meet Danu…'

'He's clean.' Shouted by the soldier; acknowledged with a wave from another soldier with stripes on his arm leaning against the bonnet of a dark green Syrian army jeep: a sergeant who spat phlegm towards the camel shit.

'Let him go.' From the sergeant; the soldier with stripes on his arm, in charge, indifferent to proceedings staged before him. 'Bring him to me.'

Nico was grabbed. He was pulled to his feet and dragged to a man with stripes on his arm. Then the smell of camel shit was gone from his nostrils and it was suddenly replaced by the smell of an English cigarette. He saw a curl of smoke from the butt end of a filter cigarette and saw a curt moustache on the lips of the Syrian sergeant.

'Anything?' From the sergeant, his question posed at soldiers on the platform of the wagon, aimed at the men in the cab rifling Nico's belongings.'

There was a shake of heads from the platform of the wagon and a dull glance from the cab of Nico's wagon.

'Is this the way that you treat my employees?' The voice was new, shouted, angry, growing louder as it seemed to near. 'Is this the way that you repay me for my friendship?' The voice rasped in Arabic, seeking conflict; and there was the soft scuffling sound of a clubfoot being dragged relentlessly along the ground.

'Danu!' From the sergeant; surprised, leaning against his jeep. 'He is your man?'

'Of course he's my man. He's driving my wagon, is he not?'

'He is new, Danu. We thought him a thief! We thought him a stranger in our valley. We thought him a Mossad spy.'

The scuffling foot stopped. Danu laughed, pulled the sergeant from his jeep, hugged him, and then clapped a hand on the back of the sergeant. 'A Mossad spy!' Danu laughed aloud, bent double, held out the palms of his hands and then hugged the soldier who was holding Nico tight. 'May Allah kill a thousand times the evil shit Mossad man who touches the soil of the Bekaa and touches the soil of the Lebanon.' Danu spat to the ground then stamped his spit on the ground with the heel of his strong boot. 'Cursed Mossad!' Danu laughed. 'Nico is my man.'

The sergeant chuckled. Then the chuckle grew to a laugh. The Syrian soldiers saw their sergeant laughing and they joined in. Suddenly, they were all laughing.

'You do your job well, my friends,' said Danu. 'But no, Nico comes this week, maybe next week. Nico works in our shop with my father. He carries our pot urns and drives our wagon in Istanbul. Today we have problems so Nico drives all the way here, for the first time, to collect our pot urns. A Mossad spy?' And there was another laugh from Danu as he limped towards Crosby, dragging his clubfoot behind him. 'Nico, come! These brave men are good soldiers. It's nothing personal, you understand. These men look after my business and me. These men look after the Lebanon and the Bekaa. They are my good friends.'

Crosby exhaled, blew out his fears and said, 'I thought your friends were going to cut off my balls and feed me with camel shit.'

There was a raucous laugh from the sergeant. 'We cut off the balls of the Mossad spy,' he roared, and the Syrians laughed, free in a moment of release from the boredom of the day. 'Like this.' The sergeant withdrew a double-edged dagger from a sheath on his belt and whipped it through the air, inches from his own throat. Then he replaced the dagger and laughed. 'Sorry, Danu. You have a present for me, yes?'

'I always bring you presents,' said Danu. 'I could not work safely in the valley if it were not for you. You keep out the thieves and strangers who plague our land. I always have presents for my brave friends.'

The sergeant clapped his hands. 'Good, Danu. It is good.'

'Nico, go to my wagon. Check the travel papers and check my load. The soldiers will sign the papers that cover our load. No problem! Go, Nico. Do as you are told while I spend time with my friends.'

'I didn't see you coming,' said Crosby.

'I arrived when you had your face in camel shit, Nico.' There was a childish giggle from the soldiers again. 'My wagon is parked over there. Go, Nico. Check the papers and the load. Do as you are told or you won't be paid.' There was a pleading in Danu's one good eye and a vice-like grip on Crosby's wrist. It was an order given, a plea for obedience.

Withdrawing, Crosby saw Danu's wagon parked some thirty yards from the crossing, inside the Lebanon. He walked towards Danu's wagon.

'My friends,' said Danu. 'I have French perfume taken from a tourist who should have known better than to stop in the desert. I have English cigarettes borrowed from a tourist who stopped for a leak and was frightened shit-less by the howl of a young jackal. I have a camera from a German woman who stopped to buy my amphora and laid her camera at my feet. Sad day! It was the only thing that was laid that day.'

The Syrian soldiers howled with laughter.

'I liberated these things as I walked in the desert,' smiled Danu. Then he laughed aloud and conspiratorially quipped, 'I also have a little weed, a little hashish, the crop was good, but I think you should not have these things if you bother my driver. I need my driver. Without my driver I cannot come with French perfume, English cigarettes, a German camera, and the golden hashish of the Lebanon.'

There was a thin threatening smile from the sergeant who was not amused.

Danu laughed. 'But then I know I could not walk without the help of my brave soldier friends.'

Then there was a nod of approval from the sergeant. The threat in his grin was gone and boredom was gone from their faces. The fun had been had at Nico's expense. The fun had been had at Danu's expense, pathetic servile creature that he was.

Danu wore sandals and he was robed. He wore a red and white-flecked keffiyeh fastened on his head by a two-strand dirty black cord that wound around his temples. The keffiyeh was triangular in shape and one corner of the keffiyeh trailed towards his shoulder and was tucked into his robe so that the cloth covered half his face. The black eye patch that covered his left eye peeked out from beneath his keffiyeh. Dragging his clubfoot to a jeep, Danu spilled the contents of his robe onto the bonnet.

English cigarettes were grabbed by the sergeant and pocketed with a smile of satisfaction. Sold! French perfume was lifted, unscrewed, dabbed on the back of a hand, smelled, and inspected. Sold! An infantryman who spent his life asking for papers grabbed a German camera. The camera was checked for film and pointed at the others. Smile please! There was a click and laughter from the soldiers assembled. Sold! There was hashish wrapped in the thin leather of a goat. The hashish was taken, inspected, smelled, held to the light, weighed in the hand, sampled. Sold!

When the auction was over, Danu pocketed the meagre proceeds of his plunder. There were a few pounds that would ensure his return, soon; a few pounds that had probably been stolen by the Syrians in the first place. A few Lebanese pounds that were a token bauble for a pathetic creature with a clubfoot and an eye patch.

Nico's papers were signed and returned. Then there was a wave from the sergeant, a fired engine, a cloud of dust, and the Syrian soldiers were gone.

When the dust settled Danu said, 'You are a fool to come, Nico.'

'I'm sorry, Danu.'

'You are a fool to enter the Lebanon. They could have killed you.'

'I never intended to enter the Lebanon. I came to the border crossing to meet you. I have questions to ask.'

'Border crossing?' Danu was exasperated. 'Nico, you are ten kilometres inside Lebanon, you fool. Did you not see the signs? Did you not know you were inside the Lebanon?'

'No, I've driven all night and all day, Danu. I'm dog tired, dead on my feet. I thought I was...'

'You thought wrong. Those Syrians could have killed you. You are a ten-minute drive from the Bekaa valley and they could have killed you without a thought. They could have squeezed the trigger, blown your head off, ripped the clothes from your back and sold your wagon in the streets of Beirut. The jackals of the night could have feasted on your body, you fool. You were a fool to come, Nico. You must never come again, Nico. Never!'

'I'm sorry, Danu, but I have questions to ask.'

'My father how is he?'

'Too old, too frail and he smokes too much. But then he is well and he sends the love of a father to his son in the desert.'

'He is not a fool like you, Nico. He is not a fool who walks into the home of another without an invitation. He is not fool enough to go where he is not safe.'

'I'm sorry, Danu, It is important.'

'Your questions?'

'Namir is gone from the valley. Namir is an assassin. You must tell me all that you know of Namir. You must tell me all that you know about the training camp in the Bekaa valley.'

'Do you not read my words in our amphora?'

'Yes, I read your words but they are thin and weak, Danu, and they lack the depth of your understanding that I need to know.'

'Trivial?'

'No, not trivial, Danu. Your words were good but they do not tell me enough.'

'What do you want to know?'

'Danu, why did Namir leave the valley?'

'Namir is a killer, it is said. It is obvious why Namir has left the valley. He will kill. Your questions sound trivial; too trivial for a man to risk his life in the desert of the Lebanon. I only know trivia, Nico. Pay my father and leave us alone. I can only give you trivia that I hear.'

'It is trivia that I want to hear, Danu.'

'Namir goes to kill for a tablet. It is the reason he leaves the valley.'

'Kill for a tablet? What do you mean?'

'Come, we will walk and we will talk. Then you will drive your wagon back to Istanbul and you will hug my father for me.'

'Which part of the valley of the Bekaa is their training camp? Who else lives in the training camp? Who is their leader? How many terrorists are there? What do they look like? Can you describe these terrorists for me? What kind of arms do they have? How many guns?'

'Your satellites are no good?'

'Not when they hide in the caves, Danu.'

Smiling, Danu shook his head.

'How do you know Namir is gone from the valley, Danu? How do you know he will kill? When did he leave the valley? What is this tablet that you speak of? Is Namir alone? I have a list of questions in my head.'

'Come, Nico. I will talk with you and tell you of Namir. I will tell you where their camp is and I will tell you of the men and women in their camp, but you must never come in that wagon again. It is too dangerous, Nico. You were lucky I knew that corrupt sergeant. Had it been another, you would be dead. I could be dead and the flies would have your body to feast on along with that camel shit'

'Namir, I need to know about Namir and I've got to get back to Istanbul as soon as I can.'

'You are not Mossad, are you, Nico?' There was a pause when his words had been spoken and then Crosby looked uncomfortable. 'I thought as much. My father was right. Are you American or British, Nico?'

There was a reluctant sigh and a movement of Crosby's eyes away from Danu's face. 'I cannot tell you such a thing, Danu.'

There was an empty silence in the air; a silence that lingered, a silence that had closed their conversation down, ended.

'You move in a strange world, Nico. You move in a world where you use a half-truth as a passport. Your passport is no good anymore. I deserve to know the truth.'

'What the hell! I prefer English cigarettes,' said Crosby as he looked Danu straight in the eye once more. 'The truth is I've never tasted an Israeli brand, Danu. I've never been to Tel Aviv and I've never been to New York. I'm an Englishman and I work for....'

'Why should I trust you, Nico? English? American? CIA? Nico, you are a fool of a man and a liar.'

'Do you have a choice after all this time? There will never be peace in these lands if there are men like Namir. We fight a war against such men. So I am a fool and a liar but am I a fool and a liar because I work for peace in your lands?'

Danu walked away, dragging his clubfoot, scuffling on the ground, and turning his back on the captain of intelligence. There was a pause with only the sound of the wind, soft, blowing through his long dark hair as it wafted from his shoulder blades. 'Our lands?' said Danu, quizzically. Turning slowly, Danu looked into Crosby's eyes. 'Okay, Nico, or whatever your name is. I will tell you want you want to know. My trivia is important, yes?'

'Yes, Danu.'

Nico, Namir is from the camp of tents. He goes to steal a tablet and kill a man. Namir is not alone…'

10
~ ~ ~

Dateline: 6th September, Present Year: The City of Carlisle.

Whatever had happened during the night was finally over. The early morning streets were damp and deserted now, yet an eerie symmetry seemed to linger where derelict shells enclosed their dark secrets. It was as if time had shrouded the estate with a cloak of denial, as if history had locked a savagery from the past into a wind of change that had come, seen, and then moved on, unrepentant, unforgiving. Now all that remained of a restless stormy night was a sombre drizzle.

Driving through the estate in her rusting van, Louise glanced at some gable ends scrawled with the black jagged paint of anti-establishment graffiti. Then, slowly passing an overturned, vandalised car, she saw a burnt out bus shelter still smouldering in the aftermath of violence and mayhem. She drove on, bypassing the desolate park, broken bottles littering filthy pavements, and bricks and cobbles that lay abandoned on the road. She knew there had been trouble through the night and wondered which elements had inspired such a bout of wanton, selfish destruction.

At the cross-roads Louise turned left, then left again, selected first gear, crawled, and finally manoeuvred onto some wasteland. There was a splash of a tyre in a puddle as she reversed carefully into position. Snatching at the handbrake, she stopped near to a thrown-away refrigerator and noticed its broken door hung from a rusting hinge. Quite deliberately, she parked as close as she could to a broken bough drooping from a nearby dying tree. A limb of the tree had slumped to the ground and its remaining leaves, and the twisted angle of its broken bough, configured to secrete part of her van. Situated on a slight mound, her vantage point overlooked the junction, and was exactly where she had planned to park.

When Louise had positioned her van, locked its doors and set the alarm, she climbed into the rear and yanked at a carpet. Rolling back the thick mat, she pulled at a latch, opened up the belly of her van and exposed a false compartment. Dropping into the belly of her van, she slid the false floor above her head. Alone in the belly of her van, she was hidden beneath the floor, concealed in a false compartment, with only a buzz box for company. It was very cramped.

Twisting her body, Louise lay on her back and inched her way to a control panel where she activated the buzz box. Flicking a switch, she heard the soft murmur of electronics taking over. Then all the dials lit up and bathed her breathing space in fluorescent red. Pressing more buttons, she heard a yielding click from an optical instrumentation panel fall into line.

Apertures for her spy-glasses and telescopic lenses were hidden in the lighting units of her van, and secreted in the front radiator grille of her rusting old van. The lenses and electronic interface ran from the van's lighting units and radiator grille to the van's optical instrumentation panel. At the instrumentation panel they were disentangled in a bank of tiny television screens, which were embedded into the van's false compartment. Of course, her van was heavy and cumbersome to drive, but it had been Boyd's idea and she had told him it would not be a problem. The belly of her van sank the rusting monstrosity to the extremities of its springs and axles, but she had not argued with Boyd at the time. She thought her van was a little cramped, but it was more than adequate for the job in hand.

Removing a headset from a hook near the instrumentation panel, Louise smoothed the carphones across her hair and heard that infernal low buzz quietly invade her ears. The sound of electronic gadgetry had earned the nickname 'buzz box' and it had been that way since the first time she had worn her earphones. Another finger clicked another switch and a directional sound location system trickled into play. Her idea, endorsed by Boyd. In the radiator grille of her van, hidden from the public eye, a powerful but tiny microphone twitched and listened. The product of her microphone rippled through the electronics into her van's belly, and then softly into her earphones. A glance at one of the tiny three inch square video screens revealed a milk float approaching the cross-roads below. Louise moved a dial, moved her directional sound location system, and listened in her earphones. A microphone hidden in the van's radiator grille prickled, angled towards a milk float, and located the noise. The sound of a radio playing far away in the milk float filled her ears. Louise reduced the volume until she was satisfied her skull would not explode.

Turning her attention to her telescopes and spy-glasses, Louise adjusted her image and focused on the cross-roads. Eventually she selected a spy-glass holding the best view of the street below. Then she angled her spy-glass towards her target. With her free hand, she angled the directional sound location system towards her target and looked into a tiny video screen that revealed the street with its launderette and terraced houses.

From the mound of land upon which she was parked, Louise could penetrate the entire street and with a random flick of a switch she could select three hundred and sixty degree visibility. With a flick of a switch she could see what she wished, could hear what she wanted, and could record on a tiny video screen the events she saw.

Now she really was undercover. Louise was on covert surveillance, living in the belly of her van, waiting for those three foreigners to appear in an image on her video screen. She would see them, she would listen to them, and she would record their presence. When she was sure she had found them, sure she had located their house, she would move closer and hone her instrumentation panel to perfection. Until then she would live cramped and she would live on target until her target was penetrated to perfection.

The milk float turned into the street that cradled a launderette: the street that housed the decomposing body of a heroin addict called Trish.

Suddenly, the milk float stopped.

A driver in a white coat stood out from his milk float and gathered three bottles of milk in his hands. Whistling, he began delivering to houses in the street. Louise listened to his tune and his bottles clacking. Then she heard the front door of number twelve shut tight behind a man who wore blue overalls, a flat cap, and carried his lunch to work in a Tupperware box.

A newspaper boy and a postman would come soon. Her street would soon be alive. She waited, cramped in the belly of her van.

She thought herself a second class woman in a high-tech van.

Suddenly a signpost loomed in his face and a wheel crunched on a patch of loose gravel. Crosby was slipping away into dark oblivion. Startled, annoyed with himself, he wrestled with the steering wheel. The back of his wagon shook and his pot urns bounced as the tyres bit in anger.

God, he was so tired. Crosby wound his window down and took a deep breath of fresh clean air. Clean air sank into his face and a breeze snapped at his skin, rousing him from his drowsiness. He ran a hand across his face, pressed an index finger and thumb into the corner of his eyes, killed the sleep, and then drove on, straight ahead.

A momentary error had brought him to his senses. He checked his watch. He was running against the clock and he was running out of time. He had to get back to his office in Istanbul and report his information on that secret chattering machine.

Pressing hard, he willed himself towards Istanbul. He drove and thought of a report he would send. Thinking about Danu, he wondered if Danu was a double agent. He had been pleased when Danu had pulled him from the clutches of that Syrian army patrol, but he had not liked what had happened then. He did not like the bartering of his life against a stolen camera, hashish, and English cigarettes. It was as if Danu played a game he did not understand and was not a part of. He wondered if Danu lived by his wits every day, wondered if he might have sold him as the spy that he was, had it suited the Arab Jew. Was Danu the kind of agent that might exchange his life with Hamas or Hezbollah or Jihad? God, had what Danu said been correct? Would those soldiers have really killed him and left him to die like a dog in the desert? With a cold chill caressing his spine, Crosby composed the message he would send on his secret chattering machine: words he would type and send down the lines to those men in grey suits in London...

From: Station Bosphorus.
Sender: G9/142/Codename Nico.
To: G9/001/Codename Ratchet.
Date-time: 06.09.00 0630 hrs
Classification: Omega Blue
Sub Classification: Top Secret
Subject: Codename Danu.
Provenance: Personal Debrief.
Circumstances: Highly volatile, extreme danger.

Content: Codename Danu confirms presence of a terrorist training camp at grid reference E315/336/673/Bekaa Valley...Break...This camp consists of three canvas six man tents, Icelandic type, coloured light green, camouflaged to brown/grey...Break... Plus one derelict building, (bomb damage apparent), situated one hundred and fifty yards east of tented area... Break... Approx. four hundred yards to north-west of bombed out building lies escarpment rising to four hundred feet above sea level. This escarpment - rock face, coloured red/brown, vegetation sparse - rises from the valley floor and carries small clusters of pomegranate trees before ground gives way to rock... Break... This rock face houses four caves wherein the following equipment is secreted...Break...Repeating provenance...Break... Codename Danu confirms presence of following from personal sighting during last forty eight hours... Forty rifles, fifty sub machine guns, one hundred grenades, one hundred small arms, fifty rocket launchers, twenty five ground to air missiles, unknown quantity of high explosives...

That sounded right, thought Crosby. Ratchet would like the latest from Danu but would consider the meeting in the desert to be trivial. Damn my boss, Ratchet, thought Crosby. Ratchet, Head of Covert Operations, Middle East Section, damn him. What did Ratchet know of all the wild dangers involved? What did he know of a Syrian Army Patrol, a rifle in his ribs and the knee of a bad-breathed Syrian in the small of his back? No, damn Ratchet: office man, Head of Section. Head of section and never been anywhere near the Middle East. Ratchet knew nothing of pomegranate groves, cypress trees and desert jackals waiting to tear you to pieces if you made the wrong move. He knew nothing. Ratchet would call the contents of his message trivial, nothing that couldn't be found out from his Israeli or American counterparts. There was nothing in this report that could be traded with the Israelis, Saudis, Americans, or anyone else, for that matter. It was such trivial information. Probable reply from Ratchet? Site already known. Noted! Value of meeting? Marginal! Suggest review of Codename Danu with a view to termination of case investigation. Termination of case investigation? No way, thought Crosby. Damn Ratchet. What did he know?

He drove on, scheming a report in his mind. No, the rest of the information, which sounded trivial, might mean something to Ratchet and those who worked in Vauxhall. He thought of the words he would send...

The following personalities are known by Danu to have left a terrorist camp, located in Bekaa Valley... Break... See Para One... Break...Namir, believed born Lebanon, subject of your recent Omega Blue, wanted for multiple murders, suspected of global involvement in Middle East struggle. Wears gold stud in right ear, considered highly dangerous, brother of Yasif...Break... Yasif, brother of Namir, domiciled North West England, trained by Namir in use of firearms and explosives, trained in English language and ways of western world, wears identical gold stud to that of brother in left ear... Break... Accompanied by Rollo, half caste, mother - Syrian, father - English, born 1976, plump, may be armed and dangerous... Break... Accompanied by Aden, born 1973, fair hair, moustache, trained in close quarter assassination... Break...Reason for movement to North West England as follows... An Israeli Minister, identity not known, is travelling to Peace Talks in the United Kingdom. Minister is to attend a function in North West England and is to receive a tablet, a Jewish artefact, no further details known... This from Danu... Break... Suspect assassination attempt... Message ends.

He made Istanbul, made his office, and made his cellar. Switching on his secret machine, Crosby sent his message.

There was a low growl from an Alsatian in the park, then a bark, followed by a tug on a leash. The dog whimpered, defeated, and padded on across a weed-strewn path with its nose sniffing the ground.

Mary saw an old car in the park, abandoned, and partly burnt out. She knew it had been dumped there during the night. It was probably stolen for it hadn't been in the park yesterday when she had taken her customary walk. She pulled her leash tighter, pulled closer her Alsatian, and felt safer. Mad woman, Mary, to walk in that park.

She saw a man from afar.

He was alone and she had not seen him before in the park. Mary wondered who this stranger might be. She watched him as he strolled along a path. He was tiny in the far distance and she could not hazard a guess at his height, or his true demeanour, or the contours of his face. But the stranger seemed very small.

Walking nearer, his image gradually grew larger in her eye.

The stranger strolled casually along a path towards some wooden planks that lay across a ditch: an open ditch carrying a narrow shallow stream to the river that dominated the valley.

Mary quietened her dog, knelt down, patted her dog, caressed her dog's throat, and watched the solitary man.

Waking onto the wooden planks, the man knelt down and looked into the water below. Then he stood up, walked back to the path, and then turned and slithered down a muddy bank into a ditch and out of view.

He was gone from her sight.

Mary stood up and walked with her dog, free on its leash, towards the wooden planks that crossed the ditch. She was whistling, naturally, as if she had not a care in the world. Her dog growled low, naturally.

She could hear the man breathing.

Mary saw him beneath the wooden planks that crossed a ditch. The man was crouched, quietly examining an angled bank that ran beneath some wooden planks towards a shallow stream. It was as if he were in a world of his own. He was oblivious to her presence. She wondered if the man was looking for something, or hiding something. Perhaps the stranger was collecting a package? She really didn't know what the man was doing and for a moment she wondered if it would be better to just mind her own business and walk away. Why should she concern herself with the comings and goings of a stranger in the park?

Mary glanced at the man's neck, its thick blubber of olive-coloured skin, two layers, slack on his collar, and she saw a gold stud twinkling in his left earlobe.

She walked on, whistling, apparently unconcerned and calling her dog to heel. It was as if she had not seen the olive-coloured man, as if he did not exist.

Mary knew it was Yasif, knew from that description heard at her parties where her fairy cakes were dispensed with in return for gossip on the estate. She had not met him, but she knew it was Yasif, the gold stud man!

He remained oblivious to her.

She tugged her dog and increased her stride leaving Yasif beneath the wooden planks of the ditch. As she walked, Mary decided not to move her Shamrock plant. She couldn't wait for Louise to visit. If the 'phone at the edge of the estate was not vandalised, she would 'phone Boyd direct. Boyd would want to know about drugs gathered from a ditch or drugs buried in a ditch, awaiting collection. He would want to know directly, the good bobby that she knew him to be. Mary smiled to herself. A walk in a park and a drug cache discovered. She was happy, pleased to help in the discovery of Yasif's drugs cache as she headed for a telephone.

Ratchet read page one of Crosby's report. Trivial! There was nothing new in the report from Bosphorus, classified Omega Blue Top Secret. Nothing that couldn't be seen from a spy plane or a satellite flying overhead. Drawing on his cigar, he tapped waste ash into a crystal bowl, heaved his legs onto one corner of a walnut desk and yawned. Page one was boring, trivial. Not until page two...

At page two, Ratchet faltered, grew uneasy, dropped his legs to the carpet, and shuffled in his high back chair. A shot of adrenaline pumped through his bloodstream as he rummaged for the itinerary of an Israeli Minister. Snatching some loose papers from his desk, Ratchet checked the time in Israel and realised the Minister was already en route to the United Kingdom. Placing the Bosphorus report to one side,

Ratchet leafed through the itinerary. He read again the report from Bosphorus and compared it with the itinerary.

It hit him like a sledgehammer.

Holding the itinerary in his hand, Ratchet twisted the margins of paper between his fingers and thumbs. He wondered how he could tell a portly moustachioed London policeman what had happened. And how could he tell that man in the north? Boyle, Boyd? Something like that?

Sighing, Ratchet drew on his cigar again and then blew a circle of smoke into the air towards an extractor fan in the ceiling. He read the preamble to the visit... *'The likelihood of an attack upon the Minister can be construed as a 'low to medium' threat and security measures should be instituted accordingly...'*

Smiling, he realised how he could get out of his predicament.

Ratchet knew how to increase police vigilance, how to increase a police response to a *'threat construed'*. He would increase protection for the Minister without telling police the whole truth about Station Bosphorus. He owed that much to his agents in the Middle East. Ratchet couldn't tell police the whole truth about the government's false company, a British soldier who ran a spy network, and an Arab-Jew agent who thought he worked for Mossad but actually worked for the British Secret Intelligence Service. It would be like signing a death warrant and he wouldn't countenance such an embarrassment. It was fine to have given police very basic details of minor intelligence received, but it was far too risky to reveal specific details of such a conspiracy. It was far too dangerous for police to know about a government sponsored false company and the delivery of cannabis seeds in return for intelligence. Particularly when the Prime Minister himself was spearheading the nation's anti-drug campaign. There was the irony; that politicians pontificated on the virtues of a drug-free society while they knowingly connived with British Intelligence to distribute the very drugs they were pledged to defeat. The media would make fools of the Cabinet and Ratchet would probably be eaten alive for breakfast. And if Namir was successful in his attempt to kill an Israeli Minister on British soil then the whole sordid story would come out because the police would be the first to point their finger and remind everyone that the *'threat construed'* was *'low to medium'*, not *'high'*, as was now the case. In the corridors of power police would insist they had acted on the advice of British Intelligence, and Ratchet knew the itinerary and his threat assessment had been circulated prior to the receipt of the latest intelligence from Bosphorus. The potential political embarrassment had to be killed off, as soon as possible. If not, there would be questions in Whitehall, probably the Houses of Parliament, and his neck would be on the line. The police couldn't be trusted with such information, could they? And he couldn't jeopardise the safety of Station Bosphorus, Codename Nico, Codename Danu, and more importantly; his own neck. Ratchet, keeper of secrets, couldn't trust police with such information: Top Secret Information, Classified Omega Blue.

Reaching for a pen, he pulled the Minister's itinerary towards him. He scored out the words '*low to medium threat*' and boldly substituted the words '*high threat*', which he then underlined in red ink. Satisfied, he thought that was one way to increase a police response to a Minister's visit without jeopardising operations in the Middle East.

But there was another issue, of course. Perhaps there really was something in those pomegranate groves and cypress trees that was known by the others in the intelligence community. Perhaps there really was something out there in the valley of the Bekaa that could be sold on, swapped for the tittle tattle of an intelligence community.

He read again page two. At the bottom of the page he read an annotation from an indexer in his communications centre. For the second time that day a shot of adrenaline charged through his body. According to this annotation at the bottom of the page; there had already been a briefing about this matter. Some of this information was in the hands of the police!

A shrill coldness skimmed across his neck as Ratchet's trembling fingers reached for a telephone.

'Was he alone, Mary?'

Boyd's pencil tapped on his table, impatience, a symptom of an irritable mind.

'Are you sure he was alone? Perhaps there was someone else down there with him in the ditch?'

Swivelling in his chair, he listened to Mary's voice in his ear.

'Was he carrying anything? Did you see him take anything from that ditch?'

McMurray appeared at an open doorway, entered Boyd's office, and stood with a flimsy message in his hand.

'Of course, I appreciate your call... I don't know what I'd do without you... Yes! She's fine... Busy at the moment but she'll be in touch... How are things otherwise up on the estate..? Jo-Jo..? Yes, it's a bad business...'

Sauntering in, McMurray sat on a vacant chair, and crossed his legs.

Boyd bade farewell and replaced the telephone.

'Sorry to bother you,' said McMurray, his pipe blazing a smoke screen. 'But I thought you should see this.' He handed a flimsy over to Boyd's outstretched fingers. 'It's just come through on the wire from the Metropolitan police. Your friends, I presume!'

Boyd ignored McMurray's comment and read the words, which had been sent down an electronic wire to the far reaches of the north. Reaching for the Israeli Minister's itinerary, he compared the words and realised the change. '*...The likelihood of an attack upon the Minister can be construed as a high threat and security measures should be instituted accordingly.*'

No explanation, thought Boyd, but a threat against the Minister had been increased from low to high and the word '***high***' had been underlined and printed in bold italics. Why?

'Have you read this?'

'Yes, I have, Boyd,' said McMurray. 'It changes things. Perhaps you were right at the briefing…'

'How do you mean?' interrupted Boyd.

'I mean perhaps you were right to be rather forceful in your approach to these security measures, Boyd. No matter; it's water under the bridge now. These orders from you friends in London clearly indicate we need to tighten up our procedures. Construed as a high threat! Can't remember ever receiving such a message before. Very strange! Most unusual! A call to your friends in London will probably tell us why.'

'Stop calling them my friends in London, Mac. There's no need. I reckon this will have come from the Foreign Office or the Ministry of Defence. I don't really know. But my stomach tells me we'll be told only that which we need to know.'

'Make a call, Boyd. Rattle some cages. Why is the threat construed now high when yesterday it was low?'

'I know what to do, Mac. I'm not an idiot.'

Boyd picked up the 'phone, dialled a number, waited, and listened to a monotonous tone. Tapping his pencil on the tabletop, Boyd was irritated and, in a sense, a little angry; annoyed that he had not been personally consulted about alterations to an itinerary and additional security measures that would be needed. It would mean that they would have to double up on everything. More officers on look out. More officers searching, protecting, watching. And more money drained from his dwindling budget.

Looking up, Boyd saw McMurray smiling sarcastically.

Jutting his pipe towards Boyd, McMurray said, 'Your problem, I believe, Chief Inspector Operations!'

Boyd's 'phone was answered. The call was diverted to a moustachioed London policeman who could offer no explanation. Boyd crashed his 'phone to its cradle.

'I'll try again later but I suspect the shutters have just been put up. We'll have to live with it, Mac.'

'Most unsatisfactory,' muttered McMurray. He rose from his seat and inspected the bowl of his pipe. 'Mmm... Most unsatisfactory, Boyd. They can't do that to us. We deserve to know why the threat assessment has changed.' He walked away leaving Boyd with a flimsy and a problem. At the door, McMurray turned and said, 'Have you ever thought that your friends might just be clouding the issue a little. Find out why the changes have been made, Boyd. If anything goes wrong with this visit they'll eat you alive. It'll be Chief Inspector Billy Boyd hung out to dry. Not some faceless, nameless bureaucrat in London. Just my thoughts, Boyd. Suit yourself, it's your problem, but it's most unusual. Mmm... Mark my words. Most unusual!'

'You can say that again,' said Boyd.

Studying the itinerary, Boyd examined his plans for protection, for searching, and for watching. Then he looked at his budget, pencilled some financial figures in the margin, and shook his head. He was running out of money. There wasn't going to be enough money in the pot for all that needed to be done. Billy Boyd pursed his lips and crumpled the flimsy in his hand, lightly. Something was going to give soon.

Colleagues of Ratchet were not inclined to describe him as a sombre man. However, he was reputed to approach his paperwork in a silent, dignified manner, often working well into the night when the comparative silence of his office seemed to fine tune his mind. It was as if he devoured each document sent to his desk in a way that sometimes beggared belief. He would dissect each paragraph of a report, separate all the sentences for individual analysis, and taste each word until he understood why every dot and comma had been so assembled by the document's writer. Then, and only then, would he allow himself time to savour each and every morsel of a worthwhile intelligence report. It wasn't at all surprising, therefore, to find him locked into a special branch intelligence report written by a detective sergeant from Newcastle on Tyne.

Headed *'Yasmin-Al-Amin'*, the report told of a young woman who had entered the United Kingdom legally some years earlier. She had been checked by Immigration officials and allowed to remain in Britain for six months. Travelling under a Jordanian passport, it was noted that Yasmin was of Palestinian origin having been born in an Arabic suburb of Jerusalem.

Crumpling the report with his fingers, Ratchet nodded approval at the work of a Geordie copper. The detective sergeant from special branch went on to explain that Yasmin was, in effect, a Stateless person. He revealed how Yasmin had moved to the north east of England and eventually secured full time employment in an estate agent's office. Proving herself proficient, she successfully applied for leave to remain in the United Kingdom indefinitely. The Immigration authorities had agreed with her request following an interview, which revealed nothing untoward. It was not until a series of burglaries occurred that the diligent sergeant became really interested in Yasmin-Al-Amin. Some twenty six burglaries had occurred during a two year period on the north east coast between Blyth and Whitley Bay. It appeared that almost every month a break in occurred at the home of either a serving or retired member of the armed forces. Strange, as it seemed, only items of uniform, occasionally cash, were stolen. But on one occasion a handgun had been plundered and the sergeant had begun his investigation in earnest. Within a couple of weeks, he discovered that the residents of all twenty six burgled homes had, at some time or other, used the estate agent's office where Yasmin worked. Carrying out background enquiries into the staff working there, the sergeant soon discounted any theory of a criminal conspiracy within Yasmin's office. Indeed, her fellow employees were found to be of good character and sound integrity. But Yasmin-Al-Amin? Yasmin was a strange character, solitary at times, and of Stateless origin. Just a hunch, but the sergeant had placed Yasmin under surveillance on her days off. Initially, two officers had been assigned to watch her movements for a total of sixteen hours one weekend. Hardly a major operation, more of a fishing expedition, thought Ratchet, as he absorbed the report.

On the third weekend the sergeant's men reported that Yasmin had travelled to the Metro Centre in Gateshead where she had met a man with Arab looks. She was observed handing over a package and surveillance photographs were taken. The mystery man had been followed to his car and its registration number had been obtained. Driving off in a black Mercedes, the police followed their mystery man to

Newcastle railway station. Here the man met with four men in a black BMW. Three of the men were Arab looking and the fourth appeared to be a young Englishman. Yasmin's package had been handed over to the occupants of the BMW, which had driven off. Police opted to stay with the mystery man in his Mercedes and eventually he had driven south onto the A1 where they allowed him to carry on his journey unhindered. A succession of enquiries through a number of different government agencies revealed Yasmin's male friend to be Mahmoud-Is-Quarti, a chauffeur with an expensive Kensington address. Discreet enquiries revealed Mahmoud drove for an Embassy in west London. Of course, the detective sergeant didn't know it, but Ratchet carried a top secret file on Mahmoud-Is-Quarti. Coloured pink, the A4 file detailed Mahmoud's links to the Palestinian Liberation Organisation.

None of this proved either Yasmin or Mahmoud were involved in burglary. Such conjecture was now insignificant as far as the special branch detective sergeant was concerned. The detective sergeant had set the ball in motion and asked the question now forming in Ratchet's mind. Yasmin? She was a spy, wasn't she? Furthermore, who were the men in the BMW?

Ratchet drummed his fingers on the desk and studied the black and white surveillance photographs. Oh yes! He liked a little intrigue. Ratchet would soon prove she was a spy, sent by the Palestinian Liberation Organisation to infiltrate British society, to listen and to watch, and pass on tittle tattle to her handler, Mahmoud-Is-Quarti. And the men in the BMW? Ratchet looked again at Crosby's messages from Station Bosphorus. Yasif? Namir?

Game on, thought Ratchet with a smile. Game on.

*

11

~ ~ ~

Dateline: 7th September, 2000: Heathrow Airport, London.

Emerging from a carpet of fluffy white cloud, the Israeli pilot checked his instrument panel and intercepted the glidescope that would guide him safely to the threshold of Heathrow's active runway. Moments later, the El Al aircraft touched down to the reassuring screech of rubber kissing tarmac. The Minister of Foreign Affairs for the State of Israel had arrived in the United Kingdom.

Immediately, there was the soft hum of an engine as a narrow wheel-based transporter carried forward its flight of stairs. As soon as the pilot had turned at the end of the runway and taxied to a standstill near the entrance to the VIP terminal, the flight staircase docked with the fuselage and a door swivelled open. First to appear was the Minister's principal personal protection officer. The bodyguard wore a plain dark suit, white shirt, navy blue tie, and an obligatory pair of black rimmed sunglasses. No more than five feet nine inches tall, he was, however, quite bulky round the shoulders and chest. His granite face was finished off with a solid square chin that complimented his rugged features but did little to attract him to the female form.

The bodyguard stood at the top of the staircase in a dark void, which temporarily shielded his charge from public view, as his eyes scanned Heathrow's restricted apron. He saw silent maintenance vans, static fire rescue trucks, and bright red liveried police cars: the ones that carry the elite Metropolitan Police Firearm's Unit. Stepping out into the sunlight, he noted the placid demeanour of assumed security radiating from the assembled vehicles. Then his eyes searched Heathrow's rooftop and sought out the sentries he had insisted upon. There was a nod of quiet approval as he appreciated the presence of armed police where Heathrow's building line met the morning sky. A begrudged smile formed on the bodyguard's lips as his eyes retreated from the rooftops back towards the apron. There were armed police at every conceivable vantage point and he wondered for a moment how many undercover SAS troopers were mingling with the civilians in the arrival and departure lounges. Then, here and there, he took in the profile of a police dog sniffing the ground, and the contours of a machine gun hugging the chest of a bullet-proof vest.

A black Rover with darkened windows ambled forward and stopped at the bottom of El Al's mobile staircase. A passenger door

200

opened and a portly moustachioed gentleman stepped out, smiled, and nodded towards the Israeli bodyguard. The moustache then allowed his jacket to flap open slightly and reveal the butt of a pistol, which protruded from a holster slung casually beneath his armpit.

Israel forced a begrudged smile of approval. The bodyguard's smile seemed to acknowledge London's response to a high threat construed. Without a further glance at the London moustache, he turned into the dark void and said aloud, 'Come!'

As the bodyguard began to descend El Al's flight of stairs, the Israeli Minister appeared at the aircraft door. Dressed in a grey suit and smiling broadly, he followed his bodyguard down the steps to the waiting Rover.

Two more bodyguards, wearing identical dark suits, appeared directly behind the Minister and followed him closely down the stairs. It was as if the Minister was cocooned in safety: one bodyguard in front and two behind, and each step they took were careful and measured: almost rehearsed.

More bodyguards appeared from the body of the aircraft and then there was an entourage of secretaries, aides and hangers-on, carrying briefcases and hand luggage. More cars, some with diplomatic number plates, arrived on the apron behind the black Rover and within minutes the visitors were into the cars and moving off.

Outside the airport, at the entrance to the security cordon, two police motor cyclists slid in front of a signed police car and the Rover containing Israel's Minister. Gear changes and the raised drone of car engines announced the high speed escort to Chequers, the country retreat of the British Prime Minister.

In a nearby car park, Namir sat in his hire car: a Vauxhall.

Watching, he switched on his dashboard radio, unfolded his dark driving spectacles, placed them on the bridge of his nose, and took it all in.

Forming a rough circle with his thumb and index finger, Namir extended his arm before him and trapped the image of the black Rover in a circle made by his fingers. Then Namir allowed his index finger to drop as he reduced the circle and focused his eye on the rear offside window of the black Rover: the place where the Minister was seated. Moving his arm, in tune with the Rover, Namir laughed and under his breath quipped, 'Chicken shit, English! Easy, but only when I'm ready.'

As the convoy gathered speed towards a roundabout near Heathrow's exit, Namir waited for the last of the entourage to pass before firing his car engine and coolly, casually, joining the traffic flow.

The Minister of Foreign Affairs for the State of Israel had arrived in Britain. Despite lavish security, his arrival was quiet and without pomp or circumstance, but the laid back Namir was watching and waiting, studying the police response to a threat construed, and now the assassin from Bekaa Valley was following the man he intended to kill.

Pressing the digits on his mobile 'phone, Boyd engaged the encrypted mode. 'Where are you now?' He angled his head and held the 'phone closer to his ear... 'Mary 'phoned. I need you in the park...'

Shaking his head, Boyd said, 'No! I need you there now. Right now!'

He shook his head again. 'No, forget that. Trust me. Follow my instincts. Get into that park. The target is a set of planks over a ditch...'

Boyd listened and then said, 'That's right. Wooden planks! Listen to me carefully. Near the rickety old bridge you'll find...'

A short time later, a rusting old van, creaking on its cumbersome springs, lumbered to a standstill near the cross-roads on the outskirts of the estate. The van's indicators flashed and then the vehicle slowly turned right and made its lethargic way towards the park and a rickety old bridge.

The van's driver yawned. She was just a slip of a girl really: the young woman who was driving the rusting heap through Carlisle.

Ugly black smoke belched from an upper bedroom window as raging flames lashed a blood-chilling devastating tongue outward and upwards towards a black plastic gutter and a sloping tiled roof. On the weed strewn path of a barren garden below, a young fireman slowly retreated from the burning derelict as his hose slithered and snaked behind him while he fought to contain the terrifying inferno.

In the park, behind the derelict house, a crowd had gathered. Only thirty strong, but growing by the minute; it was baying callously at the collection of fire engines that had gathered on the streets near the heart of the estate. A youth with an unruly mop of ginger hair proudly stepped forward to the cheers of his drug-crazy friends. Screaming and chanting his nickname, 'Ginger! Ginger! Go on, Ginger,' the mob was demented; for this was the day on which hollow heroes were made. An empty vodka bottle was produced and filled with stolen petrol. A lighted taper was inserted into the bottle's neck and then Ginger ran down a cut between two derelict houses and threw his missile towards a fire engine. Smashing on the ground, well short of its target, burning liquid perished on the stark tarmac as the crazy deranged mob jeered at the hapless Ginger.

As if in competition with Ginger, an older man, with a shaven head and a drooping beer belly, stepped forward. 'Like this!' he shouted, and promptly hurled half a building brick into the windscreen of a fire engine.

There was a whoop of laughter and a raucous cheer from the crowd as the Fire Chief immediately pulled his men back to the centre of the road, away from the burning derelicts, away from the raging fire and the baying mob of lunatics.

Suddenly, the mob was out of the park and into the roadway, bearing down on the fire-fighters and their emergency tenders.

There was an angry panic in the air when the Fire Chief bellowed into his radio. Then a siren was heard and a posse of dark blue police vehicles arrived at the scene, lights flashing, sirens blaring, and it was only lunch time: the pubs were hardly open.

Disgorging their passengers, the vans lined up, three a breast, and trundled slowly towards the mob. Behind the vans walked Boyd's team, but Boyd was nowhere to be seen. He was absent and always seemed to be busy elsewhere when the pressure was mounting, or so a sergeant in one of the vans had said. Boyd's unit carried circular Perspex shields and wore blue NATO style crash helmets, but they seemed to be holding back, not looking for confrontation at all. Indeed, while sheltering behind their police vans, Billy Boyd's Bobbies seemed to be positively out of the game. They were plodding along at a leisurely pace, too few, and too late.

Slowly, the vans moved forward, protecting their men and women as they gradually inched down the street towards the growing crowd. Smoke swirled skyward and nearby flames licked at another rooftop as the fire grew. Then a hail of bottles and stones were thrown from the mob into the police ranks. Another windscreen exploded and with a whoop and a cheer the mob turned and ran into the park with Boyd's men apparently happy just to clear the streets, to frighten the offenders away by their mere presence.

Things were getting out of hand and the timid police response had been noted by the mob, Yasif, Aden and Rollo.

Stepping back into the shadows of a nearby derelict house, Yasif nodded quietly to an older, shaven-headed man who ran next to a ginger-haired youth. Smiles were exchanged and a thumbs up sign was made by Ginger as Yasif watched the police vans stop on the tarmac with the pedestrian pace of their plodders behind.

In control, Yasif was ahead of the game and ahead of the police as he scuttled quietly from the area, gone from view, and Boyd was still nowhere to be seen…

Chequer's black iron gates opened wide as two police motor cycles peeled off and the tyres of the lead patrol car bit deep into the ashen grey gravel. The security convoy had arrived. As a black Rover, containing Israel's Minister for Foreign Affairs, headed towards the Prime Minister's welcoming committee, a dark grey Vauxhall came to a standstill on the approaches to the famous country retreat.

Namir checked the Vauxhall's mileage and then looked at his wristwatch. Pulling the road map and a pencil from a glove compartment, Namir traced the route from Heathrow to Chequers. Amazingly, he thought, the route was reasonably straightforward. It was more or less as straight as the crow flies. There had been no deviations and no silly attempts to ward off any would-be followers. The security convoy had relied purely on flashing headlights, blue beacons, sirens, high speed, and arrogance - a fatal concoction enjoyed by police the world over; and exploited only by men like Namir: killers of men.

On his map, on the route, Namir wrote the location the convoy had passed every fifteen minutes. With the intervals clearly denoted on his map, Namir removed two black and white passport-sized photographs resting behind the sun visor. He took one last look at the snapshots of Yasmin and Mahmoud before placing them in the pull-out ashtray. He flicked a cigarette lighter and ignited the edge of one of the photographs. Within seconds the pair were burnt to ashes. Namir knew the faces well enough and had committed them to his memory. Depressing the clutch, he selected first gear, smiled, and made for the nearby main road.

Very soon, he would visit the site of one of his options: the railway bridge over the dual carriageway. There was little doubt that when Israel's Minister of Foreign Affairs returned to Heathrow, then the same return route would be taken from Chequers. Situated some five hundred yards from the dual carriageway, Namir had selected the perfect place to kill a man. As the Minister's Rover slowed and turned from the main road onto the slip road, there, that's where he would do it! That's where he would pull the trigger! For just a second or two the Rover would be crawling at a very low speed when the ninety degree turn at the junction was negotiated. That was the spot Namir would take the Jew's life. One shot fired from a throw away sniper's rifle dropped at the scene; then a short sprint down the railway line, over the wire fence, and into the Vauxhall parked on a country lane. He would be gone, and the Minister would be dead.

Namir's finger and thumb twiddled with the volume control on his car radio. Loud music boomed from the dashboard as he drove away with the killing ground firmly in his mind. It was the chosen ground and he had made the choice.

By early evening, the mob was again orchestrated. Much larger now, the mob appeared briefly, threw stones at shop windows, hurled rocks at passing cars, and withdrew like lightening when police vans appeared.

They were like desert jackals, that mob, hiding amongst alleyways and walkways then rushing out into the open and savaging their victim. Like jackals, they plundered, burnt, and vilified, and from the battlements of Carlisle's castle, three miles away, two men and a dog stood as a thin haze of black smoke gradually fanned out across the estate.

'We should be there, Cross,' said Bannerman, looking out towards the estate and a ravaging tongue of flame that stretched into a twilight sky. 'Boyd needs to get it together and put that bird out of his mind.'

'Which bird?' asked Cross.

'He was talking to some woman on the 'phone the other day when we were in his office. Randy sod thinks I didn't hear but he's always on the 'phone to her.'

'Boyd said, no,' reflected Sergeant Cross, his eyes also watching the black smoke and swirling flames that seemed to threaten the very existence of the approaching night.

'That was before he'd lost control,' argued Bannerman, annoyed. 'Very soon he'll need every man he can get hold of, but he'd be the last one to say that,'

'And when that happens he'll call us,' replied Cross. 'Until then we do as we're told and get on with this search.'

'Come on, let's get up there and get stuck into them. We can do it!'

'No,' mused Cross, quietly. 'We'll follow Boyd's orders. I'll back him for now. Come on, I'm going to do the perimeter walls again.'

'We should be there!'

Sergeant Cross ignored him, failing to respond.

'Rocky! He could have had Rocky taken away from you and put down. But he didn't. Doesn't that count for anything, Cross?'

Cross stepped away, knelt down and fingered Rocky's neck, and then walked away along the battlements with Rocky at his heel.

Bannerman turned to follow, to restrain Cross, to hold him and shake him and make him see sense, but he let him go. Thoughtful, Bannerman looked again at the smoke smudging the sky and a ribbon of flame gradually painting an awesome array of orange across the rooftops of the new estate. No wonder it was the place where no one wanted to live. Then Bannerman, standing by the battlements, clenched his fist and hammered it down onto the mortar of a forgotten century. 'I should be there,' he said, words lost on the wind that suddenly whispered from the Castle Keep.

Trying to smile an air of confidence and authority was never easy, particularly when you knew your back was against the wall and the Press were baying for your blood. Yet with a straight eye into a television camera, Boyd answered his critic, 'No, I don't agree with your comments. This young man did not die at the hands of the police. Indeed! I'm satisfied that Jo-Jo's death is drug related and, furthermore, I expect to make arrests very shortly.'

A microphone threatened Boyd's lower lip once more as a television reporter stepped forward and pierced the air with a further question…

'Of course,' replied Boyd. 'We take all allegations made against police officers very seriously, but I can categorically say that these insinuations are false'

Another question from another camera angle…

'I have no intention of suspending either of the officers concerned.'

Another journalist spoke, stabbing to the heart of the matter…

'Bannerman and Cross remain on duty. In fact, they're assigned elsewhere, but the dog that you mention is not owned by the police. Can I make that quite clear?'

And then there was a babble of questions, hurting, wounding, pointing, twisting, and searching for a story for tomorrow's front page…

'I give you my word, gentlemen. I will hunt down Jo-Jo's killers and bring them to justice. In the meantime, I ask that members of the public stay indoors and allow us to proceed with our enquiries.'

The babble encircled him, bedevilled him, and then the subject changed abruptly as Boyd felt the pressure and wiped a drop of sweat from his forehead...

'I'd hardly call it a riot, but yes it may be a public response to the alleged manner in which Jo-Jo died. I prefer to think that evil forces are behind an unruly element hell bent on causing trouble... Yes, it is an appropriate time to call for calm and good order... Yes! Force will be met with force if calm is not restored.'

More questions raged, more persistent...

'Yes,' said Boyd. 'I meant that. Force will be met by force. Now, if you'll excuse me, ladies and gentlemen...'

Boyd, besieged and bewildered by the media, pulled a cable from his lapel, severed his communications link with the television network, and walked away from the cavalcade of news people. Shrugging, exasperated, Boyd took a sigh that was somewhere between relief and frustration.

A camera lowered, a journalist smirked and pointed skyward, and then a reporter remonstrated with his network colleague as Boyd walked away with the smoke and fire raging in the backdrop.

Out there, in the dark, the buzz box was hell. There was just a frantic jabber of electronic garbage as the television networks perplexed the electronics in her old rusting van. Louise activated her infra-red cameras and settled down to watch a rickety old bridge across a shallow stream that led to the Eden. The video screens flickered with static and honed in to the deserted bridge of wooden planks. Boring! It was like a played-out soap that had run its course and was waiting for the plug to be pulled. There was no fire here, no petrol bombs, no shouting and swearing. It was just a totally silent existence, lying in the belly of a surveillance van.

Jeopardise his sources in the Middle East? Never! Not for anyone. Ratchet knew Namir was the kind of fanatic who would take pleasure in becoming a martyr for the cause. But Ratchet wouldn't tell the Geordie copper who had uncovered Yasmin and Mahmoud who they really were. And, for that matter, he wouldn't let on to Boyd in Cumbria what was about to happen.

Ratchet's hand moved across his desk and unlocked a small red velvet box. From inside the box he removed two small Chinese exercise balls. Nimbly, he played the balls between his thumb and fingers and watched the two balls rotate in his palm. Balance, it was all a question of balance, thought Ratchet. Israel's current government was seen to be out of favour with it own electorate. Indeed, the government was seen as positively dove-like. All talk of peace. No sign of a skirmish with the Arabs, just posturing and hot air. Now the Israeli opposition? They were a different kettle of fish, much more hawk-like. Yes, that was the key issue in the whole matter, wasn't it, thought Ratchet. Balance. Doves against the hawks. First you back one and then the other. By so doing you could play them of against themselves and maintain a balance in the Middle East. One had to assert western influence wherever one could. Smoothly, the exercise balls rolled across his finger. Perfect balance.

*

12
~ ~ ~

Dateline: 8th September, 2000: The Estate, Carlisle.

Small and compact, Boyd's mobile police station was little more than a portable cabin bolted to the rear of a flat back wagon, which had been painted regulation police blue. Nevertheless, a short flight of well-worn, grimy metal steps led to a reasonably sized office area. Inside, a handful of detectives were busy sifting through reams of papers: witness statements, press cuttings, completed questionnaires and house to house enquiry documents. At the rear of the makeshift incident room a bank of telephones occupied Boyd's murder squad and there was a dry white-board screwed to a wall. Photographs of Jo-Jo and details of his last known movements were scrawled on this board. A series of dotted red marker lines connected Jo-Jo's photograph to the titles *'Forensic'* and *'Associates'*, and in a deep Royal blue colour someone had neatly written *'Suspects'*, with a list of names in black beneath. Next to the word *'Forensic'*, a photograph of a .38 calibre handgun occupied space beneath the title *'Murder Weapon'*: a fact no doubt gleaned from a ballistics report identifying the type of bullet responsible for ending Jo-Jo's life. A police radio whispered from one corner of Boyd's cabin and there was a soft hum from a mobile generator, which was situated underneath the vehicle and powered Boyd's unit with an array of wires. On a work surface dominating the interior of Boyd's office a collection of plastic trays, full of paperwork, and half a dozen mugs of stale coffee and cold tea witnessed the mad methodology of murder investigation in the late twentieth century. Yet it was exactly what Boyd had ordered: a versatile cubicle that could be moved quickly to any given geographical location where a team of officers needed to work close to a murder scene. In this case, it was situated right at the core of the investigation.

When his 'phone rang, Boyd seized the instrument and listened to the Chief's voice complaining about lack of progress: 'Why haven't these foreigner types been arrested and charged with Jo-Jo's murder? We must centre on the need to look positive in the eyes of Joe Public and achieve a good result in double quick time. We need to adopt a multi agency approach to the investigation,' said the Chief. 'There's a saying, isn't there? To disperse responsibility is to dilute accountability,' offered the Chief.

When, eventually, and without losing his delicate temper, Boyd asked for additional manpower, there was a silent interlude on the other end of the 'phone. When Boyd asked for a Press Liaison Officer to be seconded to deal with the media on his behalf, to take the pressure off his shoulders, there was a low grunt followed by a lengthy sermon on how to juggle responsibility during this crucial time of insufficient resources. Then there was only silence and Boyd slammed the infernal telephone down on its cradle and swore under his breath.

No sooner had he dealt with the top man when McMurray rang: 'The Chief will be ringing you if he's not already had a word. I've told him what I would have done had I been in your shoes. He's after your scalp. You'd best get Bannerman and Cross out of it completely, Boyd. You need to prove them innocent beyond any shadow of doubt, not just some fancy police fingerprint expert espousing about marks in blood scrawled on a wall. That's not enough for the Coroner! Come up with the goods or it's back to jeans and tee-shirts.'

And then McMurray had laughed down the 'phone and Boyd hadn't the energy to hit back right away. McMurray too had a list of awkward, penetrating questions from the local media and there was a deep sense of rivalry apparent when McMurray again made it clear that he'd told the Chief how he would deal with the situation. They'd argued again. Not so much argued as sparred, in the verbal sense, and neither had won nor lost.

All the time Boyd was talking on the 'phone, he knew nothing was being done. Boyd felt exasperated as he finally banished McMurray's voice and pushed away the telephone. Damn machine, he thought. Damn those interfering, meddlesome twerps. They were more interested in their own agendas than gathering the truth. Or was he wrong and just being a pratt to himself?

Pinching the bridge of his nose with his finger and thumb, Boyd seemed to drive out unwanted fatigue gathering in the corner of his eyes. Sighing, he dropped a pile of papers into a vacant tray and turned towards the sound of footsteps rattling the metal steps. Bannerman and Cross had just arrived.

'We're getting nowhere, boys. It's just a long plod and there's no light at the end of the tunnel. Plenty of suspects though but no hard evidence. Least, not enough for a conviction. I think I know Jo-Jo inside out by now but we're no nearer to catching his killer than when we started. I can tell you what he had for breakfast and I can tell you his life style inside out; but the last twenty four hours of his life still remain a total mystery.'

'It's the usual way, isn't it?' offered Bannerman. 'Any nearer to finding those three foreigners mentioned on the briefing board?'

'Not yet,' replied Boyd. 'But I've got an observation post set up on one of their drug stashes. I'm jut keeping my fingers crossed they show soon. They look a good bet for this but we'll know better when we've got them inside.'

'An observation post! Whereabouts?' asked Cross.

'The Intelligence Unit is looking after it, Cross. You don't need to know. Sorry, but you know my rules!'

Cross nodded as Bannerman asked, 'Anyway, boss, you called us in. How can we help you?'

Boyd took a mouthful of black sugary coffee and said, 'I wondered how the search teams were getting on at the museum? I need to keep a handle on this damn visit tomorrow. I can't forget that, just because we've got a murder and sporadic rioting on our hands. Despite what others may think, I actually know what I'm doing.'

'But we're stretched to the limit, boss,' replied Bannerman.

'Like a piece of knicker elastic waiting to snap. Why don't you tell the Chief that next time he stops by, and McMurray, for that matter, tell them what you really think?'

Bannerman's eyelids rose slightly as he caught Cross's eye.

'Sorry! My problems, not yours,' apologised Boyd. 'What about the search teams, Sergeant Cross?'

'Fine! They're on their third rummage and we've just put one team onto doing the outside of the building. You know, litter bins, post boxes, anywhere a package might be left innocently.'

'Good!'

'What's more, the bomb disposal boys have just arrived from the army and they've gone up to the museum to advise our lads.'

'Excellent! Now what about that route? Do you boys know it backwards yet?'

Bannerman stepped forward, nodded and said, 'Like it was the back of my hand, boss.'

Boyd smiled approvingly as Bannerman handed over a sketch and added, 'this is the Minister's route and here's where Cross and I suggest you strengthen our weaknesses with some additional uniforms.'

Bannerman unfolded his plan, smoothed it across Boyd's desk and said, 'Here and here!' Jabbing at his paper with his fingers, he continued, 'The convoy will be ambling at slow speed at this point and we need a uniform at those traffic lights to get us through without any hold ups. We're not stopping for anything!'

Casting his eyes quickly over Bannerman's sketch, Boyd nodded his agreement. 'Okay, the motor bike escort can look after that.'

'Fine!' said Bannerman. 'Anything else?'

'The murder weapon's history is starting to take shape,' offered Boyd. 'The gun was stolen from a Major Foxton's house on the north east coast near St. Mary's lighthouse. That's somewhere near Whitley Bay, I understand. His house was burgled earlier in the year. He's ex army. I've sent CID to interview him and speak with the local police. Something may come of it, who knows?' '

'Sir!'

Boyd turned sharply towards the radio operator and engaged her quizzically.

'They've started again. The patrol units report a large group of youths - one hundred plus - on the edge of the estate. They're apparently armed with pick axe handles and two yobbos are carrying a case of milk bottles.'

'Petrol bombs?' suggested Cross.

'I would guess so,' agreed Boyd. 'Radio the Response Unit to attend and bring those other teams onto the estate. Tell them to rendezvous with me near the old post office. We'll go in mob-handed this time. It's about time we sorted this crazy mob out once and for all.'

'About time,' smiled Bannerman.

As the radio operator flicked a switch and spoke into her mouthpiece, Boyd collected his hat from a coat peg and stood up. 'Come on, boys. Let's take a look, shall we?'

'Us?' asked Bannerman. 'Us?'

'Yes! Us!' snapped Boyd. 'Come on!'

Stepping out of the mobile police station, Boyd, Bannerman and Cross made their way towards a police van parked nearby. There was a click of Cross's fingers and Rocky scrambled from beneath the metal steps and leapt into the rear of the police van.

Shaking his head, Boyd said, 'The dog's not driving. Okay?'

'I'll drive,' explained Cross.

'Can you smell it?' asked Bannerman, pausing for a moment as he looked towards the estate.

Boyd stopped in his tracks and took in a deep breath. 'Yeah! I know what you mean.'

'It's the smell of trouble,' said Bannerman.

Heading north with the Potteries behind him and the concrete jungle of Lancashire's motorway system ahead, Namir slid into top gear and overtook a line of slow moving vehicles. An authoritarian male voice spoke excitedly from a radio embedded in Namir's dashboard: The winds were dying; a bout of clear skies and a warm front was heading in from the west.

Carving through traffic, Namir drummed his fingers on a leather steering wheel and casually glanced at his mobile 'phone occupying the vacant passenger seat. His 'phone was switched on, illuminating the way north, pointing towards the serenity of Cumbria's lakes as Namir drove north to kill a man.

Cramped in a red fluorescent light! Louise was so confined with her legs stiff and her mouth dry. All night she'd watched and listened, and all night she'd nothing to report to Boyd. Now she fought sleep as the full light of day invaded the dead ground in front of her rusting grey van. Perfectly placed, Louise carefully caressed a dial and expertly panned her cameras the full length of a pathway that led to the wooden planks, which crossed over a shallow stream. Nothing! A few rabbits had caught her eye during the night and one or two night birds had pecked at the soil bordering the weed-strewn path. Perhaps they'd extracted an errant worm or a juicy insect for a late night feast. Then, when night had died and her infra-red cameras had done their bit, Mary had announced early morning with a walk through the park with her Alsatian. Her Alsatian had barked at a rabbit and jolted Louise's sense to come alive once more as she began to slip into a careless doze.

Yet Mary hadn't stopped at Louise's old van, wouldn't know Louise was watching from the belly of a broken down, clapped-out wreck; wouldn't be allowed to know such a thing. Mary was in her house now, at home, watching from behind her bolted door and drawn curtains the angry crowds gathering in her street. Peering from behind a tired-looking, potted Shamrock plant, Mary was frightened when she heard the mob chanting Bannerman's name!

On waste ground near an old post, not far from a launderette, Boyd listened to his radio reports and then swiftly removed a map of the estate. Unfolding the map, he spread it out across the bonnet of a police van.

'Four vans, four teams. Team one... Insert here. Team two... Here.'

They crowded round, listening to his plan, watching his finger strike the map.

'Team three... Here... Four... Here... The rioters are making towards the park. We'll cut them off there... At the cross-roads... Surround them... Hit them hard and hit them fast. Disperse them! Then I want lots of arrests. Okay?'

There was a mumble of uncertainty from among the ranks and then Cross asked, 'You with us, boss? I mean out front, boss?'

'Right at the front, gents!'

There was an exchange of glances from among those in the unsure ranks of blue and then an audible murmur was heard: 'Now we'll see what he's made of.'

The remark was lost on Boyd who was studying his plan.

'If he's out front, he's not undercover.' A snide remark heard but then gone.

'Why four different insertion points, boss?' asked Bannerman.

'Perfect planning prevents piss poor performance, Bannerman,' smiled Boyd.

'Are you taking the Pee's, boss?'

Then there was sudden laughter and smiles as Bannerman and Boyd seemed to capture a needless moment of banter.

'No boys,' replied Boyd, 'I'm taking the ground. Come on. Let's do it.'

There was a throaty growl of engines firing into life and then four vans began to shake gently as Boyd's squad loaded themselves into their vans, fully briefed as to the operation about to take place.

Cross floored the accelerator pedal as Rocky yapped in his ear and wagged his tail ferociously.

'A little music, Mister Boyd?' ventured Sergeant Cross.

'Why not, indeed, Mister Cross?' quipped Boyd. 'A symphony, perhaps.'

A flick of a switch by Cross activated a blue rotating light and a powerful noisy klaxon. The convoy drove off, lights flashing, klaxons blaring, and the tail of a dog flapping against a window pane immediately behind Cross's head.

'Sorry, it's Rocky's favourite,' quipped Cross.

Louise heard the footsteps' first!

A gentle padding sound on the pathway into the park invaded her ears from the directional sound location system. Louise adjusted a dial and then three men came into view on one of her tiny video screens in the belly of the van. Walking quietly, purposefully, the three men were headed towards the wooden planks across the stream. Suddenly she was alive as she strained her eyes to identify the trio. Sweating - God, she was so warm in the tightness of her van. A bead of sweat formed on her forehead and then smoothed across the furrow of her brow before sloping towards her high cheekbone…

On the edge of the park, Boyd's van slewed to a halt in the centre of the road. Cross wrenched its handbrake on tight and then immediately threw his hands up to shield his face as a building brick unexpectedly blew the windscreen into smithereens. The brick collided with Boyd's face, glancing his cheek. He gasped in pain when, at the same time, a sliver of glass nicked his chin and a trickle of blood ran towards his throat.

Then a ginger haired youth appeared from no more than ten feet from where Boyd was sat and hurled another brick towards Boyd's van. The brick fell short of its target and it bounced from the bonnet onto the ground.

'Out' screamed Boyd, dabbing blood from his throat.

There was a rush of sliding doors and a twang of plastic riot shields as Boyd's squad hurriedly gathered at the rear of the van.

'Time to rock and roll,' shouted Bannerman.

'Oh no!' replied Cross as Rocky scampered away from the men.

Hidden behind the open doors of the van, Boyd's squad sheltered from a barrage of missiles that drilled downwards from Ginger's direction.

'Line it up,' ordered Boyd.

Suddenly there were no more mumblings of irritation or smirking faces as a dozen blue uniforms extended their shields before them. Leather gauntlets smoothed into dark blue fatigues. Lightweight calf-length black boots awkwardly cushioned the ground as Boyd removed an old fashioned wooden truncheon from a side pocket in his trousers.

'Visors down!' ordered Boyd

There was an abrupt rush of adrenaline darting through the bloodstream when it became obvious that this was no drill. It wasn't a drill. No, it was the real thing and the air was dark with flying bottles and stones that rattled the roof of Boyd's van.

Then, growing loudly, the sound of a jeering mob baying for Bannerman's blood was heard.

Mystically, the van began to roll from left to right on its springs. Surprised, aghast, suddenly frightened by the unknown, Boyd reluctantly retreated backwards as the springs of the van squealed in anger and then, angrily, the nearside wheels of the van lifted from the ground.

Sweat rolling down her cheeks, Louise focused her dials and her cameras, and honed into the target she had penetrated.

'Gold stud… Left ear… Male.' She was whispering; her voice had let her down in the final triumph of her task. She coughed, tried to find some tone in her voice, and then snapped 'Shit!' into her microphone. She was on the wrong radio net!

Nothing for it, no alternative, she would have to break into the main net and contact Boyd right away. Flicking the radio switches, Louise pressed a red button on her console and delivered a high-pitched radio signal into Boyd's ear piece.

Boyd, far away, was in the wrong place again! Boyd, far away, was nowhere near the park, near the wooden planks, which crossed a shallow stream that carried three olive-coloured men. Boyd had been looking for them, had told her to go on target twenty four hours until she found them. Now she'd found the olive-coloured men and Boyd wasn't responding.

'Second class man. Second class Boyd!' She screamed into the radio.

Louise released an emergency signal and began talking into her radio. 'Message for Chief Inspector Boyd from Lima One… Urgent… Male answering description of target one…. Middle Eastern extraction, Arab looking, swarthy, five feet eight inches tall, proportionate build… There are three of them but this one has a gold stud in his left ear and he's carrying a black plastic bag… It's a gun… I'm sure it's a rifle and it's…'

Abruptly, the radio net collapsed and her video screens went blank. The red fluorescent light died, plunging the buzz box into darkness. Pitch black, she frantically fingered her dials and twiddled the switches on her console. But the buzz box was dead and there was a tongue of flame lashing violently at the van's underbelly.

The flame had burnt yellow at first, from a Molotov cocktail thrown minutes ago: a petrol bomb, which had been thrown from the edge of the park by a mindless moron who had selected a rusting, old, clapped-out, abandoned van as his target. Now a tongue of flame beneath Louise's van grew to a deep orange that merged into an evil blue edge where fire scorched the underbelly of her van. The grass beneath Louise's van was smudged black as smoke began to engulf every little hidey-hole that cradled her. She didn't know it then, couldn't know what was happening beneath her, but Louise was slowly being burnt alive. Beads of sweat grew like a stream of water on her neck and soaked her skin with cold fear.

'Don't you go worrying on PC Bannerman, Mister Boyd. It's just his way, his way of announcing his arrival so to speak,' offered Sergeant Cross with a wry smile, buttoning his chin strap and tightening his black leather gloves, workmanlike. 'Do you like music, Mister Boyd?'

'Aaaargh... Aaaargh....'

Bannerman's breathtaking cry bounced from the walls of the van and resonated into the estate where no-one wanted to live.

And then louder still... 'Aaaargh... Aaaargh...'

It was his battle cry. It was Bannerman: loathsome, frightening and formidable. When Bannerman's voice boomed from inside the police van, the chassis rocked from left to right in an awesome, terrifying display of controlled agility. It was as if the van was alive, had taken on a life of its own, with a rocking, rolling gait and a voice of thunder booming from within.

'Holy shit!' mouthed Ginger. 'What's that?'

A half brick slid from his slender fingers and fell to the ground as Ginger stepped backwards and his face turned pale.

Open-mouthed, Boyd heard Bannerman screaming, saw the rolling van, and saw a ginger haired rioter apparently stopped in his tracks.

'That's rock and roll, Mister Boyd,' said a deadpan Cross. 'Old fashioned music but it brings a tear to your eye, does it not?'

'Why didn't you tell me about Bannerman's party piece, Cross?'

Looking directly ahead, without so much as a glance at Boyd, Cross replied, 'Rules! You didn't need to know the rules, Mister Boyd.'

Boyd chuckled. 'Do you ever get cross, Mister Cross?'

'Not so you'd notice,' replied Cross, turning towards the van.

Inside the van, Bannerman had planted both feet into the angle where floor and side panels meet. Similarly, his hands, wide apart, gripped the underside of the roof. Fingers splayed out, his body gyrated from left to right and his muscles bulged, orchestrating the movement of the van. Then his voice unleashed its monumental cry and his muscles finally relaxed as the tilting of the van gradually subsided and came to a standstill.

Blowing out hard, Bannerman jumped from the van dragging his shield and fastening his helmet above close-cropped ginger fuzz.

'Ready, Mister Boyd,' shouted Bannerman.

'I'm glad you're on my side,' replied Boyd, shaking his head. 'Maybe the Chief and McMurray were right after all.'

'Pardon?'

'Forget it, Bannerman. '

Bannerman walked into line and then Boyd marched to the front and beat his shield with his truncheon.

'Forward!' ordered Boyd.

'Where are the others? The other three units aren't here,' mumbled a voice in the line. 'Why doesn't that stupid pratt wait for the others?'

Rocky barked and fell in behind Cross, bounding and yelping.

'Forward!' Another beat from Boyd's truncheon pounding plastic.

'They'll be here,' growled Bannerman.

'Are you sure?' Another grumbling, mumbling agnostic.

'Forward!' ordered Boyd.

Boyd was ten steps ahead of everyone else with his visor down and his truncheon beating against the inside of his shield, and Rocky was barking and scampering at the rear of a line of marching men.

'Forward!' ordered Boyd, oblivious to those behind him as the beat of his truncheon on the shield grew.

When Ginger and the mob saw the van rocking and rolling, they didn't know what to make of it. When they saw Bannerman, all six feet five inches of solid muscle and gleaming skull, they were immediately apprehensive. Some were even strangely terrified at the sight and sound of a screaming giant. For most of the rioters, Bannerman had only been a name fed to them: a name that had been flashed across a television screen and a newspaper headline. They didn't all know him; just the true locals amongst the crowd of demented. Now Bannerman was real and he was physical; oh so physical; and he was walking forward, not running away. He really was a big hard man! When the mob saw Boyd marching with his truncheon beating out the tempo on the inside of his shield, they couldn't work out what was happening. They'd never seen anything like it before. They were dumbfounded and leaderless and suddenly they were all caught on the hop.

'Now!' screamed Boyd, setting off at a run. 'Forward!'

An agnostic march became a reluctant trot and then their trot became a full-bloodied gallop as police stormed towards the rioters and the cross-roads where Boyd had planned their trap. Boyd's beating of his shield grew louder and the shuffle of leather boots on tarmac became a pounding in their brain. Rocky barked, scampered, wagged his tail, and then barked again. It was as if Boyd was out there in front leading his men while Rocky trailed behind the line of shields snapping and barking at those pounding heels. It was comical in a way, almost farcical; with a stressed-out, jaded, one-time undercover officer trying his best to drill a downhearted pack of disbelieving men. But then they'd found their leaders that day. Suddenly they were frightening and magnificent as they bore down on the mob with their truncheons outstretched before them and their shields challenging the very presence of the rioters.

Then there was a symphony of klaxon's and sirens filling the air as three other vans lurched into the streets and disgorged their passengers at the cross-roads. Trapped inside Boyd's square, there was nowhere to run as Boyd's precise and perfect planning decimated the unruly.

Ginger was first to fall, pushed aside by Boyd's shield and trampled underfoot by Bannerman.

'Forward!' Still Boyd blasted orders, as yard by yard they took back the ground, his truncheon raining down, his free fist punching flesh, his whole body committed to the onslaught.

A milk bottle smashed on tarmac! Burning fuel escaped its stubby neck, flaring wildly, attacking a line of advancing blue uniforms. A long shield was thrown to the ground, smothering the flames and denying oxygen that fed a sinuous fire. In a matter of seconds, the fire was dead. With a spirit of vitality, they were on the move again.

'Forward! Forward!' But now it was Bannerman, Cross and Boyd's agnostics who were shouting the charge.

As their speed gathered there were no more petrol bombs flaring on tarmac and no more shields thrown to the ground. Yard by yard, Boyd's line of shields closed with the mob. Within minutes, Boyd's square had compressed the rioting mob into a hapless bunch of lack-lustre nomads. As police closed with rioters, a score of arrests were made. But the square eventually broke and fierce hand to hand fighting followed as a posse of police reinforcements, led by McMurray, arrived at the scene.

McMurray jumped from a Transit van and almost tripped on the kerbside when he landed. Regaining his balance, his first response was to point at Bannerman and Cross and try to mouth an admonishment from a set of lips that had seemed to cease functioning. When McMurray saw Rocky prancing and barking, his bottom jaw dropped and he shook his head in disbelief. McMurray was speechless; but then he pointed towards Boyd. McMurray's arm was outstretched, following Boyd, waving at his rival who was now running away from the fighting down a cutting towards the park. When, at last, McMurray found his voice, he shouted, 'Bannerman, Cross… Boyd… The radio…Who the hell is Lima One?'

Disregarding McMurray, Boyd was already running at full pelt into the park with his truncheon waving and his shield flapping in the breeze.

Bannerman and Cross saw Boyd's fleeing figure and watched him run down the cut into the park.

'The radio… McMurray's on about the radio,' shouted Cross. His middle finger relocated a radio ear-piece lodged in his right ear. 'Someone from the Intelligence Unit has hit the emergency signal… Boyd…'

'It's Boyd's observation post,' screamed Bannerman.

They were like sprinters out of the blocks chasing Boyd through the melee into the park towards a slender wisp of smoke that drifted skyward.

Boyd could smell fumes from the old grey van as he bounded down a weed-strewn path as fast as his legs would carry him. Dropping his shield, too heavy to carry, he increased his speed. Unclipping his helmet, awkward, he threw it down and screamed, 'Louise!'

Flames licked at the underneath of Louise's van, encircled its side panels, and melted the rubber seals that protected its windows.

His truncheon bounced from the van's front windscreen as the build-up of smoke inside seemed to deny access to a screaming Boyd. He clenched his fist, drew back, and punched a side window with all the strength he could muster. There was a shower of glass when the window immediately surrendered and Boyd hurriedly reached inside and unlocked the door handle, blood seeping with cut.

'Louise!' screamed Boyd again, delving inside the van.

Bannerman and Cross arrived as Boyd began coughing and spluttering. Pulling at a carpet in the rear compartment of the van, ignoring swirling smoke and acrid fumes, Boyd looked at Bannerman and shouted, 'Louise! She's in here!'

'Oh God!' replied Bannerman, and then with a surge of bodily strength he was inside the van tugging at the carpet with Boyd. A catch was found and turned, hurriedly, and then Boyd dragged Louise out of the buzz box into the body of the van.

With a wrench a rear door was pulled open, a cloud of black smog escaped to find freedom in the park, and Cross leaned inside and helped pull Louise to the ground.

'She's dead!'

'No, she isn't breathing!'

Boyd laid Louise on her back, undid her collar, arched her neck, and began blowing air into her mouth. Meanwhile, Cross was feeling Louise's carotid artery. Searching for a pulse, he flashed a glance at Boyd and then began pumping his hands on Louise's chest in time with Boyd's mouth to mouth respiration.

'Come on, girl,' said Cross, depressing her sternum. Turning into his radio microphone, Bannerman blurted, 'Control... At scene... Ambulance required pronto... One down... One of ours, I think... Not sure...' Bannerman's eyes questioned Boyd's face.

Boyd nodded and screamed, 'Yes! She's my U.C.,' confirmed Boyd. 'She's a U.C... An undercover officer!'

Bannerman radioed, 'One blue down. She's one of ours.'

He was dissecting Tebay Gorge and climbing Shap Fell at seventy-five miles an hour in the fast lane. He was beneath Shap interchange with Hardendale Quarry disappearing in his rear view mirror. He was speeding along the M6 at Lowther Park on a fast downhill stretch towards Penrith. He was through Catterlen interchange and bearing down on Southwaite Services. He was thirty minutes from the estate in Carlisle and Namir was talking to Yasif on a mobile 'phone. They were both laughing.

Once paramedics arrived, some five or so minutes later, Louise was whisked off to hospital, leaving the Fire Service to douse her old grey van and police to restore normality to the estate. Trundling down a weed-strewn path that bordered a narrow stream, a paramedic fitted an oxygen mask to Louise's face and gradually stabilised her vital signs. Threading through the embittered cross-roads the ambulance crew noticed an array of abandoned stones and milk bottles lying in the gutter. Here and there, policemen stood guarding handcuffed prisoners as they waited for more vans to arrive to remove them to cells in the police station. One policeman was knocking out ragged edges of broken glass from a shattered windscreen: at least one missile had found its mark; and a few rioters and police were nursing black eyes and bloody noses. Yet it was strangely quiet as if in the aftermath of battle some bizarre modicum of strangled peace had been restored to the bitter streets. Klaxons sounded and blue lights flashed as the ambulance made for the hospital with Louise flat out on a stretcher.

Boyd and his fellow rescuers watched the ambulance leave as the strike of a match was followed by a cloud of smoke and a pungent odour of pipe tobacco. 'Bannerman, you'd best take Chief Inspector Boyd down to the hospital as well,' ordered McMurray. Then, turning to Boyd, McMurray said, 'Get them to take at look your face, Boyd. And your hand, what on earth have you done to it?'

'A van window ran into it,' winced Boyd. 'Will she make it?'

'Your undercover lady, we'll soon know,' offered Bannerman. 'Come on, let's get down to casualty and find out. They can fix your hand while Cross and I see about your Louise.'

'Sounds good to me!' gasped Boyd. 'But she's not mine. She's ours and she's been providing vital tip-offs for months now. But you're right. She's one of my undercover officers and she's a bit special really.'

'Why didn't you tell anyone?' asked Cross.

'Because to be truly effective she needs to be on her own.'

Nursing his injured hand, Boyd made towards the cross-roads with Bannerman and Cross. Rocky trailed obediently at Cross's leg, tongue drooling and tail wagging. Pausing for a moment, Boyd asked McMurray, 'What brought you here, Mac?'

'I was listening to my radio when I heard an emergency signal override everything else. Then I heard your squad calling a baton charge. It all seemed to happen at the same time. It was crazy for a while. It went berserk! Anyway, I thought you might need some help so I emptied the police station of the lame, sick and weary and got here as fast as I could. Sorry! I know I've broken the habit of a lifetime but I expected you to be thankful for the presence an experienced man like myself.'

'I wish I hadn't asked,' replied Boyd.

'Apart from that, the Chief asked me to keep an eye on you,' mocked McMurray. 'Something about monitoring the budget!'

'Bollocks! But I'm glad you came, Mac,' replied Boyd, offering his good hand.

Boyd's hand was taken, grasped firmly, and shaken by McMurray.

'Actually, there's something else you should know, Boyd.'

'Go on, Mac.'

'Your search team has hit the jackpot! A suspect package has been found at Tullie House. Bomb Disposal has cordoned the area off and evacuated the building.'

'A bomb?'

'I presume so.'

'That's all we need,' said Boyd.

'Yes, well you asked them to search the building, Boyd,' said McMurray. 'You surely can't complain if they find something. That was the whole purpose of their expedition, wasn't it?'

'Fine!' replied Boyd. 'Bannerman! Cross! Let's get down there. Mac, can you tidy up here for me?'

'But of course. I think I ought to ring the Chief and let him know of our success though. Don't you? Looks like we've killed this disorder off in one foul swoop, Boyd. How many prisoners would you say, so far?'

'Fifty plus,' interrupted Cross. 'But we're not finished yet.'

'Over fifty prisoners, good God! They'll be stacked up in the cell block like...'

'Your problem,' interrupted Boyd. 'Not mine.'

'By the way, Boyd. How did you persuade the Chief to sanction overtime payments for the troops?'

Spinning on his heel, Boyd pulled a face, choosing to ignore Mac's question. Crossing the road, they climbed into Cross's van and drove off towards the hospital. As they negotiated the cross-roads, Boyd caught sight of two young constables who, between them, guarded four prisoners. The prisoners were shell-shocked, desolated, handcuffed, and sitting on a kerb waiting for transport to the cells. Both policemen saluted Boyd as he passed by. Turning, looking back, Boyd recognised one of them to be a young constable he'd admonished during his very first briefing at Carlisle police station - for being scruffily dressed, as he recalled. With a huge grin, Boyd extended a *Thumbs Up* to the youngster who nodded with a smug, satisfied smile growing across his face. They drove on. But then a sergeant threw up a salute followed by another constable and suddenly Boyd was something approaching a hero in their eyes - well, not quite a hero, but close enough to have earned a modicum of respect - or so it seemed. Even Rocky seemed to be whimpering with humility.

The salutes didn't go unnoticed by Cross who caught Bannerman's eye. 'Looks like you've made a bit of a hit then, boss,' said Bannerman.

'A bit of a hit? No, Bannerman. They've just found their feet, that's all,' replied Boyd, quietly.

They drove on, leaving the dark estate behind them and finding the main road into the city. As Cross turned at a junction, a blue Ford flashed past containing three men.

'It's them!' snapped Cross, excitedly. 'Look!' He wiggled a finger at the fast disappearing Ford. 'Front nearside passenger seat! Gold stud, left ear. Arab!'

Bannerman shouted, 'Take them, Cross.'

Rocky was up on all fours, barking again.

Dropping a gear, steering firmly to the left, hard on his accelerator pedal, Cross was through the junction and into the chase.

'Definitely the left ear then?' mused Boyd, as the van lurched.

'No doubt about it, boss. I never forget an ear,' quipped Cross.

'How could you!' chuckled Boyd.

'Don't rattle them, Cross,' advised Bannerman. 'I'll get on the radio. Penny to a pound there's a murder weapon in that car!'

'Gently does it, Cross' ordered Boyd; only to receive an icy stare from the driver. 'Well, let's not frighten them. You know what I mean.'

One quarter of a mile is all it took Cross to move directly behind the Ford. Activating his headlights, Cross said, 'Sorry, but they're going to take off any minute. I can feel it. Where's the intercept.'

'They're on their way,' replied Bannerman. 'It's an armed response vehicle. They'll be with us any moment.'

As an armed response vehicle came into view ahead of them, the Ford suddenly pulled out of a line of traffic and swung right into a narrow street. Accelerating hard, the Ford pulled away from Cross who wrestled with his steering wheel, then braked and swerved to miss an oncoming post office van. Temporarily balked, Cross shouted, 'Told you so,' and then snatched a lower gear as his van took off after the Ford.

At a hill crest, the Ford's four wheels lifted from the tarmac and then bounced squeamishly on cobbled stones as the road surface changed and broadened out towards another junction. Left then left again, both the Ford and Cross found themselves on a dual carriageway with an armed response vehicle in tow struggling to carve through traffic.

Lights flashing and horns blaring, Cross gunned his van as the Arabs tried desperately to escape.

Approaching a bridge over the River Caldew, the dual carriageway ceased at a junction controlled by traffic lights before it continued again towards Carlisle castle. But at these traffic lights a slow moving brewery wagon sauntered through an amber light causing the Ford to brake violently to avoid a head-on collision.

'They've lost it,' yelled Cross, and Rocky barked in agreement.

The Ford's bonnet suddenly dipped and the back end swung round in a spin. Fighting to control his vehicle, Aden had inadvertently put his car into a skid. The wheels locked up and all four tyres screeched noisily before the Ford glanced a fleeting blow to the offside of the brewery wagon. The Ford then mounted a pavement, spinning out of control, collided with a lamp-post, and careered towards a wall. There was a colossal smash when the Ford demolished the brickwork and dived into the icy Caldew below.

Coming to a standstill nearby, Cross, Boyd and Bannerman ran onto the pavement and peered through the hole in the wall. The front of the Ford plunged headlong into the river and then quickly submerged in the water that soon engulfed the three Arabs.

Submerged, Aden mouthed a terrified silent scream as he continued to struggle with his steering wheel in a futile attempt to somehow float the vehicle back to sanity. Rollo died instantly: his neck was broken when his head thumped into the car's windscreen. In the rear of the Ford, Yasif tried in vain to open his door and swim to freedom. But the pressure of the Caldew denied him his liberty. Yasif's fatal mistake was to roll his window down. Yasif and Aden drowned in the waters that rolled into the passenger compartment and took their lives.

Watching the surface of the Caldew for what seemed an eternity, Boyd saw there was no sign of life from the submerged vehicle. The waters smoothed over the Ford and rippled gently as they meandered towards a confluence with the nearby Eden.

Coldly, Boyd said, 'Better get a diving team here to recover the bodies. No survivors!'

When a major from bomb disposal carried out a controlled explosion on a suspect package located near the entrance to Tullie House Museum, Boyd, Cross, Rocky and Bannerman watched an almighty eruption of leather, metal and plastic as the parcel was ripped into a thousand fragments. Ever cautious, bomb disposal had caused an electromagnetic ray to pass through a locked and abandoned Delsey briefcase in an endeavour to identify what was contained inside. A subsequent photographic image, obtained from this x-ray function, revealed nothing but a mass of what appeared to be metal wires running around the extremity of a plastic container. It wasn't until after the detonation occurred that the same army major was able to say that the suspect package was, in fact, a music stand. Subsequent revealed the music stand belonged to a local student attending a social function inside the premises. It would be the last time she would forget where she'd momentarily put down her briefcase and music papers.

By the time debris had been swept away from the front of Tullie House, a diving team was plumbing the depths of the Caldew and most of the prisoners from the estate had been incarcerated in cells for the night. Daylight was fading fast and night was rushing in. It was getting late; but not too late for Cross's van to finally pull up in the hospital car park.

Reaching casualty department, at last, Cross headed for an automatic vending machine and fed its greedy mouth with a handful of coins until three plastic containers of black sugary coffee appeared. Handing one to Boyd, Cross said, 'You need to get that hand fixed before it swells anymore.'

'I think it's just my knuckles, actually,' replied Boyd, sipping his coffee. Then, with a doubtful smile, he said, 'Could be arthritis?'

Weary, totally exhausted, they were escorted inside to find Louise recovering in a cubicle. Boyd smiled at her and motioned to his companions. 'Louise, this is Cross and Bannerman. Boys, this is Louise.'

Nodding, Louise asked, 'And who's this then?' She bent down and stroked Rocky. 'Friend or foe?'

'Definitely friend,' replied Cross. 'He likes you. I can tell.'

Rocky was licking her hand, playful.

'Thanks for pulling me out of the van back there.'

'No problem!' Cross was immediately taken with her. 'We all thought you were done for.'

'Well you all thought wrong. I passed out and I've coughed up half a ton of smoke from my guts since. But I was always with the plot, gents.'

'Good for you,' smiled Cross.

'What kept you, Mister Boyd?' she asked, slightly annoyed. With a hint of sarcasm in her voice, she said, 'I've had half an hour with an oxygen mask, two x-rays, three aspirin, and a pregnancy test while I've been waiting.'

'A riot, a suspect package at the museum and three Arabs,' laughed Boyd. 'Anyway, how are you?'

'Ready for home; what's this about the Arabs? Did you get them?'

'Not exactly,' said Boyd.

'What do you mean - not exactly?'

'There was a chase. They crashed and ended up in the Caldew.'

'You mean they escaped?' asked Louise, zipping up her jacket.

'We're pretty sure they're dead!' said Cross. 'Stone dead I would say.'

'Did you recover the rifle?'

'What rifle?' asked Boyd. 'I don't know what you're talking about.'

'You got my message…'

'What message? I heard your emergency signal and I presumed you were in some kind of trouble.'

'Trouble!' she snapped. 'Bit of an understatement, Mister Boyd, if you don't mind me saying. Some bastard used my van for target practice, by the look of it. I'm lucky to be alive. Five minutes more and I'd have been fried to a cinder. No, my message was simple and straight forward. The three olive-coloured men turned up at the drugs cache. One of them, the one we think is Yasif - the one with the gold stud in his lug hole - he was carrying a big plastic bag. It looked like a gun to me. It was a rifle. I shouted it in on the Intelligence channel but when there was no response from you…'

'Let's get this straight,' said Bannerman. 'You were watching a drugs cache but the suspects were identical to the Jo-Jo murder suspects. Right?'

'You are quick, Bannerman. Does Cross do the thinking in your team or do you both leave it to the dog?'

'Settle down, Louise,' said, Boyd, an edge of authority creeping into his voice. 'Twenty four hours is a long time to stay on target and I know you must be stretched to the limit but tell me how you know this man had a rifle. You said he was carrying a black plastic bag. There's a difference.'

'I don't know where they came from. One minute there was nothing, the next they were there on the path in front of me. They crossed over the wooden planks. The one we think is Yasif was carrying a plastic bag. It wasn't just a bag though. It looked like two bags sellotaped together and it was long enough to carry a rifle inside. Yasif dropped underneath the bridge and went down the banking. When he reappeared a few minutes later, he wasn't carrying the bag. He wasn't carrying anything.'

'So he was hiding a bag of drugs in the bank underneath the tiny bridge?' asked Bannerman.

'No. It wasn't drugs,' said Louise. 'Too big. God, the bag was three or four feet long. Can you imagine what weight of drugs that would hold? No, he wasn't collecting drugs but he sure as hell was leaving something for someone to collect.'

'Doesn't sound anything like a drugs drop,' said Boyd.

'And you didn't actually see a rifle, Louise,' pointed out Bannerman. 'It's supposition that it was a rifle and not something else.'

'You're right but I just think it was a rifle,' argued Louise.

'Why?' asked Boyd.

'Gut feeling!'

'Funny,' interrupted Cross. 'I was reading one of those spy thrillers not so long ago. One of those paperbacks. Le Carre, I think it was. The spy was using a - what did they call it - A dead letter box?'

'Mmm… Not quite the same analogy, Cross, but close enough,' said Boyd. 'I like it. If your theory is correct then Yasif left a gun at a predetermined drop-off point. Is that what you mean?'

Cross bent down and started to fondle Rocky's neck. 'Yes, I think that's exactly what I mean.'

'First rate! Soon as I've got my hand fixed we'll check it out.'

'Just one thing, sir,' said Louise.

'What's that?'

'I'm not sitting watching it again. Not for anyone, okay?'

'Okay!' smiled Boyd.

'Let's hope it's not a wild goose chase,' chided Bannerman. 'You might be an undercover officer but it's just your guess that it was a rifle.'

'Have you seen the time?' suggested Cross, preventing an argument, suddenly protecting Louise. 'We've a lot to do and not long to do it in. There's a rifle adrift and the Minister's here in twelve hours time.'

An old grey river carried a silver sheen of moonlight as the day drew to a close and a white support bandage was applied to Boyd's hand.

*

13

~ ~ ~

Dateline: 9th September, 2000: Tullie House Museum.

Pacing back and forward in front of the museum entrance, Boyd was impatient. He'd arranged to meet Louise and Cross first thing. Now dawn had recently broken and there was no sign of his comrades. He was gradually growing somewhat irritable but nevertheless decided he ought to try very hard at controlling his emotions. It was best behaviour day, which explained why the polish on his shoes was quite exceptional and the creases in his uniform were razor sharp. In control of his feelings, for the moment, Boyd paused and took time out to reflect on the security arrangements he had made.

Security? Security was always a farce, thought Boyd. However, on this occasion it had been changed midway through proceedings. The threat level was now *'construed as a high threat'*. As such, security matters were well and truly out of the ordinary. For seldom did uniform police deal with security that was construed as a high threat. The Minister would have a Special Branch bodyguard, perhaps his own Israeli bodyguard for that matter, but they weren't responsible for ground security. These bodyguards weren't responsible for security at Carlisle airport; a drive to the city centre, a walk inside a museum, and a return journey to the airport. At least, not on this occasion. Really dangerous security assignments were usually dealt with by those elite personal protection officers from Special Branch, the Anti-Terrorist Squad, the Royalty and Diplomatic Protection Group, very occasionally Special Forces; but seldom the ordinary rank and file of the British uniformed police. Boyd paused, deliberately thinking of those words on that flimsy: those words that originated from someone in British Intelligence. It was an absolute 'unadulterated farce', thought Boyd. One minute the threat level for the visit was 'low to medium,' the next it was 'high', and no-one seemed able to account for some faceless Arab terrorist called Namir. So what was the true relevance of Namir missing from the Lebanon? Where was the Lebanon? A thousand miles from Carlisle? Five thousand miles? Boyd didn't know and he hadn't thought to ask how far away the Lebanon was. At that London briefing, they told me only what they wanted me to know, thought Boyd. They withheld the whole story for matters best known to themselves. But who are 'they'? Why can't 'they' tell me everything I need to know so that I can do my job to the best of my ability? Are 'they' deliberately blindfolding me and tying one hand behind my back? Fine, to hell you with all, thought Boyd. Then he'd decided to do things his way. Approaching the matter warily, he, Boyd, decided to adopt high profile policing methods in order to dissuade any would-be killer from murdering an Israeli Minister on his patch. Boyd reached such a conclusion because he didn't like the sound of Namir missing, a thread of complacency he'd detected at his London briefing, and that London moustachioed copper who'd belittled his visit from the far north. Apart from that, Boyd had felt it in his insides on the train near Crewe. He'd had a premonition that this man, Namir, would come. He'd felt it in his bones from the very start. Now he was getting nervous and it was beginning to show.

Shaking his head again, Boyd continued to pace back and forward.

It was the day of the Minister's visit, and the day the Tablet of Masada was to be returned to the people of Israel. All this would be done in full view of the people of Carlisle and a host of television cameras, which would broadcast proceedings into an estimated fifteen million homes when all the networks had transmitted the daily news. It was best behaviour day.

Bomb Disposal had retired to their quarters for a well-earned nap and the night shift was about to give way to the morning crew. Boyd's search teams had finally completed all their tasks and handed over responsibility for security of the museum to a detachment of uniform officers. Indeed, smart blue uniforms were very much in evidence with officers stationed at every conceivable entrance.

A council van was parked nearby and two police officers were supervising its presence. From the rear of this van, two council employees were unloading a collection of metal barriers, to be used to control pedestrians. Once linked together, these barriers were to be positioned on a pavement near the museum entrance. The crowd, and for that matter, the media, would have controlled access to the Israeli Minister. They would be close enough to see the important man; but not close enough to touch him. Boyd knew this was important because a last minute change of plan meant the British Foreign Secretary and the Defence Secretary would now be in attendance. ITV, BBC and SKY were all covering the event live, with CNN , NBC and the American networks taking 'links'. What had started out as a low key affair had turned into a photo' opportunity for an important handful of government officials. Or was it a freebie 'plane ride to England's most north-westerly outpost under the guise of a cultural exchange? Politicians, thought Boyd. Who needs them? But the fact remained that the Press would have a field day if anything went wrong, and that was something Boyd didn't want.

Standing on a pavement, looking out towards that broad expanse of castle green, and those Norman battlements towering above the sweeping grass, Boyd's eyes anxiously scanned for the unexplained and unimaginable. Best behaviour day could very easily turn into Boyd's bad day; if things didn't go right.

Boyd didn't want a bad hair day!

Bannerman approached with a cheery smile that hid the fact he'd only snatched a couple of hours sleep. 'Morning, boss. Sorry, I'm late.'

'Everyone's late this morning, Bannerman,' replied Boyd. 'But then it's still not too late to run through those last minute checks.'

Bannerman groaned and said, 'There's fifty-three prisoners still in the traps this morning and they aren't going anywhere. The cells are creaking at the hinges, rammed full. The boys and girls at the nick think you're tops because you led the charge against that mob.'

'So much for the boys and girls, Bannerman. I need men and women. What do those old-timers think?' laughed Boyd, yet his voice carried a soft but earnest tone.

'That you're going to muck it all up today and make a complete pratt of yourself, Mister Boyd.'

'Thanks, Mister Bannerman. You're so kind.'

'You did ask.'

'Not quite the answer I was looking for.'

'The old-timers! I presume you mean anyone who's been in the job five years?' chuckled Bannerman. 'Well, they reckon you've scored one out of three.'

'One out of three! What do you mean?'

'Canteen crack says you've killed our riot but you've not proved Jo-Jo's murder and this Israeli visit is nonsense. They think you're making them a laughing stock. If this farce continues, look out! They can make life difficult for you if they decide not to like you, Mister Boyd.'

'Good job they don't know you've turned into my spy then!' whispered Boyd.

'Put it this way, boss. There's a secure V.I.P zone created at Carlisle airport. For God's sake, some say that anyone travelling out of Carlisle airport is a V.I.P because they only deal with a handful of flights a day. And that route into Carlisle? It's crawling with armed police. There are sharpshooters going into position on every nearby rooftop and this museum's been searched so many times, it's as clean as a whistle. They've had this V.I.P visit up to their ears, boss.'

Boyd was listening but his eyes were roaming the castle battlements.

'Before I forget. Here's a list of guests and civic dignitaries.' Bannerman waved a flimsy list of paper in Boyd's face. 'They've been checked inside out by Special Branch. By the way, the sewers have been cleaned, the flower beds dug over, the lamp posts painted, and the Irish Sea has been cordoned off in case of submarine attack. And, just in case, we've got a platoon of Gurkhas on standby in the canteen.'

'Very funny,' said Boyd. 'Over the top?'

'Yes, boss. You're well and truly over the top but then you've known that from the start.'

'We can throw a security blanket over this place until the cows come home, Bannerman, but I can't stop people coming and going. It's a free country. Carlisle's a city with a population just under a hundred thousand and half of them are going to drive down this road at some time today. Over the top? Probably, but then it's not their responsibility, is it? Looking after an Israeli Foreign Minister whose life is threatened!'

'No, Mister Boyd, but that's what you get paid for - Making decisions!'

'Tell me what I've forgotten, Bannerman. That's why I'm standing here first thing this morning wondering whether or not I really should cordon the Irish Sea off. There's an air exclusion zone above us, so why not the sea?'

'Talking about water, boss. The diving team have recovered three bodies from that wreck in the Caldew.'

'Anything?'

'A silencer from the pocket of a jacket worn by an Arab-looking gentleman with a gold stud in his left ear - Yasif.'

'Can ballistics do anything with a silencer?'

'Too early to say, but by lunch time today I bet forensic tell us one of those Arabs' fingerprints match those found scrawled in Jo-Jo's blood at the murder scene.'

'Sounds about right. I agree. Does that make it two out of three, Bannerman?'

'It might even things up a bit.'

'Anything else in that car? Drugs? Black plastic bag? Rifle?'

'Cupboard's bare.'

'Well,' said Boyd. 'We could always run a book on which one of the Arab's fingerprints is scrawled on the wall.'

'You serious?' asked Bannerman.

'U.C joke, sick humour works at times.' Boyd exhaled loudly and walked away from Bannerman towards a council van. Resting his bandaged hand on a metal barrier, Boyd turned and said, 'Here's one for you, Bannerman. It's three o'clock in the morning and you're in charge of a diving team. The diving team have just dragged a car from a river. They remove three bodies and find a silencer. Well, they're expecting to find a silencer because that's the word on the street.'

'I don't follow your drift,' said Bannerman, quizzically.

'I'll put it like this. If our diving team found a water-tight bag containing a couple of kilos of heroin would we know about it or would it be the best kept secret this side of Tebay Gorge?'

'You said I was in charge. Theoretically, that is.'

'So?'

'Don't doubt my integrity, Mister Boyd, or theirs, for that matter. You've come to far too quickly to destroy a faith you're in the process of creating?'

'Moralistic, Bannerman? Maybe, you need a rest.'

'Maybe you need a rest, or maybe we both need a rest. I'm not sure anymore.'

'So where do I go from here, Bannerman?'

'Trust your people, Mister Boyd.'

'You mean I have a choice?'

'Okay, boss. What if there were drugs in that submerged car and our divers snaffled them?'

'Then Louise could have been wrong about that rifle and you might be right. Supposition, you said. You said that Louise was guessing when she thought Yasif was carrying a rifle in a big black plastic bag. Was she guessing when she said it was sellotaped? In all that excitement, she may have been wrong.'

'In which case, that rifle might not have existed and that bag could have contained drugs! That was the idea behind your observation point, wasn't it, boss? The intelligence pointed to a drug cache. So why are we talking about a rifle?'

'Seems like I need to believe someone before it's to late, Bannerman,' said Boyd, 'If Louise was right, then there's a rifle missing and I've got intelligence that speaks of a high threat against a foreign visitor. If Louise is wrong, then has a massive drugs cache just been stolen from right under my nose? Or am I being unkind to everyone?'

A van screeched round a corner and pulled up sharply in front of Boyd and Bannerman. Cross was driving but Louise wound her passenger window down and leaned out. 'Morning, Bannerman! Hop in, Mister Boyd. Sorry we're late but…'

'Forget it, Louise. Everyone's behind schedule this morning. Morning, Cross.'

'Sir!'

Boyd glanced at Bannerman as he stepped towards Cross's van. 'Thanks, Bannerman. Brief the teams when they arrive, as arranged, then make sure they're in position in good time. We'll be back before you know it.'

'Where are you going?' asked Bannerman.

'To do something we should have done last night, Bannerman. Search that bank under the bridge in the park.'

'Good luck then, but remember what I said.'

Boyd smiled, nodded, and said, 'I'm just tired, that's all.' He squeezed in beside Louise as Cross drove off. 'Best behaviour day?' he muttered to himself.

Honoured guest, David, had dressed in his best blue suit and he was looking forward to his day in the limelight. Ironic that after all these years Carlisle City council had sought him out and invited him to attend Tullie House on the very day the Tablet of Masada was to be presented to an Israeli Minister. Mind you, thought David, it was only right that such a thing should happen. It was he who had found that Tablet in the first place. He was the one who had identified that artefact as the Tablet of Masada. Yes, he would look very smart in a line-up outside the museum entrance. He would be first to shake hands with the Mayor of Carlisle, of course, then he would be introduced to the Israeli Minister. Proud, David had decided to revert to his native tongue as soon as formalities had taken place. It was a big day for David, and he was a principal guest.

Combing his hair, patting down a stray unruly lock, he looked into a bathroom mirror and smiled at his reflection. Then he combed his beard and carefully placed a black trimmed hat on his head.

Yes, David thought, it was going to be a very big day.

With a tug of a blanket, Steve tried to block out the deafening noise of an alarm clock blasting in his ears, invading his privacy.

Snuggling beneath his covers, he wrapped an arm round his wife's waist, cuddled tight into her back, and shuffled his pelvis into her buttocks.

'Time to get up,' she responded, murmuring sleepily.

'Too early,' he yawned. 'Five minutes more.'

'No. Time to get up, Steve, now. Come on.'

'Rather go fishing,' he whispered. 'Or perhaps...' His hand began to slowly tickle her thigh. Then he guided his careless fingers towards her naked navel and began to sensuously caress her skin.

'You can forget that,' she snapped, suddenly awake.

An elbow dug into his ribs. She reached from their bed and slammed a button on the alarm clock, killing that infernal, unwanted shrill.

'We've got an invite to a big knob's do. Now get up, Steve. Get dressed, and get a move on.'

'Mmm...' He was virtually oblivious to it all. 'Five minutes more.'

'If it wasn't for you, Steve, there wouldn't be any rock to return to those Jews.' She sat up instantly, shook out her hair, and then stretched. 'It's your big day, Steve. You found it in the Eden. Remember?'

'Mmm...'

'You're the top man today. My dirty little dredger; top man.'

She slipped from their bed leaving Steve buried beneath a pillow and a mound of blankets. Finding her slippers and a dressing gown, she said, 'Today, my darling husband, you are a very important person. Today you're going to stand next to the Mayor and explain to that Foreign Secretary chap how you discovered history. You're top man, Steve.'

She made for the bedroom door.

'Five minutes, Steve. That's all you've got then I want you up. I want you looking your best.'

'Mmm...'

'Put your church suit on, Steve. The dark pinstripe. And take my camera. We'll show our photos to the vicar and his wife at the next church social.'

'Camera?'

'Yes, the camera! There's a colour film on the sideboard.'

'Mmm...'

'Shall I wear my blue dress or the pink one?'

'Mmm...'

There was a soft footfall as she stepped across the hall and entered the bathroom. She pulled the string of a light switch and flooded the room in fluorescence. Removing her robe, she ran her bath and salted its water with something smelly and pink. There was a splash of water from the bath and she yelled, 'Five minutes, Steve. Then put that kettle on.'

Turning over in a half sleep, Steve mumbled, 'Rather go fishing...'

A university scarf hung from a plastic hook on the back of a kitchen door. The scarf was old, tatty, and a shade grimy. It looked as if it hadn't been worn for quite a while; unlike a nearby pair of Wellington boots and a black duffel coat. The morning's *Times* was folded in half and propped up on a pine breakfast table. The newspaper was precariously wedged between a silver-coloured sugar bowl and a half-empty china milk jug. From a nearby corner unit, a small transistor radio was playing orchestral music; not quite loud enough to spoil an early morning conversation between man and wife.

Jeremy, knife and fork poised at the ready, finally attacked his bacon and egg while he took in the day's headlines.

'It's not on the front page, darling,' he said, shovelling a finely cut square of rasher into his mouth.

'I didn't expect it to be. Did you, Jeremy, dear?' she chided.

'Well, I thought what with all that security and everything.' He carefully sliced a tough rind from a rasher of bacon and pushed it to one side. 'Not to mention the history of it all, darling.'

'Hardly front page news for the Times, dear. Not for the tabloids and certainly not for the Times, Jeremy.'

'Well! Best be off soon, I suppose, darling,' replied Jeremy, applying a sprinkle more salt to his bacon, toying with his food really, unnecessarily.

'Finish your breakfast first, dear. You know how you like to get something substantial inside that stomach of yours. Sets you up for the rest of the day, you keep telling me.'

'Not at all that hungry this morning, darling,' admitted Jeremy.

'Excitement, perhaps, dear?'

'Don't be ridiculous, woman,' chuckled Jeremy. 'Can't remember the last time I was excited.'

'Me neither,' she chortled under her breath.

'Pardon! Did you speak, darling?'

'Nothing important, Jeremy. It was only a little something.' She chuckled again.

Pushing an egg around his plate, he asked, 'Are you coming with me? This invitation is addressed to us both.'

'Suppose I ought,' she replied. 'But you're just a clumsy museum curator, Jeremy. Don't go getting any fancy ideas above your station.'

'Me, clumsy!'

'Yes, dear. You!' She admonished.

Jeremy stopped eating and looked up. 'Well, aright then. Perhaps! But this invitation says it wants me to be there. The man who came from those council offices made it very clear. If it hadn't been for me no-one would have kept the Tablet of Masada. Don't you realise that, woman?'

'Yes, of course. But you were a clumsy student then and you made a mistake, dear. You were shilly-shallying about as usual. Don't you remember?

'We weren't even married then. I'm surprised you can remember.'

'Like it was yesterday, dear.'

'Actually,' said Jeremy, conspiratorially, 'to tell you the truth I was never too sure. Thinking back, best thing I did was to put that rock in the museum vaults. I knew all along it was an altar of some kind.'

'Jeremy,' she said. 'There you go again. Don't create a hubbub. Shilly-shally! Shilly-shally! What will the mayor think of us?'

'I don't know but if you don't stop chattering and get a move on, we'll be late.'

'Mmm…' she said, and poured herself another cup of tea.

The Times newspaper fell backwards and one of its pages fell into the yolk of Jeremy's egg.

'Now look what you've done, woman,' he scorned. 'You really ought to be more careful.'

'Quite…' she said and sugared her tea viciously.

Shamrock is a delicate three-lobed tiny clover and a native of Ireland. When Saint Patrick first landed on the island of Ireland, centuries ago, he used a Shamrock plant to illustrate the doctrine of the Trinity. He told anyone who cared to listen to his teachings of Christian theology that this beautifully formed trifoliate clover reminded him of the Father, Son and Holy Spirit. All three tiny leaves came together to compose a perfect clover and, as such, a Shamrock reminded him of one Supreme Being: for indeed, that was the very essence of his religious teachings.

Shamrock is also looked upon as a symbol of good luck, but when watered in a pot in a house on the edge of an estate in Carlisle, it meant only one thing: Mary Forsyth was at home.

Mary, or Mad Mary, as Boyd and Louise occasionally referred to her, was dressed in her best bib and tucker: Black broad-brimmed hat, adorned with ridiculously long synthetic feathers; a three-quarter length black dress, set off with a mother-of-pearl brooch; and a lilac knee-length coat, which altogether took at least ten years off Mary's appearance and made her look like 'the belle of the ball'.

Placing a water jug to one side, she readied herself. Buttoning her coat, she selected matching gloves, an appropriate leather handbag, and set off into the city. She would stroll in summer sunshine to Tullie House and stand next to those awful metal barriers. She would watch the civic proceedings that so much had been made of in the local press. She wasn't at all central to the visit, hadn't even been invited, but the weather forecast was good and there would be bands playing and the local regiment, The King's Own Border Regiment, was marching. Something of a spectacle, it was not to be missed, and she was looking forward to taking her place amongst those enthusiastic tourists and interested sightseers.

Taking a leash from a drawer in the hall, she whistled, collected her Alsatian and set off to walk.

Crosby was on the net in his office in Istanbul. Surfing the world-wide web, he clicked his mouse and dragged his cursor, here and there, looking for news items. He'd decided to monitor proceedings by accessing the BBC on Line service. More reliable than his own communications' systems, he would have his eye on the news within minutes of it being reported.

As his screen came alive, he glanced across at his encrypted machine. Why hadn't Ratchet replied to that Top Secret Omega Blue? Surely there would be further questions for Codename Danu? Or had British Intelligence missed something? Surely not?

In the park, Cross and Rocky were standing on a bridge of wooden planks that crossed a tiny stream. Ankle deep in water, courtesy of Cross's Wellington boots, Boyd was shaking his head and muttering something about not getting his hands dirty.

'There's nothing here, Cross,' shouted Boyd. 'But it looks to me as if the soil has been disturbed recently.'

'Do you mean a big hole, boss?'

'Over two feet long! But I wouldn't quite describe it as a hole.'

'Why's that?'

'No depth! Well, the ground has been disturbed alright. But that's just what's puzzling me. Looks like a shallow trench has been dug out by hand and then covered over with loose foliage. Grass, weeds… Ouch! And some thorns!'

'I suppose it's too late to advise you to wear your gloves?'

'I am wearing them, Cross, and yes, it is too late.' Boyd was removing an evil-looking thorn from the wrist of his leather glove. 'Looks like Louise was right about this, after all.'

'But if she's right then you can hardly call them professionals, boss. I mean, it's not the best place to hide something and if it was a gun, or something like that, then you'd have to say they must be rank amateurs.'

'Shallow trench? Rank amateurs? You may be right at that. But then…'

'What's bothering you, boss?'

'Depends how long they were leaving something. If you were burying an article for a long time then you'd hardly choose this place. That said, if it was just a quick drop to avoid direct contact with someone then yes, I suppose it's a good place. And they say the best plans should always be what?'

'Simple,' replied Cross.

'Yes, simple. No frills.'

'Well, no-one comes here anymore, do they, boss? Not to this God -forsaken place. It's an ideal place to leave something for someone, particularly if you don't want to meet that person.'

They stood, both lost in their own private thoughts, trying to fathom it out.

'When I was a U. C: an undercover officer,' said Boyd. 'I got into all kind of scrapes. Often I used to think I was the criminal. I suppose I was really, thinking back.'

'So?' asked Cross.

'So there were times when I thought the baddies were onto me. I used to watch my back. You know, I used to check that I wasn't being followed or set up into something' There was a slight pause and then Boyd smiled, nodded his head and said, 'and if I ever thought I was being followed I used to go to places where no-one else ever went. That way I could see everybody and everything around me.'

'And that's why someone came to a park where not even the kids play,' mused Cross. 'It makes sense, so it does.'

'Exactly! Not even the kids come to play here and it's ideal in some ways. It's the only bridge in the park; easy to find if you were giving someone instructions. Just say you were giving someone instructions on the 'phone... Easy?'

'Someone like Jo-Jo? For instance.'

'Could be. But he's dead. But Namir? Namir is still missing.'

'Who? Never mind,' said Cross.' You can hardly call it a bridge really, can you?'

'Agreed, but it all depends on why you're leaving something and how long you're going to leave it.'

Cross said, 'If that was a bag of drugs then you're talking one hell of a wedge of money's worth.'

'And you wouldn't leave high value drugs lying about like that, would you?' asked Boyd.

'Do you need a hand down there, boss?'

'No thanks. Just pull me up. I don't want to end up on my backside in this water.' Boyd pushed out a hand and was grabbed by Cross. With a tug, Boyd made the bridge and felt the comfort of dry wood beneath his feet. 'No, Cross. Something's been hidden there. Not drugs, that's for sure. Whatever it was, it's not there now.'

Louise appeared with a portable video camera. Rocky scampered to meet her and she fingered his neck when he pranced at her feet. 'Down, boy,' she said.

'Well?' asked Boyd.

'We're in luck. I've salvaged my videos from the van and I've got my proof.'

'Good, girl,' said Boyd. 'Lucky that van didn't burn out then?'

'Very lucky!' exclaimed Louise. 'Do you want to see?'

'Indeed we do,' said Boyd, enthusiastically.

Louise inserted a video cartridge into one side of the camera and pressed *'play'*. Moments later an image on her screen showed a footpath into the park and then the bridge. A few seconds later, three men appeared walking along the path. One of them was carrying a long black plastic bag, which appeared to be sellotaped to another plastic bag. The man was wearing a gold stud that was just discernible in his left ear. He dropped from the bridge, down the banking towards the stream, and was out of sight for what seemed like half a minute.

'That's brilliant,' said Cross. 'How on earth... I mean, that was no ordinary surveillance van, was it Louise?'

Louise looked at Cross and then at Boyd. 'No!' She said.

'Well, I'll be...' said Cross, looking at the images flickering on Louise's television screen. He looked again and gasped when three men appeared back on the wooden bridge, minus black plastic bags. Then they were gone and the images went fuzzy and the screen eventually blacked out.

'Satisfied?' asked Louise.

'First class!' said Boyd. 'That puts it beyond question. You weren't mistaken and you weren't...'

'Hallucinating?' asked Louise. 'That's what you all thought, wasn't it? That I was overcome by smoke and was hallucinating because of the exhaust fumes and all that.'

Boyd slowly nodded and said, 'It crossed my mind. But you've proved that what you said happened really did happen. That's first class.'

'Not second class, Mister Boyd.'

Boyd smiled, shook his head and said, 'First class.'

'Where does that leave us?' asked Cross.

'It means that Louise's black plastic bag was long enough to have a rifle hidden inside. It means that it was buried for a short time and now it's disappeared. There was no black bag recovered from the wreck in the Caldew, so...'

'It really is missing,' said Cross.

'Probably removed from the banking by whoever within an hour or two of being left in situ by Yasif,' said Louise.

'Which means if it was a sniper's rifle, then there really is an assassin loose,' said Cross.

'A faceless terrorist called Namir, according to my national security sources' reflected Boyd. 'We haven't even got his description.'

'You mean there really is a killer loose and it's not just you playing it up for your friends from London?' asked Cross.

'Come on,' said Boyd, urgently. 'It all figures, doesn't it? This is the drop zone for a contract killing. The killer's called Namir and he's already collected his rifle. It'll be a snipe from a rooftop. How long have we got?'

'Long enough for everyone to worry about your sanity,' said Cross.

'Louise?' said Boyd. 'With me or against me?'

'What the hell!' She said. 'My cover's blown now anyway. What have I got to lose? If we're right then it's first class. If not then...'

'I know. Second class,' said Boyd.

Thirty thousand feet above sea level, Israel's silver aeroplane glided effortlessly through Britain's crisp morning air.

Closed eyes, smooth face, composed, Israel's Foreign Minister eased back and allowed his neck to flop gently to one side as he enjoyed his snooze. Not for Israel was there any idle chatter with Britain's Secretary of State for Defence. Neither was there the likelihood of an exuberant exchange of mutual interests with the British Foreign Minister. Copious amounts of fine white wines with the American contingency at Chequers, the previous night, had seen to that. Welcome British passengers? Undoubtedly, yes. But very shortly all three senior politicians would be required to emerge from the aeroplane's belly and smile politely for those cameras. Until then, there would be a just but comparative silence. There was plenty of time to be on their best behaviour; but not just yet.

Three ministers snoring did not detract from the vigilance of Israel's chief bodyguard. When he heard the engine pitch change, he knew that his pilot had throttled back. Not long now, he thought. Not long before they landed at some remote airstrip in Cumbria. Carlisle, wasn't it? Not long before the visit started. With luck, they'd all be back on the wine by mid afternoon.

There was a very slight dip of the port wing when Israel's aeroplane began her final approach to one of the north-north-west's finest airports.

Screeching to a halt, Boyd leapt from the van as Cross snatched the handbrake and shouted instructions into the radio microphone. 'All units! Watch the high ground. Chief Inspector Boyd reports new intelligence. We've a sniper on the loose! All units! Watch the high ground.'

Instantaneously, Louise was out of the van and onto the pavement with Cross and Rocky following closely behind.

A short time ago the streets had been empty, save for last-minute preparations. Now there was a military band lining up and a sparkle of shiny metal flashed from a musician's trombone. A big bass drum was being hoisted onto a soldier's chest and there were some Union Jack flags being waved loosely by children in the crowd. These streets were gradually coming alive with people queuing to watch the marching bands and the promised pomp and circumstance of the day. A luscious red carpet had been rolled out and stretched from the museum entrance to the kerbside. Two podiums had been erected and were separated by three enormous tubs of colourful flowers. One podium was decked with the Union flag; the other bore the flag of Israel. Each podium carried thick black wires from microphones that were fixed to gold-rimmed lecterns, and there was a loudspeaker system fixed to a museum wall to boom out speeches to a growing crowd of sightseers. No waiting cones were spaced out along the road and two traffic wardens were ushering traffic onwards. No-one was allowed to saunter, never mind stop, and there was an air of excitement seeping through the assembly when the Mayor and civic leaders arrived in a couple of black limousines.

Bannerman appeared in the museum entrance and walked the full length of the red carpet, much to the annoyance of a bespectacled council official who tried to shoo him from an undisturbed pile.

'Problems, I hear,' said Bannerman.

Boyd was looking left, right and centre as he answered the big man. 'Bannerman, you said I should trust my own people. Well, Louise has convinced me. There's a hole in a dike up at that park, beneath the bridge, and we've got photographs of three dead Arabs leaving a rifle for someone!'

'You sure, boss?'

'It's a long story. Trust me!'

Cross nodded and said, 'He's right. There's a hit man somewhere in that crowd.'

'Just what we need,' replied Bannerman. 'Suggestions?'

'Is everything okay inside?' asked Boyd, indicating the museum.

'Clean and secure,' came Bannerman's swift reply.

'Checked the podiums and those damn wires?'

'A major from Bomb Disposal has checked everything you can see, and more besides.'

'But did he check those rooftops?' asked Boyd.

'No, but we've cameras on the museum roof and the castle keep. We've already taken the high ground. Don't worry, boss. Everything's going to plan.'

'Where's the V.I.P. party now?'

'They're on the final approach,' replied Bannerman. 'They'll be with us in about forty-five minutes, thereabouts.'

'Okay! Louise - Get into that crowd and check every face you can see. Search anyone who's carrying a bag or looks at all suspicious. Bannerman - I want you to stand on that kerb at the exact point the Minister's car stops. When he gets out, I want you to stand so close to the Minister that you can smell his breath.'

'He'll have his own men with him, surely?'

'Yes, but I bet none of them are as big as you.'

'Sounds like you want me to stop a bullet, boss?'

Boyd twisted a face, smiled and said, 'That's about right, Bannerman. I get paid for making decisions and you get paid to stop bullets. Cover his back all the way down that red carpet. I'll be right in front of him.'

'That's comforting, but his bodyguards aren't going to like that. Not one little bit. It'll spoil the media shots.'

'To hell with them. This is my patch. Walk with me down the carpet, Bannerman,' and then, 'Sergeant Cross - Get me those binoculars from the van and then take Rocky and get into the castle. I want you on those battlements. Pronto!'

'I hear you,' replied Cross, returning to his van hurriedly. Cross flicked his fingers, gathered Rocky to his heel, and jumped back into the police van.

Boyd spun round and looked up at the rooftops. He could see his sharpshooters positioned exactly where he and Bannerman had planned they should be. An uneasy feeling trickled through Boyd's body. What if that plastic bag had also contained a fake police uniform? Hadn't a shop window been smashed with a beer keg? Wasn't that a theatrical shop, or something of the kind?

'Ah, Boyd!' It was McMurray. 'Glad you could make it. Everything under control?'

'Not quite, Mac. You heard my news on the radio?'

'A sniper?' McMurray pulled a face. 'Really, Boyd. Hasn't this lark gone far enough? If there was a threat from the Arabs then it died last night in the Caldew.'

'I don't think so, Mac.'

'Never mind. As soon as this damn visit is over, we need to talk. The Chief is playing holy hell at those overtime payments you've authorised. You're in danger of breaking the bank, Boyd. There is a budget you know.'

'Well, let me worry about that,' replied Boyd.

'The Chief wants you in his office first thing tomorrow morning. Perhaps you'd care to explain things to him?'

'I'm off tomorrow, Mac. Holiday! Remember? Tell you what; tell the Chief I'm going running. See what he thinks about that?"

Leaving McMurray appalled at the prospect of explaining the inexplicable to the Chief, Boyd walked off, his eyes penetrating windows, his mind in torment.

Four hundred yards away, as the crow flies, there was a slight movement from a wrist. Then a finger gently brushed a switch and an eye focused a telescopic lens. Boyd appeared in the cross-hairs of a sniper's rifle. Seconds later, the cross-hairs found Bannerman, a podium, and an entrance through a museum door.

The 'plane touched down and disgorged its precious cargo onto the apron. Minutes later, they were walking through the arrivals lounge and shaking hands with an airport manager, the Lord Lieutenant, and his entourage. Once outside, there was a wave towards a small crowd on onlookers, a pose for a local television network, and they were off. They were into a fleet of bullet-proof cars and out of a secure area onto a network of minor country roads. With a wail of sirens and a flash of lights, motor cycle outriders carved a path through traffic.

'Boss!' shouted Cross, 'Binoculars.'
'Cheers!' replied Boyd, spinning round. Cross handed them over. Looping a leather strap over his head, Boyd removed the glasses from their case raised them to his eyes. Focusing rapidly, he said, 'We've got about twenty minutes if we're lucky. Any ideas?'
'He's got to be Arab, hasn't he?'
'That's my guess, Cross. Would you know one if you saw one? I mean they're not black and they're not white. Silly, I know; but their skin colour is in between.'
'He won't have blond hair, will he?' quipped Cross.
'No,' replied Boyd. 'Not unless he's dyed it.'
'So, distinguishing marks nil?'
Boyd was scanning the assembly. He picked up Louise walking along the rear of the crowd apparently checking out any bags that had been abandoned on the ground. He saw the museum curator with a woman he took to be his wife. He saw Mary Forsyth and her Alsatian; a lady wearing a pink dress standing next to a man he presumed to be her husband; and a young man who was dressed as a Jew with a long beard and a black trimmed hat. The crowd was obviously growing by the minute, he thought. Changing his attention, Boyd saw a sharpshooter on a nearby roof.

Relaxing his glasses, Boyd said, 'If it is Namir then try this for size. Terrorists work in small cells. Usually no more than five or six-handed. Yasif had a thick neck and wore a gold stud in his...'

'Right ear,' interrupted Cross with a mocking smile.

'No. Left ear,' cracked Boyd. 'Someone told British Intelligence that Yasif and his friends were in the same terrorist cell. Three of them have done nothing more but cause mayhem for us. They've diverted attention, caused confusion and paid with their lives.'

'And probably left a rifle for a killer,' said Cross.

Boyd was scanning the crowd again. 'Crazy, isn't it?' He said. 'Weird! Drugs! Murder! What for?'

'To stretch us to breaking point,' replied Cross, his steel grey eyes suddenly alive and bright. 'That's the only logical conclusion, isn't it? If you hadn't finished off those riots last night, where would we be now? Here or up on that damned estate?'

'It's a mad, stupid, incomprehensible mind, Cross - The criminal mind.'

'Is Namir related to Yasif and company?'

'Don't know. London, contrary to popular theory, has been less than forthcoming. In fact, they've been no help at all.'

'How kind,' quipped Cross, sarcastically.

Turning towards the castle battlements, Boyd lifted his glasses and zeroed in on the castle keep. There was a trivial flash across his field of vision: a critical dot of vivid gold sparkling from someone's head up there on the battlements of an old Norman fortress. Then it was gone and a flash sunlight rushed behind a passing cloud.

'Stud!' exclaimed Boyd. 'Must be!'

'What?' asked Cross.

'Something flashed in my glasses. A gold stud up there on those battlements.'

Cross was striding across the road with Rocky in front of him, slobbering from his mouth. Walking up the castle drive, through the castle green, Cross turned when Boyd let his glasses fall to his chest and shouted, 'Right ear!'

The convoy was on the main Brampton to Carlisle road. Six motor cycle outriders dissected their way through traffic to the ancient Roman city. They were fifteen minutes from Tullie House. They were trouble free and the going was good.

Once beneath an outer gate-house, inside the castle complex, Cross was faced with decisions to make. Left or right? Directly ahead of him, there was an extensive asphalt parade ground, which was surrounded on two sides by administration blocks bearing the names Ypres, Gallipoli, Arroyo, Arnhem and Alma. Cross took a right, walked over a bridge over a ditch, and made his way towards the remains of the Half Moon Battery. Centuries earlier, on this site, the semi-circular bastion boasted a battery of cannon and small arms' fire, which had protected the castle's inner bailey wall against would-be invaders and a host of malcontents. Looking upwards towards a bruised and battered castle keep, Cross saw another flash and honed in on a metal barrel of a rifle. He shook his head and sighed when he saw a police sharpshooter wave a welcome arm towards him.

Boyd, thought Cross. Boyd had seen this sharpshooter's rifle glinting in the sun. Trust him to get all excited about nothing. A gold stud, for God's sake! Boyd can't even sort out which side everyone is on. That sharpshooter is one of ours!

Rocky was wagging his tail and scampering along a stone path that led away from the portcullis towards the Captain's Tower. He was enjoying himself in a wide-open space, sniffing out invisible rabbit, chasing phantom shadows. Cross followed and found himself standing in the inner bailey of Carlisle castle. Ahead of him there were three buildings, the Magazine, the Militia Store and the Regimental Museum. The castle was the headquarters of the King's Own Royal Border Regiment and it was apt that the Regiment's band should be playing nearby. Above Cross loomed the keep and an English Heritage flag fluttering from a flagpole in a very slight breeze.

There were only a handful of tourists standing on the inner bailey wall - the castle wall-walk. Directly opposite Tullie House, they were watching proceedings at Tullie House museum. There was a Japanese couple, or were they Chinese? Cross didn't know. There was a teacher and a small party of school children carrying sketch books and pencils, but they were leaving and making their way towards the parade ground. Not the best place for a sniper to position himself, thought Cross. It was quiet, yes. But there were too many people about, and it appeared there was only one entrance to the castle: beneath the portcullis: the route Cross had just taken.

Cross neglected these three buildings and the keep and followed Rocky up a flight of stone steps towards the Captain's Tower. At the top,

Cross paused and allowed his eyes to wander along the battlements. The cupboard was bare again. More decisions?

Outside Tullie House, Carlisle's Mayor was at the front of a line, standing near a red carpet and two podiums, ready to greet three very important guests. Beside her stood her senior town councillors; her Town Clerk; a museum curator and his wife; a dredger and his wife; and a young Jew called David.

In front of the podiums, a mahogany table had been brought out of Tullie House and placed at the end of the red carpet. A resplendent blue velvet cushion was resting on a wooden surface. Nestled cosily on a velvet cushion sat a mahogany box. Its hinged lid was open revealing the Tablet of Masada in all its glory. A private security guard, tall, broad and burly, stood beside the box; his eyes watching the Tablet, his mind fascinated by its crude craft work.

The civic party and their guests were all on their best behaviour, smiling and laughing, exchanging polite small talk; and gradually being surrounded by the swelling noise of a nearby crowd. Amongst the assembly, Mary Forsyth was tugging an unruly, bored Alsatian on her leash while trying to wave a tiny Union Jack with her free hand. People behind the barriers were beginning to grow a little impatient until the band struck up a chord. With a thundering rendition, the band of the King's Own Royal Border Regiment burst into life. There was loud applause and more flag waving when the Regimental band began to march along the front of the museum.

Military steps to military music. Glorious tunes of old from a proud regiment.

Cross turned his back on the Captain's Tower and walked away from the direction of Tullie House, towards the remains of Queen Mary's Tower: the furthest point from Tullie House and the place where Mary Queen of Scots was once imprisoned.

Rocky barked and set off at a gallop. He barked again and snarled his teeth.

High in the castle keep, a man dressed in a police constable's uniform deliberately flicked his safety catch and allowed his fingers to curl round a trigger guard. Beside him lay the unconscious body of a young policeman.

Leaning hard to his offside, headlight flashing, a lead motor cycle outrider was negotiating Hardwicke Circus. Then they were round the roundabout and through some traffic lights and onto a dual carriageway.

Two minutes later six motor cycles peeled off and a convoy of black limousines arrived at Tullie House.

Israel's chief bodyguard vacated his front nearside passenger door as soon as the lead car drew to a standstill. In a trice, the bodyguard opened a rear nearside door and ushered Israel's Foreign Minister from the vehicle and onto a pavement! Behind the Israeli car were two more black limousines: one carried Britain's Defence Secretary, the other carried the Secretary of State for Foreign Affairs. Carlisle's visitors had finally arrived.

The band ceased marching when they reached a yellow painted line on tarmac. A precision marching display, timely indeed. As the entourage emerged from a convoy of bullet-proof cars, the band ceased playing and brought a sudden, unexpected hush to proceedings. There was a slight pause as the Mayor stepped forward and shook hands, welcoming his guests to the ancient city.

Standing quietly, a boorish twist as far as some of the crowd were concerned, they listened to the Regimental band playing the opening bars of the National Anthem.

They'd arrived and Boyd and Bannerman were ignoring the honour of the National Anthem as they moved into position, taking close order on Israel's Minister.

As melodic strains of a National Anthem reached the castle battlements, a telescopic tube revealed through its cross-hairs the head of the Israeli Minister for Foreign Affairs. A safety catch was off. A rifle was levelled and held firmly into the assassin's shoulder. His fingers were caressing the cold metal of a trigger guard. As the cross-hairs honed into the centre of a skull, four hundred yards away, one finger moved a mere centimetre and touched a trigger. Then, suddenly, the figure of a tall policeman called Bannerman blotted out those cross-hairs and the Israeli Minister was hidden from view.

Taller than the intended victim, Bannerman moved in behind the Israeli, to the annoyance of a bodyguard, and closed with him. Israel's Minister turned, looked at Bannerman, and was slightly startled at the prospect of a uniformed policeman standing so close; but he decided not to object since the National Anthem was playing and everyone seemed to be steeped in austere dignity. More discomfiture followed when another policeman stood immediately in front of him. Israel's Minister shook his head, annoyed: the nobility of the day was being displaced by two pompous, idiotic policemen who were stifling his movements.

The music eventually died and the Mayor beckoned a beleaguered Israeli Minister towards his podium; and the Tablet of Masada.

His walk was slow and stifled, each step laboured by the unnecessary presence of two fat-headed policemen who seemed intent on spoiling his great day.

There was a beam of sunlight breaking through some fluffy clouds above. A ray of light struck the Tablet of Masada and its flint work beamed and shone in its brilliance. It was beckoning Israel forward, crying out for its true owner to take it back to the lands where it belonged. A security guard retreated, moved away, his duty done; leaving the Tablet of Masada all alone.

Yet somewhere in that flint work, that exquisite noble pattern, there was a young Zealot's work. Young Jacob was inside that Tablet, was he not? Wasn't young Jacob's finery on display, calling, beseeching, pleading to be taken away from the false Gods of Rome? Wasn't Eleazar ben Jair in there somewhere, smiling, paternal, nodding to Israel to step forward and claim its rightful property? Wasn't Hussein repentant? Wasn't Alexander standing on the banks of the Eden dominating a pile of shields, his vinewood staff rigid, and his voice calling Israel - Forward, Forward?

The Mayor laid a hand on her podium and her foot reached onto the first step.

Rocky saw him first.

Namir, wearing a policeman's uniform, was crouched inside the remains of Queen Mary's Tower at the end of the castle's curtain wall. He was hidden from celestial view at an abrupt right-angled turn in the wall-walk of the Norman battlements. Using a sharply cut turret to his best advantage, he was positioned directly above a tiny grille door of the Dacre Postern Gate. He was lying in wait, adjacent to the remains of the city wall. A gold earring quivered from his right ear when his finger took its pressure on a trigger.

'Contact!' shouted Cross into his radio. 'He's got a gun. It's a shoot!'

There was a bark from Rocky and Namir flinched for a second, unsettled. It was enough to prevent that crucial first shot.

'Go, Rocky!' screamed Cross. 'Go!'

The Labrador was running, striding, and bounding, full stretch in all his magnificent glory.

Namir breathed out, ignored Rocky, and squeezed his trigger.

Rocky leapt and bit deep into Namir's arm as a soft and silenced crack rifled from the barrel of Namir's weapon. Cross was running as fast he could but Rocky was biting and pulling at Namir's arm: tearing and ripping, gruesome in his attack. Five strides, four strides, three strides, and then Cross threw himself headlong at Namir. The rifle fell from Namir's hands and tumbled to the ground below. In a confused, panic-stricken, terrifying half turn, Namir tried desperately to remove Rocky from his upper arm as Cross bounded headlong into his body.

There was an eerie, uncanny scream from Namir's lips when he, Rocky and Cross, lost their balance from the force of Cross's onslaught. Tilting backwards, Namir careered through a turret and fell from the battlements to the castle green below, pulling Cross and Rocky with him.

In the pandemonium that followed, no-one was subsequently able to adequately account for what really happened, or who did what to who and why.

Only Boyd and Bannerman reacted immediately to Cross's radio signal. With Cross's cry, 'Contact! He's got a gun. It's a shoot,' Boyd turned and grabbed hold of the Israeli Minister's suit jacket. Hauling the Minister unceremoniously towards the comparative safety of a museum entrance, Boyd was aware Bannerman was directly behind the Minister and pushing him in the same direction. They were moving forward swiftly, guiding the Israeli Minister to safety. They'd positioned themselves to take the assassin's best shot! They were bullet stoppers!

Israel's chief bodyguard turned to face the crowd. Thinking that was where an attack was coming from, he withdrew his handgun and pointed it into a sea of faces. The crowd screamed! Waving his gun frantically at an invisible enemy, he pushed Bannerman and the Minister towards the safety of the building.

The Minister resisted at first but when Boyd shouted at the top of his voice, 'Armed attack!' the Minister acquiesced to Boyd's every movement.

Mary Forsyth screamed when she saw the Israeli bodyguard's gun waving like a wet lettuce leaf in a deniable salad. All she could see was the barrel of his gun and panic on his face. There was more screaming and Mary's Alsatian barked angrily at the bodyguard and tried to climb over a barrier.

The Mayor was stepping from her podium, but not quite quick enough. Boyd bustled her out of her way, pushing her to one side as he pulled the Minister towards safety. Instantaneously, the Mayor fell unceremoniously from her podium and crashed into a tub of flowers.

A shower of radiant blooms and a dust cloud of fine potting compost sprayed across the red carpet.

Louise was shouting, 'Down! Everybody down!' But to no avail.

Then a woman in a pink dress rendered an ear-splitting screech when a man standing beside her clutched his chest and staggered into her. Blood seeped from the Town Clerk's shirt where Namir's bullet had entered his chest. Later, they would presume that Rocky's timely intervention had been enough to sway Namir from his true target. Unbalanced by Rocky's leap, Namir's bullet had diverted an inch above the Minister's head and plummeted into the town Clerk's chest cavity.

Another woman screamed and children began crying, unable to comprehend what was going on. The Regimental band scattered like leaves in a wind and a big bass drum snapped from a soldier's chest and rolled forlornly across a yellow painted line in the tarmac. Bobbling away, the drum had a life of its own.

Louise leapt over a barrier and ran towards the Town Clerk.

Staggering awkwardly, firstly dropping to his knees, the town Clerk succumbed face downwards onto the red carpet.

Louise turned the town Clerk over and was anxiously attempting to stem the blood flow with her hands as soon as she realised what had happened.

Jeremy sprinted to the museum door, leaving his wife to fend for herself. There was complete chaos with frenzied people running here and there in blind panic. In the ensuing melee, a mahogany table was knocked over by Jeremy, who then tripped over a collection of black microphone wires. A cushion billowed upwards and a hinged box jumped into the air and discharged its ancient passenger. The Tablet of Masada crashed to the ground. There was a scatter of dashing feet and an incensed lunge from a throng of frightened people. There was a bloodstained carpet, an upturned flower display, and people rushing hither and thither in a pathetic attempt to escape the inexplicable.

There was complete pandemonium at Tullie House, and the nation's television cameras captured the pictures.

Curiously, unseen, unrehearsed, a hand reached down and picked up the Tablet of Masada. Three fingers smoothed across its flint work and pocketed the Tablet without so much as a word to anyone.

It wasn't long before the minister was inside the museum and he was safe.

It was nearly five minutes before some kind of order was regained. That was when a police sharpshooter ran from the castle keep and found Cross lying on the castle green. Cross called for an ambulance for himself and pronounced Namir dead. They'd both tumbled from the castle battlements. Namir had landed on the grass below first, and Cross had broken his fall on Namir's prostrate body. Cross managed to stand up before he promptly collapsed to the ground again. In agony, it didn't take him long to realise he'd broken his leg and fractured a wrist. Namir, on the other hand, was as dead as a doornail with a stark, horrified look etched into his greasy face.

Rocky was nowhere to be seen. Rocky had yelped and barked and then hit a patch of grass with a mighty bump. With Cross dazed, in severe pain, and eventually surrounded by a crowd of well-wishers and first-aiders, Rocky merely limped away into the park.

The minutes ticked by and the media had a field day. It was an hour before anyone realised that the Tablet of Masada had been stolen!

The cause of it all, The Tablet of Masada; crafted by a Jewish Zealot; stolen by a Syrian archer; lost by a Roman centurion; found by an English Protestant; had been stolen by an unknown hand.

*

14

~ ~ ~

Dateline: 10th September, 2000: The day of Boyd's run.

Weary, Crosby pressed the 'shut down' button on his high-tech Pentium computer and wiped fatigue from his eyes. So much for Press reporting on the Internet, he thought. Oh, yes! There was a report, hours ago, regarding an incident involving a diplomat in Northern England. Unconfirmed accounts revealed how two members of the public had been killed in a series of tragic accidents during a cultural function staged at a museum. Someone had fallen from a castle wall, but nothing had been reported about the other death. It was just tittle-tattle at this stage. There was no firm substance embroidered in the words and there were too many questions left unanswered. Nothing substantial enough for Crosby to get his teeth into. Nothing that was going to keep him awake for the rest of the day.

Time for bed!

Crosby would sleep the rest of the day. He was tired beyond belief and he wondered if an opportune moment to visit an optician would arise in the near future. His eyes were truly gritted from a long night facing a flickering computer screen, all to no avail. By the looks of it.

Leaning across to a wall socket, Crosby powered down his computer. Standing, he sighed deeply and walked towards his encrypted machine. Bending down, he checked his machine and saw a green light flashing monotonously from its bed. Yes, it was still functioning correctly. He felt reassured.

He tapped his machine thoughtfully and wondered for a moment where Danu might be; and what Danu was doing at that precise time?

Dragging his listless feet, Crosby decided against sending a request for information. London would tell him all he needed to know when the time was right. Wouldn't they?

He walked quietly out of the room. As he reached the door, his finger automatically sought a light switch and plunged the room into darkness.

He was gone from his office.

Five minutes later, a green light shone brightly and his encrypted machine burst into life and spewed out an urgent message.

In an office overlooking central London, Ratchet felt somewhat uneasy. Nervous, apprehensive, he was virtually white about his gills; although his heartbeat was a little faster than he would have wished it to be. A warm, centrally heated office did nothing for his body temperature. He was perspiring and he paused a moment to briefly wipe a drop of sweat from his forehead. Hot days, warm nights, and a faulty central heating system did little to aid his composure. Opening a window, he sucked in some fresh air and trusted his body would cool down soon. Then he returned to his desk and toyed with the end of a fine cigar and a crystal ashtray.

Casually, almost with relief, as if he'd finally realised how to solve a dilemma, he took a sheaf of papers, fixed them with a paper clip and placed them inside a green-coloured portfolio. He pursed his lips and reached for a telephone. Having made his appointment, he dialled again and ordered a taxi to meet him at the end of the street in thirty minutes time.

In conclusion, he secured his portfolio in a wall safe, locked it, and set his private combination.

An hour later, a taxi pulled into a kerbside at Park Lane, and Ratchet got out. Paying his taxi fare, he sauntered into Hyde Park and left the hum of Mayfair traffic and the noise of a bustling city behind him.

Once inside the park, he walked quickly towards a bandstand situated near The Serpentine boating lake. The sun was shining fiercely and it was a day for scantily dressed joggers and an occasional youth riding a skateboard. A sparrow unearthed a worm from a strip of soft grass, and made a meal of it.

At the appointed place, Ratchet shook hands with his contact from the Israeli Embassy. They both knew each other, of course. Ratchet was a senior British Intelligence officer specialising in Middle Eastern affairs. The man he had encountered, by arrangement, was a senior member of Mossad: The Israeli State Security Organisation.

They walked into an expanse of deserted green and talked softly to each other. Yet in that comparative open space of a green and luscious park, they could see everyone around them. They were totally unhindered from the constraints of the nearby bustling capital. Talking softly, without any show of emotion, it was if they had arranged to meet in private; in this very private place.

In London, there were few such places: Hyde Park was only one of them.

Strolling in gentle sunshine, it looked as if two gentleman business acquaintances had met by chance. As their conversation wore on, they eventually strolled down Lovers' Walk in the direction of Hyde Park Corner. Here the noise of traffic grew stronger and the life of a throbbing city beckoned once more.

At the end of Lovers' Walk, they stopped abruptly at a statue. The Israeli was nodding, emphatically, agreeing, gesturing with his hands. Then he listened to Ratchet and their voices remained low. The man from Mossad took a sharp of intake of breath and then smiled politely. Ratchet returned his smile and they turned to appreciate the splendour of the statue. They were chuckling, for no apparent reason other than the presence of a statue.

Finally, they both shook hands once more and walked off in opposite directions. As Ratchet walked past the Achilles Statue, he paused and bent down. Scratching his heel, he realised he must have picked up a piece of grit on his walk.

Her Shamrock plant didn't need a trivial amount of water to feed its adequate roots. Indeed, it didn't need watering at all. But that wasn't going to stop Mary Forsyth from tending her beloved plant.

She set down her water jug, puffed out its tiny clovers with her fingers, and looked out into her street.

There was bright sunshine and a sparkling novelty creeping along black tarmac into an unfriendly park. But today, it was as if things had changed. It was as if people just might be able to walk in peace again. Perhaps some good had come of it all, despite the Town Clerk's injuries. Perhaps her estate would be better now.

Of course, she'd started it all with her call to police about that suspicious black Beamer and three olive-skinned men. She hadn't done it for money or self esteem. She hadn't done it for any false prestige or to curry favour with authority.

No, she was a simple woman leading a simple life.

She'd done if because of that maverick policeman Boyd, initially. The one who'd returned those horrible garden gnomes to her years ago: gnomes that had been stolen from her garden. But when she'd thought about it later, it wasn't because of Boyd she'd made that telephone call. No, it was because she'd wanted to improve the quality of life for herself and the people living on her estate. She'd decided to make a stand, to make the difference.

That's why she'd made the telephone call!

In the aftermath of violence, there was an awesome serenity about the place that had to be seen to be believed. Her quality of life had been improved.

She looked out of the window from behind her Shamrock plant and looked towards a park that was once desolate.

Soon, the children would come to play.

McMurray was on the 'phone to the Chief.

'Well, I can only apologise on his behalf, sir... No! Boyd insisted on taking his holiday, sir. Tells me, he's going running, but I don't believe him...'

McMurray set his unlit pipe down in an ashtray.

'Precisely, sir... You can't play about with a budget like that! I mean, things have to be discussed, approved, authorised. One shouldn't just rush into unnecessary expenditure!'

Shuffling in his seat, McMurray tried to make himself more comfortable. A tobacco pouch was removed from a uniform pocket and flopped onto his table near an ashtray and pipe.

'Well, I thought we did very well indeed, sir. I told Boyd right from the start to adopt high profile techniques... Yes, it was my idea, sir... Boyd is a little inexperienced in these things. Don't you think? Thank God he took my advice, that's all I can say...'

A match was sought, found, struck against a box. Then the light was blown out when the tone of the Chief's voice changed.

'Pompous! Me? Surely you don't think I'm over the top with my comments, sir... My attitude...? Well, I... Well, I... If you'd let me get a word in, sir... No, I don't know what you mean... Stealing someone else's glory...'

McMurray's large posterior shuffled uneasily from one buttock to the other. Then he started to sweat a little when the Chief began to irritate him.

'Well, of course... Yes, I fully support Chief Inspector Boyd, sir... No, I don't think that at all, sir. He's a fine officer, sir. I've said that all along, sir...'

McMurray suddenly went quiet for a moment and felt quite sick in his stomach.

'Me! Arrogant? I consider myself to be a typical senior officer...'

A pipe and an ashtray were thrown from a table and bounced from a wall.

Hospitals have an uncanny knack of spreading an odour of clinical preparedness into the world's atmosphere. There's always a smell of cleanliness in Carlisle hospitals: an unearthly smell that can't be found anywhere else on this planet, and its presence in one's nostrils defies worthwhile explanation.

Imprisoned in an orthopaedic bed, Cross's leg and his wrist were receiving expert medical attention. A bottle of blackcurrant juice and a basket of fruit sat on a nearby table. Bannerman was extolling the virtues of life with Boyd. There was a story of panic and a story of broken flower pots and compost all over a red carpet. There was a story of a museum curator falling over a microphone and... God, he did go on, thought Cross.

Louise was laughing and ignoring their bad stories. It was a way of life with them. Speak only of the funny or you'd go mad in a very short space of time. Louise was tickling Cross's toe with a feather and his steel grey eyes were zeroing in on her freckled face.

Cross was angry at her tickling and broke in... 'Where's Rocky?'

Danu was walking in the desert valley of the Bekaa, blissfully ignorant of matters that had unfolded thousands of miles away in an old roman city he'd never even heard of. He was dragging his club foot and carrying a stolen video camera inside the folds of his djellaba. There were also a few squares of cannabis for sale in one of the folds and he wondered if he might make a sale soon.

Danu struggled towards a pitch of Icelandic tents and a row of derelict buildings. Above him, there was a cluster of pomegranate trees and a small copse of cypress trees rising above the valley bed and looking down on the terrorist training camp. As Danu approached the four hidden caves, which housed a quantity of explosives and terrorist weaponry, there was a soft familiar hum above.

Danu dragged his club foot more quickly and clutched an amphora to his side. Looking up, skyward, his good eye searched for an aeroplane. It was a little early today: a surveillance aircraft flying over the Syrian army positions, he presumed.

Danu didn't see the pattern of cluster bombs and assorted missiles that bombarded the Bekaa valley in a salvo of hatred and revenge. Neither did Danu see six Israeli jets swoop low in formation over the camp and finish off any survivors with a catastrophic hail of cannon fire.

Danu felt the first terrific impact on the ground.

Blown into oblivion, Danu was killed in the opening seconds of an Israeli air strike. Minutes later there was an almighty eruption from the inner belly of a cave complex when an Israeli missile penetrated the earth, found a dozen boxes of high explosives, and blew up the final legacy of Namir's deadly lair.

In London, a telephone rang on a broad expansive desk. His hand lifted the instrument and held it to his ear for a matter of moments.
A smile formed his lips. An expression of gratitude was voiced and then the 'phone was returned to its cradle.
Ratchet stood, walked to his safe, dialled his private combination, and removed a green portfolio marked Danu - Bosphorus. In the centre of the portfolio, Ratchet read the words he had once written: Top Secret - Omega Blue.
Turning to a shredder in one corner of his office, Ratchet shredded its contents into obscurity.
Deniability has a metallic, earthy sound.
Drumming his fingers on the desk, Ratchet read again the report from a special branch sergeant in Newcastle. Then he took another folder and endorsed the front - Yasmin - Top Secret - Omega Blue. Ratchet would turn her. He wasn't quite sure how, probably money, a new identity, and a promise that she could live safely in the western world for as long as she wanted. After all was said and done, she surely wouldn't want to return to the Middle East after enjoying the trappings of the west. No, he would turn her. She'd be a double agent soon, and, with luck, she would expose Mahmoud's weaknesses. Mahmoud would follow and soon Ratchet would have increased his stranglehold on the Arab network working in Europe. A little prowess, that's all it took. Yasmin first, then Mahmoud. Ratchet secured the folders and removed the Chinese exercise balls from their velvet box. Balance, that's all it was.

*

Boyd was gone from the fisherman. He was running in the park. Leaving the Sheepmount behind him, He padded over a bridge crossing the Caldew and settled down to an even-paced jog. To his right, the land dipped into a basin of luscious meadow stretching towards tennis courts and a putting green before the mighty buttresses of Carlisle castle rose to dominate the backdrop. To his left, the land dropped away slightly to a rough pasture, which leads to a river bank and a gently flowing Eden. Boyd was running along Mayor's Drive and he was approaching exhaustion. Passing a statue of Queen Victoria, Boyd slowed to a canter and realised he was well and truly out of breath. Limbs aching, heart thundering, he broke right down to a gentle stroll and placed his hands on his hips in silent resignation. Sucking in a dose of oxygen, he saw a tunnel ahead of him. It was quite a long tunnel, as far as Boyd was concerned, and it extended the full width of the Eden Bridge above. He could hear a soft throb of traffic above crossing from the centre of town towards Stanwix.

Stepping from Mayor's Drive, near the entrance to the tunnel, Boyd sauntered towards the old grey river. On the opposite side of the bank, he could see Edenside cricket ground and houses rising up into Stanwix. Kneeling down, he scooped cold water into his mouth. It tasted good, refreshing. He drank his full. As he drank, Boyd realised he was kneeling next to a sand bank. The sand bank rambled beneath the Eden Bridge and ran parallel to the tunnel he had reached. Should he run on tarmac through the tunnel or should he run along the sand bank? Both routes would take him to the Sands car park and then he would be able to run north towards his home.

As he pondered on his decision, Boyd felt a sudden presence and knew he had company.

Rocky was at this side, limping; sad-eyed, and looking for comfort.

'There you are, boy,' said Boyd. 'We've been looking all over for you. Where did you go?'

Boyd stroked his neck and made a fuss of Cross's pet.

'Let's have a look then?'

Rocky lifted a paw and Boyd casually inspected a pad.

'So, I'm not the only one who picks up unwanted thorns, Rocky.'

Holding the Labrador's paw, Boyd extracted a spike from soft flesh.

'Better now?'

Rocky scampered away and then returned sharply, tongue drooling as usual, happier now. The niggling pain was gone from his paw.

Boyd knelt beside the dog.

'It's over now, Rocky. All I have to do is get you home to Cross. He'll look after you. I'm glad it's over. I didn't mean it to end that way...

The Town Clerk, I mean… I think it was my fault when he was shot, Rocky.'

Rocky's head nudged into Boyd's knee as he craved for affection. Boyd obliged with another caress, stroking Rocky's head between the ears.

'You see, Rocky, I was so busy looking after the top man I forgot about the little guy. I saved the top man, sure enough, but the Town Clerk!'

There was the beginning of a solitary tear in Boyd's sad eyes.

'It's all my fault. This is where it all started for me, I'm sure. Still, we can't be morose forever, whatever the circumstances, Rocky.' Boyd faced the river and stroked Rocky's hair. It was so peaceful there: calm, tranquil.

David walked towards them. They talked, then Boyd reached into his bum bag and they turned and walked towards the river. Then they parted.

Boyd took a stride towards the tarmac path, and then he faltered. He wasn't afraid of the tunnel. After everything he'd been through lately the prospect of choosing which way to run was really quite refreshing. It was just that he could hear a wind circling and whimpering in the tunnel of despair.

Boyd turned and made his way along the sand bank. It was a little bit muddy to start with but directly under the Eden Bridge the texture of sand changed and became dry and flaky. Boyd's trainers kicked up a minor dust storm as he jogged along by the side of the river. Rocky was with him, soon to be reunited with Cross. But for now Rocky was scampering in the sand and disturbing its solitude.

Boyd wondered how long it had been since anyone had run along the sand bank in such isolation. He wondered how it had looked centuries ago, when it had all started. He even wondered if there had been sand bank there, centuries ago, nestling beside an old grey river at the dawn of time.

In the beginning there was only peace and solitude. There wasn't even a single footprint in the sands of time. No, there was just a desert and a million grains of sand that held no memory of before and no prediction of the future. Until man was born.

The jogger and a Labrador disappeared into the mist enveloping the Eden valley.

David walked towards the tunnel, which would take him beneath the Eden Bridge, alongside the River Eden. The tunnel was long and dark, ominous, foreboding, perhaps filled with an uncertain future. Reaching inside his pocket, David removed a piece of rock: a tablet, and placed it in the palm of his hand. Personal protection from a long ago time? Perhaps the flint work and the carved Menorah would light his way, guide him through the dark passages of time, protect him, heal him, and keep him safe?

    There was a glint, a mystical flash of light, as David walked through the tunnel and into the centuries of time.

*

The Legacy of the Ninth
~ ~ ~

I ran as the wind, my body and spirit in harmony.
Tiring, I jogged across the Moor.
Breathless, I slowed to a walk.
Spent, I sat, resting against the rock of Hadrian.

Closing my eyes, I drifted in fatigue.
Drifting! Slowly drifting down the abyss of my mind,
Slipping backwards through the centuries of time,
Eyelids in surrender. Darkness! I dreamt.

Marching! Behind my Tribune in Roman might,
I saw green wastes beyond the river bank.
Those fields of Stanwix beckoned,
'cross a multitude of roaring heathen Picts.

Marching! Ten cohorts in my Legion.
I felt the pilum in my hand,
A shaft as smooth as ebony,
An iron point to thrust in battle nearing.

Marching! Each with shield held high,
I felt the gladius slap against my thigh,
Its killing edge encased,
Asleep, within a leather sheath.

Marching! Yet in the Eden mud, I lay, fear, uncertainty,
Defeat! We could not breach those banks.
Our Standard fell! And all around me fought Luguvalium,
For the Glory of the Ninth.

And here, I met my early death,
For here, did fall my noble Ninth,
T'was here, my Roman Legion perished,
But here, in Eden's waters deep,
I left my legacy...
~

Extraction from 'Sunset' A Collection of poetry by Paul Anthony

Also, by Paul Anthony

The Fragile Peace... by Paul Anthony

A thriller of violent prejudices and divided loyalties.

This Ulster novel reaches to the very roots of sectarian life and death. Written by a member of the security forces, it penetrates behind the media-screen to reveal a human landscape that is unknown, yet startlingly believable...

Everything is here, from the glamour of hi-tech intelligence work to the despairing pub-talk of men locked in the past. Trace the origins of these relentless tit-for-tat killings, often starting in childhood and see how the lives of vastly different people may be mysteriously linked forever against the fatally beautiful backdrop of Northern Ireland...

... 'A bomb will explode in Downing Street in half and hour'...

The chilling Ulster accent, echoing a world of grey streets and grim death... The correct password, confirming a deadly threat to the UK government.... As more Irish republicans come to the negotiating table, one fanatical group sets out to smash the peace talks beyond hope. Highly trained and well-armed, they have the power to strike a devastating blow at the very heart of the establishment, but the police keep intercepting their plans – until they gradually realize that one of their own number must be a double agent.

When you read this topical thriller, you'll see why this crime-fighting author had to use a pseudonym

Published by Janus Publishing Company, London
www.paulanthonyassociates.co.uk

Also, by Paul Anthony
Bushfire… by Paul Anthony

~

'Bushfire' is a terrifying thriller of greed and deceit. The action spans the oceans, from Colombia to the British Isles and is set against the inferno of a raging drugs' culture…

'The waves gave way to the rocks, and the rocks gave way to the pebbles, and the pebbles gave way to the sand. The waves rolled onto the sand and went back to the pebbles, and the rocks, and rolled again. Only the waves and the rocks, and the pebbles, and the sand, saw them coming. They were alone and unseen when the morning broke and they had arrived'…

….'Trident ran free to cruise in the fathoms of uncertainty, to stay loose to join the fray, and when called upon to serve, they would be there'…

…'In the Vanguard…To Vanquish… To be Vengeful…
To be Victorious'…

Revised Second Edition Published by Paul Anthony Associates
www.paulanthonyassociates.co.uk

Also, by Paul Anthony
Sunset… by Paul Anthony

~

'Sunset' is a collection of poetry from a crime-fighting author who has previously published fictional novels on policing, terrorism, and the raging drugs culture.

Written under his pseudonym, he traces the life of a relaxed carefree teenager in the Sixties to a man at the dawn of the Twenty First Century. The journey captures an age of experiences; peaceful and pleasant, violent and murderous.

The voyage from one century to another smoothly results in a unique portrayal of the era in which we live. From love and romance, war and peace, sorrow and surrender, to private tears and unknown fears, *Paul Anthony* delivers a roller-coaster of poetic emotion in his third book 'Sunset.'

Published by Paul Anthony Associates
www.paulanthonyassociates.co.uk

Coming Soon….
G'Nigel the Gnome…

~

'G'Nigel the Gnome' is a story for children detailing the exciting adventures of G'Nigel, a common garden gnome who lives on a patio, beside a fish pond, near a magic well… and much more… He's such a grey coloured garden gnome. What can be done to make him colourful? Perhaps the children playing in the garden can help.

This is the first book in the 'Paul Anthony' 'Bedtime Stories' Series for children.

Published by Paul Anthony Associates
www.paulanthonyassociates.co.uk

Printed in Great Britain
by Amazon